"You smell like sex."

Devyn leaned down toward Bride, moonlight caressing him as though it couldn't help itself. Maybe it couldn't.

"The dirtiest kind of sex, at that—which just happens to be my favorite." His thumb traced her palm.

A shiver slid the length of Bride's spine. He was flirting with her, wickedly so. Though she had no desire to flirt back—really—she forced herself to say, "Wow. Already we have something in common." One thing she knew about men. They were more likely to help a woman if they thought they'd get something in return. "That's my favorite kind, too."

That put a surprised sparkle in his amber eyes. "Isn't this just my lucky day, then?"

Turn the page to read praise for Gena Showalter and her novels of danger and desire . . .

GENA SHOWALTER

SEDUCE THE DARKNESS

POCKET **STAR** BOOKS

New York   London   Toronto   Sydney

Pocket Star Books
A Division of Simon & Schuster, Inc.
1230 Avenue of the Americas
New York, NY 10020

This book is a work of fiction. Names, characters, places, and incidents either are products of the author's imagination or are used fictitiously. Any resemblance to actual events or locales or persons, living or dead, is entirely coincidental.

First Pocket Star Books paperback edition July 2009

POCKET STAR BOOKS and colophon are registered trademarks of Simon & Schuster, Inc.

For information about special discounts for bulk purchases, please contact Simon & Schuster Special Sales at 1-800-456-6798 or business@simonandschuster.com.

The Simon & Schuster Speakers Bureau can bring authors to your live event. For more information or to book an event contact the Simon & Schuster Speakers Bureau at 1-866-248-3049 or visit our website at www.simonspeakers.com.

Designed by Jill Putorti

Manufactured in the United States of America

10 9 8 7 6 5 4 3 2 1

ISBN 978-1-4165-3164-7
ISBN 978-1-4391-6364-1 (ebook)

To Lauren McKenna, whose amazing insight blew me away. This book couldn't have been possible without you.
To Kelli McBride. He was always yours. Except for the few times he was mine. But mostly he was yours. And mine. Fine, he's all yours.
To my three Walters: Jill Monroewalter, Kresley Colewalter and PC Castwalter. Pillow fight, anyone?
To Deidre Knight, who's always in my corner.

PROLOGUE

Devyn de bon ci Laci, prince of the Targonia Royal House, drew his knees to his bare, dirty chest for warmth. Though he told himself over and over to stop, his shivering didn't cease. He was fifteen summers, yet every time he was shoved into this cell, he felt like a child again. Lost, forgotten.

You are a prince, and have been promised to Princess Mika since birth. You disgrace our family every time you even glance at another female. His father's voice filled his head, the disappointment and disdain as fresh as before, and still enough to destroy him.

He'd learned at a very young age to lower his gaze when anything female stepped into a room he occupied. He'd learned to hold his breath so that he wouldn't smell their sweet scents, learned to inch away from them so that they could not even brush his shoulder with their delicious warmth.

But sometimes, he was ashamed to admit, even the *thought* of those things brought the traitor between his legs to attention, aching, filling, silently begging for contact. Any contact. Even the rasp of clothing would make him moan, desperate.

"Shameful," he muttered, echoing the reproach he'd heard too many times to count. A reproach that always preceded being sent here to "consider the depth of his betrayal."

For this newest indiscretion, he'd been as careful as always. He'd been reading in the library—a text of newly discovered worlds—wishing he were far, far away. Wishing he were anyone other than who he was, when a servant his age, but very female, had entered.

Servants were not supposed to talk to him, weren't even supposed to look at him, but she'd noticed him and had gasped in surprise. He'd glanced up. Rather than race from the room as was the custom, she'd stayed. Rather than pretend he hadn't spotted her, he'd stared, breath trapped in his lungs, skin hot and tight, mouth watering. His pants, already too tight, had strained against his growing manhood.

How pretty she'd been, her skin suns-kissed, her dark eyes heavily lashed, her breasts straining against her robe. When her lush, pink lips had curled in greeting, his heart had nearly beaten its way from his chest. He'd wanted to rush to her, put his hands all over her body, lick her and kiss her and thrust into her the way a prince was only supposed to thrust into his wife. But she wasn't his wife, would never be his wife, so his guard, never far from his side, had pushed her from the room and called for his father.

How long ago had that been? How long had he been here, trapped in this cell? He'd lost track of the days. All he knew was that he was cold, enveloped by a sphere of thick darkness, denied any sound but the ring in his ears, and alone, forbidden to know the touch of another. In the last, he was greatly familiar. But to lose his other senses, as well . . . it was a torment beyond comprehension and one he'd sworn never to endure again. No matter what he had to do to avoid it.

Devyn laughed bitterly. *I am a failure, even in that.*

Hinges creaked, the first noise to greet his ears in so long he nearly moaned in pleasure. But to moan would have invited more punishment, so he pressed his lips together. A second later, a small beam of light shoved its way inside his cell.

Devyn blinked against it, his eyes tearing in pain yet also rejoicing. Finally!

"What do you have to say for yourself?" his father asked, devoid of emotion. Always devoid. Still the sound was welcome, quieting that frantic ring.

"I'm sorry. So sorry." He strove for a calm tone, as unfeeling as he was supposed to be. "I should not have looked at her. I knew better, and I know I'm dishonorable for the way my body reacted. I tell you now, it will never happen again. I swear it."

"That's what you said last time."

"I didn't feel this . . . shame before." A lie. The shame never left him.

That earned him a nod of approval. His first. It warmed him. "The little whore was tossed into the streets where she belongs," his father said harshly. "She's lucky I didn't kill her."

"Yes, Father." He knew better than to say anything else as he drew his knees tighter against his chest. His nakedness would offend, earning him another punishment, even though his clothes had been ripped from him before he'd been forced in here.

"Do you wish to be a good king? A good husband our people can respect and admire?"

"Yes, Father." Another lie. He did not want to be king. He did not want to be prince. He wanted to be free. The desire was an ache inside him. An ache he'd learned to ignore.

"Then you, more than any other, must control your baser urges, Devyn. Otherwise you are no better than an animal." There was a pause, a hardening of his father's stance. "Otherwise, you are no better than your mother."

His mother, another female he wasn't allowed to see or touch. But sometimes he heard her, laughing gaily in another room, feet shuffling as though she were dancing. Always he shouted for her in his mind, but she never heard him, never called for him, never tried to sneak a hug. "Yes, Father."

A sigh crackled between them, and then a bundle of clothing was flying through the air. Each piece slapped against his face, tickling his faithless skin, his arms too weak to lift to catch them.

"When I discovered how you had thrown yourself at that servant"—his father's tone was sneering—"I summoned the princess. Finally she has arrived. You will be wed today. And so help me, if you ever look at another female, if that beast between your legs ever shows itself in public again, I will kill you myself. I'd rather you were dead than a disgrace."

CHAPTER 1

Bride McKells meandered along the crowded street in the pulsing heart of New Chicago, moonlight and multihued shop lights blending together to create a sparkling canvas of dream and shadow. Chaos and calm. Red brick buildings stretched at her sides, each fairly new, no clear, breakable glass or blink-and-it's-in-flames wood in sight. A shame. She loved peeking into shops and imagining owning whatever was being sold just as much as she loved the smell of pine.

Neither of which she would be enjoying anytime soon. Windows were now made of dark "shield armor," and wood was scarce.

After the human-alien war, everything had had to be rebuilt for strength and durability, even while resources had been limited, the world a shell of its former self. Good-bye extraneous use of pretty glass and sweetly fragranced timber. Now, almost eighty years later—eighty years in which Bride had barely aged—everything was comprised of unattractive, dirt-scented stone.

Not a bad smell, but when paired with the reeking

public . . . Ugh. Every day it worsened. Perfumes and
body odor, flowery laundry soaps and car exhaust. And
food. Oh, God, the food, the spices. Her too-sensitive
nose wrinkled in distaste. McBean burgers, fried chicken,
and the ever-popular syn-milk. . . the list could go on and
on. *Mind on the task at hand, or you'll puke.* Already bile
rose in her throat, burning.

Deep breath in, hold . . . hold . . . deep breath out.
Men and women, both human and nonhuman, bustled
in every direction, some in a mad rush to reach their
destination, some as unhurried as her. Only difference
was, they were shopping for clothes and shoes. Bride was
looking for her next meal: warm blood from a live, jugular tap.

Unfortunately, tonight's buffet was lacking. As usual.
All those smells . . . *Back to that already, are we?* The bile
threatened to spill over.

She supposed, to a human, finding a tasty meal among
this stretch would be the equivalent of picking between
oversalted pasta, the charred nibblets left in the bottom
of an oven, or stale toast seasoned with week-old mayon-
naise. Again, ugh. But hungry as she was, weak as she
was becoming, she needed to feed. Soon. No matter how
crappy the buffet.

Lately, though, she couldn't eat indiscriminately without severe consequences. Most blood—human or otherworlder, it didn't matter—now left her writhing in a dirty
alley, vomiting and moaning in pain for hours. Why, she
didn't know. She only knew it had started about a month
ago and had yet to abate.

If she'd known another vampire, she would've asked

what was going on. But did she know another vampire? *Nooo.* Except for movies and books, she'd never even *seen* another of her kind.

She hated—*hated!*—not understanding her own body.

Just one bloodsucker. That's all I need. Were they dead? Was she the last? Her earliest memories were of herself, alone, always alone, walking the streets of New Chicago, just like she was doing now, the words "Bride McKells" tattooed on the inside of her wrist, lost, hungry, starving actually, stumbling and finally falling against the pavement.

A human male had scooped her up without a word—intentions unknown, even now—and Bride's gaze had locked on the vein fluttering along the column of his neck. Her mouth had watered, her teeth had sharpened, and the next thing she'd known, she'd bitten him, gulping back every drop of crimson nectar she could. He had collapsed, but she hadn't released her hold on him. He had spasmed and gasped and fought, but still she'd maintained her grip. Only when he had stilled, his vein as dry as an empty cup, had she moved away.

Her strength—instantly restored. Her eyesight—unbelievably perfect. Her hearing—exponentially better. Her sense of smell—too strong, sickening, but filterable. Her touch—ultra sensitive.

Her guilt—raging.

She'd been a child in mind and body, perhaps no more than eight human years, starving, tired, desperate, and feeling utterly abandoned. Yet even with her limited understanding she'd known, beyond any doubt, that she'd just wrongly killed a man. And sadly, he hadn't been the last. Several years had passed before she'd learned to control her urges, to disengage before swallowing that final, life-taking gulp.

Now, nearly a century later, she should have been a wrinkled hag, doddering and senile, but she looked twenty-one and was stronger than ever. The people around her had aged, of course; most had even died. A few years ago, she'd had to fake her own death and come back as someone else. She could have traveled somewhere else, but hadn't. The only person she'd ever loved was here, somewhere. So here Bride would stay.

"Hey," a male suddenly said, keeping pace beside her.

Startled, she flicked him a glance and sized him up in less than a second. Sandy-colored hair, brown eyes. Young, probably early twenties. Several inches taller than her. Clean shaven. Looked about as dangerous as a stuffed animal. But if he was anything like her, he sewed razors into his shirtsleeves and pant pockets, proving just how deceiving looks could be.

"Sorry to rush at you like that. 'Cause I know it's uncool to approach a woman who's alone at night, but I'm not creepy or anything," he added, palms raised as if that proved his innocence. "I swear."

She quickened her steps, preferring a murderer to the sales pitch she suspected was coming. "Sorry, I'm broke." And sadly, that was the truth.

"I'm not selling anything," he said. "Swear to God!"

"All salesman say that—right before they reveal an item I just can't live without." That never changed, no matter the era or season.

"Okay, maybe I am trying to sell you something, but it's not what you think. Honest."

It never was. She sucked in a breath, preparing to use her voice voodoo and compel him to leave, when she caught the vaguest hint of grilled chicken, cloned of course, and white rice. Nothing else. No spices. No other scents to clutter up her nose and burn her belly.

Bride cast him another quick but assessing glance. Clearly, he was fresh from an enzyme shower, not a speck of dirt on him. His heartbeat was strong, his energy levels high. The moisture in her mouth increased.

Maybe she'd be able to keep him down.

The thought was heady. *Appearances are deceptive, remember?* Maybe he'd make her sicker than ever. Only one way to find out. She softened her expression. "So what are you trying to sell me, hmm?"

"Well . . . me. Only, I'm available free of charge." Twin pink circles painted his cheeks, and his pulse kicked up another notch. Desire wafted from him, barely discernible, but there all the same. "I, uh, noticed you back at Sid's and thought I'd introduce myself."

"I wasn't at Sid's tonight." Last night, sure. It was her favorite hangout, a local bar that catered to sensitives— otherworlders who were as overwhelmed by smells as she was. No perfumes were allowed. No illegal cigarette smoke.

She was a regular, and the otherworldly patrons assumed she was a human with a fetish. Yeah, that made them leery of her, but she let them assume it. While humans and aliens might cohabitate, that didn't mean they were comfortable with each other yet. But better to be feared than hunted. If nothing else, old vampire movies had taught her that.

"I know you weren't there tonight, but I saw you yesterday and then again as I was walking out tonight and you were, uh, passing by. So I ran after you," he admitted with a self-deprecating grin. "Impulse. Gets me every time. I'm Tom, by the way."

Points to Tom for being brave enough to approach her. She hadn't been asked on a date in months and had begun to think something was wrong with her. But . . . wait. She hadn't noticed him last night and wondered why he hadn't approached her then, if he'd been interested in her. Why now? Because she was on her own, seemingly helpless?

So suspicious! "What are you doing hanging out at Sid's? You're not the usual patron."

His cheeks reddened again.

Ah. Trying to nail otherworlder ass. Should have known. A classic pastime for today's youth. No wonder his scent was so unassuming. He'd picked up a sensitive before and knew how to go about it. "And you decided to come after me, huh?"

"Well, yeah. I'd really like to get to know you."

"Get to know you." Code for "fuck your brains out and never call you," perhaps. God, when had she become so cynical? Since her last boyfriend had dumped her for being moody and secretive, and her rebound *hadn't* called her, she supposed. "Why didn't you try and get to know me last night? Since you noticed me, I mean."

He swallowed, even missed a step and tripped forward. Thankfully he righted himself before he fell. "I was there with someone else and couldn't get away. But she was just a friend, honest."

Just a friend. Right. *And I wouldn't like to nibble on your carotid.*

Bride twisted to the side to avoid slamming into a woman in a hurry, a woman whose heels clacked faster and faster against the pavement in a booming rhythm that made her cringe. After a decent meal, she would be able to control the volume in her ears.

Her gaze slid back to Tom. Why not? she thought. He was young, but he probably wouldn't put up a fight when she came at him with fangs bared. He might actually like it. Kids were kinky these days. Of course, that would mean avoiding him for the rest of his life.

She could erase the memory of her eating habits from his mind if she only drank from him once. But if she were to go to him for a second helping, his mind would begin to build an immunity against her "forget me" suggestions. He would remember her and what she'd done, and word about what she was would leak. Spread. That's why she'd never been able to drink from her boyfriends, and why she'd had to sneak away every night from her only live-in to find a meal. That's also why he'd considered her secretive and ultimately booted her from his life.

Eating from the same buffet was a mistake she'd made a few times before the war, and each time she had been chased by cross-holding, holy-water-throwing, stake-wielding fanatics. Ironically enough, the war had saved her, wiping out the very people who'd wanted her dead.

"I'm thirsty," she said. "Wanna get to know me over a drink?" *Funny, Bride. Very funny.*

"Hell, yeah!" His eyes darkened, those chocolate irises

overshadowed by the dilation of his pupils. "Anything you want, anywhere you want it."

If he only knew . . . "Great. I—" A familiar scent suddenly drifted to her nose, and she stilled. Frowned.

Tom noticed and backtracked, his smile fading. "Everything okay?"

Bride closed her eyes as she inhaled again, sorting through the sea of fragrances and locking in on one. Slowly she exhaled, then inhaled again. Sure enough. There it was.

It was a fragrance she'd encountered only a few times the past two decades, a blend of aged pine and smooth morning sky. A fragrance that belonged to her childhood friend, Aleaha Love, a girl—woman now—she hadn't seen in sixteen years. A friend she had wept for, missed, needed, and never stopped searching for.

Finally, blessedly, Aleaha was nearby. Had to be.

"Sorry. Maybe we'll do that drink later." Despite Tom's protests, despite her growing hunger, Bride leapt into a sprint, dodging people, shoving them out of the way when necessary. Her heart slammed against her ribs, as fast and hard as the high heels she still heard drumming inside her head, and sparked a burning pain in her chest. *Calm down. You know better.*

"Hey," someone snapped.

"Watch it," another growled.

At one time, she and Aleaha had been inseparable, relying on each other for survival. Bride had protected and provided for the girl, and Aleaha had staved off the loneliness. Because Bride was a vampire and Aleaha a shapeshifter, both of them had feared being captured, studied.

Tortured. Didn't help that they'd been poor and dirty, as disposable as garbage. They'd had to live in the shadows.

One day several policemen had chased them for sneaking inside the homes of the rich and stealing food. Bride had hidden the younger girl, leading the cops away from her. But when she'd returned, there'd been no sign of Aleaha. Not there, not anywhere.

Now Bride's gaze swung left and right, scanning the masses for any hint of her friend. Not that she expected to see her. One touch, and Aleaha could assume the identity of anyone, her appearance becoming theirs. *Where are you, Leah Leah?* Swiftly Bride breathed in and out, the scent of pine and sky intensifying. She was on the right path.

Excitement pounded through her, and the burning in her chest increased. The few times she'd encountered her friend's scent, it had never been this potent, and she'd soon lost the trail. Was this the day she'd meet with success?

So many times she'd imagined presenting Aleaha with all the things they'd dreamed about but Bride had been unable to give her. Fancy clothes, soft shoes, and so much food the girl's stomach would burst. She'd imagined whispering and laughing in the dark with the only person who knew what she was but loved her anyway. Just like they'd used to do.

She'd imagined showing Aleaha the new tricks she'd learned, the different abilities that had revealed themselves, one by one, springing from a place deep inside her. A place protected by thorns and fire, so that she couldn't get past it to see what else lurked there. But she'd tried, oh, had she tried. Many times. And every time, the pain had almost killed her. Finally, she'd given up and now left that turbulent place inside her alone.

Unless she experienced any emotion too strongly, that is. Then the thorns and fire sprang up on their own. Too much pleasure brought pain (not that it detoured her). Too much pain brought more pain. Too much sadness, too much anger, too much happiness—pain, pain, pain. *Which is why you need to, what? Calm down.* Being incapacitated held no appeal.

Aleaha's wonderful smell was so strong now, she discerned two scents wrapped together, both somehow familiar . . . she was almost upon the source . . . but there was no longer any women in sight. Was Aleaha guised as a male? Where could she— Bride crashed into a solid, unmoving wall of muscle, air gushing from her parted lips. She stumbled backward, hit someone else and bounced forward, nailing the wall of muscle and brawn yet again.

That second time, her knees gave out and she tumbled to her ass. As she sat there, panting, she realized Aleaha's scent was now all over her. Had she truly found her? Bride's excitement became as hot as fire in her veins.

The man—Aleaha?—turned, his lips curled into an annoyed frown. Down, down he gazed, a lock of dark hair falling over his forehead. When he spotted her, his eyes widened and his frown lifted into a what-have-we-here grin. Bride's excitement drained, as did the burning. There was no recognition in that gaze, no ethereal outline of Aleaha beneath that face. But what a beautiful face it was.

Bride, always a lover of art, experienced a wave of feminine appreciation. His eyes were bright amber, honey mixed in cinnamon and fused by fire, surrounded by decadent black lashes. His skin looked as if it had been dipped in a pot of opalescent glitter. That glittery skin should have made him appear weak, girly. It didn't. It somehow added to his I'll-kill-anyone-anytime-anywhere-and-laugh-while-doing-it air.

Clearly, he was an otherworlder. Though which race, she didn't know. Whichever one, she had to wonder if they were all like him: perfection wrapped in dazzling and sprinkled with every woman's fantasy. What would his blood taste like? Would she be able to keep him down? Her mouth watered, and her fangs elongated.

He had a wonderfully sloped nose, sharp cheekbones, and a stubborn jaw. His dark brows were slashes of menace, yet tempting all the same. His lips . . . a portal to heaven, surely. They were lush and pink and promised unimaginable pleasures without saying a word. He knew it, too. He radiated utter confidence, absolute strength, and that I'll-do-anything wildness.

As she stared up at him, his smile took on a wicked edge, knowing and sure. He was nothing like shy but horny Tom, the boy-man she'd just abandoned. Dressed completely in black, this man seemed every inch the night warrior. Ready to slash your throat without a moment's notice.

In his case, looks were not deceiving. Without a doubt, he was dangerous.

"Well, well. Aren't you a pretty thing?" he said, offering her a hand. That voice . . . deep and raspy and just roused from bed, as perfect as his face and body.

As people buzzed beside them—the females staring

at him in openmouthed wonder, the males giving him a wide berth—Bride tentatively accepted his aid. His warm fingers curled around her wrist, and he easily hefted her up.

When she gained her bearings, she realized he'd tugged her forward so that they were only a few inches apart. He did not release her hand. Her smaller height placed her gaze right at the steady pulse in his neck, and her mouth once again watered.

Concentrate. Bride raised her chin and forced herself to look him in the eye. "You smell like my friend Aleaha Love. Do you know her?" Wait. What if she'd changed her name? He could have been with her and not even known it.

"I smell like a woman, hmm?"

At least he didn't sound insulted. Merely amused. "Yes."

"Well, *you* smell like sex." He leaned down as if he intended to share a secret with her, moonlight caressing him as though it couldn't help itself. Maybe it couldn't. "The dirtiest kind of sex, at that. Which just happens to be my favorite." His thumb traced her palm.

A shiver slid the length of her spine. He was flirting with her, and wickedly so. Though she had no desire to flirt back—really—she forced herself to say, "Wow. Already we have something in common." One thing she knew about men. They were more likely to help a woman if they thought they'd get something in return. "That's my favorite kind, too."

That put a surprised sparkle in his amber eyes. "Isn't this just my lucky day, then?"

"You never answered my question. Do you know Aleaha Love?"

"I know many women, but their names escape me right now. I so want to solve this mystery and become your hero. Perhaps your friend and I use the same perfume."

"She doesn't wear perfume, and I doubt you do, either." Even though so much time had passed since Bride had seen Aleaha, she knew her friend would never douse herself in any kind of body spray. Aleaha had to be as desperate to find Bride as Bride was to find Aleaha. She couldn't believe otherwise. Aleaha was the one person who would never have walked away from her willingly. They'd become family, relied on each other.

"Perhaps, then, it's a coincidence that we smell the same."

"Perhaps." Her shoulders slumped. He could very well be a shape-shifter like Aleaha, and all shape-shifters could very well produce the same fragrance.

"I didn't expect you to agree. Darling, coincidences don't just happen. We need to put our heads together and think up some kind of explanation for this extraordinary occurrence. I do my best thinking in bed. You?"

She laughed; she just couldn't help herself. The man was incorrigible. "Another thing we have in common. Thinking in bed. Alone." Letting him assume a little some-some was possible was one thing. Outright agreeing to it was another.

"Alone." He *tsk*ed under his tongue. "Now that's just silly." His gaze fell to her mouth, and his pupils dilated. "What race are you, darling?"

She felt what little warmth resided in her cheeks drain away and finally tugged her hand from his. Had he seen her staring at his pulse? Had he sensed the growing hunger in her? "I'm human. What race are you?"

"Targon." He chuckled, the most erotic chuckle she'd ever heard. "But seriously, pet. What race are you?"

"I'm human," she insisted, then returned to the only subject that mattered. "My friend. You smell like her." Bride had heard of Targons. They were a warrior race—big surprise—and all of them possessed brown hair and eyes. Or so she'd heard. If that was true, Aleaha wasn't a Targon. She had green eyes. "Why?"

One of his brows arched, and she feared he meant to rebuke her again. Then he shrugged as though he didn't care what they discussed. "I've just left a female's bed. Two females, actually. But neither used the name Aleaha, I don't think. Someone shouted 'Oh God' several times, but that's not helpful to you, is it? Anyway, I digress. I'm ninety percent certain I'd remember your name, if you were so inclined to give it."

She wondered how she'd laughed at his flirtation a moment ago. The man was frustration incarnate. "Think back. Are you sure you didn't cry out their names in the heat of passion?"

"I'm sure. But I can describe their birthmarks and wax preferences. Hair and eye color would be a bit harder, since I wasn't paying attention to that area."

Disappointed, Bride shook her head. Having him describe his partners wouldn't do any good, since Aleaha could look like a thousand different people. "Did you stop and eat anywhere afterward? Maybe rub up against the person sitting next to you?"

"No and no. Now, your name," he continued smoothly. "I hinted before, but you didn't give it to me. I guess I'll have to be direct. Tell me."

"I'm Bride." Damn it. Why had she given him her real name? Why hadn't she told him Amy, her new identity? "Can you take me to the women? I'd like to see them for myself."

"So persistent. I like that. By the way, my name is Devyn. Not that you asked." His lips edged into a frown, but another spark ignited in his eyes. This one, if she wasn't mistaken, was of curiosity. "Why didn't you ask for it?"

"Because I didn't care to know it." So much for flirting for the info. "Now. Can you. Take me. To the. Women?" *Careful, or your irritation with him will drive him away.*

His frown intensified, but then, so did his curiosity. "Yes. I can. Will I? No. I won't. So let's discuss something else. Like why you didn't care to know my name. In case you haven't noticed, I'm gorgeous. Everyone wants to know my name. Everyone."

Great. He was one of *those*. Conceited, narcissistic. Too bad he'd already used up her patience. There'd be no pandering to his ego.

She reached up and fisted his shirt. It was soft, almost as if it were made from cotton rather than the synthetic blends most people were now forced to wear. He must be wealthy.

"Take me to the women," she said. "I need to see them."

"Are you jealous of them?" he asked hopefully. "Do you want to kill them for having a go at me? Darling, we just met. That's silly. It's the girls after you that you should want to slay." He brushed a strand of her hair behind her ear, leaving a trail of fire. "Not that I'll be able to find one as lovely as you."

Frustrating man. "Of course you won't find anyone as lovely as me," she said, adding dryly, "No one compares to me. I'm all you'll be able to think about for the rest of your life. You'll be heartbroken that you let me get away, and perhaps you won't ever recover. Now that we've got that established, let's talk about those women you were with. If you won't take me to them, fine. At least tell me where you left them. I'll check them out myself."

One corner of those gorgeous lips twitched, as though he were fighting a grin. Of course, he ignored her demand. "You forgot to mention that all the women I've been with were merely practice for the day I met you."

"That's so obvious I wasn't sure it needed to be stated. Now. Where did you leave the women?"

His head tilted to the side as he studied her, those lips still twitching. "You don't desire me, do you?"

"No." Truth. He was gorgeous, as he'd said, the egotistical bastard, but his attitude grated.

Of its own accord, her gaze dropped once more to his neck. Well, maybe she desired his blood. He wasn't human but he was equipped like one, his vein fluttering faster than before. The hunger she'd battled all day increased exponentially. *You can't drink him here. Too public. Besides, you're with him for a reason, remember?*

Perhaps she could force him to tell her where the

women were. Even if they were gone, their scents would have lingered. For a while, at least. And if Leah *had* been there, and the scent still remained, Bride could follow her trail.

"I've lost you, darling," Devyn said, his amusement intensified for some reason.

"What? Oh, sorry." When she pulled herself from her musings and focused on him, a gasp escaped her. No longer did the night sky and golden moon frame his erotic face. Somehow he'd moved them both to an empty side street. To her knowledge, they'd never taken a step. Silver stone stretched all around them, lines of gang graffiti warning them away.

"How did you do that?" she asked.

"Do what?" He blinked, acting harmless, those long lashes like feathered fans.

"Move us." As if he didn't know.

Rather than try and deny it, he waved his fingers, saying, "Magic. Now, why don't we go somewhere cozy and get to know each other, hmm? We'll have sex and discuss your friend."

Her second offer of the day, though this one was more blatant. She wouldn't run away from this one, however. "How long ago did you leave those women?"

He uttered a long-suffering sigh. "I lied when I told you I liked persistent women. I'm this close," he pinched two of his fingers together, "to spanking you. Would you like that?"

"Enough!" Exasperated, Bride reached up and cupped his jaw, forcing his gaze on hers. "Listen, you. You're going to do everything I tell you to do." There was power in her voice now, soft thrums that wafted between them. "You're going to—"

"Wait." He frowned again. Even stiffened. But his eyes didn't glaze over, and his muscles didn't slacken, as was supposed to happen. "Say that again."

Fru-strat-ing. "Stop talking and listen to me. You will—"

"Do everything you tell me to do. Yes, I know. You're a vampire, aren't you?" he asked, and there was disappointment in his tone.

First, why wasn't he obeying her? Second, he knew what she was without seeing her bare her teeth? Disappointment wasn't the usual reaction she received. Terror, yes. Awe, sometimes that, too. Intrigue, even. Third, now would be a good time to beat feet. He knew what she was and could try and stake her.

Bride remained rooted in place, though, fury sprouting, growing, burning through her. She would face him and she would hurt him if necessary, but the bastard was going to tell her what she wanted to know. "Like I told you, I'm human. So just tell me where you left those women, damn it! I mean them no harm. I only want to talk to them."

"I've had a vampire," he said, ignoring her. Again. He wrapped his fingers around her wrists and lowered her arms away from his body. "I'm afraid you'll have to look elsewhere for dinner."

Wait. He'd had a vampire? That meant there were others out there. That meant she wasn't alone.

Her mouth fell open as excitement returned and blended with her fury, this time billowing through her on a cloud of astonishment. Each emotion was so strong, the thorns in her chest sharpened, joining the fire, but she hardly noticed them. There were others out there! Blood drinkers, just like her. People who could tell her why she now sickened when she drank. People who could teach her how to use her powers without weakening.

"You're not going anywhere," she told Devyn, once again grabbing onto his shirt. Her nails cut past the material and into skin. "I have questions, and you *are* going to answer them."

"It would have been my pleasure, if you had been what I'd thought. I collect different species of women, you see, and like I said, I've had a vampire. A few of them actually. I don't need another." Again, he jerked from her hold. One step, two, he backed away from her, almost upon the crowd. "A pity. I enjoyed your resistance."

"What do you think you're doing? You're staying here." Jaw clenched, Bride moved toward him. Her voice of compulsion obviously didn't work on him, but she'd grown up on the streets and had had to learn how to defend herself. Taking him down wouldn't be a hardship. "Tell me about the vampires of your own free will or I'll force you. *Then* I'll drain you."

He arched a brow. "I thought you were human?"

"Now I'm just pissed." She kicked out her leg, knocking his ankles together. He stumbled to the side, and she reached out and captured the back of his neck, using his momentum to swing and bash him against the brick wall. Breath whooshed from him, his eyes going wide with shock.

"Now you listen to me, you piece of shit." She slapped her hands at his sides, getting right in his face.

"I've had enough of your flirting and denials. You will tell me what I—"

"Stay still," he said, and every muscle in her body locked down. "Sorry, darling, but even though you took me unaware and I'm highly impressed, this restaurant is closed. Besides that, you can't force me to do anything I don't want to do."

She couldn't move. Her body couldn't freaking move. "What the hell?" she shouted, trying with all her might to uproot her feet. It was as if her boots had been glued to the pavement. "What did you do to me?"

"It's a little trick of mine. But don't worry." Grinning, he ducked under her arm. "You'll be able to move soon enough."

"I need to talk to you, damn it, and ask you some more questions. Questions you *will* answer."

"I only answer questions when the one doing the asking is naked, and as we won't be getting naked anytime soon . . ." Another of those disappointed sighs. "If I wasn't in a hurry, you might have been able to make me forget I prefer variety. As it is, I'm late and have to go. But do dream of me, darling."

That dirty, rotten bastard! How dare he! "Leave, and I'll come after you. I swear I will."

"Won't do you any good, I'm afraid." And with that, he disappeared amid the churning crowd.

Bride was unable to follow and all the madder for it. *He's going down,* she thought darkly. *In every possible way.*

CHAPTER 2

Devyn, king of the Targons, released the delightful woman from stun the moment he was too far to sniff out and find. It was difficult. Her energy molecules were like nothing he'd ever encountered before. Glimmering, almost overpowering . . . probably addictive. Already he craved another taste of them. But he prevailed, letting them go with only the slightest twinge of remorse.

The ability to force bodies to obey their every mental command was one of the reasons his people were so prized as warriors here. They could literally stop an army in its tracks and slit the soldiers' throats before a single fist or sword was raised.

Most humans were frightened by the skill. Some, like the agents of AIR, Alien Investigation and Removal, liked to utilize it for their own gain. The vampire, well, there'd been fire in her eyes. The girl had wanted answers—and perhaps his blood—in a bad way. His skill, not so much.

He grinned. She'd been hungry for answers, yes, and he'd denied her . . . there at the end she'd wanted to gut him, he was sure of it.

Only once before had a female resisted him with such fervor. Only once before had a female radiated such fury at him. Only once before had a female gotten the better of him and manhandled him with such force. That another had intrigued him, on all counts.

What's more, this one had mentally left the conversation a few times, and he'd wondered what thoughts drifted through her head, distracting her. Women simply did not dismiss him like that. Not since his father had died and he'd gone a little wild, doing everything he'd ever fantasized about doing to the females in his household—and so much more.

It might have been fun, bedding the vampire despite her origins, he thought, then shrugged. Nah. The more time he spent with her, the more she would have become like everyone else.

You sure? First moment he'd seen her, he'd meant to leave her without engaging her. Everything about her was designed to blend into a crowd. From her mousy brown hair to her unassuming hazel eyes. From her pale skin to her average height and curves.

Until he'd begun to see beyond the mask.

As he well knew, some races were able to "glammor" themselves, hiding their beauty with the commonplace so that no one would pay them and their actions any heed.

The more he'd looked at Bride, the more he'd seen the truth of her. She was a mélange of colors. She possessed long, jet-black hair, and her eyes were like dazzling emeralds. Her skin was dusted with rose, and her lips were a brilliant scarlet. A lush and dewy, ripe-for-a-kiss scarlet. And the energy swirling inside her . . . it was stunning, as bright as the sun and unlike anything he'd ever encountered.

That's what had gained his notice and convinced him to stay. That delectable energy, snapping and sizzling around her. Then she'd rebuked him, hadn't even wanted to know his name. In that moment, he'd become determined to win her. A challenge had seemed like a nice change of pace.

Then he'd discovered she was a vampire. Devyn sighed. He hadn't lied to her. He'd already had a vampire, two actually, and more of the same held no appeal to him.

If only The Voice hadn't given her away, he might have continued to convince himself she belonged to a race he'd never before come across. But her sweet timbre had gone low and husky, a hypnotic hum pulsing from every word, beseeching him to listen, to do everything she asked.

Unfortunately for her, he'd encountered The Voice before, and hers was weaker than most. When Devyn discovered an ability that could potentially bring about his downfall, he worked and trained until he learned to defeat *it*. Exactly what he'd done with The Voice. It had taken months, but his mind was now immune to secret suggestion.

Oh, the expression on her face when she realized he would not be doing as she'd wanted. Priceless. He chuckled, remembering.

What was she doing topside? Vampires lived underground, hidden from the rest of the world. They only emerged twice a year to collect food—aka humans—and not even their exiled were sent to the surface to live. Because of this, most people still considered them the stuff of myth and nightmare. Devyn only knew about them because he'd once participated in slave auctions, buying females for his collection.

And no, he'd never forced his purchases to sleep with him. Anyone reluctant to be with him, he set free. So far, though, there'd been only one who'd rejected him. Eden Black, a golden-skinned Rakan and the woman he'd remained on Earth for, hoping to bed at least once. The woman who loved him—like a goddamn brother. His chuckle was wry this time. One day that would change; she would leave her lover and seduce Devyn. He was sure of it. Until then, he would simply continue to play with the vast supply of females here to distract himself.

Bride, with her don't-touch-me attitude, was a lot like Eden, he realized. Maybe he *should* have bedded her. He could have pretended he'd finally won Eden's affections.

He frowned. *I've had vampires, and I don't want anymore, remember? Even if I'm pretending they're something else.*

One of the auction traders had managed to snag two bloodsuckers who'd been on the hunt, and high bidder that he'd always been, Devyn had acquired them. Actually, the two had worn those glammored masks of plainness, and no one else had been interested in them. But they'd dropped those masks for him and him alone, which was how he'd learned such things existed.

They'd spent several weeks with him, and they'd told him much about their society. Very archaic, he thought, much like his own world had been. There was a royal family, and everyone else lived to serve them. Those who broke the rules were harshly punished. He wondered if the current vampire king knew of Bride's whereabouts.

Surely not. Living among the mortals was forbidden because it could leak the secret of their existence, bringing humans and otherworlders to their door. Perhaps war. If little Bride was discovered, she would most likely be killed for placing her brethren in danger. Oh, well. It wasn't his problem.

Devyn turned a corner, his friend's apartment building coming into view. One of the newer structures, it boasted sturdy stone and metal that could withstand fire and air strikes long enough for the people inside to evacuate safely. Not much to look at, but the people of Earth cared more about safety than aesthetics now. After they'd fought the war of the species, he couldn't blame them, though he did prefer the open beauty of his own planet, Targonia.

A planet he could return to, and often did, but one he no longer ruled. Thank God. Oh, he still had his title, still had his army, but as interplanetary travel had become more prevalent, his people had been introduced to life without a monarchy. Some had wanted to leave, travel the galaxies through interworld wormholes, while some had wanted to stay, but all had wanted to govern their own lives. So he'd let them, because he'd been tired, so tired, of ruling. Of being an example of all that was "pure."

Not that they'd seen much of his purity those last few years.

Now, he spent most of his time here on Earth. Helping AIR. At one time, an alien aiding the very people who policed them would have been laughable. But over the past year, the powers that be had realized the only way to control certain dominant races was with, well, certain dominant races.

AIR liked having Devyn on their side, and they paid him very well. Though the money wasn't the reason he stuck around. He didn't need it. Being king came with certain privileges, and one of those was the cash to set himself up on whatever planet he desired in the style he was accustomed. He stuck around because of the agents he worked with. Eden, of course, was included in their numbers.

For the first time in his vast existence, he was treated as an equal. No one lived their life based on what he said or did. No one was scandalized or humiliated by the actions of him and his "beast." No one bowed to him—except the females, when he asked. Excluding Eden Black. And probably Bride. Damn it. He had to stop thinking about her. She was gone, out of reach.

Here, he wasn't a leader, an example, or a marital prize. He was simply a man who enjoyed sex, fighting, and freedom. In that order.

Sex. The single word elicited an image of black-as-night hair, eyes of brilliant green fire, lips stained red with blood. Every muscle in his body hardened. Did no good, trying to keep her from his mind. Why'd the little firecracker have to be a vampire? Variety was the only thing that kept him sane, the only thing that kept the pain of his palace days, of being denied *everything*, beaten to the back of his mind.

He stomped up the steps and entered Dallas's building, the cool night air giving way to warmth and laden with the scent of lemon cleaner. There was a lounge area complete with two chocolate-colored couches and a matching chair, a coffee table and a cream-colored rug.

Not the wisest of choices, as the pale fabric was already stained with dirt. Dirt. He shuddered. He was a clean freak and wasn't ashamed of it, even though he knew the preference stemmed from the frightened, cowed, utterly repressed boy he'd once been.

Behind the half-moon desk of monitors, the security guard nodded, clearly expecting him, allowing him to pass without a word. As he pounded up the stairs to the fifth floor—no cramped elevator for him, thank you—he enjoyed the burn in his thighs. Physical exertion of any kind was always a pleasure.

A pretty girl, probably in her early twenties, stopped and gaped when she spotted him. She was human, with pale hair and brown eyes. A little plump, but he liked and welcomed all shapes and sizes, all colors and consenting ages. *If* he hadn't sampled the race before, that is. Sadly, it was becoming harder and harder—not in the literal sense, unfortunately—to find new bed partners.

"Hi," she said, a little breathless.

He nodded in greeting, but didn't smile, didn't flirt. No reason to lead her on. Like vampires, even lovely, colorful, tease-just-right vampires, he'd already had his fill of human females. They were boring. "Whacking off," as Dallas would say, was more fun.

Her gaze bored into his back all the way down the hall. Maybe that was because he'd frozen her in place. He never gave his back to a person without doing so. It was habit now, from his palace days when rebels would have done anything to cleave his head from his body. Or maybe it was because she was imagining him naked and would have raced over to flirt with him if allowed. Either way, he freed her only when he was in front of Dallas's door and she had his profile.

Dallas Gutierrez was already standing in the opened

entry, eyes narrowed, arms stretched out to block Devyn's forward progress. He was a handsome man with dark hair, dark skin, and eyes so pale a blue they were almost translucent. He wasn't quite as tall as Devyn, but was just as bulked with muscle.

"You're late," Dallas said, clearly irritated. "The girls have already left."

"I know. I ran into Macy, Mishka, and Mia a few blocks down. And my God, that's a lot of *M*'s." Apologizing would have meant he regretted where he'd been and how long he'd taken, and he didn't. "Security call and let you know I was on my way up?"

"No." There was a wealth of resentment in that one word.

Which meant Dallas's psychic abilities were growing stronger—abilities the agent had only recently acquired and despised with every ounce of his being. The more powerful his abilities, the less breakable his bond to the alien responsible for them.

A while back, Dallas had been shot with pyre-fire. There'd been a hole in his chest, his skin and organs charred and unable to regenerate. Kyrin en Arr, an Arcadian king, had sliced his own wrist and fed Dallas his blood. That blood had saved Dallas's life, causing his body to supernaturally heal. And now, Devyn knew, as he saw a future he'd never been able to see before, Dallas feared the blood inside him was turning *him* into an alien.

"Aw, you sensed me," Devyn said to lighten the mood. "I'm touched. I wonder if that means we're meant to be together forever."

"Fuck you."

"Proof we aren't really meant to be together, I suppose. My mate would never talk to me like that."

Dallas bared his perfect white teeth in a scowl. "Can you take nothing seriously?"

"There'll be time enough for serious when I'm dead." Truth. His father had ruled for two hundred years, concerned only with his reputation, bound by the opinion of others. And his father had died, not a laugh line on his face, mourning all that he'd missed, all that he could have had.

On the flip side, his mother had lived for her own happiness, no one else's, and she had died with a smile on her face, her merriment imprinted on every wall in the palace.

At that time, Devyn had been more like his father. Joy had had no place in his life. Only duty. Only honor. He'd wed the female that had been chosen for him. He'd attended meetings and ceremonies, on time and dressed as benefiting his station. He'd led the army but had never fought with them, his precious, stainless life too important to risk injury. He'd sat on his throne and issued judgment for crimes, deciding who would live and who would die when he'd never truly lived himself.

He hadn't played games, and after all the punishments he'd endured, he hadn't so much as looked at another woman after his marriage. Not even when said wife viewed sex as the same filthy pastime his father had. She'd vomited the first and only time he'd placed his ugly "thing" inside her. So he'd kept his desires in his pants, thinking, what kind of example would I set, pledging my life to one yet lusting after another?

When he'd seen the regret in his father's eyes as the once rigid, sanctimonious man gasped his final breath, saying, "Everything I could have done . . . ," Devyn's entire outlook had changed. He'd severed ties with his frigid queen. Divorce, it was called here. He'd begun training with his men and truly leading them. Sometimes, when his dick had hardened, he'd stroked it. Sometimes he'd even lain with the servants—however filthy that made him.

Occasionally shame had come gunning for him, for the things he'd done to himself, for the things he'd done to his lovers, but he'd come to see that shame as his enemy and had fought against it with all his might.

The more things he'd done and the more women he'd taken, the more he had realized the bliss of diversity. A desire to sample anything and everything had overtaken him.

Now the shame no longer plagued him. Not even a little. He did what he wanted, when he wanted it. Bed two sisters at the same time? Why not? String a female up and whip her as she begged for orgasm? Sure. Go at it in public? Any time, any where. He would not die with a single regret.

"You reek of determination," Dallas said, cutting into his musings. "What the hell are you thinking about?"

"The past."

"That's never good."

No, it wasn't. "Gonna make me stand here all night?" He loved human slang and used it every chance he got. Made him feel more like a man, his royal parentage a distant memory.

"Maybe. You'd deserve it."

Being late because you were enjoying a three-way wasn't a crime. It was a reason to celebrate.

Perhaps Dallas the Somber needed a three-way of his own.

"I predicted you'd be here," Dallas said, "and here you are. There was nothing in my vision about you lingering. I can shut the door in your face and not change the future in some terrible way."

"Really, it doesn't get any better than predicting my presence. Your luck must be changing." Usually the agent's visions were bleak. Like the time he'd seen a woman—a half-human, half-machine cyborg—killing their friend Jaxon. When he tried to change the outcome, it had been *Dallas* who'd almost killed him.

Since then, Dallas's mood had been harsh, black, the man hard as shit to please. The only silver lining was that Devyn had found something new to bed: a cyborg. Mental note: be on the lookout for a black-haired, green-eyed, half-machine woman. Even a brown-haired, hazel-eyed one would do, killing two female birds with one long, hard stone.

"You're doing it again," Dallas said on a sigh. "Winking in and out of the conversation. Only this time you're smiling like an idiot."

"You would be, too, if you were imagining what I am."

Dallas rolled his eyes. "I don't want to know what's in your head. If I hadn't seen the dirty, downright nasty way you fight, I'd think the only things you were capable of doing were having sex and thinking about sex. Now, I want to know why you were late."

"I was tied up." Again, truth. He'd allowed his partners

to anchor his wrists and ankles to the bedpost. They'd liked the thought of having him at their mercy, and he'd liked the girls doing all the work. Not that he'd been helpless. That, he would never allow. But he'd let them think he was vulnerable, and they had pleased him for it.

The agent studied him and shook his head in exasperation. "You might as well return to your women. Like I said, the girls have already left."

They'd agreed to meet today and discuss the latest threat to New Chicago. Damn if there wasn't always a threat. "You know I never return to a woman once I've had her. So let me in and tell me what was decided during the meeting. Meanwhile, I'll entertain you, there's no denying that, and you'll stop acting pissy. It's win-win."

Another sigh. "You don't deserve it, but fine. Come in." Dallas moved to the side.

"You're as vengeful as a woman, you know that?" Devyn said as he passed him.

There was a growl, and Devyn's lips twitched. So easy to provoke, his friend was.

The apartment was as messy as always. Well, except for the time Devyn had paid two hookers to clean it. Naked. But the spotlessness hadn't lasted long. Wrappers and beer bottles were scattered throughout, along with dirty clothes and weapons. The leather couch Devyn had bought Dallas could barely be seen under the chaos.

Grimacing, Devyn kicked his way to the kitchen and grabbed a beer. He didn't pop it open until after he'd plopped into the recliner. Something hard dug into his back, but he didn't bother to move it. He'd only encounter something else, he was sure.

Dallas fell into the seat across from him and propped his ankles on the small stone table, dislodging a computer notebook and sending it to the floor with a *thwack*. He didn't bend down and pick it up.

Messy as he was, Dallas usually took more care with his equipment. Something more than simple anger at Devyn's tardiness was at work here. Had to be. Devyn's gaze sharpened on him. There were lines of strain around Dallas's eyes and mouth, and his T-shirt and jeans were wrinkled, stained, and cut. He'd lost a little weight. His hair hadn't been brushed in a week. Maybe a month.

Guilt joined the beer, swimming laps inside Devyn's veins as he gulped back a few swigs. While he'd spent the last two hours fucking himself stupid, his closest friend had been stressing about something. "Tell me what's going on, and I'll fix it," he said. It was a vow.

Though he only lived for his own pleasure nowadays, he couldn't walk away from a friend in need. He would regret it, and Devyn never did anything he would regret.

Dallas scrubbed a hand down his face. "I'm not sure you can fix this."

"Tell me, anyway."

"Remember Nolan?"

"Of course." Nolan was a new breed of alien called the Schön. They were beautiful and deadly, and they had come to Earth, destruction hot on their heels. Everyone they'd bedded, everyone their blood had come into contact with, had soon become cannibals. Once-loving humans had morphed into flesh-eating murderers. They'd also died slowly and painfully, the virus eating through *them*.

AIR had managed to capture Nolan and kill several

of his brethren—as well as everyone infected—and that should have been the end of it. But "should have" meant nothing. Now the queen of the Schön, the woman responsible for the virus and the greatest source of its power, was on her way to this planet.

When she would arrive, no one but Nolan knew, and he wasn't talking. AIR only knew that she *would* come, and she *would* kill. Already she had destroyed several worlds, for the more people she infected through sex and bloodletting, the longer she lived, keeping the disease at a minimum inside her own body. Same with her army. Same with Nolan. If they didn't pass the disease on to someone else, and then someone else, and then someone else, they too became cannibals.

It was a vicious cycle.

"You ready for this?" Dallas asked.

"Lay it on me."

"Nolan escaped AIR."

Okay. No, he hadn't been ready for that. "Shit. How long ago?"

Dallas glanced at the clock hanging on the wall. "About fifteen hours."

"And no one realized until this afternoon when Mia called the meeting?"

"That's right."

"How is that possible?" The guy had been locked in a state-of-the-art facility, complete with fingerprint IDs, retinal scanners, and weight- and heat-sensitive tiles, all of which should have caused the alarms to screech to life the moment he stepped outside his cell. Again, "should have" sucked ass.

"God only knows. He's out there, probably screwing his way to good health while infecting innocent women, who then infect their lovers. If that's the case, this thing is going to spread fast. So fast we might not be able to stop it."

Devyn placed the now-empty beer bottle atop the stack of unfolded laundry beside him. "Think the Schön will want revenge against Jaxon and Mishka?"

Mishka, the cyborg Devyn wanted a go at but wouldn't make a play for because he did not poach his friend's females, ever, had befriended and betrayed Nolan, all to protect Jaxon. Saving the world from that sadistic disease by locking Nolan away had been a side benefit.

"Revenge?" Dallas shrugged. "He didn't seem the type, you know? He was more concerned about falling in love before he died than truly hurting others. I mean, I got the sense that he didn't enjoy infecting his lovers and only did it to survive."

Love. Devyn barely stopped himself from rolling his eyes. Love could be found in the arms of anyone, anywhere, if only people would abandon the silly idea of monogamy. What was the point of giving yourself to only one? Boredom, that's what.

"I'm guessing a patrol has been sent out to look for him," he said.

"Correct. So far, no sighting. Who knows? Maybe I'm wrong, and he's not out there screwing everyone he meets. Maybe he's keeping to himself, hoping to die with a little dignity. You know, without an AIR audience. Or maybe he caught a solar flare home." Solar flares were what opened the wormholes that allowed the travel between the planets. That was how Devyn so easily moved between this one and his own. "There's been no new case of infection."

"None that have been reported, at least." One thing Devyn knew about those in power: they kept secrets. Many women could have been infected by Nolan and eliminated by the government already.

And one thing Devyn knew about men: they liked to have sex. Nolan needed sex more than most, not just for pleasure but for survival. He was sleeping around, keeping himself strong, no doubt about it. There would be no dying with dignity.

"Nolan didn't return to his planet," Devyn said. "It was wiped, remember? All of its people were either infected or killed. And then, of course, the infected traveled to Eden's planet, Raka, wiped it, then ventured here. We have to catch him, and we have to kill him this time."

Dallas shook his head. "We can't kill him. He's the only one who knows about the Schön queen we'll soon be fighting. Speaking of, I wish there was a way to send the bitch a message. Come here, and we'll hang you with your own intestines."

Devyn, too. "We've questioned Nolan repeatedly. Hell, I even tortured him. He never broke and managed to keep every one of his secrets. And the fault was not mine. I'm a damn good torturer." It wasn't something he usually enjoyed, but he'd been the only one for the job. Touching Nolan hadn't been an option. Spilling his blood hadn't been an option, either. The disease inside his body was alive, with a will and agenda of its own, and it only left a host when another was nearby.

Devyn had not wanted to become one of those hosts. As he could force objects to move in the same way he could force people, manipulating their energy, he'd been able to shatter every bone inside Nolan's body without ever setting foot in the room.

"It's time to end him," he added, "before he begins a pandemic."

Dallas scoured a hand down his tired face. "That's what we decided, as well."

Wait—what? "Then why the hell'd you hassle me about keeping him alive for his secrets?"

"Mishka spent an hour trying to talk us out of killing him. She cried, Dev. Real damn tears." The agent leaned his head against the back of the couch, staring up at the ceiling. No one was tougher than Mishka, who had once had a chip in her brain. A chip that had forced her to do things she hadn't wanted to do. Murder people she loved, have sex with people she didn't. Only recently had it been removed. "I wanted to cut out my heart and give it to her. Now you waltz in here, late, and state as pretty as you please the very thing we had to fight her for."

"One, I'm late for everything but what really matters. And two, had I been here, we both know her tears wouldn't have affected me." Tears never affected him. It was almost like he was missing the sensitivity gene or something. For sex, he could *pretend* like he cared that he'd upset a female. But actually care? No. Emotions, he'd learned from ruling his people and being responsible for their fates, were foolish. Wasted, even. "Now, why don't you tell me what this is really about."

Silence. Thick, heavy. Then Dallas laid his arm over

his eyes and said, "It's Kyrin. Ever since he saved my life, there's been a desire to please him inside me—and it's not from gratitude! Anything he says, I feel compelled to do on a cellular level. Like the blood inside me knows it used to belong to him and wants to cater to his every whim."

"You're talking as though the blood is alive, as with the Schön."

"Maybe it is. I mean, if Kyrin told me to blow him, I'd blow him, even though I don't swing that way. And yeah, I know he'd never command me to do something like that, but still. I can't stand even the possibility of it."

"Shall I kill him for you?" Devyn's loyalty belonged to this man, not to the Arcadian. Dallas had broken several AIR rules for him, placing his own career and future in jeopardy. He'd even saved Devyn's life, jumping in the way and taking a blade meant for Devyn. Of course, the agent's new Arcadian blood had caused him to heal quickly, but that hadn't lessened the impact of the gesture.

More than that, Devyn liked him. Dallas had no inhibitions, and he was as open as Devyn was about his sexuality. Those blue eyes never judged him, and the man himself had been as desperate for a friend as Devyn had been. Mia, his last BFF, was now dating the very man responsible for Dallas's gifts—and torment.

"You'd do that for me?" Dallas asked.

"Of course." Yes, Devyn respected the enigmatic Kyrin and would hate to see him eliminated. And yes, anyone who could put up with the violent Mia Snow for more than a single bedding deserved his respect. But if Dallas wanted Kyrin gone, Devyn would take care of it, no questions asked. He owed him that much. At least.

SEDUCE THE DARKNESS   43

Wasn't like he got all emotional about his kills. To be honest, he could eliminate almost anyone with no hesitation and no sense of remorse. He'd been that way since defeating his sexual shame. With its fall, his other emotions had seemed to crumble as well. He didn't cry. Ever, for any reason. He didn't become attached to people, places, or objects, in the sense that he craved them, needed them, and had to be with them. And he certainly didn't mourn when those around him kicked it.

Perhaps, though, he wouldn't tear the otherworlder's limbs from his body and choke him to death with his own hands, as was Devyn's custom. Perhaps, too, he wouldn't sneak up from behind and slice his throat. He was fond of doing that, as well. Maybe he would challenge the alien to a fight, win, of course, and then bury the body and pretend like nothing had happened. It was the only honorable thing to do, really.

"No," Dallas said on a sigh. "Don't kill him."

"Bummer. I had just come up with a gold star plan, if I do say so myself." Devyn knew why Dallas had declined his offer. Dallas still loved Mia like a sister, and Mia loved Kyrin. The agent would never do anything to hurt her, which meant he'd never do anything to hurt his new blood master, no matter how much it might beleaguer him. "You change your mind, you let me know and it's done."

Dallas straightened, some of the tension leaving him. He even gifted Devyn with one of his wry—so rare these days—smiles. "Just for that, I forgive you for being late."

"Does that mean you're not breaking up with me?"

Snorting, Dallas launched a pillow at him. "You could be so lucky."

The small square of material slammed into his chest. Devyn collected it and propped it behind his head, getting comfortable. But damn it, what the hell was still poking him in the back? Finally he reached back, fingers wrapping around . . . a vibrator. He blinked at it. Large, pink, and beaded.

"Want to explain this?" he said, holding it up to the light and smiling.

His friend shrugged sheepishly. "Had a girl over and we had a three-way with it."

"Wait a second." Devyn tossed the device to the floor and peered over at the agent in disbelief. "Back up. Two things shock me about your story. One, you actually brought a female into this dump? And two, you had a three-way yet you're still moody? Sounds like you need a few lessons in ménage etiquette."

Dallas shot him the bird.

"You wish. Okay, subject change before you start slobbering on yourself over the possibility. When do we start hunting Nolan?"

"Tonight. The others are out there now, and we're their relief."

"Let's not wait. I'm bored."

"But I'm tired. I worked all night and haven't had a chance to catch any Z's."

"Excuses, excuses. Man up, get off your ass and grab some weapons. We're going hunting."

CHAPTER 3

Finally they caught sight of the bastard.

Devyn remained in the shadows, back pressed against a wall of peeling red paint and metal. Fourteen days of flashing Nolan's picture to everyone they encountered, fourteen days of interviewing people who might have interacted with the poisonous alien. Fourteen days of passing out their cell numbers—and having to answer the calls of supposed sightings that were really women trying to date them—waiting for something, anything to break. Fourteen days of disappointment and failure. Until now. Nolan had come out of hiding to score a prostitute.

Fitting, that sex would be the man's downfall.

They had to be careful, had to treat this situation like they were patient admirers and Nolan a skittish virgin. (Devyn happened to be very good at that.) Nolan could cloak himself with invisibility and disappear in the blink of an eye. It was a skill that had almost gotten several AIR agents killed the last time they'd dealt with him, because it was nearly impossible to win a fight with a ghost.

Earlier, before he'd actually seen the little shit, Devyn had feared he'd already made a wrong move, alerting Nolan to his intentions and causing the Schön to follow *him*. Every so often, he'd felt as if someone was watching him, studying him. Waiting. Perhaps judging. That gaze had blistered him, seemingly alive with fury.

It was as that fury had grown that he'd begun to think that maybe it wasn't Nolan. Maybe it was the vampire. Bride. *I'll come after you. I swear it,* she'd shouted heatedly. Once, he'd even thought he'd caught sight of her. But she'd been blissfully, erotically naked, more curved than possible, all rose-tinted skin, blood red nipples, and dark hair.

Because he'd caught this wondrous glimpse on a crowded public street, he'd known he hadn't really seen her. He knew women. No matter their race, they didn't traipse around naked. (Much to his consternation.) There was simply too much shame involved. (Again, much to his consternation.)

After that, though, he'd begun to look for her. Which was odd. He'd already dismissed her from his mind. Hadn't he? But he couldn't deny that a true glimpse of dark hair now sent his pulse racing. Pale skin caused moisture to flood his mouth. Green eyes caused his cock to harden painfully.

And each time his body reacted to thoughts of her, he remembered the way she'd rebuffed him. How she'd wanted no part of his (magnificent) body. Not sexually, at least.

His desire to see her, really see her, had increased.

If he put the vastness of his sensual knowledge to

work, would he be able to tempt her to his bed? He just didn't know, and every fiber of his being sparked with the challenge of finding out.

He was going to have to find her, he decided. Surely she'd succumb, just like everyone else, and he'd stop thinking about her. Exactly as he'd done with everyone else. Life was too precious to waste wondering if Bride's eyes would sparkle like emeralds when she came. If her nipples were really blood red. If she had any tattoos, birthmarks, or scars. The scars he might enjoy kissing all better. Or was kissing boo-boos an Earth custom she would hate? Had she been raised here on the surface? Or had she escaped the underground to avoid punishment for something? If so, why? And did that mean she would make love like a naughty little criminal?

He had to know. The sooner he found her, he thought, the better.

He'd use the databases at AIR, of course, but would they be able to lead him to her? All he had was her first name. And what a strange name it was. Bride. Who had named her? Why had they named her that? Was she mated?

"Can you believe the balls on this guy?" Dallas muttered. They were on opposite sides of the alley, yet Devyn heard him as if he'd spoken directly beside him. They were both wearing sweet little headsets that allowed them to communicate quietly and privately no matter the distance between them.

They were dressed in black from head to toe, and even though Devyn knew his friend's exact location, he had trouble making him out in the sea of red and shadow.

Helped that clouds covered the moon, and the closest streetlights offered only a minimal glow.

"Yeah, I can. I'd be doing the same thing." He spoke in a whisper so low not even the wind could pick it up.

"No, you wouldn't. If he screws her, she'll die. You're pretty fucked in the head, but you wouldn't knowingly kill a woman."

Not necessarily true. Many times during his marriage he'd imagined cutting his wife's heart out with a spoon and eating it in front of her. "Can I approach him now?" Devyn couldn't wait to finish off the Schön. He wanted to be looking for the vampire, and that he wasn't . . . "Huh, huh, huh? Please."

"Worse than a child." Dallas sighed. "I told you. That's not how AIR works. There are too many civilians around. We can't protect them *and* take Nolan. We have to wait for backup."

"AIR can suck it. How much longer before we get to give up on backup? 'Cause at this rate, they'll never get here. The pimp is almost done giving the price list. Nolan's growing impatient, and very soon he's going to lead the female inside, where we'll have to involve a shitload of other civilians. We have to take him here."

Would have been easier if at least one of the others had arrived, yes. Devyn didn't mind admitting that. Breean could move faster than the eye could see. Mishka was stronger than ten men combined. Kyrin could heal with a drop of his blood, and Mia was just plain mean. Eden and Macy, well, they were good soldiers, but Devyn preferred them as eye candy. But damn it, this inactivity was driving him insane.

Of course, none of the other agents would have been

necessary if Devyn's own ability worked on the Schön. Unfortunately, there were some people that were immune to his telekinesis, able to move normally when he attempted to control them with his mind.

It was strange, though. Most that had been raised here on Earth, no matter their race, he could lock on and control. Outside of Earth, it was iffy. Their energy frequencies were usually too jumbled.

"Someone should be here," he griped. "What the hell is holding them up? You made the call half an hour ago."

"What do you want to bet Mishka's the culprit? She wants Nolan alive."

"Then she should be here to save him from our wrath."

"She would be, if she thought we were competent. To her, you're a slut and I'm a bad shot."

"Right on both counts." Devyn's lips curled into a smile. It had been the last time they'd battled a Schön that Dallas had turned on Mishka, squeezing off a few rounds in her direction. Yes, he'd wanted to kill her, thinking he would be saving Jaxon from her evil intentions, as his vision had led him to believe. That's when he'd hit Jaxon instead. "Doesn't matter, though. We have to act. Nolan's pale, unsteady on his feet, and perfect for plucking."

"If we fail . . ."

"We won't."

"You're not the psychic in this relationship. If he opens fire on civilians, our heads are gonna roll."

"And that would be a damn shame, pretty as I am. Give me a minute and let me see if I can move people away from us." Pissed him off that he hadn't thought of this sooner. He blamed Bride. Damned red nipples.

Devyn propelled mental fingers out of the alley and down the connecting streets, grabbing onto every pulse of energy he could and commanding each body they belonged to, to perform the same act: turn north and keep moving one foot in front of the other.

Pulling the strings of that many humans tired him, but he fought through the lethargy until they were a good distance away. "Done. No civilians will be hurt in the making of this war zone."

"You're scary, you know that?" Dallas said with quiet affection.

"I know. It's hardly fair to others that I'm a triple threat. Pretty *and* talented."

"That's only two, moron."

"I thought it'd be rude to mention my cock."

Dallas chuckled. "All right. Here's the deal. Despite Mishka's belief, I'm the better shot, so I'll do the firing. You and Mr. Happy just sit there and look pretty."

A given. But he would be wearing heat-sensitive goggles just in case Dallas missed and Nolan did his invisible thing and tried to run. "Next time at least *try* and challenge me."

Dallas uttered another of those raspy chuckles.

"Oh, and before I forget, I think you should stun him rather than kill."

"Planned on it," Dallas said.

That was good; they were agreed. But . . . "Why not kill?" Devyn knew why he wanted the little shit alive but frozen, but he doubted his reasons were the same as his friend's.

Dallas didn't like to show it, but killing bothered him.

Devyn could tell. The knowledge was always there, dulling the light in those baby blues. That was why Devyn had wanted Dallas only to stun. When the bastard was immobile, Devyn could move in and finish him off.

Still not a drop of the Schön's blood could be spilled. Not without causing that pandemic. So he'd have to content himself with something simple, like stomping on the guy's trachea.

"I mean, we both know it needs to be done," he added when there was no reply. "We even agreed to do it. I've been looking forward to it." Did his eagerness mean he had a skewed sense of right and wrong? No. Something needed to be done about the Schön's treachery, before it was too late, and to Devyn, taking his life would be the same as taking out the trash. "Why?" he repeated.

"Mishka, man. I still remember those tears . . . I was thinking we could take him in and have Mia gas him." Since Jack Pagosa, the iron-fisted ruler of AIR, had retired a few weeks ago, Mia had taken his place and now called the shots.

"I don't think so. Too big a chance for another escape." Just as Devyn reached up to pull his goggles over his eyes, he saw Nolan stiffen. Sniff the air.

Both he and Dallas stopped breathing, suspended in an oh-shit moment of internal begging. *Please don't disappear and run. Please, please don't disappear and run.*

A moment passed. Nolan remained just as he was.

"I'm pretty sure he's on to us. Initiating battle . . . now." Dallas fired, blue beams lighting up the alley.

The prostitute, tired-looking and dirty, screamed and fell to her ass. The pimp broke into a mad dash out of the alley and never looked back. Nolan was smarter, though, even sick as he clearly was with his grayish skin and sunken eyes, and dove to the side, the beams soaring just over his shoulder.

"Mishka was right," Dallas breathed, already firing again. "I'm bad."

Again, Nolan rolled out of the way, his body twisting unnaturally. This time, he withdrew his own pyregun and started hammering at the trigger. Good thing Devyn had moved the innocent out of the way. The otherworlder's beams were yellow, which meant he was shooting to kill. One touch from them and flesh would melt, muscle would turn to ash, and bone to lava.

Not everyone would be as lucky as Dallas and have an Arcadian swoop in to the rescue.

Devyn dropped to the ground, finally jerking the goggles in place. His vision tunneled to pitch, then two slashes of red became visible in front of him. Nolan and the girl. He kept his gun on stun. If the girl was human, it wouldn't affect her. If she was alien, she would freeze in place for about twenty-four hours, able to see and hear everything around her but unable to move. No fun, but better than dying.

He fired at both slashes. One, he hit. One, he missed. Didn't take a genius to realize he'd hit the girl. She scrambled behind a Dumpster, even though the beam had knocked her back against the wall, absorbing into her body. She was human, after all. That might add a few complications. Humans tended to throw fits about this kind of thing, whereas aliens didn't want to make waves and draw attention to themselves. Especially where AIR was concerned.

"Shit, man," Dallas panted through the earpiece. "This is bad."

"I know." How the hell was Nolan able to anticipate the timing and direction of the beams and move before they nailed him? That was not a skill the otherworlder had possessed the last time they'd fought him.

Dallas continued to fire, though his shots were all over the place, as if he didn't know where to aim. Nolan must have gone invisible. With the goggles, it didn't matter. Devyn saw his every move. Watching him was like watching a fluid, lethal dance of ducking, rolling, and gliding.

"Twelve o'clock," he instructed the agent.

Dallas aimed, fired. Missed as Nolan again dodged. Over and over they repeated the process. Devyn supplied the coordinates, Dallas fired, and Nolan darted safely away. Dallas couldn't wear his goggles while Devyn wore his, because *someone* had to keep an eye on real life.

"What now?" Dallas demanded. "Do we approach?"

"Not yet. Fast as he's moving, he's not winded enough and could dart past us. We'd lose him along the city streets. Right now he's feeling pinned, and that's to our advantage."

Nolan stopped at the side of the building, his elbows jerking back and forth as though he were pulling on a door. He was, Devyn realized. Probably hoped to escape the area without having to rush the agents aiming at him.

"He's trying to open a door."

"I already melted the ID pad," Dallas shouted. "It's not gonna open, Nolan, no matter what you do. So why don't you just surrender peacefully and come with us?"

"I need a woman, and you weren't giving me any," the otherworlder growled as he zigzagged through the cramped space. "I'll die if I go back."

Whaaa. Had Nolan always been such a whiner? AIR's cells were well lit. The otherworlder hadn't been stripped and shoved into a cold, black hole. Hadn't been denied all sensory perception. "We can't let you run wild."

Dallas must have been following the sounds of the alien's hoarse inhalations, because his shots were mere inches from their target. "You infect people. Innocents."

"I didn't pick an innocent this time. I picked a woman who's already dying."

"Yeah, and how many people would she have taken with her if you'd infected her?" Dallas asked.

"No more than she already was."

"But those people would have infected more, and the people they infected would have infected more."

"Try and run, I dare you." Devyn narrowed his focus on the backside of the alien's glowing red form. Maybe, if he aimed at a piece of him rather than trying to nail him in the center, he'd actually hit the center if Nolan dodged the right way. A lot of ifs, but worth a chance, at least, 'cause damn. He was losing, and he hated to lose. "The closer you are to us, the harder it will be to dodge us"—he hoped—"and we all know it." Kind of.

Nolan paused, teetered to the left, as if he knew another shot was coming.

Devyn squeezed the trigger, angling the barrel of the gun at the last second. Finally. Contact. Nolan slammed into the wall and slid to his ass, the beam soaking into his side. But there wasn't time to congratulate himself on

a job well done. Nolan didn't freeze. He shook his head and pushed to his feet.

How. The. Hell?

"Damn it!" Devyn was the one to curse this time. "It didn't work. Stun has never not worked." He glanced over at his friend, seeking guidance. What should he do? But rather than ask, he sucked in a breath. Where there should have been only one red light, one body, there were two lights. Two bodies. And he couldn't tell which one was Dallas. *Who* the hell?

He ripped off the goggles, stilled. Only one body greeted him. Dallas's. His friend was looking at Nolan, firing one shot after another, and hitting the otherworlder dead center in the chest.

The otherworlder had given up on invisibility and was looking down at his own body in wonder, as if he couldn't believe he was withstanding stun either.

Devyn drew the goggles back over his eyes, focusing just behind Dallas. Once again, there were two slashes of red, indicating two people. One seemed to be inside the wall.

Again, he tore the goggles off. Again, only Dallas was visible. Another invisible Schön? No, couldn't be. They couldn't *become* part of an object. Could they?

He was afraid to freeze whoever it was, afraid the man—or woman?—would be killed or stuck in the wall for twenty-four hours, and Devyn would have to wait to get to him. Or her. More than that, a dead person couldn't answer questions, and Devyn suddenly had a million.

More than losing, he hated mysteries.

"No matter what I do, keep your attention on Nolan. Also, move away from the wall," he told Dallas quietly. "You've got a shadow."

"Need cover?" Dallas inched to a stand and eased to the center of the alley.

"Please."

"Let's talk about this, Nolan," his friend said to the otherworlder to mask Devyn's actions. "Surely we can work something out."

"Yeah, like my death."

"You're the one who escaped."

"I told you. It was that or die. I'm not ready to die, damn it!"

With Dallas out of the way and approaching Nolan, Devyn inched toward the wall. Strangely enough, the red light seemed to be coming toward him, as well. Keeping his gun trained with one hand, he once again shoved his goggles out of the way with the other. Sure enough, the wall was moving.

Then a woman's shape began to take form, though her skin was the exact pattern of the red brick behind her. Even her hair boasted that dusty red as it fluttered in the breeze. His eyes widened, and his breathing quickened. Bride. Here she was, right in front of him, blending into her surroundings like a chameleon. He hadn't known such a thing was possible, had never seen it done before.

Slowly the bricklike pattern faded, leaving the pale nakedness he thought he'd glimpsed this morning but had convinced himself was nothing more than a mind trick. How wrong he'd been. She had indeed been following him, watching him. *Idiot. Fool. You pride yourself on your knowledge of the opposite sex. You should have figured out the truth.*

"Told you I'd find you," she said smugly. She rubbed between those magnificent breasts, as if something pained her. "Lucky you, I caught sight of you this morning, talking to a group of models leaving a photo shoot. Big surprise. Moment I heard there were models in the area, I knew you'd be nearby."

Knew him so well, did she? Well, he might have heard about the model shoot himself, and that might have been why he'd gone to that side of town, but he'd been asking those women about Nolan, not screwing them blind. So there. *You are indeed a fool.*

"Come on," she said with a laugh and darted around the corner, away from the action. "Let's play."

Devyn followed, calling, "Stop." He hated leaving Dallas alone with Nolan, but it couldn't be helped. Bride had trailed him all day. Had heard his conversations about Nolan. She now knew things she wasn't supposed to know. Things the public *couldn't* know.

Thankfully, she stopped, faced him. Her skin and hair were now silver, the color of the stone behind her.

"What? You're eager to talk now?" she asked, and this time her voice was as smooth as silk.

"It *is* my lucky day, pet," he said, because he didn't know what else *to* say. Shock was pounding through him, sharp and potent. Shock . . . and desire. She was here, and she was naked. "We're together again at last. Did you dream of me?"

"If by dreams you mean night terrors, then yes."

He should stun her, he thought, brain finally kicking

into gear. Yes, stun. *Hello, Dev.* He doubted AIR would mind if he froze her and chained her to his bed. As long as she wouldn't be spilling secrets, they'd be happy.

Without alerting her to his intentions, he aimed, squeezed the trigger. Blue beams illuminated the front of the building.

Like Nolan, she dodged out of the way. Damn it! How were they doing that? Clearly, Devyn needed to learn how to do it so that he could combat it when others did it.

A sexy chuckle escaped her. "I've evaded more pyre-fire over the long years than you can possibly imagine."

"Oh, really?" He fired again, even as his mind latched on to all the energy inside her. He'd controlled her body once; he could control it again. "A naughty girl, were we?"

Again, she dodged. Again, she laughed. Until . . . he paralyzed that energy, and thereby her body, and she ceased moving. Dear God, the power inside her . . . it was a beacon to him, a shimmering drug of light and dominance.

For a moment, he simply luxuriated in all that electric strength, letting it wash through him, intoxicating him, making him feel invincible. There was just so much of it, each particle more astounding than the last. Surely it was enough to win ten thousand wars without breaking a sweat. And yet, he already craved more. Hungered for it.

Never had another person's energy affected him like this. Not even a vampire's. Bride had to be something more. But what?

"Think you've got me now, do you?" she said, drawing his attention.

Now was not the time to bask or ponder. "Think? Silly girl. I know so."

"You should have taken me to the women, like I asked. Now you're going to give me the answers I sought, and a whole lot more, or you'll never see the otherworlder again."

An empty boast, but cute all the same. "I do like your spirit."

"Then you should love this."

Before his eyes, her body seemed to explode, to break apart, a black mist shooting from where she'd stood. He lost his hold on her and wanted to sob.

"Bride," he called, but the thick mist was moving . . . faster . . . faster . . . swirling together and heading back around the corner.

Once again, Devyn followed her. "Dallas, man, duck!" he shouted, when he saw that she meant to slam into his friend, who was still engaged with Nolan.

As before, Dallas obeyed without hesitation. The mist soared over him. Rather than stop, turn, and go back for him, the mist continued to move forward, surrounding Nolan. Still swirling, now thickening. Dallas fired his weapon, but the beams darted straight through and hit the back wall.

Made sense. There was nothing to absorb it.

"Bride, don't touch him. He's infected. You could die. Bride!" The mist never ceased whirling. Never even slowed. Wind velocity increased, dancing his hair around his head. With it came a desperation he didn't understand, a fury he did, and a sense of excitement he couldn't deny.

Nolan tried to beat his way free, but the mist held tight, raising him up, a tornado that couldn't be stopped, and freezing him as Devyn and Dallas had been unable.

"What should we do?" Dallas rasped in his ear. "What the hell should we do? I don't even know what the hell is happening."

He had no answer. And then, it didn't matter. The mist—and Nolan—arrowed forward, out of the alley and around the corner, not even a red glow remaining.

Bride was gone.

Devyn tossed his goggles to the ground, his heart pounding like a racehorse in his chest. *I lost. I really lost.*

"We have to find her," Dallas said, his tone grave. "Before Nolan seduces her, and she becomes a carrier of his disease."

"We will." Devyn gazed at the wall Bride had stepped from and almost rubbed his hands together. *Game on,* he thought.

CHAPTER 4

Bride released the otherworlder from her swirling hold the moment she had him inside the cell she'd erected in her apartment. She'd had to leave her only window open so that she could soar through it, as well as the cage door swung wide, because she couldn't ghost through solid objects. Then she spun around his waist until everything emptied from his pockets, lifted his wallet just as she'd lifted his body, and darted out of the cell, spinning so that a breeze shut the metal bars, locking them. The wallet fell to the ground as she stilled and forced her body to piece itself back together, each drop of moisture expanding, forming some part of her, bonding to another, and solidifying.

When her feet touched the cold concrete floor, her knees buckled and she dropped. Air gushed from her lungs, and her bones rattled. She ached, God, did she ache. Her blood was thick, sluggish, her muscles shaky and weak. Black dots wove through her vision, creating a tunnel-like effect. As excited as she'd been to have finally found Devyn, she'd been battling the fires and the thorns all day; her chest, already raw, now felt like it had been scraped with a blade, doused with acid, and used as a punching bag.

"Who are you?" the man asked from behind her, clearly nearing panic. "*What* are you?"

She didn't have the strength to stand. Didn't even have the strength to angle her head and glance back at him. This always happened. Anytime she broke herself down to the equivalent of a puddle of water and then fit herself back together, she lost days of her life, unable to do anything but lay where she landed.

And weak as she'd been lately, it would probably take her longer to recover. Oh, well. It had been worth it. The shock on Devyn's face when he'd realized who stood before him . . . the stuff of dreams. She almost, *almost,* managed a laugh.

"While I like the view, could you maybe face me?" Thankfully, he was calming down, breathing in and out, relaxing. "I'd like to see the face of my rescuer, say thank you . . . maybe talk to you about releasing me from the cage? I have money. I can pay you."

Of course he liked the view. Of course he was calming. She was naked. While she could camouflage her skin and hair to look like the things around her, she hadn't yet learned how to manipulate her clothing. Which meant she had to do all her hunting bare-assed as the day she was born. If she'd been born the traditional way, that is. How the hell were vampires created? By draining humans and then feeding them tainted blood?

You're veering. Stupid weakness. "Already have . . . your wallet," she managed to work past the swollenness of her throat. The syn-leather was inches from her hand, and far enough away from the cage that he wouldn't be able to reach it. "Food. Drinks. For you." There was also a small basin of precious, very expensive water, but she'd wanted him to have everything he needed for survival while she recovered. "You'll be . . . fine."

"Thanks, truly, but that's not enough for me. I need a woman." There was a ring of desperation in his tone now. "I need sex."

That's what he'd told Devyn. That without a woman, he would die. Well, too bad. She wasn't sleeping with him. *He's infected,* Devyn had shouted. *You could die.* The thought didn't scare her; she'd never been sick a day in her life. Over the years, disease after disease had struck the people around her, but never her. She'd never even sneezed. But while she didn't fear for herself, she wouldn't allow the man to sleep with someone else, either, spreading his illness.

How, then, was she to keep him alive if he was telling the truth? "Take care . . . of . . . yourself."

"I would, but it doesn't work that way."

"Why . . . not?" She blinked until her eyes remained shut. *Stay awake. You can do it.* Slowly she pried her lids apart. Her irises burned.

Silence. Lulling, drugging silence. Beckoning her to sleep. Sweet sleep. Still she resisted.

Then, "Please. Just let me out!" The bars rattled. He must be shaking them.

"Not yet." So badly she wanted to return to the alley, taunt Devyn for what she'd taken from him, demand answers about vampires, and finally learn what the bastard knew about Aleaha.

That would have to wait, though. Either he'd find her, or she'd find him when she was able to move again. Until then . . . Her lashes fused together, practically glued this time. A shallow breath shuddered from her, taking the rest of her energy with it. Sweet sleep, she thought again. She couldn't fight it any longer. Didn't want to fight it, really. As always, she would dream of her friend and the carefree summers they'd once shared.

But as her mind drifted into slumber, it wasn't Aleaha who claimed center stage. For once, it was a man. Devyn—wild, wicked, and wanton. A smug grin lifted his lips—just as it had when he'd frozen her in place and assumed victory was his. He gazed at her with lust in his eyes, reaching for her, determined to possess her, body and soul . . .

Devyn pounded back his third single malt, neat. He and Dallas had waited in that dirty alley until backup finally arrived. Twenty damn minutes after Nolan had been captured. Part of him had expected Bride to return, to taunt him a little more and demand the answers she'd once sought from him. She hadn't.

Now, twenty-four hours later, a group of them were at the house of Jaxon, one of the richest guys in the new world, gorging on his food, emptying his liquor cabinet, and trying to decide on the best course of action.

"—telling you, she came out of the wall and looked like one big painted brick," Dallas was saying. "Then she was naked, and yeah, you should want to kill yourself for not seeing those curves, and *then* she exploded but didn't die. No, I didn't see that part, but Devyn told me all about it. She even turned into a storm cloud of wrath and wrapped around Nolan before disappearing completely."

"I had the artist at AIR headquarters do a sketch of her." Devyn drained his glass and refilled it. He didn't stop at two fingers, but gave himself the entire hand before reaching into his pocket and withdrawing a mini-console. The small black box looked like nothing more than a miniature keyboard. But after he keyed in the proper code, a blue light seeped upward, forming a flat, steady square.

Colors began to weave through the azure—peach, black, green, red. A female form took shape. And then Bride was there, as lovely as he remembered and ripe for the plucking. Her baffling level of kinetic energy wasn't visible and that was a shame. Or maybe not. The agents might have become as obsessed with her as he feared he was becoming.

After all, he'd spent the last day thinking of nothing but her. He wanted to know where she was, what she was doing, and exactly how long she could resist if he laid on the charm.

"She's nude." Dallas leaned forward, elbows propped on the kitchen table—despite the fact that it was made of real mahogany and he was rude as shit—for a closer inspection.

"Of course she's nude, dummy. That's the last outfit I saw her wearing. Anyway, that woman, our new target, is a vampire, and her name is Bride."

Macy Briggs choked on her beer, and her boy toy— new agent and otherworlder Breean—slapped at her back, his expression concerned.

"Vampire?" Mia said when she quieted. "Those actually exist?"

"What, you think someone's imagination was rich enough to create them on their own?" Normally such a smooth-as-silk voice would have been enough to send blood rushing south, thickening and hardening his cock. Today only those thoughts of Bride could do so. She'd bested him. Actually bested him. Last person to do so had been his father. Well, and Eden. Oh, yeah. And Bride, first time they'd met. Still.

He wasn't gonna let it happen again. *Game on,* he thought once more. She wanted to play, then they would play.

He would use every sensual weapon at his disposal. He would show no mercy. He couldn't. Besting that little she-devil might just be the greatest challenge of his life. She was smart—she'd found him. She was powerful—she could do that misting thing. And she wanted nothing to do with him sexually—a lie, surely. He was desirable, damn it.

No matter what was decided here, he was going to find her, and he was going to chain her to his bed as he'd wanted to do in that alley. She'd tell him everything he wanted to know: Nolan's location, how she'd done those things, her favorite sexual positions. Once she talked, the pleasure could begin.

Oh, yes. Those luscious curves would belong to him until he tired of them. He'd sate himself on her, make her scream and beg for more, give it to her—if he was so inclined—and then start all over again.

Of course, he'd have to figure out how to keep her there. No chains could hold her. And whether she could break his mental hold on her body or not, he was practically drooling at the thought of touching that energy again.

His gaze veered to the electronic composite of her, and his blood heated, burning through him with a desire he both loved and hated. There was a way to find and capture her. Had to be.

You're as good as mine, he thought, punching a few numbers and causing her image to fade. No need to sport a hard-on for the rest of the meeting.

"Vampires are like . . . cousins to my race, for lack of a better word." The pronouncement came from Kyrin en Arr, Mia's boyfriend or husband or whatever they called themselves. Kyrin was also Dallas's blood master, the Arcadian who'd saved his life.

"Vampires are aliens?" The pronouncement came from several people at once.

"Yes." Kyrin nodded. "They've just been here longer than anyone else. A long time, actually. But they are the reason the rest of us knew to come over."

"Why didn't you tell me?" Mia said, exasperated.

"Sweet, there are hundreds of races here. I answer any questions you have for me, but unless I know what information you seek, I can't provide the answers."

Her expression softened. "Well, from now on it's safe to say I want to know everything."

"How the hell did she find you? This vampire girl, I mean," Jaxon said. He was a calm, by the book (or so it had seemed) agent who never lost his temper (or so it had seemed). Then Mishka had entered his life, and the real Jaxon had come out swinging. Boy had a temper and cussed worse than Mia I-Can't-Finish-a-Sentence-without-Saying-Fuck Snow. No wonder Devyn liked Jaxon so damn much. "You're not exactly in the local database."

"I'd met her before, so she knew a wee bit about my personality. I made the mistake of going to a girl-on-girl photo shoot. Apparently she was waiting there."

"Ah. Say no more."

"Wait. Let's backtrack a little. So you've actually met one? Other than this Bride person?" Mia asked him. She'd recently chopped her black hair to her shoulders, and the cut framed her pretty face perfectly. A devil in angel's skin, that's what she was. But she'd wanted a new look to celebrate her recent promotion to commander. "A fucking bloodsucker?"

He shrugged, downed the last of the Scotch. "If by *met* you mean bedded, then yes."

Dallas rolled his eyes. "Is there a race you *haven't* bedded?"

"Yeah. Eden Black's." Eden was a Rakan, and Rakans were golden from head to toe. Golden hair, golden skin, golden irises, all of which made them look like living jewelry. Rakans reportedly smelled and tasted like honey when aroused, a fact that intrigued him greatly.

When she'd left him—without allowing him to sample her goods—he'd tried dousing a few of his lovers in honey and pretending they were Rakan, but imitation was never as tasty as the original. Imitation was also sticky.

"Breean's a Rakan," Dallas said with a laugh. "Give him a go."

The man in question scooted back in his chair, the legs scraping against Jaxon's kitchen floor. "No one but Macy may bed me."

He'd only recently come to Earth and hadn't yet learned the art of sarcasm. Poor guy.

"Breean, honey, they're kidding." Macy was pale, her hand shaky as she poured the rest of her beer down her throat. "Now, tell us more about this . . . Bride, did you say? Why'd she follow you?"

"Yes, Bride." What was wrong with her? Normally, she was unflappable. One mention of the name Bride, however, and she'd choked. Now, she couldn't stop trembling. "I ran into her a few days ago, and maybe there's a . . . small chance that I pissed her off."

The "maybe there's a small chance" earned him several snorts.

Macy rubbed her neck in agitation.

"Are you feeling well?" he asked.

"Just a slight stomachache." She chewed her bottom lip, refusing to face him. "I'll be fine."

He knew women and knew when they were lying, knew when they were uncomfortable and when they were hiding something. Macy was all of those. Did she know Bride, perhaps?

The moment the question drifted through his mind, he froze, another possibility taking shape. Could *Macy* be Bride's mysterious friend? No, surely not. But . . . Bride had smelled her friend on him, and Devyn had just run into Macy. Macy never wore perfume—at least, he'd never noticed it on her—just as Bride had claimed her friend wouldn't. And when he'd offered to describe the women he'd been with, Bride had shaken her head no, as if the descriptions couldn't help her. She'd needed to see them, up close and in person. Why? There was only one reason he could think of.

Macy could change her appearance at will, one moment a luscious blonde, the next an exact replica of even the golden giant beside her. A golden giant who had paled, as well.

Everyone inside this kitchen knew Macy was not really Macy. She was an otherworlder posing as the human model-slash-AIR-agent. But no one knew who she really was, who she'd been before taking over the dead Macy's life. Hadn't seemed important. Until now.

This can't be right. Pensive, Devyn stroked two fingers over his jaw. "Does the name Aleaha Love mean anything to anyone?" Though he asked the question of everyone, he kept his attention fixed on Macy. She'd been pale before, but now she became chalk white, the thin lines of her veins visible.

Everyone but Macy and Breean shook their head no. Those two shared a heavy look, Macy fingering the locket hanging around her neck. Interesting. If Macy wasn't Bride's friend—which, Devyn would now bet his most prized possession, aka his cock, that she was—the two were involved somehow. Was the locket something Bride had given her? Something that reminded her of Bride?

"Where'd you see this vampire?" Macy asked softly.

"A few blocks from Dallas's apartment."

"Hey, you didn't tell me that," Dallas said.

"I didn't think it was significant." Until now. To test the foundation of his theory, he added, "She was just another woman in a long line of women. Unimportant and a bother. There was no reason to mention her at the time."

Macy tensed, as though offended.

But then, so did Mia. "Insulting ass! Better watch your mouth before you lose your tongue."

"Females the world over would hunt you down and destroy you for such a travesty." He traced his fingertip around the rim of his glass. "I say we find Bride and kill her."

Macy gasped and shook her head violently.

Mia nodded in agreement.

Devyn almost grinned. Oh, yes indeed. Macy was Bride's friend. No doubt about it now.

"We cannot kill her until we find out where she's hidden the Schön," Kyrin said.

"No one will be killing her." The words left Devyn with more force than he'd intended. "I was teasing, of course. I don't want her killed."

Dallas punched him in the shoulder. "You've got a great sense of humor. Anyone ever tell you that? No? Well, that's because I was lying, and your humor sucks ass. You don't tell a room full of killers to kill someone and expect the target to walk away unscathed. Moron." He drained his whisky sour and slammed his glass onto the tabletop.

"Respect the wood or die," Jaxon said. "Mishka will have my ass if anything happens to it."

Mishka was currently out on assignment. She was stronger, faster, *deadlier*, than anyone around her, and could crush a man with a single squeeze. He *had* to get his hands on a cyborg soon. A vampire cyborg would be even better. And as Bride was more than a vamp, it was entirely possible he'd get his wish.

"Sorry," Dallas muttered, properly shamed.

Devyn patted his friend's hand. "I love when our channels of communication are open like this." He was fighting a grin. "I really do. Makes me feel so close to you. It's heartwarming. I think there's even a tear in my eye. But back to the vampire. She's mine. I'll take care of her."

Kyrin arched a brow at him. "Another morsel for your collection?"

"Yes." Truth.

"Top brass won't like it," Dallas muttered, but there was laughter in his tone.

"He's right," Mia said. "I don't."

Macy wouldn't like it either, judging by the fire now blooming in her blue eyes. "I'm sure I can convince you of the wisdom of my plan, Miss Snowball." Even if she didn't like it, she wouldn't be able to stop it from happening. "I'll give her to you when I'm done with her."

Like her man, she arched a brow. "Snowball?" Then she shook her head and waved her hand. "Give me Nolan, and *then* we can talk."

Done, he thought.

"H—how are we going to capture her?" Macy asked on a trembling breath. She was gripping the edge of the table, her knuckles tight.

Telling, how Breean reached over and squeezed her hand in comfort. The otherworlder knew, as Devyn had suspected.

Most likely Macy planned to learn his intentions, find her friend first, warn her, and send her into hiding. Understandable. Devyn would do the same thing, were the situation reversed. That wouldn't stop him from tricking Macy now, though. Nothing interfered with his objective. Ever. That would make him regret.

"I have something she wants," Devyn said with relish, "and I plan to dangle it under her nose until she finds me."

CHAPTER 5

The pounding on the door woke her.

Slowly Bride blinked open her eyes. Her vision was cloudy at first, but gradually it focused, and her apartment came into view. A single lamp burned, its golden glow providing a small circle of light. The window was still open, drifting a warm morning breeze inside and lifting her curtains. Thankfully, she was far enough away that the sunlight didn't touch, and therefore burn, her sensitive skin.

The well-worn couch, basket of folded laundry, and so-small-you-had-to-strain-to-see-it TV were where they had always been, though she was not. She was on the floor, trembling from cold and bone-deep hunger. Naked.

What the—

Devyn. The name was like an electric current inside her, and memories flooded her mind, heating her up inside and out. She'd found him, had watched that beautiful body stalk the streets of New Chicago, constantly fighting the urge to reveal herself and drink from him, savoring every delicious drop of blood he possessed, and then she'd stolen his captive, beating him soundly.

Another pound of fists echoed at the entrance. "Amy. Amy, I know you're in there!"

Bride dragged herself to a sitting position. She swiped her tongue over her lips, her mouth as dry as dirt, her teeth aching. So hungry . . .

"Finally," a relieved voice breathed behind her.

She whipped around, and had to massage her temples to assuage the sudden wave of dizziness. When the dizziness cleared, she studied her companion. He wore the same clothes she'd left him in: a button-down and slacks. They were wrinkled, stained with sweat. A plain copper necklace wrapped around his neck like a snake, tight, almost choking, causing his pulse to flutter wildly.

Mmm, a snack . . .

No. No, no, no. "You're alive," she said foolishly. And damn, her throat *hurt*. It was swollen and raw from disuse. Or had she screamed in pleasure as dream Devyn licked his way up and down her body?

And just when the hell had she begun thinking of him as a sexual conquest? He was a means to an end. That was it.

"Barely." Her captive lay on the cot she'd provided for him, facing her, his skin grayish, his eyes sunken. There were small circular wounds on his neck, as if something had tried to bite its way free of his skin.

Boom, boom, boom. "Amy!"

Shit. Had the otherworlder shouted for help while she'd slept, and was the cavalry now here to rescue him? "How long have I been out?" If she was going to be arrested, it'd be nice to know how long Devyn had had to find her.

"Four days."

Wow. Had she been human, she probably would have peed herself. Thankfully, that was not a bodily function she'd ever had to endure. She smacked her lips together, her mouth still as dry as a desert.

Time to feed. Automatically her gaze returned to the otherworlder's neck, and her still-aching fangs elongated. Blood . . . good . . . need . . . Waaaay past time to feed. *He's sick. You'll probably vomit after you drink him, anyway, weakening you all the more.* Who cared? Her body always absorbed the first few sips before the sickness hit her, which was how she'd managed to survive, and she would be stronger. Right now, even the *taste* of blood would have been enough for her. So, so good . . .

"Your eyes are glowing," the otherworlder said, but he didn't sound as if he cared.

"Damn it, Amy. Rent's overdue."

The voices snapped her out of the blood haze, and she blinked. Rent. Thank God. No arrest today. Maybe.

"Now your eyes are back to normal."

"That's good."

"Amy, I know you can hear me. I want my money, or your ass is outta here. Understand?" More banging. "I told you one more delayed payment and you were gone. Don't tell me you don't remember."

"Your name's Amy?" her captive asked. "I thought Devyn called you Bride."

"Be there in a second," she called, relieved that the otherworlder hadn't shouted for help. For his cooperation, she gave him a reward. Honesty. "My real name is Bride, yes."

"I can see how the guy at your door confused that with Amy," he said dryly. "I'm Nolan, by the way."

"I know. I heard."

"Hurry up, damn it!" the super repeated, this time grudgingly rather than furious. "I don't got all day. I'm two seconds away from letting myself in, and it won't be against the rules 'cause you're so behind."

"I said I was coming!" Bride pushed to her feet, swayed. "Why didn't you scream the roof down while I was out?" she asked Nolan.

"And allow humans to stone me while I'm in this condition?" He snorted. "No, thanks."

"Just . . . be quiet while I deal with my super. Please. If you hadn't already guessed, I'm not human, but he thinks I am and I let him think it because he's more prejudiced than most. He'd rather shoot an otherworlder than look at one." She turned and forced one foot in front of the other, closing the distance between herself and Nolan's wallet. "Swear to God, he's a piece of shit who would trade his mother for a beanburger."

"Uh, you might want to dress before you greet him," Nolan said when she bent down. "And yeah, I'd guessed about the nonhuman thing. So what are you?"

"Alien," she lied.

"Like I said, I know."

As she stood, her gaze drifted along her body. She was pale, as always, and spotted with red where her skin had pressed into the concrete. Her nipples were hard.

Was that what Nolan saw when he looked at her? Was

that what Devyn had seen when she'd stood before him? The real her? Or did they see the image she projected? Long ago, the ability to cloak herself with nondescript features had risen from the thorns and fire inside her, preventing people from picking her out of a crowd. She did it without thinking now; it was just a part of who she was, like breathing. But sometimes, as weak as she'd become this past month, she feared the shield was down and she simply couldn't sense it.

Cheeks heating, she grabbed the robe she'd draped over the couch just in case she'd been unable to walk to her room after imprisoning Nolan. Good thing. "Sorry for the show."

"Don't be. Back to my question. What *kind* of alien are you?"

Don't be. It was something Devyn would say, and it caused her heart to race. Surely she wasn't missing the bastard. "I'm the kind that's from another planet." No way she'd cop to vampire. Even otherworlders would fear bloodsuckers. How could they not? She was a parasite. "I'm a—" What sounded good? she wondered, peering at her feet "—concre . . . sha. Concresha."

"Never heard of them."

Of course not. She'd just made it up. "Doesn't mean they don't exist."

"Amy!"

Fully covered now, she walked to the door and pressed the code to open it a mere crack. Mr. Guise immediately tried to push his way inside.

He growled at her. "Open it wider and let me in, little girl."

"You don't need to come in to collect your money."

"Well, I want to talk to you."

"So talk."

After a moment's pause, he backed away. Even chuckled darkly. "I know you don't have no money, so I thought we could work off the debt another way, if you know what I mean."

She rolled her eyes. He'd been trying to get her into bed for a year. He was a balding, greasy perv. The perviness and the grease she could have overlooked, but not the comb-over. Or, to be honest, the stench of rot that always accompanied him.

But hungry as she was, even Guise was starting to look good. His pulse was slow but steady, a taste-me beat. "No need for me to take one for the team." Her tongue was so swollen the words were slurred. "I can pay you properly." She hoped.

She flipped open Nolan's wallet and gasped. So much money. So . . . pretty and green. It was more than she'd ever seen in one place.

"Just think about it," Guise said, reaching his pudgy fingers through the crack and sifting them through her hair. "You could spend your money on something like food or clothes."

"Tempting, but no." Her fingers shook as she thrust the bills at him. She kept her lashes fused, just in case her eyes were glowing again. Usually, she could control it. Only when she was reaching the starvation point did it happen automatically. "That should take care of the rest of the year."

He looked down at the wad of bills, then up at her, then the bills. "But . . . but . . ."

More satisfied than she'd been in a long time, even when she'd bested Devyn, she pressed the button to close the door in his stunned face, then jabbed her thumb against the ID to engage the lock she'd had installed—a lock Guise could not open at will. She was grinning widely as she turned and pressed her back into the metal.

"You're pretty when you smile," Nolan said weakly.

Her gaze shifted to him. Once, he'd probably been handsome. His bone structure was total perfection, his body tall and packed with just the right amount of muscle. But now, ashen and bruised as he was, he just looked pitiful. "Thank you, and thanks for the loan, by the way."

A choking sound bubbled from his throat. A laugh? "Please, you won't pay me back."

No, she wouldn't. She couldn't work during the day, her skin was too sensitive, and she couldn't hold a job at night since she needed to hunt. She had to steal what money she could. "Thanks for the gift, then."

"You're welcome." He sounded sincere.

"Listen," she said. "You seem like a nice guy despite the fact that you had AIR gunning for you. I want you to know that I don't plan to hurt you."

His gaze locked with hers, grim but determined. "If you don't want to hurt me, you have to let me go."

Did she look stupid? "Do you have a terribly infectious disease?"

"Yes," he said, shocking her. She hadn't expected him to answer honestly.

"Then you understand that I can't let you loose on the streets." She rubbed a hand over her forehead and sighed. "I need to take a shower, but maybe we can talk afterward, okay? I'll tell you my plans for you."

"I'd like that."

"I'll hurry." In her bedroom, Bride brushed her teeth, rushed through an enzyme shower, and quickly dressed in jeans and a T-shirt. Took her ten minutes. Ten minutes she used to breathe deep and get her hunger under control. Finally she dragged a chair in front of Nolan's cage, her fangs retracted. He hadn't moved an inch. "I'm back. Now, before I tell you what's to be done with you, why don't you tell me why Devyn wants you?"

His eyes, once most likely a vibrant blue, were now dull and glazed with pain. "Do his plans affect yours?"

"Yes." If Devyn *didn't* want him as much as she suspected he did, she would have no use for him.

"At least you're honest." The shoulder not pressed into the cot lifted in a weak shrug. "Devyn wants me because I need sex, and I need sex because Devyn wants me."

O-kay. Great. That explained everything. "Let's try a different angle. Maybe break it down for me like I'm a five-year-old child."

"Nope. I answered you, whether you realize it or not. Now you have to answer something for me. Why did you take me from that alley?"

Easy enough. "Devyn has something I want. A few things, actually." And he *would* give them to her. First, he would take her to the women he'd bedded that day. Would do no good to go to the place he'd sexed them up. The scent was long gone, she was sure.

If neither of them was Aleaha, she would make him take her to everyone he'd been around that day. Then, he would tell her everything he knew about vampires. Maybe even introduce her to the ones he knew.

"And you plan to trade me for these things?" Nolan asked.

She played with the hem of her shirt, but didn't shrink from his gaze. "Yes. In a perfect world I would have captured him and put *him* in the cage, but this isn't a perfect world, and I had to make do with what I could." She was grumbling.

"Why didn't you? Lock him up, I mean?"

"Nope. Your turn to answer something. Did Devyn plan to kill you, or simply capture you?"

"I don't know. My guess is capture. My queen is on her way to this planet, and Devyn, along with the rest of AIR, is desperate to know when and where she'll arrive."

Then Devyn wanted him back for more reasons than she'd realized. Did life get any better than this? "Your disease—"

"Is deadly, yes. If that's what you planned to ask. AIR expects me to let it eat away at my body, destroying me. They don't understand that I just want to live. Like everyone else, I just want to live. And . . . love." His voice dripped with sadness. "I've never fallen in love, and that's something everyone deserves a chance to experience."

"I've been alive a long, *long* time. Trust me, you're better off without the emotion. It just leads to hurt."

"Nevertheless."

Well, she'd warned him. That's all a girl could do.

"Your turn to answer," he said. "Why didn't you just lock up Devyn?"

"Originally, that was my plan. That's why I erected the

cage. But as I was watching him stalk you, I realized that if he can freeze me in place, he can also force me to move the way he wants, so he'd just have me unlock the cage, defeating the purpose of bringing him here. I didn't relish the idea of being at his mercy in my own home."

"Smart girl. So if you could lock him up without having to worry about his taking over your body, would you let me go and lock him up in my place?"

She thought about it; she really did. Because, God, it was tempting. This guy could help her. Devyn hadn't been able to manipulate his body the way he'd done hers, and with Nolan's help, Devyn probably wouldn't be able to manipulate hers anymore. But in the end, she couldn't do it. Couldn't free this otherworlder, no matter the reason. By his own admission, he was infected with something dangerous and contagious, and she couldn't willingly unleash that upon the unsuspecting world. A girl needed to eat.

With the thought, her shoulders slumped. Why couldn't she eat like before?

"No need to answer," he said with a sigh. "I can read the decision in your eyes."

Perceptive man. "So how'd you dodge those pyre-beams? I can do it, sure, but I've been doing it for a long time. Which also means I've seen a lot of aliens over the years. I've never seen one move like you. And yeah, I could still see you when you shed your color."

He regarded her intently for a moment, as though an internal battle was raging inside his mind. Finally, his shoulders lifted in another shrug. "Don't let my weak appearance fool you. The disease I told you about?

It's a being inside of me, a parasite that grows stronger while my health declines. It told me when and where to move."

A being that spoke to him? Poor guy needed a psychiatrist, she thought, then blinked. He'd dodged those beams, something she had already admitted she'd never seen another person do. And while he did appear near death, he didn't look crazy. "Did this being also help you absorb those stun rays rather than lose control of your body?"

Slowly he grinned and glided a trembling finger along the necklace he wore. "That was all me, baby."

That grin lit up his face and erased the grayish tint to his skin, offering a glimpse of the devilishly handsome man he'd been before. "How? The necklace?"

"Necklace?" He frowned in confusion. He must not have realized he'd been playing with it. "Oh. Nah. It's just a pretty decoration," he said. "But like I said, I'll tell you how I did it if you release me."

"Not gonna happen."

His jaw hardened. "Then this conversation is over."

"Fine. Have it your way." Sighing, she stood. "I have to leave for a little while, anyway."

Before she could face Devyn again, she had to feed. Keeping the entire meal down would be nice, as well, but miracles were few and far between nowadays. At least her desperate body would quickly absorb those first few sips of blood before the roller-coaster ride of nausea began.

There was a flash of panic in Nolan's eyes. "Where are you going?"

"My fridge is empty, and I need to grocery shop."

That's what her live-in boyfriend used to say. Thankfully Nolan didn't search the kitchen for said fridge. She didn't own one. Besides, her statement wasn't technically a lie. She needed food. "Do you like wine?"

"Yes."

"Then we'll share a toast before I go." She crossed the small space into the kitchen, cutting her palm with the razor in her shirtsleeve as she walked. She held tight to every precious drop until she pulled a glass from the cupboard. The moment she opened her fingers, a pool of blood trickled from her and lined the bottom. Too slowly for her peace of mind, the wound healed, flesh weaving back together and finally sealing shut.

"What are we toasting?"

"Devyn's downfall." She filled the rest of the glass with her most expensive red. The thought of drinking blood would be abhorrent to him, she knew. It was abhorrent to everyone but her. But he needed something—besides sex—to heal him, or he might not last out the day. Hopefully her blood would do the trick and not turn him into a vamp or kill him outright, as most movies and books claimed.

She'd never shared her blood with anyone for those very reasons. While she would enjoy having another vampire running around, hunting with her, drinking with her, Aleaha was the only person she'd ever loved enough to attempt it on—but she'd also loved the girl enough not to do so. Too risky. Guess she'd find out what happened to people who drank her blood when she returned.

When she faced Nolan, she saw that he was sitting up, arm outstretched through the bar. Waiting patiently. She hurried over to him, careful not to slosh a single drop over the side.

"Aren't you going to have a glass?" he asked.

"Of course." Red wine was the only human beverage she enjoyed. Back in the kitchen she poured another tumbler full. She rejoined Nolan and they held up their cups in unison. "To Devyn's downfall."

Together, they drained the contents.

The red liquid slid down her throat, warm and smooth, but not what she needed. At least her stomach remained calm. "Glass, please," she said, holding out her hand. If he were to drop it and cut himself, well, that wouldn't be good.

Though he was scowling at her, he relinquished possession without incident.

"Thank you."

"You're welcome." He eased back on the cot and stared up at the ceiling. "Will you at least leave me a game or something? Any more from the stupid voice in my head, and I'll welcome a lynch mob."

"I don't have any games. You should nap. Might help you heal."

"That's what I've been doing for four days, and as you can see, I haven't healed."

Guilt wound through her. She'd wanted to capture him, yes, but not torture him. "What if I switch on the TV?"

"Fine." He waved his hand in dismissal, but she noticed the action was stronger, less shaky than any he'd made before. Was her blood already working, or was he excited at the thought of watching television and simply didn't want her to know? "Whatever."

She almost laughed. A "Yes, Bride, thank you, Bride" wouldn't have been amiss. Men. After she'd angled the screen toward the cell and found him a decent station— *As the Otherworld Turns* was playing—she crossed her arms over her middle. "Do you need anything else?"

"Freedom would be nice."

"Besides that."

His gaze pursued her, lingering on her breasts, between her legs. "How about your body?"

"Besides that."

A moment passed while he considered his other options. "You know what sounds really nice about now? Not just Devyn's downfall, but his head on a platter."

Slowly she grinned. "I'll see what I can do."

CHAPTER 6

For three days, Devyn kept Macy in his sights. He even escorted her throughout the city at all hours on the pretense of searching for Bride, never telling her that she was merely his bait. She'd been more than happy to join him. She had no idea he kept her on a deliberate path, planting her scent along select buildings and shops.

To his consternation, Bride never revealed herself, and he never felt her eyes on him. Didn't matter. One way or another, he would draw her out of hiding. He was determined. He'd give this one more day, then think of something else to do.

"Ready to move on?" he asked.

"No. I texted Breean when I realized where we were headed, so he's on his way here. Besides, we've just been going in circles," Macy said, frustration dripping from every word.

They were in front of his brand-new apartment complex, the top floor purchased for his and Bride's exclusive use, for the second time that day. They had been here twice yesterday and four times the day before. For some strange reason, he was struck by the urge to "think" about their next plan of action every time they reached this point. And yeah, he'd taken Macy inside a few times, straight to the door that would later become known as Bride's Surrender.

Now he studied her, this former model, now an agent, who was unintentionally aiding him. Sunlight bathed her, highlighting the delicacy of her deceptively innocent features—the girl had a temper and had once slit her own boyfriend's throat. Her skin was creamy and rich, but more than that . . . surely not . . . couldn't be. Except, the more intently he looked, the more he was sure he saw a second, startling layer to her. As though she wore a mask. Like Bride.

Devyn intensified his focus. Maybe he'd never looked closely enough to notice the nuances of her, but he was looking now. Finally *seeing*. At first glance, Macy's eyes were large, a mix of blue and silver. A cap of pale hair framed her face. Her nose was small, and her cheeks rounded, like a cherub's. Now he could see a wider set of *green* eyes. A longer nose, slimmer cheeks. *Dark* hair.

Bride, too, had dark hair. Bride had green eyes, as well, though hers were a brighter, lighter shade. Were the two more than friends, perhaps? Were they sisters? Macy wasn't a vampire, but then Bride, with all that sparkling energy and the ability to turn into mist, was definitely more than a vampire. As he'd already surmised. He just had to figure out what else she was. Couldn't be cyborg, as he'd hoped. Wires and metal couldn't change into water.

"What?" Macy asked, shifting uncomfortably. "You're staring."

He forced a flirtatious chuckle. "You're pretty, is all."

"Macy," a male voice called.

Both of them turned.

"Breean," she said with relief. "You made it."

The golden giant's pace increased. When he reached the agent, he pulled her away from Devyn's side and into his arms. Devyn sighed. Possessive, jealous men were a nuisance. He hadn't been that way over his shrew of a wife, and he wouldn't be that way over one of his many lovers. Ever.

To show possessiveness or jealousy was to stake a claim over a specific female. And to stake a claim was to give up the right to enjoy other females. He shuddered.

Macy twisted in her man's arms, facing Devyn. "Like I was saying about going in circles. No matter what route you take, we always end up here. I'm not stupid. There's a reason. Tell me."

Very well. He'd give her a reason. It wouldn't be the truth, but it would be a reason. "You caught me. I'm thinking of buying property on this side of town and was using company time to scout the area." Best lie he could come up with, but he delivered it smoothly. Lying was second nature to him, maybe because it was just another form of flirting.

The only thing he refused to lie about was what he would do to those who wronged him or his friends. When he made a threat, he saw it through. No hesitation. That, he'd learned from his father. A lesson he'd actually taken to heart. Better that people feared and respected him than underestimate and attempt to hurt him.

"Devyn!" Macy said. "I can't believe you. You've been wasting my time for your own gain."

That's it. Get angry. Maybe the stronger her emotions were, the stronger her scent would be. Bride would finally catch a whiff and start running, as desperate to reach the girl as she'd been when they'd first met. Maybe more so, now that she was so smug about capturing Nolan.

Devyn had been sleeping in the new apartment every night, waiting. Alone. Maybe tonight would be the night they were reunited.

"My bad." Dallas, his partner in this delicious crime, was due to—

Ring, ring.

Perfect timing. As if he didn't know who was calling, he glanced at his cell's ID and tried not to grin. "I have to take this," he told Macy. "You know how Dallas gets when I ignore him."

She nodded stiffly, her irritation with him clearly undiminished. "He's such a pouter."

Macy's power of observation was greater than Devyn had assumed.

Doing his best to appear grave, Devyn flipped open his cell and placed it to his ear. "Devyn, king of the Targons and prince of pleasure, speaking. How may I help you?"

"Funny," Dallas said. "You're sounding chipper."

Of course he was. Macy—and now Breean by association—were his puppets. Which meant, Bride would soon be his puppet. Only, he would enjoy pulling her strings. And then wrapping those strings around her wrists and ankles and anchoring her to a bed. And then licking her entire body. And then slipping and sliding inside of her while she shouted his name.

"You couldn't have," he said for Macy's benefit. "Again? Seriously? And you're on her trail now? Tell me, is she wearing the same outfit as last time?"

"You mean skin?" Dallas barked out a chuckle. "Macy right beside you?"

"Affirmative."

"Ohhh, affirmative he says. You know I love it when you talk shop."

To Macy, Devyn said, "Dallas thinks he found the vampire. Again. I can't leave—did you *see* that skyscraper?—but he'd love some backup. You interested?"

"Yes," she rushed out. "Is he sure this time? Last two nights, we tailed humans. They looked like her, or rather, what you described, sure, but I'm tired of failure."

"You sure this time?" Devyn asked Dallas.

"Affirmative."

That did have a nice ring to it. "He's not, but he doesn't want to take a chance." Devyn allowed some leeway, just in case they needed to relive this scenario tomorrow. "He's happy to go alone, though, if you—"

"No! No, we'll go. Find out where we should meet him and then tell him not to do anything until we get there. He does remember what happened the last time the two of you acted alone, yes?"

Devyn relayed the message and rattled off their coordinates. Paused. "No worries, Mace," he told the agent. "He's nearby and is happy to pick you up again."

Breean was frowning. His eyes were narrowed, but he remained silent.

"I thought they'd see through you in a heartbeat," Dallas said in his ear. "I guess I have to choke down another of those Sweet Munchkins." There was disgust in his voice. Rather than use money, they wagered with pastries. Out-of-date, stale, not-fit-for-the-homeless pastries. Loser had to eat one in front of the winner. "Sometimes you're scary brilliant, have I told you that before?"

"I'd argue the word *sometimes,* but yeah. You're right."

Another laugh. "I'll be there in two." *Click.*

Sure, he could have let the couple walk away and not sent them with Dallas to track this latest "sighting," but he didn't want the girl's scent spread too far and wide. Hopefully, being inside a vehicle prevented such a thing.

Thinking about the spreading of Macy's scent had him wondering how long Bride had been searching for her. Weeks? Years? If so, why hadn't Bride smelled her until now? He'd tried to subtly question Macy about her own past, but the girl had been tight-lipped. She had to be, he supposed. With an ability like hers, she'd probably been hunted most of her life.

Devyn pocketed his phone. "Like I said, Dallas is nearby and will be pulling along any . . . minute. Ah, there he is."

A black van with tinted windows eased to the curb. Because of the tint, Dallas couldn't be seen, but Devyn imagined his friend grinning from ear to ear. Made him want to grin himself, thinking of Dallas happy and amused. It was much better than imagining the agent wallowing in self-pity over that whole blood master issue.

Macy stepped toward the van, the sun stroking the brass of her necklace and glinting in his eye. The necklace. Oh, oh. Devyn jerked her into his body for a hug, stealthily removing and pocketing it. How could he have forgotten about his insurance policy? Well, hopefully it was an insurance policy. "Good luck, darling."

"Uh, thanks, Dev." Awkwardly, she patted his back.

Breean growled low in his throat, and for a moment Devyn feared he'd been found out. But the warrior merely tugged the female from Devyn's clasp and ushered her into the waiting van.

With the passenger door open, Devyn was able to catch a glance of Dallas in the driver's seat. The agent was indeed grinning, white teeth gleaming. He wore a hat that shadowed his eyes, camo pants, and a camo shirt that revealed the new (and scabbed-over) skull-and-dagger tattoo on his right forearm.

Devyn had a matching tattoo on his own arm. They'd drunk too much last night and had thought the identical marks would be funny.

They weren't.

"Nice outfit," Devyn said with a grin of his own. "Planning on hunting the clones on government land while you're out and about?" Clones. Animals.

"Maybe." He was also chewing gum. "You guys ready to chase down a bloodsucker or what?"

"Let's do this," Macy said, slapping Dallas's head rest.

There would be hell to pay when this was over and the truth revealed. Macy would be pissed that he'd used her to capture her friend, which would piss off Breean, which would in turn piss off Mia, because Breean was a powerful warrior and her new favorite.

Devyn could call things off now and prevent the reaming he would surely receive.

Without pause, he shut the door and waved them off. He was whistling as he strolled inside the building.

Bride slunk through the unfamiliar apartment, remaining in the shadows. Her eyes cut through the darkness with the precision of a knife, taking everything in and weighing her options.

Thankfully there wasn't any furniture, so she didn't have to worry about knocking anything down. The air was musty, as if the room hadn't been occupied for some time. *Where are you, Leah Leah, and why did you come here?*

Aleaha's scent was all over the building and had led directly to this room. After Bride had caught the familiar fragrance a few blocks down, she'd given up her fruitless search for that bastard playboy Devyn and concentrated on her friend instead.

She was embarrassed to admit she almost *hadn't* switched gears. The urge to find Devyn, to gloat about her victory, to spar with him again, was strong. Besides, she was almost positive he couldn't be as decadently handsome as her memory painted him. Couldn't be nearly as witty or flirtatious. Yet only when she'd smelled his scent mixed with Aleaha's had she finally changed her objective.

What were the two doing together? Were they lovers, as she'd first thought? Did they live together? Devyn's flirtations had seemed so practiced, Bride hadn't thought him capable of commitment. Not that having Aleaha as a semi-permanent or even permanent lover equaled commitment. But if they *were* together, he was definitely a cheater and Aleaha needed to know.

In and out Bride breathed, as quietly as possible. There was a window, but it was closed, blocking out the night's symphony of racing cars, pedestrians braving the streets, and criminals hiding in corners. The deeper she maneuvered through the apartment, the weaker Aleaha's scent of sky and pine became and the stronger Devyn's, like sun-dried sheets and rain.

Damn it! Her grip tightened on her daggers. A half-way strong grip, too, now that she'd eaten. Well, some. As before, she'd kept down the first few sips but had thrown up the rest.

Mind on the task at hand. You more than anyone know the price of inattention. That's how those policemen had caught her sneaking inside those mansions all those years ago. That's why she'd had to hide Aleaha. Why she'd lost Aleaha.

Okay. So. Time to regroup. Aleaha had been here, but she hadn't stayed for long. Ten minutes, tops. Was little Devyn not as skilled a lover as he clearly liked to believe? Was he a slam-bam-thank-you type?

Bet there was a piece of furniture here. A bed. Proof of his priorities.

There was a fire in Bride's blood, burning her veins, scorching each of her organs. A fury that had nothing to do with the thought of Devyn sleeping with her friend and everything to do with her friend's future happiness. Really. Clearly Devyn was the kind of guy who left only heartbreak in his wake.

That fury also poked and prodded at that molten,

thorny place inside her, the place her powers were buried, the intense heat of *its* flames making her anger seem comprised of ice. She had to stifle a pained moan. She knew better than to let herself become too worked up. When she did, those flames spread and those thorns grew branches, each destroying her bit by bit. If she wasn't careful, she would soon be praying for death.

I'm calm. I'm happy. After all, I found Devyn. She would finally get to gloat.

Remaining smashed against the wall, Bride angled her body and peeked down the hall. Empty. Darkness. Silence. Devyn's scent—stronger than ever. There were two doorways. As she breathed deeply, her heart pounding erratically in her chest, she tiptoed forward. He was here. He had to be.

She passed the first doorway, giving the bedroom only a cursory glance. Empty, as well. Finally she reached the farthest entrance and paused. The door was closed. Was Devyn inside? Sleeping, holding some little tramp in his arms? Waiting for her?

She'd warned him, told him she would be coming for him, and he was obviously a warrior, used to strategy and battle. He was even working for AIR in some capacity. An agent, perhaps? He was daring enough. Nervousness joined the lingering thrums of fury.

Lord, she'd picked a hell of a target. One that could lock her away or kill her, no questions asked, she thought, a cold sweat beading over her skin. *You knew the consequences. You came here anyway. Don't wuss out now. Answers are worth any risk.*

He had to be expecting her, had to know she'd find him

again. So how should she do this? Bust inside, knives at the ready? Sneak inside and try to catch him unaware?

There was no time to reason it out.

In the snap of fingers, her mind separated from her body, her limbs no longer hers to command. Of their own accord, her fingers released their grip on the blade hilts and the weapons thumped to the ground. One of her arms reached out and pressed the button that opened the door. Her feet moved one in front of the other, forcing her to enter the darkened space.

He was awake, and he was controlling her. She'd known this could happen, but had come anyway. *Worth the risk,* she reminded herself, gritting her teeth and trying with all her might to petrify her muscles and lock herself in place.

If only she could fight past the thorns and the flames to see what other abilities were buried inside her, rather than waiting every few years for one to spring up on its own. She suspected the others were strong, stronger than Devyn's, desperate to explode, to overtake her. But she just couldn't get to them, even now, when they probably would have saved her.

"You certainly took your time," a familiar voice said huskily. Without a rustle of clothes or a single movement, the overhead light switched on, golden beams chasing away the shadows. "Black becomes you, pet. It's like you're enveloped by storm clouds."

And there he was. Sitting in a plush leather chair in the far corner, Devyn was relaxed, sipping a glass of amber liquid. His dark hair was mussed, as though he'd run his hands through it a few times. His eyes, the exact color of his drink, glittered dangerously. Like her, he wore a black T-shirt and black pants.

A large king-size bed was the only thing between them. A bed with black silk sheets and velvet-covered chains attached to the head and footboards. Her jaw clenched even as her nipples hardened, her mind momentarily lost in the naughty things that had probably happened in that bed.

Oh, no you don't. She would not allow her body to ready. He'd think her desire was for him. And it wasn't. Really.

"Where's Aleaha?" Her voice trembled, mortifying her to her soul. "I know you've been with her."

He finished off his drink. "Please. Have a seat." With a tilt of his chin, he motioned to the bed. "We have much to discuss."

Rather than force her to obey, he released his hold on her. "You're not going to compel me to do it?"

"Now that would be rude, wouldn't it?"

Devyn, her freeze 'em and leave 'em guy, was concerned with being rude. Laughable. But she had something he wanted, so of course he would play the I'm-your-friend card. Her eyes widened. That's right. She had Nolan. *She* was in control right now. No need for her powers, after all. Smiling smugly, she sauntered to the bed and plopped onto the edge, facing him.

His gaze fell to her lips, and he inhaled sharply.

Was he thinking of kissing her?

"I want them all over me," he said.

Holy hell. The answer to her question: yes. "The chains are a bit much, don't you think?" she said, ignoring his comment but unable to hide her breathlessness. "It's not like they could keep me down if I decided to leave." It was a reminder of her victory over him, meant to put him in his place.

He didn't back down. "True." Nor did he sound concerned. "I have a feeling you'll willingly lock yourself up, though."

She would have snorted, but couldn't quite manage it. If ever there was a man who could convince a woman to play kinky bondage games, it was probably this one. But no matter what, she couldn't give herself to Devyn. The moment she did, he would lose interest in her. His kind always did. And she needed his interest. It would, hopefully, keep him malleable during their negotiations.

What makes you think he's truly interested in you, anyway?

I've already had a vampire, he'd once said, as though the thought of bedding another bored him. Maybe his interest in chaining Bride up and ravishing her stupid was feigned. Intended to soften *her.*

"Aleaha," she said. Her friend was the main reason she was here; she wouldn't forget. "Where is she?"

"Does the name Macy Briggs mean anything to you?" he asked, once again ignoring her.

Was he serious? "Macy Briggs the model?"

"She doesn't model anymore, but yes."

"No. Should it? Oh, wait. Let me guess. She's one of the women you screwed that day." The last lashed from her, harsher than she'd intended. "I thought you couldn't recall their names."

"Sheathe the claws, darling. I've had a model and

wasn't impressed. Macy isn't my type, so no, I haven't had her."

"How sad for you." One day a woman needed to put this man in his place. Grind up his heart and scatter the pieces all over New Chicago. The female population would be the better for it. *I would be better for it.*

"So tell me, did you fuck Nolan?" Again, he didn't sound concerned.

That . . . irritated her. But only because it meant he didn't want her as she'd supposed, so she wouldn't be able to use his desire against him. Really. "No. Near death isn't my type."

"That's good. Did he bleed on you? Spit on you?"

"No."

"You're sure?"

She laughed without humor. "I think I'd remember." Unless she'd been asleep when he'd done it. Her shoulders sagged. "Why?"

"You'll catch his disease if you come into contact with any of his bodily fluids."

A shudder rocked her. Whether Devyn was telling the truth or not didn't matter. Just the thought of possible contamination had her vowing to keep her distance from the imprisoned otherworlder. She'd never been sick a day in her life, true, but that didn't necessarily mean she was immune to *everything*.

"Tell me where he is." Finally, emotion. White-hot anger, barely leashed. Devyn didn't care about her escaping his clutches or who she slept with; he only cared about where she'd placed his enemy. "You never should have taken him. You placed yourself and everyone around you in danger."

She had no loved ones, no family or friends. "Don't worry. I'll tell you where he is. After."

One of his brows arched in question, but he didn't look surprised by her announcement. After all, she'd already warned him. "After what? I bed you?"

"Please," she said dryly.

"Now you're begging. We're on the right track."

She gritted her teeth, that burning pain flickering in her chest. *Stay calm.* "After you've taken me to Aleaha. After you've answered my questions about vampires. *After* you've apologized for leaving me immobile on that street. Only then will I tell you where Nolan is."

Now his brow crinkled adorably. Wasn't fair! Everything he did was a seduction. A temptation. "One, if you want to see your friend, you'll pay *my* price. Two, why would you want answers about vampires from me? I'm not a vampire. And three, I never apologize."

Deceptively casual, Bride leaned back on her elbows, placing her hands near her waist, where she'd stashed several other blades. "One, you'll take me to Aleaha or you'll never see Nolan again. I shouldn't have to repeat that one over and over. Nor should I have to tell you that I will *not* be paying you anything. Two, because you've clearly met a vampire before, and I haven't. And three, we'll see about that."

Not surprisingly, he ignored everything she'd said. "I like this new pose." His hot gaze perused her, lingering on her breasts, between her legs, perhaps imagining licking her, sucking, biting. Or was that just wishful thinking on her part, idiot that she clearly was? When his eyes locked with hers again, his pupils were dilated, black overshadowing amber. Perhaps not so wishful, after all. "Lovely. Stay just . . . like . . . that." Then he shrugged. "Or don't. Whatever."

Argh! First he'd seemed to want her. Then he hadn't. Then he had. Now he didn't again. Which was it? "Let's start with the easiest. The vampires. Who are they and where do they live?"

He traced a fingertip over the seam of his lips, and her entranced gaze followed the movement. Her own lips even puckered, suddenly wanting to press into his. "You've truly never met one?"

"No," she said raspily. How was he affecting her this way? Making her crave things she shouldn't? "I haven't."

"That means you were raised here." Attention never leaving her, he set his now-empty glass at his feet and straightened. "Interesting."

By "here," did he mean New Chicago? Had vampires simply settled in another state? "Yes, I was. I've never left New Chicago."

"A new twist." He scrubbed two fingers over his stubbled jaw, the very picture of intrigued male. "Perhaps we can trade information."

"Men must like that game." Nolan had wanted to play, too. "Good thing for you, I'm all for it, as long as you don't ask me about the otherworlder."

"Oh, I won't, pet. There's no need. Not anymore." Leaning forward, Devyn tossed something at her. "You'll simply bring him to me."

Bride caught it by reflex alone and held it up to the light. A necklace. Obviously cheaper than Nolan's with dull, scratched metal links and a scuffed emerald stone hanging from the center. Breath froze in her throat, frosting up her lungs. "This belongs to Aleaha." She knew because she'd stolen it and given it to her one Christmas.

"I know."

Her lashes lifted, and she leveled a piercing glare at her tormentor. "You have her." A statement, not a question, laced with disbelief, fear, and grim expectation.

"Oh, yes. But the question is, what am I going to do with her? Which in turn raises another, more important question. What am I going to do with you?"

CHAPTER 7

Devyn had relished his words, every last one of them, eager to watch Bride's reaction to them. What was he going to do with her? Anything he wanted.

First, Bride's mouth floundered open and closed, not a sound leaving her. Then she pushed out a heavy breath, as if she were trying to calm herself down. *Then* she narrowed her eyes at him, murderous intent glowing in their emerald depths.

"Where is she?" Bride demanded. Gone was any hint of her earlier breathlessness. Breathlessness that could have sprung from desire . . . or anger.

"We'll get to that," he said smoothly.

She wound the links around her neck, the motions jerky. "What have you done with her?"

Devyn kicked his feet out, crossing them at the ankles. *Why, I sent her to a motel room fifteen miles from here, where she has been watching another room for any sign of you.* "Again, we'll get to that. I believe I once mentioned that I only converse while naked."

Those lush red lips parted on a gasp, and he almost

laughed. He'd known he would enjoy this, but the *depth* of his enjoyment surprised him. She was everything he remembered, yet so much more. Beautiful, witty, and oh, so charming. She was also a fighter by nature. Proof: she'd hunted him down. Twice. Proof: she'd captured Nolan when he and Dallas had been unable. Proof: she sat on the edge of his bed, the chains surely taunting her, but she didn't run away.

He found himself curious about her past, about what had shaped her into the strong, vibrant woman she'd become. A woman who knew nothing about her own race, but a woman who was desperate to know everything. A woman who loved her missing friend with a loyalty that astounded him. Most people turned their back on their loved ones the moment their own lives were placed in danger. Bride plowed through that danger with no thought to her own safety.

He liked that. He liked her. She'd entered the apartment smug and eager, just as he would have done were the situation reversed. Would she have reacted as he had, though? He'd sensed the emotions pulsing off her, and they'd short-circuited his brain, causing great waves of arousal to sweep through him. Dark and carnal and consuming. Blood had left his head, then his limbs, and flowed straight into his cock. It had yet to leave.

"I'm not stripping," she finally said, breaking the silence. Each word dripped with quiet rage. "But I hope you feel free to do so."

"Oh, I do." And he would. Maybe. He hadn't yet decided how far to take this round. Her reactions would dictate his. "But ladies first."

Devyn pushed mental fingers into her mind, clasping onto the energy required for movement. As each time before, hers was spellbinding, enough to drown him with power. For a moment, she resisted, doing her best to shove him out and reclaim her rightful property. But he'd been doing this for so long, it was as simple as breathing. People, objects, it didn't matter. If he could hold the energy, he always prevailed.

The more people he controlled, the harder it was to force individual movements. Usually he'd resort to locking them in place or moving them in the same direction, as he'd done in that alley. It was just him and Bride now, however, and she was his to do with as he pleased.

"Take off your shirt." He didn't need to say it aloud to make it happen, but he wanted her to hear his voice and feel her body respond accordingly, unable to stop herself. Hopefully, it would become habit and she would later do what he wanted without his having to exert any energy of his own.

Her eyes narrowed further as her fingers gripped the hem of her shirt and yanked it over her head. The material lifted her hair, and that amazing black silk tumbled back down, landing on the smooth expanse of her shoulders . . . covering her bra . . . probably tickling her stomach.

She retained a tight grip on the material. "Is this the way all AIR agents act? Like dirty perverts?"

"I'm only an agent when I feel like being an agent. Right now, I only want to be a dirty pervert."

Her nostrils flared in renewed—and far more potent—anger, her eyes bright with sudden . . . pain? "Well, does this make you feel powerful, forcing a defenseless woman to your will? Revealing a body she'd rather hide and shaming her?"

For a moment, only a moment, he paused as his own sense of shame washed through him. Bride's words were nearly a mirror of his father's. *Bodies should never be revealed*, the man had always said. *It's degrading . . . disgraceful.*

Devyn scowled, shoving at the memory and the emotion until both left him. There was nothing degrading or disgraceful about nudity. It had taken him centuries to realize that, to not hate himself for his love of the female form.

Bride didn't believe it, either, he told himself. How could she, when she'd traipsed the streets naked? This was simply her way of fighting back with the only weapon she currently possessed: her intelligence.

"You have no qualms about exposing those decadent curves and that delicious femininity. I know this because you gave me the peep show of a lifetime in public."

She returned his scowl.

"Now be a good girl and drop the shirt for me."

When the fabric hit the floor, there was a clank. He arched a brow in question.

"Razors," she said, chin lifting in challenge. "Check if you want. Maybe I'll luck out and you'll cut yourself."

"Typical vampire. Desperate for my blood." If only she would have lied. He could have punished her. Perhaps made her bend over for a spanking. He did enjoy giving those. "Were the razors for me? Did you plan to mar my pretty face?"

"I carry them with me everywhere I go, moron, and I never said you were pretty."

"I'm exquisite, then. Come now, you can't deny it," he added when she opened her mouth to protest. "Your hard nipples speak for you." Or spoke of the coldness of the room, but whatever. "Tell me, have you ever cut someone with them?"

"My nipples?"

He barely managed to hide his grin. Imp. "No. Your razors."

"Yes." She'd sounded offended that he'd had to ask.

Adorable. He enjoyed her more with every second that passed. "Who?"

"Like I remember all their names."

"Did you do it for sport or defense?" Not that he cared. He'd bedded sadists before. Had actually gone through an all-sadist-all-the-time phase. No longer were they his favorite type, though. He'd grown tired of the hitting and the biting and the scratching. Blah, blah, blah, boring. But as he'd already decided to have this woman no matter what, he'd man up and endure if she needed to hurt him to climax. "Well?"

Her chin lifted another notch, and she stared down at him through the exotic fringe of dark lashes. "None of your business."

"Hint taken. You don't want to talk, you want to finish stripping. Well, who am I to argue with a determined woman? Stand and take off your pants. They're too binding anyway."

She was on her feet, tugging at the stretch pants, and growling low in her throat a second later. "That's not what I meant, and you know it."

"We'll work on our communication later." For his own

amusement, he forced her hips to wiggle as she slid the tights to her ankles. White panties, plain but the perfect match to her bra. Nice. Unexpected. He would have bet a Sweet Munchkin on red lace. He liked the innocence of the white, though.

"Enjoying yourself?" she snarled.

He propped his elbow on the arm of the chair, then rested his chin in his hand, one finger rubbing over his jaw. "Very much so."

Once again her eyes followed the motion of his fingers. He almost smiled. Imagining slicing him or kissing him?

"Have you slept with Aleaha?" she asked.

"No. I just discovered her. Would it bother you if I had?"

"No." She ran her tongue over her wonderfully sharp teeth. "I don't care who you've been with because I'm never going to be among their numbers. I just didn't want to think of my friend heartbroken over the likes of you."

"The likes of me. What a sweet thing to say, as I know you meant that in the very best sense." He reached behind him, pulled his shirt over his head, and tossed it aside. "Have you slept with Nolan?"

Her mouth dropped open, her gaze zeroing in on his new tattoo, then his nipples. They were small and brown, perfect for licking. Or so he'd been told. When her focus lowered to the ropes of muscle lining his stomach, then his navel, she gulped. The reaction pleased him because for once, he didn't have to wonder what thoughts were dancing through her head. Just then, she wanted him.

"No answer for me?" he asked huskily.

"I, uh, what did you ask me?"

Keep looking at me, pet. Keep wanting me. "If you'd slept with Nolan."

"Oh. Well, I already answered that earlier."

He knew that, but repetition was the best way to catch a lie. To his consternation, she switched her attention to just over his head. And not his favorite head, either. Determination pulsed from her.

"Better him than you, though," she said.

If he were a lesser man, he might have crumbled at that point. Being shot down for a dying, contagious criminal . . . it was disgraceful. "Just so you know, his disease is really another life form, an otherworlder a part of yet separate from him, who will invade your body if given the chance, turning you into a cannibal if you fail to infect others. That would mean I'd have to kill you without enjoying you, and I really want to enjoy you."

"First, Nolan explained that to me. Second, I've never been sick. And third, do you always give little Devyn what he wants? Even when the girl in question isn't interested?"

"What a silly question. The girl is always interested." But no one had ever fought it like Bride. Well, except for Eden, but he suddenly couldn't recall why he'd desired her. "Now be a good girl and walk over here and sit on my lap."

The muscles in her legs bunched and strained as she struggled against his mental hold. And for a moment, she actually managed to remain in place. She shouldn't have been able to do it, no one should have, but he would be lying if he said her strength didn't make him proud. All too soon, his will prevailed and she was gliding toward him. Sweat beaded on her skin, glistening like diamonds in the golden lamplight.

"Pretty," he said.

"You're a bastard, you know that?" she choked out as she stopped just in front of him.

"Wrong. My parents were mated when I was conceived." And considering his father's dislike of nakedness and arousal, it was a miracle he'd been conceived at all. He'd wondered over the years if his father really was his father. With the number of lovers his mother had had—lovers the king had not been able to keep out of the queen's bedroom, no matter how hard he'd tried—anyone male could have created him. "Now sit."

Finally Bride was there, resting on his lap, her ass pressed against his thigh.

He craved deeper contact. Did she? "Place your hands on my chest and straddle me."

The heat of her palms nearly scorched him. And when her knees were anchored to the back of his chair, her legs riding alongside his, her panties hovering just over his straining erection, he moaned. His hands settled on the flare of her hips. How perfect she was, smooth and pale like cream.

"I'll kill you for this," she said.

As her gaze was glued to the pulse at the base of his neck, her words slurred as her tongue pushed against her fangs, her pupils dilated, and her expression hungry yet somehow soft, the threat lacked true menace. "You'll kill me with pleasure, is my bet." Just to see what she'd do, Devyn released his mental hold on her hands. She didn't shift them away, but continued to gauge the erratic rhythm of his heart. "I hate to break it to you, pet, but the fact that you want to kill me that way isn't a surprise. I suspected. Bet you're even damp right now."

"Argh!" She balled her fingers into a fist and pounded at his chest like it was a punching bag. "Can you take nothing seriously?" When she realized she'd moved on her own, she blinked down at her hands, wiggled her fingers.

He barely had time to register the wickedly satisfied gleam in her eyes before she'd slapped him. The force of skin zipping over skin stung, but that didn't stop his grin from forming.

When she reached up to do it again, Devyn grasped her wrist, preventing the action. Rather than take control of her next movements with his mind, he brought her palm to his mouth and tenderly kissed her hammering pulse. She allowed it. A shiver rocked her, and her core brushed his penis.

"Do you want to continue our conversation or get right to the loving?" he asked, trying to cut back another moan.

There were several beats of silence. He couldn't guess what thoughts were rolling through her mind. He knew what he wanted her to think, though: she shouldn't want to want him, but want him she did.

Women loved temptation . . . forbidden fruit. Devyn was both of those things, and he knew it. He was a blatant womanizer, shameless, unapologetic, and totally lacking in moral fiber. Many had tried to tame him, and every one of them had failed. He simply wasn't tamable, though he did love for women to try.

"I want to continue the conversation," she finally said, the words like velvet-covered steel.

Pity.

She licked her lips, the pink tip of her tongue swiping back and forth and giving him all sorts of ideas. That tongue, circling the head of his cock. That tongue, laving his testicles. That tongue, riding up and down his shaft.

"Do you give yourself to so many women because you're trying to fill a void?" she asked. "Were your parents mean to you or something?"

"There is no void," he snapped. He was what he was, and there was no more to it than that. That she'd pegged his parents was irrelevant. "Now enough of that." He wouldn't let her ruin the mood he'd gone to such pains to set. "Are you thirsty? A proper host always sees to the comforts of his guests." He angled his head, giving her a better view of his throbbing pulse.

Again, she paused. Again, she licked her lips. "No, thanks." Trembling, slurred again. Her palms flattened on his chest, her nails digging deep. "I had a lot to drink before I came."

Tendrils of something dark swept through him, and he gripped the arms of his chair to prevent himself from gripping her and shaking her. Who had she drunk from? A man? Had she slept with him, too? Vampires often fed and loved at the same time, each act increasing the pleasure of the other.

The thought of this challenging female sinking those teeth into someone else, the thought of that wet sheath riding a cock other than his, should not have bothered him. *Didn't* bother him, he assured himself. He had not been jealous a day in his life, and he wouldn't start now. That would have meant he desired more than a few sweet hours with Bride, and he didn't. He was merely disappointed, for he'd hoped to be the one to feed and sleep with her tonight, and now he'd have to wait.

"Fine, then." The grinding force of his tone surprised him. "We'll jump right to the questions. Where's Nolan?"

"You told me you didn't need to know that anymore. I agreed to continue our conversation because I thought we were going to talk about the vampires."

"We were. I changed my mind. If you want answers of your own, you'll give me what *I* seek. Where's Nolan?"

"My apartment," she gritted out. "Where's Aleaha?"

"A motel. Where's your apartment?"

"Not telling. What motel?"

"Not telling."

They stared at each other for a moment.

"Well, that was informative." He sighed, making sure the warmth of his breath trickled down the valley of her breasts. Whether she allowed much more intimacy this night, she would not leave this room unscathed. His scent would be imprinted on her every cell, and she would think of him every time she breathed.

Goose bumps broke out over her skin. "Let's back away from the topic of Nolan and Aleaha for a moment. As planned. Tell me about the vampires you've met."

With her demand, the way to have her, at least somewhat, presented itself. He almost purred with satisfaction. "And what will you give me in return, hmm? You've already proven you won't give me the answers I seek."

She eyed him warily. "What do you want?"

"A kiss."

"Where?"

"So suspicious." He *tsk*ed under his tongue. "I meant my cock, of course."

A choking sound bubbled from her. "No way. Hell, no. Never. I'll die first."

"Darling, that's just silly. You can't possibly know that for sure until you try it. But I can honestly tell you no woman has ever died from giving me a blow job. They've come close to dying of pleasure, yes, but in the end they did survive, I assure you." He sighed. "If you'd rather, you can kiss me on the mouth. Though I can't guarantee you won't nearly die of pleasure from that, as well."

"You are the most egotistical man I've ever met." Even as she spoke, her gaze dropped to his lips, lingering . . . savoring? "It's beyond frustrating. I don't know how to deal with you."

"Should I pretend I'm ugly?"

"No. You should . . . oh, I don't know." Her head fell back, her back arching as she peered up at the ceiling, as if imploring the heavens for support. Her core brushed his penis yet again.

Sweet fire. "I'd think my honesty easier to deal with than another's lies."

She blew out a breath. It trickled over his skin the way his had done to hers, branding *him* with *her* scent, orchids and midnight tempests. "Maybe you're compensating for something." Before he could toss her on the floor and yell at her for even considering such a foolish thing, she added, "Fine, I'll give you a kiss on the mouth for every question you answer, but you don't get to touch me while I'm doing it."

Slowly he relaxed. "Very well, I won't touch you unless you beg." Something he was (almost) confident he could make her do.

"Like that'll happen." At least her confidence didn't seem to match the level of his. "Just so you know, you only get to collect when I'm satisfied with your answers. And you can't lie," she added in a rush.

"Deal. Don't worry, I'll be keeping score inside my head, and I'm very good at math. Example: Devyn plus Bride minus clothes plus a hard, flat surface multiplied by roaming hands equals greatest pleasure ever. When shall we begin?"

Her jaw had dropped during his equation, but she quickly collected herself. "Let's start now." Those inky locks cascaded down her arms, brushing his stomach as she faced him dead on. "Where did you meet the vampires?"

He plucked a few strands and drew them to his mouth, running the tips along the seam. "A slave auction."

"A slave auction?" Her eyes widened with equal measures of incredulity and disdain, and she jerked the hair from his clasp. "That's barbaric!"

"Yes, at a slave auction. That's two questions I've answered, which means you owe me two kisses."

"I only asked—damn it! I did ask two." She pressed her lips together in a mulish line. "I'll be more careful with my phrasing."

Pity.

"I'm assuming, despot that you are, that you bought them. And that's not a question! If you raped them—"

He rolled his eyes. "As if I need to resort to rape."

That deflated her anger. "Then why buy women? Never mind. Don't answer that. I don't want to pay the toll for it."

Toll. As if kissing him was a punishment. Silly girl. She would soon learn. He'd become skilled at many things since he'd given over to the dark side and embraced his decadent nature. "What's your full name?"

She opened her mouth to tell him, then shut it with a snap. "If I answer that, you have to deduct one of the kisses I owe you."

"But darling, how else am I to tell you everything I know about your people if I don't know everything about *you*?"

She had started to nod her head in agreement when she caught herself. He'd almost had her. "Nice try. I'll answer and you'll deduct, or I just won't tell."

Never had he enjoyed a sparring/bargaining match more. "Fair enough."

"My name is Bride . . . McKells." She held up her wrist, and he studied the black tattoo. No fancy font, just her name.

"McKells. Warrior class," he said, thinking back to the guards who'd escorted him through the underground world of the vampires. First, they'd thought to punish the two vampire females for leading him to the doorway to their world, killing them alongside Devyn. Then, they'd decided to place the decision in their king's hands. So they'd surrounded Devyn and forced him deeper and deeper into the city, not knowing he could have destroyed them all in seconds. And he would have. Dark, confined spaces didn't agree with him. Except, he'd never had sex in a cave and had decided to remain for several nights.

In the end, the king had thanked him for escorting the females back into their fold, for they were of royal blood. The king—Manus, yes, that was his name—had been fierce, jaded, yet fair. While the McKell, the leader of the vampire army and the cruelest among them, the most bloodthirsty, had petitioned for Devyn's execution, citing that they couldn't have anyone running around on the surface knowing where the vampires were hidden, the king had once again surprised his people and invited Devyn to stay for as long as he desired.

Devyn suspected the vampire king was a mind reader. That, or a psychic like Dallas, and had sensed Devyn would do them no harm and could even be relied on as an ally.

He told Bride none of that, however. She hadn't asked, and the information would cost her. "Any more questions for me, pet?" He hooked a finger under the strap of her bra and glided back and forth.

Though she was trembling, she latched on to his wrist, stopping him. "Where do the vampires live? Will you take me to them? Can they do the things I can do? How do they drink blood and keep it down?"

Okay. She had a lot. He tackled them one by one. "Underground. No. No. I don't know. That's three more kisses, plus the one you already owed me. Notice I didn't charge for the answer I didn't know. Now. You can't keep blood down?"

A muscle ticked in her jaw. "Not a full meal, no. Subtract one of those kisses, please, and then tell me how they live underground."

While he'd visited the vampires, he'd come across only

one who'd had trouble digesting the blood she'd consumed. He'd been told the poor female's husband had died, and therefore, she would die. Or maybe she had refused a . . . repression of something? He hadn't been paying the best of attention.

"Are you married?" The moment he spoke, he experienced a killing rage. Bride . . . married . . . out of his reach . . .

"No," she said after a disgusted snort.

"Have you ever been married?"

"No."

The rage vanished as quickly as it had appeared, leaving him shocked and confused. How . . . odd. He'd never reacted that way before. Clearly the disappointment of potentially losing this challenge was once again the culprit for his riotous behavior. "I thought you drank a lot before coming to me."

"I did. But I also threw up most of it. I'm living off a few sips a day. End of subject."

Actually, it wasn't. "Do you want my help?"

"I do not. Not with the drinking. So tell me about the underground."

Infuriating woman. "The underground . . ." Devyn shook off her hold and ran his hands up her sides, stopping beside the swell of her breasts. She didn't protest, didn't pull away. "It's a city, much like ours. Dark and murky, water dripping down the rocky walls of their caves. They are self-sufficient, with roads and shops and bars. They only enter our world twice a year, where they capture humans and use them as food for the rest of the year before killing them and getting more. Only a select few are sent here during the hunts, so I'm not sure how you ended up here, raised . . . alone?"

"Yes. Except for Aleaha." There was so much hurt in the words, he was momentarily speechless. "And FYI, you just lost another kiss."

He wasn't worried. He'd get it back. He just . . . He didn't like that hurt. He much preferred her angry, excited, and triumphant. Clearly she felt abandoned by her people. By Aleaha. "I wonder how you reached the surface. And no, that wasn't a question."

"I don't remember," she answered anyway. Her fingertip traced a circle over his breastbone, just beside his heart. He doubted she realized what she was doing. "I don't remember my mother or my father or if I even had a mother or father. I don't remember anything about my life before waking up on the streets of New Chicago."

"So you were young. Again, not a question."

"Yes. And thirsty. So damn thirsty."

So why couldn't she digest the blood anymore? Better question, would she be able to tolerate *his* blood?

He leaned forward and brushed a gentle kiss between her breasts. He'd meant to offer comfort, to tempt her, as well as finally planting the tiny tracking bug he had waiting on his tongue. Mostly, he aroused himself. Needing to taste her, desperate for it, he flicked out his now-bare tongue, running it over the edge of her bra and then, when she failed to protest, her skin.

She sucked in a breath, tangled her hands in her hair, and held him in place. "Wh—what are you doing?"

"Enjoying you. And now you owe me three kisses." See. Got it back.

"Damn it. Diabolical man."

An endearment, surely. As he arched toward her, he gripped her ass and pumped her forward, grinding their bodies together. She moaned; he hissed and turned his head, lips locking on one of her nipples. The syn-cotton or whatever material it was that shielded her didn't deter him. He sucked and laved it like the treasure it was, the little pearl teasing him.

"Don't you want to ask me about Nolan?" she rasped. To distract him? Because she didn't have the strength to pull away herself?

"Yes. Four kisses now, and you *will* pay up." He spread his fingers over her ass, two closing in on a place she probably didn't want him, but one day would if he had his way, the others inching toward her clitoris. If she bowed her back, he could thrum her to release. She'd beg and plead, drip in his hand. And oh, wasn't that a delightful image?

"Take your kisses now, then. Do it!" She yanked at his hair, tugging several strands from his scalp.

Slowly he lifted his head, meeting her heated gaze. Passion had wrought a rosy glow to her cheeks. Her eyes glittered brightly, dangerously; they were seductive. Tempting him. Her lips were damp and swollen from where she'd chewed them. Breath sawed in and out of her mouth, choppy and shallow.

"You want your kisses, pet?"

"Want? No. But I never welsh."

So, she still thought to deny him, did she? His eyelids slitted. If he kissed her now, with her core so close to his cock, he would take her all the way—they both knew it—and if he had her delicious little body now, she would tell herself he'd forced her. She would convince herself it had been for answers, not desire. Afterward, she would avoid him, build a resistance to him. Think of him only in her nightmares.

He would tolerate none of that. Whenever Bride thought of him, he wanted it to be because of sex, passion, and pleasure. Not shame and regret. Never shame. Never regret. He wanted her to remember this time, his words, his touch with a smile on her beautiful face. He didn't want her remembering her *duty* and frowning. More than that, he wanted her to run *to* him if he so desired in the future, not away from him.

"I'll collect my kisses, don't worry, but I won't do it here and I won't do it now. I'll let you know when and where. Promise."

Those sharp nails of hers dug into the base of his neck. "This is the last time I'll allow myself to be caught alone with you. Take them here or forfeit."

Just as he'd suspected, she thought to avoid him. Well, too bad. She'd see him again, and she'd kiss him again and then do a whole lot more. Devyn reclaimed his hold on her mind and forced her to straighten and stand, to walk backward, away from him. He didn't have the strength to walk away from her himself. Not this time. Already his body mourned the loss of her.

Mourned? Surely not.

"Let me go, damn it!"

"Listen closely, pet. I forfeit nothing. You'll kiss me when I tell you, or you'll be in breach and I'll be entitled to simply take what I want. And now that that's settled . . .

tomorrow night at midnight, you're going to bring Nolan to the pier. I'll bring Aleaha, and we'll trade."

Immediately she shook her head, but there was hope in her eyes. "I don't trust you."

Smart woman. No way in hell would he be at the pier tomorrow. "Do you want to see Aleaha or not?"

She bit her tongue, probably drawing blood. To keep from biting him? "You know I do. And if you've hurt her, I swear to God I'll cut off your balls and feed them to you."

"Kinky. But like I was saying, if you want to see her, you'll bring Nolan to that pier."

"Where I'll find all of AIR waiting for me. No thanks."

"You'll come, or you won't see her again. It's as simple as that." He shrugged, as if he didn't care what she decided. "Oh, and a little side note. I'm gonna need your cell number."

She laughed, her smile so bright it was as though the sun had just bathed her. "No way I'll give it to you."

"Then take mine. I bought a new number just for you." Devyn forced her to remain still as he stood and stepped around her. He bent down and grabbed her tights, reaching inside the slim pocket and tugging out her cell.

"If I could move, I'd slap that out of your hand. Stop controlling me, damn it!"

"Learn how to stop me yourself." He'd known she had a phone because he'd felt the energy kicking off it. Quickly he deleted every number in her address book and programmed in his own. "There. You'll have no trouble scrolling and finding me."

"Do you get a new number for all your girls, or am I just special?"

"You're special, sweet." There was a ring of truth to his tone that surprised even him, and he frowned. He released her from stun and handed her the pants, the phone stashed back inside the pocket. "Call me tomorrow at noon. I want to talk to Nolan and make sure he's still alive."

She yanked the pants from him and jerked them on. "I'll expect to talk to Aleaha."

"Sounds fair." If he'd truly planned to call her, that is. As it was, he'd have her at his mercy *before* lunch. "Any tricks tomorrow, and I'll slice Aleaha's throat like a melon." A lie, but she didn't know that.

Her hands fisted at her sides. "You're going to regret the day you met me. I'll make sure of it."

"I look forward to your attempts." So badly he wanted to force her to strip again. So badly he wanted to finally sink inside her, pounding hard into her tight, wet sheath. And she would be wet when he took her. Dripping, as he so desperately wanted. He'd make sure of it.

"Then I'll see you tomorrow night," she said softly. Deadly. "Dream of me."

CHAPTER 8

Everything Devyn had told her about vampires raced through Bride's mind as she snuck home, doubling back, taking wrong turns, careful to avoid any AIR agents that might be following her. Devyn was just the type to tell her he'd meet her for an exchange tomorrow while having someone lying in wait for her today, ready to steal Nolan rather than trade for him.

Plus, it was better to think about the vampires and her possible family link—she was part of a warrior line?—than to think about Devyn's nicknames for her—pet, sweet, darling—and how they melted her heart—so foolishly, since he most likely used them with everyone. The way she'd wanted to trace his skull-and-dagger tattoo with her tongue. The way he had kissed her bra, her skin. The way he'd touched her, and the way she'd wanted to beg for more. Beg! Something she despised and had sworn never to do again. Too many times, she'd had to beg for food for Aleaha, and too many times, people had waved her away as if she were a pesky fly.

But for more of those naughty hands, that hot tongue,

that decadent scent . . . more of everything he had to give . . . maybe. *Who are you? Never maybe. Always no.*

And what about Aleaha? Devyn had found her. How? Bride fingered the necklace she now wore. She'd been searching for years with no success. Devyn had learned the girl's name, and boom. He had her. How was he treating her? Bride was tempted to lie in wait for *him*. To follow him to where Aleaha was being kept. Except, his warning echoed through her mind continually. *Any tricks tomorrow, and I'll slice her throat.*

Any tricks . . . tomorrow. He'd said nothing about tonight.

Hello loophole.

Nervous, excited, hopeful, she backtracked once again, heading toward Devyn's building. Was he still there? He didn't live there, that much she knew. The closet had been empty. So had the fridge; she would have smelled the food.

Speaking of food, what did he eat? He smelled divine, no hint of human spice. And what did his blood taste like?

She was so curious about him, this man she'd encountered thrice, touched twice, made out with once—kind of—and now dreamed about. What made him tick? How did he live his life? Had he ever been in love?

Not that the answers mattered. Really. He was her enemy right now. If he'd hurt her friend, his throat would be ripped from his gorgeous body and tossed into a gutter, she thought, nails digging into her palms.

Physically hurting women didn't seem like Devyn's style, she reminded herself, and her muscles relaxed.

Most likely he'd screwed Aleaha stupid. *That* was more his MO. The bastard. How many hearts had he broken over the years? Did he even care about the destruction he left behind?

Not that it matters. Another reminder.

It was late Sunday night, and the streets were nearly deserted. Only a few people bustled past, a little woozy on their feet from too much alcohol. The moon was high, golden, and full. It was the kind of night she usually loved. She could meander freely, air cool on her easily heated skin, drunks ripe for the plucking. Not that she could keep beer-saturated blood down anymore, either. Even that upset her delicate stomach.

Devyn had seemed surprised and angry that she couldn't keep an entire meal down. Those beautiful amber eyes had given him away. Why the anger? He knew something she didn't, most likely. Hell, he knew a lot of stuff she didn't. If she had to trade more kisses for the answers, fine, she'd suck it up like a big girl and do it. *If* he treated Aleaha well. Everything hinged on that. Everything but the fact that she was going to drink from him. One way or another. As far as she was concerned, he owed her.

The closer she came to Devyn's apartment, the more she felt a pair of eyes burning into her back. Bride's heartbeat kicked up a notch, even as she tensed, slowed, scanning the area. One thing movies and books had gotten wrong was the fact that vampires were dead. At least, *she* wasn't. She had a working heart; she breathed. The only difference between her and humans—besides her abilities—was her need for blood rather than food.

Vamps could be otherworlders, she supposed. Or

even genetically altered humans. Either way, she *could* be killed. She'd come close a few times over the years.

Purposefully she rounded a corner, heading into a back alley that led to a maze of doors and walkways. While it was a good place to hide, it was also a good place to test her possible shadow's intentions. There were no shops here, nothing a normal person would want to see or need. There was no reason to follow her here unless she was a target.

Boxes lined the buildings, the homeless sleeping inside them. No one should—footsteps resounded behind her. Okay. She was being followed; she was a target. Devyn? AIR? Or someone else?

Don't turn, don't let whoever it is know you know they're there. Bride breathed deeply, in and out, trying to sort through the deluge of scents. Urine, waste, dirt, unwashed bodies, rotting food. A clean body, lightly cologned. Not Devyn. She would have caught a whiff of his clean-sheets-and-rain fragrance, mingled ever so slightly with Aleaha's sky-and-pine smell, no matter what surrounded her. It was probably someone he knew, though.

Grinding her molars, she swiped another corner and picked up her pace, grabbing her phone and flipping it open. She didn't have any trouble finding Devyn's number because it was the only one in memory. That dirty little shit! She didn't have any friends, but she collected numbers to restaurant deliveries. Not for the food, but for the delivery boys.

The footsteps picked up pace, too.

With a press of a button, Devyn's number was dialed. She held the phone to her ear, snaking into an open doorway, zigzagging through a building, and sprinting out the other side.

"Miss me already, darling?" Devyn's sexy voice purred on the other end.

"Couldn't keep your word and wait until tomorrow, could you? Had to sic your AIR buddy on me tonight? Is it the blue-eyed one? What's his name? Dallas? He's cute, so I might call and thank you tomorrow. He won't, though. That, I promise you."

A heavy, crackling pause. "You're being followed?"

"Oh, look. Devyn's acting innocent. Must be a fun new game."

"Where are you, Bride?"

There wasn't an ounce of humor in his tone. That . . . scared her. "And help your friend find me? Sorry. I'm not gonna tell."

"That's not my friend." There was static on the line as he spoke, as if he was talking and running at the same time. "Where are you?"

Was he telling the truth? Only person she'd ever truly trusted was Aleaha. Too many others had betrayed her, lied to her, and let her down. Course, most of those sins came courtesy of her ex-boyfriend. He'd been so sweet at first. A real doll. But because of her late-night jaunts, he'd begun to think she was cheating on him. He'd become resentful, jealous, hateful, and had decided to teach her a lesson and cheat on *her*.

A glowing blue beam soared a few inches to her right, and she gasped as she dove around a metal pole. "Shit! Whoever it is just tried to stun me. Sure it's not AIR?"

"Yes. Now give me your goddamn location."

The anger in his voice was enough to make her shudder. If the person chasing her *was* AIR, then that person could just as easily phone him and tell him where she was. He could have her location whether she gave it to him or not. The rationalization eased her objections, and Bride finally spouted off her coordinates.

"I'm on my way."

"Okay. See you—"

"Don't hang up!" he shouted.

Another beam soared past her, this one mere inches from her shoulder. She yelped, increasing her speed, feet pounding into the pavement. "Almost got me that time," she rasped. The burning started up in her chest, thorns ready to cut.

"Does stun effect you?"

"Yes." Unfortunately.

"I'm almost there. Keep dodging."

"Brilliant plan. However did you think of it?" she asked dryly. "Don't answer. We'll talk when you get here."

"That sounded like good-bye, and I already told you not to hang up."

"Sorry, but I'm going to take the bastard out, and I can't do that one-handed." *Click.* As Bride ran, she stowed her phone and tore several razors from her sleeve. Her palms were damp with sweat, but she maintained a firm grip as she swerved behind another doorway.

This time, rather than race onward, she crouched on the floor. A quick peek, her gaze cutting through the darkness like a knife, and she saw that her attacker was male. Tall, lean but muscled. Sandy hair. Boyish good looks.

Tom, she realized, and her stomach rolled. Shy, horny Tom wanted her stunned? Why?

He slowed to a leisurely stroll and raised his pyre-gun as he searched every doorway. "Come out, come out, wherever you are," he called. "I don't want to hurt you, Bride."

Bride didn't reply. She wasn't an idiot—hello, he *so* wanted to hurt her—and wouldn't give away her location by allowing him to follow her voice. Thank God she hadn't drunk from him that night. Afterward, he could have ambushed her while she'd writhed in pain.

Guess she owed Devyn a thank-you.

When Tom stepped around one of those thick metal poles, Bride jerked her arm forward, releasing one of her razors. It whizzed through the air and sliced the side of his neck. He howled, fired, free hand reaching up to staunch the blood.

The stun missed her by a mile. She used his distraction to her advantage and tossed another blade, aiming for his other side. It, too, sliced at his neck, drawing blood. Mmm, blood. So red . . . so pretty. He didn't smell as pure tonight, had eaten oversalted eggs and bread, but the dark red liquid still looked savory. He howled again, dropping his gun and covering the rest of his sensitive flesh.

"Damn it! I just want to talk to you," he growled.

"Then you shouldn't have shot at her," another, deeper voice said. A pissed-off voice. Devyn was here.

Her heart pounded against her ribs, her skin tightened, and her nipples beaded, relief and arousal blending. Every nerve ending in her body ached for another touch from him. *Maybe I am an idiot.*

"You can come out, sweetheart. Your human can't move; he's under my control. Nice shots on his neck, by the way. Very impressive aim. Next time sever the jugular, though."

Keeping a razor in hand and beaming at Devyn's praise, Bride pushed to a stand and strode from the doorway. Though she wanted to stop beside Devyn and breathe him in, she bypassed him for Tom's gun, still resting on the floor. She picked it up and sheathed it at her waist.

Devyn *tsk*ed under his tongue. "Thinking of using that on me?"

"Just adding it to my collection." And holding on to it for protection. One wrong move from him, and she *would* stun him.

Finally, she faced him. He'd pulled on a shirt but was otherwise the same as she'd left him. Sexy as hell in wrinkle-free slacks, hair in disarray, and amber eyes bright. He wasn't winded or sweating. He looked as if he'd stepped from the pages of a magazine, rather than having just sprinted a five-hundred-yard dash.

"Let me go," Tom demanded. "I'm human. I have rights."

"Not anymore," Devyn said flatly.

Bravado faded. "Please. I didn't mean any harm, and I don't know how you're keeping me still like this, but I'm willing to forgive and forget. Just let me go."

"Do you know this man?" Devyn asked her, ignoring Tom.

"Yep. Tom tried to pick me up the other day. The day I met you, actually."

One of Devyn's dark brows arched. "Heaven and hell, all in one day. Lucky girl. I take it you refused him?"

"I planned on having a drink with him, then caught Aleaha's scent and took off."

"*With* him?" Devyn chuckled. "Poor Tom." He eyed the man in question. Sweat had beaded over Tom's face. His lips were pulled into a frightened frown, and lines of tension branched from his eyes. "Denied the delectable morsel that is my Bride. I understand your pain, human. I, too, let her get away once. Now, what I don't understand is shooting at the woman days later." Every word was harsher, harder.

His Bride?

"You don't know what you're messing with, man," Tom said on a trembling breath as he tried to collect himself. "Just let me go, and we'll forget this ever happened."

"Oh, then please enlighten me as to what I'm *messing with*."

Tom's dark eyes skidded to Bride before returning to Devyn, the biggest threat. "She's a vampire. She'll suck you dry if given the chance. I know how to deal with them. I can protect you from her."

So. He knew she was a vampire. How many others knew? Was there already a mob after her, determined to stake her or burn her alive? "Why do you think I'm . . . vampire?" She couldn't keep the fear from her voice. She'd gone to such pains to hide what she was.

Tom laughed cruelly. "Few weeks ago you were seen drinking from a bum in an alleyway just like this. You were followed, information gathered. When I questioned your ex-boyfriend, I learned some interesting things about your nightly habits. And guess what? I'm not the only one who knows about you. My friends plan to sell you to the highest bidder." He turned to Devyn. "Let me go, and you can have half the profits. You don't want a bloodsucker as a lover, trust me. We'll find you something else. Something sweet and pliable."

Something, he'd said, as if the women weren't living beings. She realized he'd never truly desired her, had just sought her capture and the profit that would have accompanied it. Bastard.

"No, thanks. I'd rather send your friends a message." Devyn slid a long, sharp knife from his side, the silver winking in the moonlight.

He'd turned down money and a slave. For her. Sweetest gesture ever. That didn't mean she'd sleep with him, but wow. She might maybe kinda sorta didn't despise him now. *Like you did before.*

"Wh-what kind of message?" Tom asked, gaze glued to the weapon. If he'd had control of his body, he would have trembled, shrank back. Maybe pissed his pants. There was an unholy gleam to Devyn, as if he relished what was about to happen. As if he could already smell the blood and gore and found it heady. "How are you holding me so still? Let me go. Please, just let me go, or you'll regret it."

"I can promise you, I'll do no such thing. I never regret."

Devyn seemed to have forgotten Bride was even there, his full attention focused on his prey. And that's exactly what Tom was just then. Prey. Part of her suddenly wanted to leave Devyn to his torturing and race home. To safety. The other part of her wanted to find out who Tom's friends were, so that Devyn could destroy them, too.

In the end, she stayed. And she watched. Just in case Devyn needed assistance. Tom did a lot of crying, a lot of begging, but Devyn never relented. Merciless, cruel, he took his time, slicing, taunting, inflicting maximum pain without actually killing the human. At one point, Bride asked him if she should act as lookout and keep others from approaching, but he told her he'd taken care of that. Probably with his body-control ability.

Tom spilled blood—lots and lots of blood—and Bride's mouth watered for all of that beautiful crimson nectar. Her fangs were sharpened, cutting her gums. Still she smelled the spice, but it no longer mattered in any way. She was starving, and the human was a banquet. But she resisted. Barely. Now was not the time to gorge. Once this was done, she needed to be on her feet, not writhing and vomiting. She needed to go home and decide what to do now that others knew about her.

When Devyn cut off one of Tom's fingers, blood sprayed her directly in the face, dripping . . . oh, yes, dripping . . . begging her to taste, and she almost crumbled. Somehow, she managed to keep her tongue inside her mouth. A single taste would whip her into a frenzy; since her body always absorbed those first sips, it thought it could handle more and so it would demand more. She would drink and gulp and lap every drop from the sidewalk, unable to help herself.

Again she thought that she should leave, but Tom also began spilling lots and lots of secrets, so she remained in place, listening. Horrified. He and his friends had been slavers for years. They hadn't just planned to abduct her. They'd planned to abduct *many* women. Selling them for sex, torture, or whatever the winning bidder wanted. The rarer the species, the higher the price.

Apparently, vampires were now the pick du jour.

Names, though, Tom refused to give, and in the end Devyn carved him up piece by piece before cutting off his head and depositing it on the nearest street corner for someone to find and news stations to shout about. Tom's friends would see what had happened to him and know he'd been caught.

By then, it was an hour before sunset. Bride was covered in blood spatter, scared to her soul about slavers knowing who she was and where she lived, rubbing her chest to stave off the pain, and in awe of Devyn. Not once had he tired or hesitated. The very man who had probably charmed thousands of women out of their panties had been brutal, savage. Emotionless.

He turned to her, eyes as bright an amber as always but filled with uncertainty. "You're frightened."

"Yes." No reason to deny it.

He looked away from her. "Of me?"

She should be. Anyone who could take a life like that, hurt someone like that, was not a good enemy to have, and she'd challenged him several times already. She'd even vowed to make his life miserable. Yet right here, right now, she felt safer with him than anyone else in the world.

"No, not you. I'm afraid of the men who hunt me."

There was a beat of surprise before a slow grin spread over his face and he once again met her gaze. What a morbidly beautiful sight he was, Bride thought. He waved a dismissive hand. "When they see the news, they'll know. Mess with Bride McKells and die."

"That, or they'll come for revenge." A shudder rocked her.

His head tilted to the side in thought. "You could always room with me." The moment he spoke, his lips pursed, as if he wanted to snatch back the words.

"No, thanks. I've been protecting myself for years. I'll be fine." Most likely she'd have to move again, change her name again. Damn. She didn't want to do either. She liked her home.

He popped his jaw, an action completely at odds with the tender way he then brushed her hair behind her ear. "They won't come for you, not for days yet. When they find out about Tom, they'll meet and talk about what to do. You have time to think, to plan, so rest easy tonight. Or rather, today. We'll figure out how to handle them once Nolan and Aleaha are taken care of." He glanced up at the sky. "Much as I'm enjoying our time together, you had better go. I doubt you can tolerate the sun for long."

"You're right. It blisters my skin." It was a weakness she shouldn't have admitted to, but after everything he'd done for her, her defenses were down and the truth had simply slipped out.

"Until tomorrow, then."

She backed away, intending to leave as he'd suggested, but stopped herself before she'd even taken four steps. "Devyn?"

"Don't tell me. You want to kiss me good-bye." He sighed, waved her over. "Fine. I'll jump on that grenade. Get over here."

She rolled her eyes. "Why did you help me?" she asked. She had to know.

For a moment, she doubted he would answer. Then he shrugged. "You have Nolan. And you owe me three make-out sessions. I wasn't about to let you die and renege."

Whatever she'd hoped to hear, that wasn't it. "Uh, I owe you *kisses*. Not make-out sessions." She paused, nibbled on her bottom lip. "Will you get in trouble? For killing a human, I mean?" As an otherworlder, he had very few rights. Unfair, but the way of the world all the same.

His lips twitched. "Worried for me, sweetheart? Well, don't be. If I'm punished, I'll make you fuck me all better."

She spun around, giving him her back before he saw her smile. Fuck him all better, indeed. Incorrigible womanizer. "See you later, Devyn," she said, and strode away from him.

CHAPTER 9

Dallas Gutierrez clutched a garbage bag as he pushed through the mess in his living room, bending down and picking up trash. Cleaning. Ugh. It was something he hadn't done in months. After his near-death experience, he'd just stopped caring about the state of his domicile. Why waste precious time doing something he hated? But Devyn liked clean and neat, and Devyn would arrive any moment. He knew it, sensed it.

They hadn't talked since yesterday morning, when Dallas had taken Macy and Breean to a motel to "search" for Bride. They'd even made plans to meet for coffee at eight a.m. today, a few hours away. But Devyn was on his way even now. Lately, Dallas knew all kinds of trivial things. They seeped into his head, not visions but whispers of coming truths.

He hated it. He didn't want to know things before they happened. Little or big. Last few months, a lot of his friends had stopped calling, stopped hanging out with him. They were afraid of him and what he could now do. Predict the future. Move at speeds the human eye couldn't see. Compel people to obey him with only a single voiced command.

The speed, he actually enjoyed. He'd secretly used it on the job once or twice and was a better agent because of it. Only problem was, he couldn't have one ability without the others. Okay, two problems. His control of each ability was sketchy. Maybe because he fought them so fervently. But he couldn't help himself. When he welcomed his visions with open arms, he saw loved ones die. When he forced people to do things they didn't want to do, the guilt ate at him for days. Therefore, he tried not to use either.

Finally, though, he'd caved and tried to force Nolan to stay in that alley, unmoving, compliant, because, unlike Devyn's, Dallas's ability wasn't a manipulation of energy but an exertion of will. And look what that had gotten him. Failure. That particular power had remained dormant, Nolan had continued to move, and Dallas had had a vision of himself, as he was now, in bed with a woman he hadn't seen in months. How?

Kyrin had offered to teach and train him, but Dallas couldn't bring himself to agree. The more time he spent with the Arcadian, the more he was reminded that his will was not his own. That he was really just a slave to another.

What am I going to do? He needed to decide, one way or another: welcome all of his abilities completely or suppress them, which Kyrin had said he could do if he ignored all three abilities long enough. Either way, he needed to decide now.

For the past few hours, another vision had been knocking on his brain, demanding entrance. He'd been fighting it, but fighting brought crack-your-skull-against-the-wall headaches. So . . . embrace all? Or suppress?

Knowing the future brought both triumph and failure. Last time he'd almost killed his friend Jaxon trying to prevent a vision from coming true. But if he knew what was going to happen, he could possibly *save* a life one day.

Damn it. There were good arguments for both decisions.

He needed to do something. *Well, you can't call an old girlfriend to come over and distract you.* Because of what he'd seen in that alley, he'd already done that.

After griping him out for not calling in forever, she'd come over and they'd played naughty-AIR-agent-and-dirty-otherworlder. He'd acted like the dirty otherworlder, and she'd had no idea how perfectly the role fit him now. Every day he lost a little more of his humanity.

Now she was asleep in his bedroom. He should have sent her home after the sex, but he hadn't wanted to be alone. How pathetic.

As he continued to clean, Dallas began sweating, panting, unable to catch his breath. His ribs soon felt as if they were comprised of glass and were cutting into his chest cavity. His temples ached unbearably. *Just suck it up.* He swiped up an empty sandwich wrapper, an image of—no. No! He shoved the image away with a mental hand, not booting it out of his brain but keeping it locked inside a box. He hadn't made a decision yet.

The action caused a sharp, agonizing pain to tear through him, and he dropped to his knees. He gritted his teeth, his jaw clenching so tightly that the joints threatened to snap out of place. Nausea rolled through his stomach. *Just suppress already. Knowing the future changes the future, and not always for the better.*

What if someone I love is about to be hurt?

He lumbered to his feet as the vision tried to claw its way free. He shook his head violently, and still another pain slashed through him, doubling him over. A moan slipped from him. Too much. It was too much. If he kept fighting, undecided, he was going to have an aneurism.

Not knowing what else to do, Dallas peeked through a crack in that box. The pain eased slightly. There were two visions, he realized, each vying for entrance. One, he'd ignored for hours. The other was brand-new. No wonder the knocking had intensified.

Don't do it. Don't let them in. Ignorance is bliss, and you won't be able to mess with the future.

It's better to know. And this way, you can keep your superspeed.

The two desires warred inside him until he was shaking, almost foaming at the mouth. Every nerve ending in his body was sharpening, desperate to cut through him and escape the pain.

Don't do it. You almost killed Jaxon, remember?

Do it, do it, do it. You're wiser now. You won't hurt anyone. How many times do you have to be reminded that you could save more lives—

With a roar, he wrenched open the box. The first vision flew into his mind, colors taking shape, images forming. There was Devyn, standing in an abandoned alleyway, soaked in blood. It dripped from him—draining his life? In front of him was the vampire, Bride. She, too, was covered in blood. There were smudges around her mouth, as if she'd recently fed and had tried to wipe herself clean.

If that bitch had drank from Devyn . . . Dallas's hands fisted. But guilt joined ranks with his anger, and he squeezed his eyes shut, hoping to tamp down both emotions. *If I'd allowed the vision inside earlier, would I have been able to stop this?* Was Devyn now hurt? Dead? They'd known there was a chance Bride would erupt when she learned that Devyn had "captured" Macy, aka Aleaha, but neither of them had taken it seriously. Devyn could lock the woman in place. Besides that, females simply didn't attack Devyn. Not with malicious intentions, anyway.

Maybe Bride had learned how to defend herself against Devyn's ability, as Nolan had done. In fact, Nolan could have told her what to do. Snarling, Dallas punched the wall, leaving a hole.

Devyn's alive. He's on his way here. You know that. The panic gradually receded, and Dallas watched inside his mind as Devyn reached out and tucked a lock of Bride's dark hair behind her ear. An action of affection. Bride nibbled on her bottom lip, her fangs sharp, and peered down at the ground, shy but intrigued. Dallas relaxed a little more. Whatever had happened between the pair had been consensual and perhaps nonviolent, despite the blood. But damn, he was going to have to talk to his friend about his bed partners.

Bride turned on her heel and marched away, disappearing into the shadows. Devyn was smiling that wicked, satisfied smile of his.

Not such a bad vision, after all, Dallas thought, shoulders slouching in relief. That image faded, making way for the second. Once again colors began to take shape. Moments later, the pier came into view. A metal bridge that stretched over what little water remained, inching its way to shore.

There was Devyn, a knife in his heart, his body prone, motionless, his eyes closed, blood all around him. Bride stood off to the side, a group of men flanking her. They were holding her in place as she cried and screamed and fought for freedom.

Every muscle in Dallas's body tightened. Devyn planned to tell Bride to meet him at the pier, but he didn't plan to actually go. Had his friend changed his mind?

Dallas shifted his attention, scanning the entire area. There was no sign of himself, Breean, or Macy. He then focused on the men holding Bride, memorizing their features, their clothing.

"—on, my man." A warm hand patted his cheek. "Wake up for me. Your visions have never taken this long before. What's going on? You know I hate mysteries."

Everything winked out of focus, and Dallas almost roared. He clawed at his mind, at the dark box, desperate to learn everything he could, but nothing reappeared in the first and the second was now empty.

Okay. Fine. Dallas would write down everything he remembered about the vision, and he would reason it out, share the details with the players involved, and then do whatever was necessary to stop it from happening. He wouldn't make the same mistake as last time. He wouldn't assume he knew what had brought about the events or who had caused Devyn's . . . death.

No. *No!* Devyn would not die. There was no longer any question about whether to embrace or suppress. Dallas would embrace and ensure his friend lived.

"Wake up for your sweet Devyn." Another pat, this one harder. "That's a good boy."

Slowly Dallas blinked open his eyes. He was still panting, still sweating, but was no longer in pain. Devyn loomed over him, concern darkening his usually bright eyes. Just as Dallas had seen him in his first vision, Devyn was covered in blood. It stained his skin, his clothes.

"Okay?" he managed to work past his spasming throat.

"Me?" The otherworlder looked surprised by the question. "Why—oh. The blood. No worries. It's not mine."

Thank God. "Vampire decide . . . to eat . . . in front . . . of you?"

"Nothing like that. I'll explain in a bit. You want to tell me what's going on with you?"

Not yet. "How'd you . . . get in?"

"I peeked over your shoulder last time you disabled your alarm. Memorized your code."

Smiling despite the pain, Dallas rubbed his temples. "You are such a good friend."

"I know." Devyn helped him to a sitting position and remained crouched in front of him. "I hope you don't mind, but I sent your woman on her way. She was shaking you, screaming for you to wake up, and pissing off your neighbors."

Dallas propped his elbows on his knees, hating the way he trembled. "Not safe for her to walk the streets alone."

"That's why I called her a cab. And be prepared. If you see her again, you're going to get an earful. First she passed out when she saw me, then she woke up and threatened to call the police. I told her if she was going to hang around you, she'd have to get used to seeing me because fainting at the sight of my beauty was going to piss you off, and I'd rather cut out her eyes than piss you off."

"And that didn't go over well? Women. I'm sure the coat of blood you're wearing had nothing to do with her reaction to you."

Devyn searched his face. "Your color is returning. Good. You're going to be fine."

"I'm the psychic, but yeah, you're right."

"I'm going to shower. Make us a pot of coffee—real, not artificial, if you've got any of the stuff I bought you left over—and we'll talk when I'm done." He didn't wait for Dallas's response but stood and strode toward the back of the apartment.

Dallas, too, stood but he stumbled his way into the kitchen. He had just enough beans for a full pot. As he prepared it, he anchored his phone to his ear and dialed Mia.

She answered on the second ring. "Dal, you shit, this better be good. It's my night off."

"Yeah, it is. Good, I mean. I need a sketch artist as soon as possible."

"Why?"

"I'll share the details the moment I understand them."

"Uh, you tell me or you don't get a damn thing."

Jack, their former boss, would have agreed with Dallas

right away. Female bosses sucked. "Think of this as an early birthday present, then. It's all I want."

A sigh crackled over the line. "Bastard. Your place or the station?"

Okay. Maybe female bosses weren't so bad. Jack would have told him to fuck himself for his present. "My place."

"Two hours?"

"Perfect."

"Fuck you, I'm going back to sleep. Call me when you're ready to talk, and that better be no later than forty-eight hours, or I swear to God I'll kick your ass into next week just like Jack always threatened." *Click.*

Dallas was grinning as he slid his cell over the counter, the scent of caffeine thickening the air, frivolous and decadent. He gathered two cups, the last remaining scoop of real sugar, and a can of dried milk. Devyn liked his caffeine sweet, but refused to drink anything with synthetics. Dallas would have called him a girl, but Devyn would have viewed that as a compliment.

The smell of dry enzyme soap drifted to him, alerting him to Devyn's arrival. He turned. And sure enough, there was his friend, bent over and resting his elbows on the counter. The blood was gone, his hair perfectly combed. He wore Dallas's favorite "Size Dental Appliances Here" with an arrow pointing down T-shirt and a pair of his jeans.

"You gave me that shirt as a gift. Taking it back?"

"I'll return it. It's just the only thing you own that's made from real cotton. My skin deserves the best."

"You're such a snob."

"I'd say I'm smart for treating myself with luxuries, but whatever. Now, tell me what the hell was going on with you when I walked in."

The coffee machine beeped, and Dallas filled the two mugs. He dropped a spoon in Devyn's so that the other-worlder could stir his own shit and handed it to him. "I had a vision and was trying to sort through it. Must have gone a little too deep into my brain."

"I guessed that. What I want to know is what you saw. And why have Mia send a sketch artist over?"

"You have ears like Mishka, man." The girl could hear a feather land on a mattress from two miles away.

Devyn shrugged. "Start talking."

Dallas leaned back against the counter and sipped at the hot java for strength. First, he told his friend about the blood.

"That's nothing," Devyn said. "I killed a human."

Dallas blinked at him, at the casual way he admitted to murder. "Wait. I couldn't possibly have heard you right. Did you just say you killed a human?"

"Yeah. He was a slaver. Tried to abduct Bride to sell her on the black market."

"And you killed him? Dude, *you've* bought women on the black market."

Again Devyn shrugged, but there was something in his eyes. Something Dallas had never seen before and couldn't place. "There are others out there who know about her, but no matter how much I tortured him, he wouldn't give me their names. Probably because he knew he was going to die either way. Either that, or there weren't actually any others. Only time will tell."

There wasn't an ounce of remorse in his friend's tone. No one could kill as ruthlessly or as uncaringly as Devyn. The man saw each of his actions as a necessary duty and never looked back, never regretted. Maybe that was why they got along so well. Dallas had enough regrets for both of them.

"Mia know?"

"Not yet, but she will. I left the guy's head on Main."

Dallas's eyes widened. Devyn had made the announcement while lifting and studying one of Dallas's small black computer maps. "Tell me. Do you polish your titanium balls every night before bed, or do you just hang them in your trophy case?"

"Polish," Devyn said deadpan, tossing the map aside.

"Damn. Mia's gonna go ballistic. You know that, don't you?"

Still the otherworlder remained unconcerned. "I'll handle her."

"Not without me." No way was Dallas going to let Devyn go down for this. Because Devyn was an otherworlder, he didn't have the same rights as Dallas. If necessary, he'd take total blame. Most they'd do to him was slap his wrists. They could send Devyn away, kick him out of AIR, or even execute him. "Anyone see you?"

"Probably."

What would it take to actually ruffle Devyn's feathers? Something catastrophic, surely. "So why the hell'd you leave his head outside for anyone to find?"

"It was a message."

He arched a brow. "And that would be that Devyn of the Targons is a psycho?"

Devyn laughed. "No. Mess with Bride and suffer."

Now Dallas's brow furrowed in question. "You into her or something? I mean, *really* into her?" Devyn loved and left his women like they were no more important than a fast-food meal. To him, they weren't.

Devyn's gaze sharpened, a play of emotions flashing through those amber depths. Readable emotions. Lust, tenderness, anger, disbelief. "For now. She'll lose her appeal soon enough."

Oh, oh, oh. What was this? Finally, a reaction. And over a woman. Inconceivable. Odd as it was, though, it wouldn't last; it couldn't. Still. This just wasn't Devyn's style.

A frightening thought suddenly occurred to Dallas. When Bride lost her appeal and Devyn dropped her— Devyn always dropped the women, they never dropped him—would she wallow in fury? Entertain thoughts of revenge? Would she pay someone to hurt him? Stab him at the pier?

He drained the rest of his coffee. "Well, like I was saying about the visions . . . I had two. And the second one involved you, the female, and a knife through your heart."

CHAPTER 10

As the first rays of sunlight glowed from the sky, Bride entered her apartment, quietly closed the door, and pressed the lock pad, engaging the ID scan on the outside. She rested her forehead against the cool metal, her eyes closed, breathing deeply, in and out, in and out. Her stomach was twisted with renewed hunger, her mouth dry. She was shaky, tired.

In the background, the TV hummed softly. The air was as clean and sterile as always, the purifiers she used running at top speed. The only scent she detected was . . . apples?

Her brow wrinkled, and she drew in another breath, holding it while she studied the aroma. Sure enough. Apples. She hadn't smelled them in more than sixty or so years, but she'd never forgotten their sweetness.

Once, she'd been casing a neighborhood, trying to decide which house to rob. The war had not yet erupted, and the world had been a different place. Trees had been lush, real fruit available for purchase on every street corner. And cheap, God, had they been cheap. The pennies she'd stolen from her foster parents had been enough to buy all the apples she'd wanted. Not to eat but to smell. She'd even dabbed the juice on herself, her own version of perfume.

Would have been a perfect memory if not for the taint of the foster parents. Ugh. Demons in human skin, that's what they'd been. The authorities had plucked her off the streets, placed her in the system. She'd looked about thirteen years old—no telling how old she'd really been, though—with a "sun allergy," so no one had wanted to adopt her. She'd bounced from home to home, her refusal to eat earning her doctor visits and sometimes force-feedings that caused her to puke her guts out.

Only once had she been caught drinking blood, and it had earned her the beating of a lifetime. If she'd been human, she would have died from it. The couple responsible had called her "unholy," "evil," and "perverted."

She was taken away from them and moved to her final foster home. Sadly, the one before had not been the worst. The husband, her "caregiver," had snuck into her room one night, holding her down, intending to rape her.

Before he'd even removed her PJs, out had come her fangs, and she'd drained him dry. It was the first killing she'd ever enjoyed. No telling how many other innocent children he'd hurt. But much as she'd been proud, happy with her actions, she'd also been scared. She would be deemed a murderer, probably sent to jail. So she'd run, and once again the streets had become her home.

Then the otherworlders had begun arriving, seeming to appear out of nowhere. Panic had spread far and wide, and her crime had been forgotten. As a "human," she belonged; she was someone to protect, no matter her past.

No human had left home without a weapon of some sort, and Bride had watched innocent otherworlder after innocent otherworlder gunned down. But what no one had known was that some humanoid races had been here a while and had already integrated themselves into society. They'd taken exception to the murders of their brethren and started fighting back.

What terrible, dark years those had been. Hardly anyone had had a home; they'd all been destroyed in fires, raids, and bombings. Money hadn't mattered; there'd been nothing to buy. Not everyone had been equipped for such a life, and some had died from the elements. The too-cold winters, the too-hot summers. Bride had spent years living that way and had thrived.

When a treaty was reached between the species, rebuilding happened fast, humans and otherworlders working together. Not fully trusting each other—that might not ever happen—but using each other's skills and resources to get the job done.

"You going to stand there all morning?"

Slowly she turned, facing the cell. Nolan stood at the bars, his fingers tight around the metal, a grin on his beautiful face. Her jaw dropped in shock. Yes, he was beautiful. His skin was tan, no hint of gray, no sores. And he glowed. His cheeks had filled out and were no longer sunken. His eyes were bright, like shining silver stars.

That apple scent wafted from *him*. With the realization, a tempting question drifted through her mind: if he smelled like apples, how delicious would he taste? Her gums actually throbbed as her fangs lengthened, sharpened. She was halfway to the cage before she caught herself. *He's diseased. You can't drink him.*

Maybe I could. I've never been sick.

Not worth the risk, remember?

Damn it! Another vampire would have known whether or not she could catch such an illness. Most movies and books claimed it was impossible. They also claimed vampires exploded in the sun, and she never had. So what was fact and what was fiction?

"I'm alone all night, bored out of my mind, dripping with energy, and finally you show up but you won't say a word." There was a pout to his voice now. "This is a new form of torture, right?"

Bride found her voice, forcing the words past a slightly swollen tongue. "You look good." Understatement of the year. His beauty actually rivaled Devyn's, though he didn't make her heart race.

"I feel good." He grinned, and it lit his entire face. "Better than I've felt in years, actually."

So. Her blood had helped him. What else had it done? Defeated his disease, or just muted it for a while? Had it turned him? Again, another vampire would have known. *I hate being the lone wolf.* Or rather, lone fang. "Any unusual cravings?"

His brow wrinkled in confusion, as if he couldn't follow the thread of the conversation. "Like what?"

Like blood. "Have you wanted to drink something you wouldn't normally want to drink?"

"I'm still lost."

"Never mind." If he began craving blood, she'd know

it. He would stare at her neck, sweat when he couldn't get closer to her pulse; he would pale.

What would Devyn think of this development? Would he and his agents want to study her? Poke and prod her? Poke and prod Nolan?

"Thank you for once more not shouting for help and bringing my neighbors rushing inside," she said. Before, he hadn't wanted to be mobbed. In his former condition, he wouldn't have survived. Like this, he could have charmed his way free. That he hadn't was a blessing.

He snorted. "Why would I want them to release me? I want more of that wine you gave me. And no, that's not an unusual craving. I love wine. But this wine . . ." He closed his eyes as if just the thought was ecstasy. "My stomach settled the moment I downed it. What kind was it? What brand?"

"Uh, it's just a little something I make myself. I'm almost out, so let's hold off on more for a while." Bride slouched forward and flopped onto her couch, keeping Nolan's cell in view. He'd been by himself and on his best behavior, so she owed him. If he wanted company, she would be his company, no matter how fatigued she suddenly was.

"What do you put in it?"

"Can we not talk about that right now? I feel like I'm dying."

"You hurt? That why you're covered in blood?"

Oh, shit. The blood. She'd forgotten about it. No wonder the few people she'd passed on the streets had given her weird looks. She needed to wash it off, but standing seemed like an impossible dream. Her thighs were shaking, the muscles bunched and knotted. Too much adrenaline crashing, she supposed, and not enough neck sucking.

"I'm not hurt. Just tired."

"I take it you found Devyn," Nolan said hopefully.

"Yes." Her eyelids fluttered closed, open.

He clapped, a smile lifting the corners of his lips. "Wow. I didn't think you'd do it. Hurt the otherworlder, I mean. But look at you. Covered in the blood of your enemy. I'm misty-eyed. Honest."

Wait. What? He thought she'd killed Devyn? "I found him, but I didn't hurt him. This isn't his blood. Someone tried to abduct me, and Devyn actually helped me neutralize him."

A moment passed in silence. Then Nolan popped his jaw, irritation replacing his joy. "He helped you?"

"Yes."

"So now you think he'll never hurt you, right?"

"No, of course not." Maybe.

"I recognize that look." His tone was grave. "You're smitten."

"I'm not smitten." She was, she really was. "That's ridiculous." Devyn might have pissed her off by forcing her to strip in front of him, but he'd also rushed to her rescue.

Why had he done that? she wondered for the thousandth time. She'd taken Nolan from him, outsmarted him in front of his friend Dallas, and threatened to cut off his balls if he hurt Aleaha. Yet still he'd come, still he'd decapitated her enemy. Because she was the only one who knew where Nolan was, as he'd claimed? No, couldn't be. He wouldn't have killed Tom like he had if he'd only wanted Nolan's location.

She didn't understand him. He was a seducer and a warrior, charming yet callous, self-involved yet kind. Back at the apartment, he could have forced her to lie on that bed, spread her legs, and welcome him inside, but he hadn't. He'd given her the sweetest of kisses, the gentlest of touches, and sent her on her way.

Why? He didn't care about her. She was one of a thousand, perhaps a million, to him. A novelty. Forgettable. Right?

I want to be more to him. The desire drifted through her, and she laughed bitterly. What the hell? No way. No damn way would she allow herself to care for him and dream of the impossible. Enjoy him, yes. She owed him three kisses, and she would give them to him. Because she was honorable, not because she craved them more than her next breath. But give him more than that? Hell, no. She valued herself a little too much to willingly be used and discarded.

"Bride?"

She blinked and pulled her hazy focus to Nolan. "Yes?"

He sighed. "Thought you'd fallen asleep."

Fallen into stupidity, more like. "Almost. Like I said, I'm tired. If you want to keep me awake, tell me something interesting. Like how you were able to bypass Devyn's mind control of your body."

A calculating gleam filled those silver eyes, making them sparkle like diamonds. "Give me another glass of that wine, and I'll tell you."

Argh! "What happened to waiting till tomorrow?"

"That was your dumb idea."

She dragged herself up, stumbling along the way to the kitchen, and prepared him another glass. She was only able to squeeze a handful of drops from her palm. After she'd passed the concoction over, she flopped back on the couch, her fatigue a thousand times worse. "God, I don't even have the strength to smack you for making me move," she muttered.

Nolan downed every drop of the wine, then licked the bottom of the cup. "So. Good."

"Don't forget what you owe me."

"Very well. I told you that the disease inside me is alive. Well, it's able to learn and study and change to best defend itself. When the disease is most active, I'm weak and it's in control of me. During the battle in the alleyway, it somehow rewired my energy molecules, for lack of a better explanation. They were sporadic and swirling, so Devyn could never lock on them and force me to his will."

Bummer. No way would she allow herself to be infected just to beat Devyn. "Feel like sharing some details about your previous captivity?" Because, if she wasn't careful, the same thing would happen to her. God, what had she gotten herself into?

"Sure, why not? Beats sitting here in silence."

"How long were you locked up by AIR?"

He shrugged. "About a month. Maybe longer. Hard to keep track of day and night when you aren't allowed outside."

Bride maneuvered to her side, resting her hands under her cheek. "Are there others like you?"

"Not here. Not any longer. AIR killed them."

"And yet they saved you."

"Like I told you before, I know when and where my queen will land, so to speak." He eased onto the cot and peered over at her.

"Do you love her?" No. Wait. "You've never been in love."

Shame darkened his eyes before he lowered his lashes, blocking the emotion. "I despise her. She is the one who infected me."

"Why help her, then? You're putting the people on this planet at risk for someone you hate."

"I know." Whisper soft. "But the . . . thing inside me will not allow me to betray her. Even the thought of it causes pain a thousand times worse than any I've ever known."

Like the thorns and fire inside her? "If AIR ran tests on your blood and found a cure, would you help them over your queen?"

He was shaking his head before the last word left her mouth. "It cannot be studied. Were I to cut myself right now, I would bleed, but the disease would stay inside of me because another host is not nearby."

"Oh."

"Yes. Oh. Finding new hosts is the only way to keep it from building up inside of my own body."

She could hear the regret and torture in his voice. He hated what he was, what he did. "I know you want to fall in love before you die, but is that a strong enough reason to place the whole world in jeopardy?"

"I could kill myself, yes." He laughed bitterly. "But that wouldn't stop my queen from coming. That wouldn't stop her from creating others like me. Wouldn't stop your world from crumbling. So why not live while I can?"

Good point, in a twisted way. "All right. Well. Think of it this way. To love a woman is to condemn her to the same death you will one day suffer."

"I know." Again, whisper soft.

Yet he still planned to do it. Selfish bastard.

"I don't want to talk about love anymore," he said. "Tell me what happened between you and Devyn. He wants me back, I know he does. What did he ask you to do with me?"

She sighed. "I'm supposed to take you to the pier tomorrow night—wait, I guess that would be tonight, since it's already sunrise—and trade you for my friend." If she worked the situation right, Aleaha might be sitting with her on this very couch by the end of the day.

Nolan laughed, and this time there was genuine amusement in the undertones. "A setup, no doubt."

"I agree." Why else wouldn't Devyn have tailed her? He'd let her go so easily, without fighting for her location. That seemed completely out of character. Not that she knew everything about him. But the intensity of his determination to get what he wanted wasn't hidden. It was there, etched into every sensual line in his face.

"Are you going to take me?" Nolan asked.

"I honestly don't know what I'm going to do." And she had very little time to figure it out. But she would. And she would win.

Devyn leaned back in his chair, gazing up at the ceiling, lost in thought. When Bride had called him, he'd heard the panic in her voice and gone running. He'd decided to kill her pursuer even before he'd learned the man's purpose. He'd wanted her safe, no matter the cost. But when he'd learned Tom's purpose, rage had bloomed inside him, eating at any mercy he might have harbored.

He'd had no right to feel that way. In the past, he'd frequented slave auctions with a wad of cash and a grin. And he hadn't been undercover or on a mission. Oh, no. He wanted to sample a morsel from every race, and sometimes buying a female was the only way to acquire something new. But the thought of the proud Bride on display . . . standing on a platform, naked for all to see . . . to touch . . .

His teeth ground together. Was this how possessive men acted and thought? If so, why was *he* thinking and acting this way? It made no sense. He was a hedonist who adored variety. Yes, Bride challenged him more than any other. Yes, Bride exuded all that sparkling energy. She was resourceful, a fighter, a survivor, powerful, and had he mentioned witty? She was flirtatious and sarcastic. And strong. She'd been covered in the human's blood, staring at his open wounds with naked desire in her eyes, wanting to drink him dry, but she had resisted. Hadn't even licked her lips clean.

But surely, despite all of that, he would desire someone else soon. Surely his interest in Bride would fade rather than continue to grow. As it was, he could hardly wait to see her again.

Because of the small, nearly imperceptible tracker he'd planted on her bra, he'd been able to follow her movements on his computer. He'd known where she was when she called him. He'd headed out immediately, even though he'd needed her to confess where she was. Otherwise, smart girl that she was, she would have suspected the tracker and removed it. She'd gone in circles for half an hour and would have lost a tail if she'd had one. Eventually, though, she had gone home. Now he had her current location. An apartment a few blocks from Dallas's.

In case Devyn had been unable to lick her and just in case she'd bitten him, he'd also injected an isotope tracker into his own bloodstream. She'd never gone for his neck, though. Why? Because she often sickened after drinking, as she'd told him?

How long since she'd had a full meal?

Would she have been able to keep down *his* blood? He'd wondered before but now the question was a plague inside him. He liked the thought of a piece of himself, any piece, inside her. *Might happen soon.*

In just a few hours, the sun would be shining brightly and Bride wouldn't be able to run. He'd have her. Dallas would have Nolan. If Nolan was with her, that is, but Devyn was willing to bet that he was. Smart little Bride would have kept the otherworlder close.

A shame Bride was involved in this for Macy rather than Devyn's cock. Hopefully, he was well on his way to changing that. There at the end, she'd arched into him. He grinned, remembering, and wanted to beat his chest like the warrior kings of old. Feeling her rub against him, even slightly, had been the sweetest victory of his life.

Even better, there was more to come. Would she fight him harder than before or finally give in?

He didn't like that a soon-to-be lover had seen the dark coldness inside him as he'd ruthlessly tortured and killed that human, but it couldn't have been helped. There'd been a primitive need inside him to prove to Bride that he could protect her from any threat. That he would do whatever was necessary to ensure her safety. Like possessiveness, it was not something he'd ever experienced before, and he'd been absolutely unable to ignore it.

Was she frightened of him now that she'd had time to think about what he'd done? Before, she hadn't seemed to be. For a moment, just before he'd rendered the deathblow to the human, he'd actually thought pride shimmered in her lovely emerald eyes. As if he were already her man and it was his right to look after her. He'd liked it.

What would he have to do to engage her interest fully?

God, I'm a mess. Devyn lifted the beer he'd stolen from Dallas's fridge and drained half the contents in a single gulp. Dallas. The perfect friend. Only Dallas knew what he'd done, what he planned to do, but Dallas wouldn't rat him out. Rather, Dallas was going to help him.

They'd spent an hour talking and gazing at the holographic images the sketch artist had rendered of Devyn's supposed murderers. Only one face had been familiar to him, and it had indeed been a McKell vampire. *The* McKell vampire, in fact. The leader of the whole bloodsucking army.

Which meant, if Dallas's vision was correct—and they always were—the McKells were going to come for Bride. Probably sneak her underground. And they were definitely going to try and kill Devyn.

Was she someone's bride, and just didn't know it? Was that the reason for her name? If so, why had the husband let her get away? Why hadn't he searched the ends of the earth for her? *Too late now,* Devyn thought darkly. At the moment, she was not up for grabs.

His murder, he wasn't worried about. Now that he knew an attempt was coming, he'd always be on his guard. No one would get the better of him. Besides, there'd been other attempts—royals were always targets, and playboy royals who broke hearts like others broke bread most of all—but he'd always come out ahead. It was the idea of Bride returning to the underground, forever out of his reach, that disturbed him.

Infiltrating that dark, gloomy world without permission would be impossible. They had a millennia of security down there, and they'd never grant him permission to steal one of their own—even if he swore to bring her back when he was done with her. Therefore, he had to keep her aboveground.

He should have taken her tonight, should have scratched his itch sooner rather than later, instead of trying to prolong the enjoyment and make her crave him the way he craved her. Stupid—and a mistake he wouldn't make again. Or rather, for a third time. When they were next together, he would take her. Finally sate himself.

The thought made him grin. *Just a few more hours, lovely Bride, and you'll be mine.*

CHAPTER 11

"This place is a dump. Sure she's got him here?"

Devyn flicked Dallas an irritated glance. He was in front of Bride's door, disabling the ID scan, twisting wires and realigning them. "As if I'm ever wrong." At least, that's what he told himself he was irritated about. The affront to his tracking skills, and not the fact that his friend had insulted Bride's living space. Not everyone could afford luxury. "Now, keep your voice down."

"You're already in control of her body."

"Yes, but she's sleeping." All that sparkling energy was static. "I don't want you to wake her." She would be frightened, and too easily Devyn remembered the fear she projected while standing on that street, knowing slavers were after her. The green in her eyes had dulled, and her skin had turned so pallid he'd seen the blue of her veins. And then she'd trembled. When that woman trembled, it should be in pleasure. Only ever in pleasure. "By the way, this place is not a dump." Damn it! Why had he added that?

"I just . . . I guess when you told me vampires were real, I assumed they lived in eerie castles and stole their victims' money so they'd never have to work. Does she even have a job?"

"I'm not sure." And he didn't like that he didn't know. Didn't like that he *wanted* to know. Why did he need to know? What value would it have?

Footsteps suddenly pounded, a body turning a corner. There was a rustle of clothing and a breeze of stale beer and sweat. A pause, a muffled curse. "What'cha doing trying to get inside Amy's apartment?" The human had stopped and now stood at the end of the hall, beefy arms crossed over a protruding middle. His expression was suspicious.

Dallas flashed his AIR badge. "Amy, you say?"

"A common name to help her blend," Devyn muttered. Oh, yes. She was a smart girl. His admiration spiked. Yet again.

"She done something wrong? Or are you guys ex-boyfriends wanting a tag team?" The newcomer was sneering as if the thought both disgusted and titillated him. "Well, good luck. She don't give it away to nobody."

"Back away and forget you saw us, understand? And take a shower, for Christ's sake. You could clear a sewer."

"No. You will stay," Devyn commanded, and the man obeyed, helpless to do otherwise because Devyn had mentally locked on his energy.

Dallas groaned. "We don't have time for this."

Devyn ignored him, pivoting and moving away from the doorway and toward the human. "The fact that you know she won't give it away leads me to believe you've tried to get some from her."

Fright filled the man's beady eyes. If he'd had control of himself, he would have run. Or fainted. "I—I never hurt her."

But he'd put his greedy fingers on her, Devyn was sure. Why hadn't she compelled him away with The Voice? Why hadn't she drained him dry? Not for one moment did Devyn think she harbored an attraction for the tag-teaming moron. Which meant there were only two possibilities. Either she was too kindhearted to hurt him or too unsure of her powers. Again, the fact that he didn't know her enough to figure her out irritated him.

"I'd be doing the world a favor if I killed you," he said.

The fear sparked into panic, but the panic didn't last long. It was soon replaced by bravado. "You're a damn dirty alien. You can't hurt me without AIR jumping all over your ass."

"AIR's behind me. You saw the badge. And the only thing I'm likely to get for my next action is a pat on the back." With that, Devyn reached a mental hand inside the man's chest and squeezed his heart.

Pain contorted his pudgy features, and he gasped. His cheeks burned a bright red, and his eyes clouded over. Devyn enjoyed the sight, more so than usual, and he couldn't deny it.

"St-stop. Please, stop."

"Dev," Dallas said.

Fine. When Devyn released his hold, the human sank to the floor, clutching his chest.

"Enjoy your heart attack," he said, and then, because he hadn't wanted to leave the guy alive but was doing so for Dallas, he punted the little shit in the stomach. Air whooshed, and blood even gurgled. "Have a friend call you a paramedic. And if you ever touch Br—Amy again or suggest such a thing to someone else, or hell, even breathe in her direction, I will return and finish what I've started."

No response. But then, he hadn't expected one. Devyn spun on his heel.

Dallas had his arms crossed over his chest.

"What?" Devyn said, all innocence. "He annoyed me."

"So nearly killing him was necessary?"

"Completely."

A roll of his friend's baby blues. "Are you sure you're not in loooove with Bride? 'Cause, dude, you're like a knight in crotchless armor right now."

Devyn bared his teeth in a scowl.

Laughing, his friend held up his hands in surrender. "Fine. You hate her. Now, can we do what we came to do, please?"

"Of course." Devyn stopped in front of the ID box and frowned, only now realizing why he hadn't been able to work it as easily as usual. Someone had beaten him to it—recently, it looked like—but they had plugged the wrong wires into the wrong outlets for it to open, forced or not. Was the human still writhing on the ground the culprit? Or was it Tom, before the beheading? The other slavers, after the beheading?

Devyn had told Bride not to worry about them, and he'd meant it. Because he'd known he would be coming for her in just a few hours. But what if someone had been waiting for her? What if she wasn't sleeping, as he'd assumed, but . . . Urgent now, he twisted a few more ends together, and boom, the metal slid apart of its own accord.

Dallas had already pulled a gun and now moved in ahead of him, arms extended, barrel aimed, ready to take down any threat. No pyre-guns today. They were using semiautomatics. What the street gangs used. Devyn had been nailed in the thigh with a slug a few months ago, and it had hurt like a son of a bitch. If Nolan had to be subdued, he'd wish to God he'd been stunnable and the bullets unnecessary. They'd just have to be careful not to touch him while he was bleeding.

Devyn moved in behind his friend, not bothering with a weapon, and closed the door. If he pointed the gun, he'd fire without hesitation, and Dallas wanted a chance to question the otherworlder one last time before killing him.

"Your vamp's on the couch," Dallas whispered. "Asleep, just like you said. And damn. You were right. There's Nolan."

Thank God. He relaxed and studied his surroundings. In the far corner was a ten-by-ten cage. Nolan lay on a cot, softly snoring, more at peace than Devyn had ever seen him.

The living room and kitchen were hooked together, no doors or walls separating them. There was a couch, a chair, and a coffee table, all perched on a dark red rug. That's all that would fit the small space. The furniture was worn but well cared for, the metal polished to diminish the scratches; the cushions were covered in a violet material. Orange, blue, and yellow pillows were scattered throughout.

So many colors. Like a rainbow. There wasn't a kitchen table, but then, she didn't need one. There were no pots or pans, only a few glasses and wine bottles on the counter.

There wasn't a fridge. She didn't even try to pretend she needed to eat, which meant she didn't have guests over.

The thought both delighted and saddened him. Everyone needed friends. Even reprobates like him. There was only one door, and it was beside the kitchen. There wasn't a hallway; the apartment was too small for even that. How did she live so cramped?

Silently Devyn moved forward and peeked into the room. Her bedroom. Again, small and crammed. There was a twin-size bed with bright green covers and a scuffed dresser. Books were scattered in every direction. Real books, the no-longer-available paper kind rather than the accepted computerized versions.

Grinning, he bent down and lifted two. *A Hunger Like No Other,* featuring a half-vampire heroine. And *Marked,* again featuring a vampire heroine. A quick glance showed that a few of the other titles were supposedly nonfiction. *Vampires: The Real Story. Vampires: They Are Among Us.*

She hadn't stolen money, furniture, or clothing. She'd stolen books. They were more valuable, but he didn't think she'd done it for the cash. She truly had no idea about her heritage and was searching for information by whatever means possible.

Devyn dropped the paperbacks and stood. In the living room, Bride still slept peacefully, her figure unmoving. Dallas stood over her, his expression confused. Frowning, Devyn approached him, though his gaze returned to the vampire and remained.

Bride was still covered in blood. It matted her hair, smudged her cheeks, and ruined her clothes. She hadn't showered when she'd arrived but had slipped straight into sleep. How tired she must have been, yet she'd never revealed it to him. He felt a stirring of pride. *That's my girl.*

His frown deepened. Not his girl. Only his to use. For a little while. That's the way he preferred it. Always. Remembering how she'd swiped up Tom's pyre-gun, he bent down and confiscated it, sheathing it at his back.

"I expected . . . I don't know," Dallas whispered. "Something more."

"What do you mean?" He couldn't keep the offense out of his tone.

"With her clothes on, she's so . . . plain. Not that that's a bad thing. But she's like a different person than the one I saw in the alley and then the composite. Less, I don't know, vibrant."

Plain? She was as effervescent as the colors she surrounded herself with. A shining jewel among a sea of dull. "You're blind."

"To be honest, each time I saw her I didn't look any higher than her lovely breasts. And really, she's the first girl you've ever shown more than a cursory interest in, so I guess I expected perfection."

"My taste is exquisite." Bride was beyond lovely, with a face and form most men could only ever dream of seeing. "Better than ever."

Nolan moaned softly in his sleep, and Dallas whipped around, gun extended. He moved toward the cell, paused, sucked in a breath. "Fuck me. Look at him, Dev." The agent no longer whispered. There was too much shock in his tone.

Devyn straightened and glanced over, not wanting to leave his perch beside Bride. Now that he had her within arm's reach again, he planned to keep her there. "What is it?"

"He doesn't look sick. And if he doesn't look sick . . ."

He'd had sex. Devyn's eyes narrowed on the other-worlder, taking in the clear skin, the even rise and fall of his chest. His gaze swung to Bride, still sleeping peacefully. Had they . . . they must have. It would also explain her fatigue.

His hands curled into fists. There were no bruises under her eyes, no grayish tint to her skin. Teeth grinding, he reached down and shook her, no longer caring if he frightened her. "Bride."

When she gave no reaction, he shook her again. Harder. "Bride!"

Slowly her eyelids fluttered open, hazel irises glazed. Hazel, no longer bright emerald. Either her mask was firmly back in place, or she'd somehow lost her vibrancy. A moment passed while she oriented herself. When realization struck, she gasped. Jerked upright. Dark hair tumbled down her arms and back.

Devyn leaned down, placing them nose to nose. "Did you sleep with him?"

"Wh-what?" She scrambled backward, only the arm of the couch stopping her. She reached behind her, probably meaning to grab the gun, but came up empty.

Devyn moved with her, never letting more than an inch separate them. "Did. You. Sleep. With. Him?" The words snarled from him.

Her gaze roved wildly. Searching for a way out? Trying to figure out what had happened? "What are you talking about? How did you find me? How did you get in here?"

"I'm going to ask you one more time, and you're going to answer, or I swear to God I'm going to kill him in front of you. And you know I don't make threats. I make promises. Did you fuck Nolan?"

Confusion flittered over her a split second before she shook her head. "No. Of course not. He's diseased."

Devyn remained in place, studying her, gauging the truth of her words. The rage inside him . . . he'd never experienced so much. And for what? The thought of a woman in bed with another man? It was laughable. He never promised monogamy, and he never demanded it in return. He didn't stick around long enough.

Seriously. What the hell was wrong with him?

"She's telling the truth," a grave voice said from behind him. Nolan had awoken.

Dallas rubbed his finger over his gun's trigger. "Try something, and your brains will end up on the wall. This isn't stun, asshole. This is copper."

Nolan kept his gaze on Devyn. "It was the wine. She gave me two glasses of wine, and within an hour of drinking each, I felt healthier than I had in years."

"Try again," Devyn snarled. "Wine can't kill a disease as strong as yours."

Nolan raised his chin. "Hers can, and I want more."

"It wasn't wine, you sellout," Bride gritted. With a shaky hand, she smoothed the hair from her cheek and hooked it behind her ear. "Not exactly. I, well, I mixed my . . . blood with it."

All three men stared over at her in astonishment.

She straightened her shoulders. "Well, it helps me heal, and he was so near death, I thought I'd give it to him and see what happened. He didn't turn into a vampire, though," she rushed out.

As if anyone cared about that. Her blood. Her vampire blood had taken a dying man and propelled him into health. That, Devyn could believe. The hottest fires of his rage seeped from him.

"What are you doing here, Devyn?" she demanded.

He splayed his arms. "Isn't it obvious? I'm winning the game we were playing."

It was like a bomb detonated in her eyes, hazel scattering and leaving only emerald fury. Mask gone, he thought with a grin.

"I knew it! You tricked me. Lied to me. Told me to meet you at the pier, and then you followed me."

"Nope." He shook his head. "I didn't follow you, and I didn't have anyone else follow you. Try again."

"Then how . . ." Her features scrunched adorably as she pondered what could have happened. A moment passed. She gasped. "Somehow you tagged me with a GPS, didn't you, you bastard?"

"Yep." A slow smile curled the corners of his mouth. "Your bra. Remember the way I licked you . . . ?"

Red bloomed on her cheeks, the prettiest blush he'd ever seen. "You are such a cheater."

"That hurts, darling. Really it does." He tugged a long, thin black case from his back pocket and popped the lid, revealing a syringe of glowing crimson liquid. Bride would have leaped from the couch, but he held her down with his mind. "And how did I cheat? There were no rules."

She glared up at him. "Let me go, damn it."

"Not yet. See, with this baby I'll know where you are every second of every day for the next three months. I see you're wondering what it is. Well, it's my pleasure to tell you. This is an isotope tracker, and all I'll have to do to find you is log on to my computer."

He jabbed the needle into her thigh, and her mouth fell open on a pained gasp.

"Sorry for the sting," he said. "Ask nicely, and I'll kiss it better."

"You shouldn't have done that." A look of utter concentration descended her features. Determination. "Soon you'll wish you hadn't."

He'd seen that expression on her before, seconds before she'd exploded into mist. "Don't you dare think about misting and leaving. I have your friend, remember?"

The determination fell away, vulnerability taking its place. She fingered the necklace she still wore. "You've treated her well?"

"Of course. Treating women well is a hobby of mine."

Sparks of anger returned to her eyes, but she never again looked as if she would mist. "So what are you going to do to me?"

"We'll get to that." The fact that her blood had healed Nolan—permanently? temporarily?—would be of great interest to AIR. They'd take her from Devyn and turn her into a pincushion, no doubt about it. He wasn't ready for that to happen. "Nolan, tell us about the changes in you." His attention never veered from Bride.

The otherworlder was happy to obey. "I'm no longer clouded by the disease's thoughts. I can think clearly for the first time in years."

So. Did that mean the disease was completely gone?

"You've lied and screwed us before." Dallas swiped his gun against the cage, rattling the bars. "No way you expect us to trust you now."

Nolan lifted his wide shoulders in a shrug. "Trust me or not. Doesn't matter. But *I* know I'm free. The queen, she—" He pressed his lips together, waited, then scrunched his brow. "I think I can talk about her," he said on a shocked gasp. "I know she's . . . infected the last of her captives . . ." His eyes widened. "That didn't hurt! I can. I can talk about her. She'll come to New Chicago within the week. Exactly where and when, though? I no longer sense her, so I'm not sure."

Yep, truth or not, AIR was going to want Bride's blood.

Devyn looked over at his friend. "Give me an hour," he said. "And do whatever it takes to find out anything else he knows about his queen and her vacation here." Knowledge was power, and Devyn liked power.

Dallas flicked a good-luck glance at Bride, then nodded.

Without another word, Devyn released her from his mind-hold. He picked her up and anchored her on his shoulder while she hit, bit, and kneed him, and then he carried her into the bedroom and kicked the door shut behind him. The true fun was about to begin.

CHAPTER 12

"What the hell are you doing? Put me down!" Bride slammed her fists against the solid wall of Devyn's back. The hot silk of his skin was evident under the material of his shirt, causing her arms to tingle. A dangerous tingle. A tempting tingle. Something she should not feel for the enemy.

"Anything you say, darling." He dropped her flat on her ass. "You know I live only to please you."

Air whooshed from her lungs, and when she caught her breath she glared up at him. "You're such an ass."

He clutched his chest, just above his heart. "Oh, how you wound me. I gave you what you wanted, didn't I?"

"A dramatic ass, at that." Biting the inside of her cheek, Bride popped to her feet. She could have misted—though she needed open space to leave a room—and could have hurriedly stripped and camouflaged her skin, but she didn't. Not only because his reminder that he held Aleaha still rang through her, but also because curiosity and something else, something she refused to name, flooded her. "If you brought me in here to rape me . . ."

One of his brows arched, and there was a definite sparkle in his eyes. "It wouldn't be rape, and we both know it. Last night you were all over me, practically dripping in my hand."

Her teeth clenched. "You're an exaggerator, too."

He shrugged. "You don't have to worry about giving in to my wicked advances. Not yet. Right now you're going to strip and shower, and then we're going to talk."

She raised her chin. "Like hell."

"You will. I'll force you if necessary. And Bride," he said, his voice dipping huskily, "I hope it's necessary."

Of course he did. He was the only person on the planet who could see through a threat like that successfully. The only person who could possibly make her enjoy the fact that her will had been ignored. "I don't need to be clean to talk to you."

"Yes, you do. Right now the sight of you upsets me."

She'd been in the process of reaching behind her, feeling her dresser for a weapon. She had them stashed everywhere, just in case. But his words enraged her, and she ended up grabbing the first thing she encountered. A book. A paperback, at that. She hurled it at him, anyway, and the spine slapped against his cheek.

He blinked in surprise, rubbed his cheek, and glanced down at the book. "That was childish."

"Well, your perfect face was upsetting *me*."

"Finally. You admit how perfect I am." Gently he toed the book aside. "First rule of thievery, sweetheart. You shouldn't abuse items you work hard to steal."

"I didn't steal it." Why she told him the truth, she didn't know. His opinion didn't matter. "I saved it."

Once again he arched a brow, his gaze sharpening. "You were able to save it because you're human, and humans live for hundreds of years without aging?"

"You know I'm not human," she grumbled. Misting in front of him had pretty much ruined her "I'm human" argument. "Now stop distracting me."

"I can't help myself. I'm perfect, remember?"

Argh! Infuriating man. "I will shower, but only because I really need one." The grumble had become churlish. "But I'll do it with my clothes on." So there. *Oh, God. I really am a child.*

"Clothes off," he said.

"On. And that's that."

"I recommend that you strip." He sounded almost pleasant now, a sure sign his patience was at an end. The sweeter he seemed, she was coming to understand, the more violent he was feeling. Exhibit A: he'd been smiling when he'd taken Tom's head.

"Fine. I'll strip. But you and your stupid T-shirt have to leave." She pointed to the door. Not for a second did she think he'd actually do it. It was worth a shot, though.

"Hell, no," he said. Big shocker. "I plan to enjoy the show. And my T-shirt isn't stupid. It's a public service."

"Size Dental Appliances Here" with an arrow to his cock, meaning women could feel free to suck him. "Devyn."

"Bride. Last chance to act on your own."

She stared over at him, taking in his determined expression, the hard line of his body. If she pushed, he really would force her to do as he wanted, and she would lose control of her own actions. If she gave in, she could dictate what angle to show him—and how badly to tantalize him with what he would never have.

"Fine," she said, and sighed. "You want a show, I'll give you a show." He would watch, and he could want, but *she would not give*. The last was a reminder to herself.

He gave another of those surprised blinks.

Expected her to continue to balk, had he? Chin lifting in challenge, she slowly shimmied out of her clothing. First the boots. She chucked them at him, and he easily sidestepped. Second, she removed her pants. Third, her shirt. His pupils dilated as she unsnapped her bra and let the syn-cotton float to the ground. The matching panties quickly followed, leaving her completely bare. Well, except for Aleaha's necklace, but that didn't count.

"I was afraid I'd imagined them, those blood red nipples. My new favorite color, by the way."

"Thank you," she replied, pleased, though she was sure she wasn't the first to hear such a compliment.

That gave him pause. "Not embarrassed by my scrutiny?" The question was almost . . . hesitant.

"No." Despite what she'd told him while he'd forced her to strip that first time, nudity didn't bother her. How could it, when she had to traipse the streets of New Chicago naked but camouflaged while she hunted? Besides, she liked her body. "No reason to be. Of the two of us, *I'm* the closer to perfection."

His lips twitched. "The only way to know for sure, of course, is to study you."

She stood there, in the silence, in the cool air, allowing him to examine every inch of her. And examine he did. His ocher gaze leisurely pursued her, lingering on her small but firm breasts and those bright red pearling nipples, the tiny patch of black hair between her slender thighs, a startling contrast.

"Now for the rest," she said, and slowly turned in a circle. "Am I still hurting your eyes?"

"No," he rasped. When she faced him again, his expression was strained. He even reached out.

Got you, she thought. Fighting a grin, she backed away, shaking her head. "No, no, no. You don't get to manhandle these perfect goods."

At first, he acted as though he hadn't heard her, and stepped closer. Then a muscle ticked in his jaw, he stopped, and his arm fell to his side. "First, it's rude to brag about your beauty, and second, it's rude to deny a man the right to touch that beauty."

"How cute. Etiquette lessons from a man who told me I would want to slay all the women he slept with after me."

"It's true."

She had to fight yet another grin.

"I want you," he said, the words guttural.

"Uttered to thousands, I'm sure."

"I can't deny it." His honesty pleased her. "That doesn't mean you won't enjoy yourself."

Goose bumps spread, a silent plea for what he promised. Touch after glorious touch, sensation after glorious sensation. Heat. The forbidden. He'd give it to her, too. All of it.

"All you have to do is ask," he said, "and it's done."

You're stronger than that. "Excuse me, but I have a shower to attend to. I'm just so very dirty." Trembling, she glided from him and entered the enzyme stall. She didn't bother shutting the door. He would have opened it, she was sure.

Silent, Devyn followed. He didn't enter, though. He pressed a shoulder against the frame and peered inside as she programmed the spray to hit her at every angle. Then she turned back to Devyn, letting him watch as the mist formed around her, creating a dreamlike haze. That dry vapor dusted over her, sinking inside, cleaning her inside out, and wiping away any memento of the brutal murder the man in front of her had committed only a few hours ago. Even her hair was cleaned, her scalp tingling deliciously.

"So you're telling me that my watching you like this doesn't . . . shame you?" he asked. Again with the hesitance. What did that mean?

"That's right," she said. "Why would it?"

"Before, you told me that I was making you reveal a body you'd rather hide."

"All part of the game, tiger."

He cleared his throat, but couldn't hide the relief in his eyes. "Ever bathed in water?"

"Oh, yes. A long time ago, before the war." Now the wonderful liquid was too expensive to waste on something like bathing.

"Did you like it?"

"What do you think?"

His gaze fell again to her nipples, his lids unbelievably sexy at half-mast. "I think you did. And I can imagine you standing under the stream, hair dripping, skin glistening." He licked his lips, as if he could already taste the droplets on her. "Invite me in." His voice sounded as though it had been pushed through a grinder, savage with the force of his arousal.

Like every other woman of his acquaintance, she was sure, Bride found her resolve to resist weakened against his appeal. Foolish, but there it was. But unlike all the others, she would not give in to her desires. Old as she was, as long as she'd been around, she'd learned how to suppress her own needs. Wasn't that difficult, really, since the thorns and the fire plagued her even during sex. Pain always blended with her pleasure, her climax both a blessing and a curse.

"Beg," she told him. He wouldn't do it; she knew he wouldn't. She also knew it would horrify him to think that that's what she wanted. He would back down.

He rolled his eyes. "Invite me in, Bride."

"I told you. I will when you beg."

That air of nonchalance melted away, just as she'd predicted, and the muscle in his jaw started ticking again. "I don't have to beg for a woman."

She grinned sweetly. "Then you'll never have this one."

There was a beat of silence. "We'll see." Angry, determined.

Oh, yes, they would.

He grabbed the bar above him, back arching just a bit. The movement caused his T-shirt to ride up, revealing a patch of glittery skin and hard muscle. His jeans were tight against his erection, the tip straining above the waist and glistening with a bead of moisture.

"Is denying us both your way of punishing me for besting you?" he asked.

He was mouthwatering, but she forced herself to shrug indifferently. "Maybe just a little."

"I can make you forget that you lost. Swear to God."

"I'm sure that you could. Just as I'm sure I could make you forget your own name."

That caused his nostrils to flare. "You're that good, are you?"

"Someone once told me it's rude to brag." Though she was already clean, the spray continued to fall around her. She didn't switch it off. Her head tilted to the side as she studied him more intently. "Question. Do you ever worry about the hearts you're breaking? Or children being conceived with some random stranger?"

He shrugged, as indifferent as she had pretended to be. "If I break a woman's heart, I showed her a good time while doing so. And children? No. I never worry about them. One, it's rare for two different species to procreate, and two, I take precautions so that I don't have to."

She laughed, but there was no humor to the sound. "Precautions aren't foolproof, you know. They're—"

"Indeed foolproof," he interjected. "The drug I take comes from my planet. It's a remedy that has worked for thousands of years, killing the little swimmers before they can leave my body. Why the question? Do you want me to give you a baby?"

"Hardly." Look how raising Aleaha had turned out.

The shower finally ended, but Bride still didn't exit. The drops of mist faded, removing all pretense of a dream. Reality was stark, but so much better. She could see Devyn clearly, the disarray of his hair, the tension tightening his mouth. In intensified desire?

"Enough talk about love and kids," she said. Because sometimes she *did* ache for those things, but never would she reveal such a thing to this man. "What are your plans for me, Devyn?"

His lips twitched into that half-smile she was coming to love. "First, I'm going to fuck you."

So crudely put. Such a sexy smile. Both clouded her mind with thoughts she couldn't afford and weakened her knees. "I will not sleep with you." Another reminder. For both of them. And hell, was that really her voice? Low and raspy? "I believe we discussed that you need to be punished for betraying me, setting me up, and following me."

He *tsk*ed under his tongue. "I never said I wanted to *sleep* with you. And please, feel free to spank me."

"Go get a paddle, and I will."

"Certainly. Then it will be my turn to punish you. It's only fair to mention that you stole a prisoner from me."

"You're keeping my best friend, my *only* friend, from me."

Now his eyes narrowed, top and bottom lashes fusing. Wow. His humor had faded so quickly, lightning fast, it was shocking. It shouldn't have been, she supposed. He did it often, switching from one extreme to another in seconds. "You'll get to see her, don't worry."

"When?"

"Soon."

"When?" she insisted.

He bared his teeth in a scowl. "Today."

Today? The single word echoed through her mind, and joy burst through her. So much joy she barely noticed the sting in her chest. Aleaha Love, in her arms, warm, sweet, real. Breathing her in, hearing her lilting voice. If not for the slight twinge of disbelief threading through her, Bride would have started dancing. "Really? This isn't another trick?"

"No trick. Now come here." He crooked his finger at her.

Happy as she was just then, it was harder to fight his appeal. "No. You come to me." Just to taunt him, she cupped her breasts and pinched her nipples to redden them further. Mistake. A lance of pleasure streamed through her, and she moaned.

Devyn expelled a ragged breath. "You're killing me. Let me take over."

"No." She traced her fingers down the plane of her stomach and straight to the core of her, fingers wiggling suggestively. *Careful, easy. This is for his benefit, not yours.* She watched him through slitted lids. There was a determined gleam in his eyes, and for a moment, she thought he might enter the stall despite their byplay.

He didn't. "You owe me a kiss," he said. The words hissed through his teeth, a demand. "And I'm collecting. Now. Don't even think about denying me."

"I won't." She couldn't. He'd already painted the picture of the two of them in her mind, his lips on hers, their tongues dancing. Gulping, she dropped her arms. Stepped toward him before she could stop herself. A kiss, only a kiss. She owed it to him, but she wouldn't allow anything more. She couldn't.

He backed away from her.

She paused, frowned. "Is this another game?"

"No."

"Well, do you want the kiss or not?"

"Yes. So come get me."

She stepped forward, but he once again backed away. This time she followed. He stopped at the edge of the bed and sat.

"No variety," she now *tsk*ed under her tongue. "I expected better of you." Too easily did she remember the last time he'd had her in that position. She'd straddled him, felt his erection pulse against her core, and she'd wanted to ride him. She'd wanted to forget that a quick bedding accomplished nothing but momentary gratification. That it meant nothing to either person involved, yet ruined all their further dealings.

He pursed his lips in question.

"Last time you had me sit in your lap, too. I'd think a man of your experience would know how to—" There wasn't time to finish her sentence. He'd jolted from the bed, grabbed her by the waist, and flung her around. She landed on the bed, bouncing up and down.

He was on her a second later. "You want variety?"

Again, there was no time to reply. He flipped her over and positioned her on her hands and knees, naked ass in the air and pointed toward him. Perhaps she shouldn't have antagonized him. There had been fire in his eyes, and every muscle pressed against her was hard, velvet-covered steel. She could smell him, a wildness to that rain scent. A wildness that teased her nose, heated her blood.

He leaned over her, propping his weight on one hand while the other clasped her chin and angled her face closer to his. Immediately he swooped in, his tongue plunging past her teeth and deep into her mouth. His flavor was sweet and smooth and hot, branding her tongue.

As his erection rubbed between her cheeks, he released her chin and cupped her breast, rolling the nipple between naughty fingers. The kiss continued. Desire pumped through her, heart hammering against her ribs. Her fangs elongated, and if he wasn't careful, they would cut his tongue. She would taste his blood, and it would be good, so good, she knew it would, and then she would bite him, suck him, drain him. The urge was already there . . .

She tried to pull back, just a little, needing some time to calm down, but he wouldn't let her. He thrust that tongue deeper, harder. And when it scraped one of her sharp canines, and a bead of blood did indeed form, sliding down her throat, it was heaven. Sweet, calming, warming her stomach and spreading . . . spreading . . . all over her, branding her organs, her every cell. Strengthening her. Nothing had ever tasted so succulent, somehow soothing her hunger.

"Beg for more," he panted.

More of his kiss? More of his blood? Desperately she wanted both. "No." Even as she spoke, she was biting at his lips, trying to draw him back to her mouth to take what she wanted.

"Beg, damn you."

"No!"

He flipped her over. He was still clothed, so the soft material of his pants rubbed against her skin as he plunged his tongue back inside her mouth, taking over, claiming her. His hand slid down her body, and he delved two fingers inside her hot, wet core without asking permission.

Moaning, she arched into the touch, sending him deeper. His thumb circled her clit, making her quake. All the while, he continued the kiss, just as before, his addictive flavor consuming her. All the while she bit at his tongue, taking more of his blood. Loving it, savoring it.

"Beg." He pressed her clitoris, hard, and she shuddered.

The touch wasn't enough to send her over the edge; it was just enough to make her reckless. Achy, needy. Her chest burned, and those thorns cut at her, but still she clung to him, nails deep in his back, hips writhing, head thrashing. *"You* beg *me."*

A third finger joined the play. In and out, in and out, they moved, mimicking the motions of sex. "I'm not the one who needs to come."

"Yes, you are." To prove it, she reached between their bodies and cupped his thick, straining erection.

He sucked in a breath.

Her gaze latched onto the pulse hammering wildly at the base of his neck. God, she wanted to bite him. Wanted, needed, more of his blood. It was powerful, addictive, those little tastes no longer enough, her hunger no longer soothed. Would she be able to keep down more than a few sips? Only one way to find out . . .

Time to stop this. She was too close to falling. "This is more than a kiss." She sounded drugged, her tongue swollen. "Only promised you a kiss."

"Beg me, and it can be a lot more, whether you promised or not."

A bead of his sweat dripped onto her, hot and sultry.

"I won't beg. I won't." *Take what you want.* Whether the demand was for her or him, she didn't know.

He pulled his fingers out of her.

She nearly cried. Every nerve ending in her body was sensitized, waiting, ready to experience climax, and he'd pulled away! The thorns sharpened with her outrage, and she suddenly wished she could rip them out and use them on *him*.

"Beg," he said.

"Fuck you," she snarled.

He breathed in and out, ragged, shallow, his eyes shooting fire at her. "That's what I'm trying to do!"

"Well, you're not trying hard enough."

With a growl, he swooped back in, tongue plunging, teeth scraping hers. The heel of his hand returned between her thighs, offering more of that delicious pressure while his fingers dove back into her. "Do it, then. Take what you need."

"I will." Trembling, writhing, hurting, she bit down on his tongue once more, unable to stop herself, sucking, swallowing every bit of blood she could. The climax hit her, slamming bone deep, soul deep, her muscles twitching, body grinding, hurting, thoughts splitting apart, flying.

A scream ripped from her. A scream of pleasure and pain. Heaven and hell. Wonder and regret. She clawed at his back, shredding his shirt. She thrashed, she writhed even harder, she cried some more—but she didn't beg.

"Are you hurt?" he asked when she quieted, his tone broken, the cracks filled with disbelief.

"Kind of," she managed, not really wanting to explain. "But it's good, it's good. Don't stop."

He jerked his fingers from her—*bastard, not done flying!*—and tore at the denim covering his cock. Palm wet from her arousal, he gripped himself, hips pistoning back and forth, hand moving up and down. The glitter of his skin brightened, became blinding, a white light that signaled the end of life. Death by pleasure.

Now just as desperate to watch *his* pleasure, Bride leaned up and nicked his jugular, drawing only the slightest heavenly bead and rubbing whatever pleasure-chemical her teeth produced into the tiny wound. He stiffened, stilled, a roar splitting his lips and echoing in her ears. On and on he shook, seconds blending into minutes, minutes to a necessary eternity.

Finally, both of them collapsed. His weight smashed her into the mattress, but she didn't care.

His skin ceased its glowing, and she gazed up at him, dazed by what had just happened. Lines of tension still branched from his eyes, and his lips were set in a mulish frown. But his eyes, oh, his eyes. They were pure amber fire, glowing like his skin had, lighting up the room. His breath sawed in and out, and sweat still poured from him.

As she watched, he lifted his hand, bringing his fingers to his mouth. Their combined essence gleamed there. He licked away every drop, completely uninhibited, and it was the most erotic thing she'd ever seen.

"Delicious," he muttered, briefly closing his eyes and savoring.

Do not relax your guard. Well, any more than you already have. "Your friend might burst in any second, thinking I killed you."

"Nope. He knows I can take care of myself." Devyn anchored his fists beside her temples, locking her in place. Concern was seeping into his expression. "Are you embarrassed by what happened?"

She frowned. Again, he was concerned about shaming and embarrassing her. Why? "Should I be?"

"You came. On my fingers."

And that was a bad thing? "What about you? Are you embarrassed about the way you came? I mean, you masturbated on me."

Twin circles painted his cheeks, but he shook his head in denial.

How odd. Something about his reaction was off here, but she just didn't know what it was or what it meant. Still, she couldn't help but be proud of herself. A man of his experience had come without sinking inside her. He must have been intensely aroused.

"Do you regret what happened?" he asked.

"Do you question all of your lovers like this?"

A muscle ticked in his jaw. "Do you. Regret what. Happened?"

Did she? Now she knew his taste and already hungered for more. She would never again be able to look at him without thinking of the pleasure they had shared. That angered her. But regret it? "No." She didn't.

"Good. Because you owe me two more kisses, and I have every intention of collecting. Soon." He rolled beside her and drew her into his body, holding her close, fingers playing with her hair, then tracing paths of fire down her arms.

She tried to disengage, but he tightened his grip. His

chest was firm and slick against hers. "I don't owe you a damn thing. This little excursion paid you in full."

He stiffened. "This little *excursion* counts as one kiss. One. I still remember my name, and I believe you promised I wouldn't."

"You are so annoying."

He sat up and stared down at her. "No. I'm confused. I have no idea what to do with you. You confound me at every turn." Frowning, he scooted to the edge of the bed and gave her his back. "Get dressed. I'll take you to see Aleaha."

CHAPTER 13

Devyn was baffled by himself.

Bride hadn't begged him to bring her to climax, but he'd done it anyway. He'd been helpless to do otherwise. He hadn't been able to walk away. Yeah, after his father died and he'd conquered his guilt, he'd taken any female who had even opened her legs and touched himself any time the desire struck. *He'd* been the one begging, but back then, he'd had no control. He'd hated himself for that weakness and had learned restraint. Iron restraint. Restraint that had not broken until today.

Restraint Bride *did* possess.

She had wanted his blood, but she had only grazed his neck. She'd contented herself with little beads from his tongue. She'd wanted sex, but she'd contented herself with his fingers. Such willpower . . .

He was disgraceful. He'd left his clothes on, hoping to dull his own desires. That plan had failed. As it was, he'd almost died from the pleasure. He suspected actual skin-to-skin contact really would kill him.

What a way to go, though, right?

As many women as he'd been with over the years, and as much control as he usually displayed, he shouldn't have reacted to this one so intensely. His body didn't seem to understand that. He'd smelled her sweetness, seen her lean curves, and had craved everything she had to give. He'd *had* to taste those lush lips, had to hold those soft breasts, caress that smooth stomach, finger that hot, wet sheath.

What was it about her that so entranced him? He needed to figure it out so that he could combat it. He'd once thought it was the challenge of her, but Eden Black had turned him down time and time again, and he'd let Eden go without a single regret.

Maybe it was the way she constantly surprised him. He'd expected her to hide her body; she'd flaunted it. He'd expected her to cave under his sensual assault; she'd flourished. The braggart had even made him laugh. What was next? Making him drool for her? Well, he was a king. He drooled for no one!

"Don't leave this room," he growled, standing and adjusting his clothes. Then, for good measure, he stalked to the door, opened it a crack, and called, "If she leaves this room, shoot her."

Behind him, Bride gasped. He didn't turn and face her. He stepped into the shower stall with his clothes on and pressed the code for a thorough cleaning.

He'd come in his pants. How mortifying. At least she hadn't mocked him about it. Hadn't even seemed to mind. He'd wanted to sink into a black hole when he'd realized what he'd done.

The enzyme spray settled on his skin and clothes, burrowing deep and scrubbing away the evidence of his too-eager desire. When he reentered the bedroom, Bride was exactly where he'd left her, only she'd pulled on a fresh pink T-shirt and a pair of jeans. They looked good on her. Made her look young and innocent. Macy's necklace still circled her neck.

There was a rosy blush to her skin, a determined gleam in her emerald eyes. Her cheeks were fuller than he'd ever seen them, and that stopped him short. She'd kept his blood down, he realized.

He nearly grinned in satisfaction.

She opened her mouth to speak, but he cut her off with a raised hand. "Did my blood make you sick?" He already knew the answer, but he wanted to hear her admit it.

"No."

There was no stopping his grin this time. He leaned against the wall, arms crossed over his chest. "Guess that means you need me, huh?"

"Don't go thinking you're special," she said. "I only had a few sips, and I can keep such a small amount down no matter who I drink from."

His grin morphed into a frown. "Do you want more?"

"No," she said, but glanced at his pulse.

A lie. She wanted more, she just didn't want to want it. As soon as the hottest fires of her hunger returned, she would *have* to take more. And there'd be only one vein available to her. His.

"You ready to go?" he asked, unable to mask the return of his satisfaction.

She nodded hesitantly. "I want to see Aleaha, but it's daylight. I can't go outside without blistering."

Silent, he eyed her. Then he sighed. He hadn't thought of that. He wasn't used to considering another's wants and needs. "Very well. I'll have her brought here."

She crouched forward, her legs tucked under her and her weight on her knees. Her hands twisted the denim of her jeans. "By someone you trust not to hurt her, right?"

"Believe me, the woman bringing her here would never harm her." Macy, he knew, wasn't into self-inflicted pain.

Bride frowned in confusion but nodded. In her mind, Aleaha was still a prisoner.

Devyn made the call. The moment Macy/Aleaha answered, he said, "I've got her. No question this time. We're at the Legacy Apartments, top floor." He hung up before she could reply. "She'll be here in half an hour, is my guess. Which means we've got thirty minutes to burn. You and I are going to talk." He had a feeling Bride would mentally shut him out the moment she saw her friend free and happy.

"Your blood helped Nolan, so AIR is going to want to test it," he told her.

"No." She shook her head violently.

"They won't lock you up." Yet. He wouldn't let them. "But helping them is the only way to save your life. You did commit a crime."

"No!"

He splayed his arms in helplessness. "I'm afraid you don't have a choice, sweetheart. You took something that belongs to them, and anyone else would have fried for it by now. But I know them. Because of your healing blood, they'll bargain with you."

Another shake of her head, inky hair flying. "I don't need to bargain. You're forgetting my abilities."

Before his eyes, her skin changed color, her arms turning bright green to match the comforter around her, her face turning gray to blend with the stone wall framing her. Even her hair lightened to that silver shade. Only her clothing gave her away.

"Don't mist," he growled.

Slowly her skin and hair returned to normal. "I'm not going anywhere. At least for now. I want to see Aleaha."

He relaxed. "What if I told you Aleaha is an AIR agent? Would you be so quick to deny the agency's desires?"

She laughed, and it was like bells were tinkling merrily. "Aleaha is not AIR. No way."

That laugh . . . His cock twitched. "Why? Because she's a shape-shifter?"

Bride tensed, stilled.

"That's right. I know what she is. She took the form of an AIR agent, liked the job, and remained on the team."

Her nails elongated, becoming little claws that dug into her thighs and drew blood. "If anyone hurt her when they found out what she was, I will hunt them down and drain them."

Such loyalty. He'd already admired her for it, but that admiration grew. "They like having her on."

That mollified her somewhat. "If you captured a favored AIR agent, they would have come after you. Are *you* now being chased?"

"We'll get to that in a minute. First, take your nails

out of your legs." If anyone was going to hurt her, it was going to be him. Only when she obeyed did he continue. "Help AIR, Bride. Willingly give them some of your blood for testing, and I'll find you a vampire to talk to."

She opened her mouth. Shut it. Bit her lip and rubbed at her necklace as she considered his offer. "Why should I? If my blood cured Nolan, AIR will take more and more from me until there's nothing left. I'll die and won't be able to question the vampire. And if it doesn't help him, they'll have no use for me. They'll lock me away or stake me, and I still won't get to question the vampire."

He rolled his eyes. "You've read too many books. They won't stake you."

"You didn't see the human-alien war. I did. I was there. Innocents were slain in the streets simply because they were different. I possess powers that would scare the shit out of every single agent. They will never be comfortable with me."

Good point. Not that he'd tell her. "Who knows? They might try and recruit you. They did me."

She uttered another of those sweet, sultry laughs. "Me? Working for AIR?" She shook her head again. "Show me where the underground doorway into vamp world is, and I'll think about aiding them."

"Nope. Sorry. Your people live by a code of rules, and the most important of those rules is to never leave the underground. It's to keep humans from finding them. To them, you broke that rule, or someone broke it for you. Either way, it's a crime punishable only by death." More than that, Devyn still had the composites of the McKell warriors in his pocket. Dallas's vision made him think they would come to the surface for her. But they couldn't come for her if they didn't know about her.

"Clearly you visited and left the underground, yet you weren't killed."

"The king had his reasons," was all Devyn said.

Her teeth ground together, those sharp little fangs slashing at her gums. "How are you going to find another vampire if they're forbidden from coming up here?"

His stare became piercing. "Twice a year, several *do* come topside. For food. Sometimes those hunters are caught and sold at slave auctions."

The words settled between them like heavy stones, dragging them into the dark, thick mire of memory.

"I'm not going to a slave auction," she bit out.

"Not as a slave to be sold, no."

Every muscle in her beautiful body tensed. Was she pissed? Jealous? He wanted her to be jealous. Which was odd. He truly did despise jealousy in his lovers. He never allowed it or tolerated it. But Bride wanted so little from him, gave so little, he was latching on to every scrap she threw his way.

Looks like you'll be wiping away drool, after all. His jaw hardened with the thought. Hell. No. He was desired and craved throughout the galaxies. He was not a whipped schoolboy panting after a specific piece of ass.

"You're angry," she said with surprise. "Why?"

There was a sudden, frantic knock at the front door, and as it echoed through the bedroom, Bride paled and scrambled from the bed. She didn't bolt from the bedroom, though, but stood unsteadily, eyeing the exit with trepidation.

"What's wrong?" he found himself asking, anger forgotten. *Do not approach her. Do not put your hands on her.*

"Do—do you think that's Aleaha?"

He nodded, hoping that would soothe her. "I'm sure of it."

"She's early, and I'm not ready." Bride licked her lips, still not budging from that spot. "What if . . . what if she ran from me, all those years ago, and has been hiding from me?"

Her uncertainty reminded him of the boy he'd once been. The boy who had put on his best clothes and snuck into his mother's wing of the palace to give her a birthday present. The boy who had knocked on his mother's door, hoping, praying for a smile, even a hug, when he gave her the picture he'd drawn for her. The boy who'd had to throw the gift away, because his mother had looked at it, thanked him, and placed it back in his hands before shutting the door in his face.

"She likes you, sweetheart. I swear it. She's been searching for you, intending to save you from my wrath."

More knocking.

"Coming, coming," Dallas shouted from the living room.

"Why did it take me so long to find her, then? Why did I only recently discover her scent?"

She looked so vulnerable, Devyn's heart actually swelled in his chest, aching, grinding against his ribs. He was at her side before he realized he'd moved, wrapping his arms around her and drawing her close.

She rested her head in the hollow of his neck, her tremors vibrating into him. Her night-wild scent wafted

to his nose, and he breathed deeply. The silk of her hair
tickled his chin. He'd never held a woman like this. Just
held her, an offer of comfort with no expectation of sex.
As her hands gripped his back, as though she wanted to
step inside him, be a part of him, he wondered why he'd
resisted such a thing. This was paradise.

"Yo, Dev," Dallas called. "Macy's here, and she's about
to claw my face off for holding her back."

"Then say good-bye to your face. We're not ready."

A frowning Bride drew back. "Macy?"

"Remember. Aleaha took Macy's identity. Just be glad
her boyfriend, Breean, isn't here. You'd have to endure an
interrogation before touching her."

The frown faded, leaving her vulnerable again. "Does
Breean know who she really is? Does he treat her right?
Is he rich?"

"Yes, he knows, and yes, he does. He loves her. And
why do you care if he's rich?"

"We promised each other we'd never marry anyone
who was poor."

"He's rich." *I'm richer,* he wanted to add, but didn't.
His finances didn't matter, as he'd never remarry. "Are
we ready now? Macy will be happy to see you." If Macy
turned him into a liar and did not welcome Bride the
way she deserved, he was going to kill her. Slowly, painfully.

"Yes."

"Send her in, Dal," he finally called. Even as he spoke,
he moved away from Bride. His arms tingled where they'd
been in contact with her.

The door flew open, and Macy raced inside. When

she spotted Bride, she gasped and stopped. Her hands tented over her mouth.

Bride gulped, then nervously licked her lips. Devyn had watched her take down a human slaver. She hadn't flinched or betrayed a hint of nerves when he'd killed said slaver in front of her. But now, she was eaten up with worry. Over a friend who might not love her anymore.

His chest started aching again.

And when tears filled her eyes, he almost fell to his knees. Tears had never affected him. How could they? Giving in to them would mean he was involved, not just with his body but with his mind. It would mean he harbored affection for the crier—affection he didn't understand or condone. But here, now, seeing Bride's emerald eyes liquefy . . . he was struck with the urge to do anything and everything in his power to ensure she never had reason to cry again. What the hell?

"Did you hurt her?" Macy suddenly demanded of him.

"No," he said. "And I won't." Maybe. "And before you ask, no, she's not a prisoner." Yet.

The women looked at each other. Both remained silent, as if they were too afraid to speak.

"Hello, Aleaha," Bride finally said, gaze intense. "You've grown."

A trembling Macy nodded. "Hello. You're just the same."

When one of those tears splashed onto Bride's cheek, Devyn stepped toward her, meaning to comfort her again. But with a joyous cry, Macy suddenly ran past him and threw herself into Bride's arms.

"It's you. It's really you."

Bride's gaze met his for a split second, wonder in their

depths. Then she was hugging Macy with all her might, crying harder, laughing, twirling. "I can't believe I found you. I've been looking so long. So damn long. I only stumbled on your scent a few weeks ago."

"I've been looking for you, too! I was afraid something had happened to you."

"Where did you go that night?"

They were talking over each other, but somehow he understood every word.

"One of the officers had hung back while the others chased you," Macy explained. "He found me and dragged me to their car. I escaped before they could lock me up, but someone else grabbed me and knocked me out. I woke up in a plane with other kids being carted God knows where. I had to take the identity of a guard, but managed to free the kids before working my way back to New Chicago. I looked for you but couldn't find you. I was afraid my scent had been buried underneath all the new identities I'd taken, and I guess I was right. You only just started smelling me again, and I only just let myself be me again. Well, me and Macy. Breean helps me."

"Oh, Leah," Bride said, and Devyn had never heard her use such a gentle, loving, fiercely *motherly* tone. "I'm so sorry! Did anyone hurt you? Tell me their names, and I'll find and kill them."

"I'm fine, I'm fine. But what about you?" Macy cupped Bride's cheeks and studied her face. "Like I said, you're just the same, just as lovely."

"And you're ten times as lovely. Look at all that dark hair, those bright green eyes. And you have the breasts you always dreamed about having."

The two shared a laugh.

So she could see the woman underneath Macy's skin, Devyn realized. Impressive.

"When I learned Devyn had found you, I almost died. I'd been searching, had no luck, and suddenly he was on the hunt to bed you. Did he hurt you?" Macy demanded.

"No." Her cheeks flushed to a pretty pink, and she flicked him a glance.

He shrugged, sheepish. He'd never made a secret of his desires.

"Oh," Bride said. "I have your necklace." She removed it and anchored it around Macy's neck.

The two women returned to their conversation, and he continued to watch them, strangely happy with the way things had turned out.

His phone vibrated, and he dug it out of his pocket. The number belonged to Breean. He was moaning inside as he answered.

"I knew you would do the right thing," Breean said without preamble.

"You knew I had Bride?"

"I knew you were close to finding her and using my woman to do it. But I let you, because the end result was all that mattered."

"And if I had betrayed her?"

"I would have killed you."

It was stated so simply, Devyn knew the big guy had already planned it out. Just in case. Couldn't blame him, really. "You would have tried," was all he said.

Breean chuckled. "You underestimated me once before, my friend, and I locked you up."

That he had. In the end, Devyn had still won. "You know, I'm starting to like you. We should hang out more."

Breean choked, his breath crackling over the line. "I won't bed you. Now or ever."

Devyn rolled his eyes. "As if you're handsome enough to win the likes of me." The thought of being with someone else, however, slipped into his mind and refused to leave. Bride was affecting him, and he didn't like it. Perhaps if he bedded another woman, he'd stop thinking of Bride so intently. Perhaps he'd stop this cursed softening. Once more, tears would no longer affect him, and jealousy would no longer delight him.

Yes. That's what he'd do. Just as soon as he turned Bride over to AIR.

CHAPTER 14

Bride hadn't seen Devyn in days. Three days, eight hours, and twenty-seven minutes, to be exact. Three days, eight hours, and twenty-seven minutes she'd spent inside AIR headquarters.

Though she'd committed a crime by stealing Nolan, she wasn't a prisoner; they'd oh, so nicely asked her to stay as Devyn had told her they would. They recognized her abilities and wanted her happy, but they also wanted easy access to her. Had she insisted on leaving, they would have caved on the issue, she was sure, but she hadn't. She stayed for Aleaha, who visited her every day. Or rather, Macy. That was the name her friend now used, so that was the name Bride needed to call her. By citing Macy as the reason for her compliance, she hopefully made Macy look good to those in charge.

Wasn't like it was a hardship to stay. She had a comfortable bed, a small dresser with her changes of clothes, a portable enzyme shower, and a fridge and microwave for bags of plasma. Yeah, she was a pincushion, poked and prodded every few hours. It wasn't such a bad deal, though. The agents were surprisingly friendly and had honored her request for them not to wear perfume around her.

So . . . why hadn't Devyn checked on her?

She knew the answer to that, she thought, fuming. He'd had her. He'd won. Like she'd suspected, once a man like him got his target in bed, he became tired of her. The bastard. God, what a fool she was. She should have resisted harder.

She paced the length of her cell, her boots digging into the tiles. There'd been talk about him. She knew Devyn had taken some stupid female out on a date. A date! With the otherworlder, there was only one way that could have ended. In bed. Naked. Doing the things she and Devyn had done in *her* bed. Only more.

Doesn't matter. You knew it would end this way. Still, her fangs and nails were elongated, and what little blood coursed through her veins was like white lightning, sizzling, raising the fine hairs on the back of her neck and razing her chest.

Think of something else before you combust. She knew several AIR agents had moved into her apartment to keep track of Nolan, too afraid to transport him. How was he? Still healthy? She hoped so. He wasn't a bad guy.

The only door to her cell slid open, and three female agents strode inside. One of them clutched a plastic basket filled with needles, tubes, and bandages.

"Time for another withdrawal already?" she moaned. She should tell them no more needle sticks for a while, but she did want them to find out if her blood was indeed a cure for Nolan's virus. If Al—Macy were ever infected, she wanted the cure available immediately.

"Yep, we're here for a little more juice," one of the

girls said. "Sorry." A pause, a frown. "You look paler in person than you do on the monitors. Plasma not to your liking?"

"No." At this rate, she'd be drained by the end of the week. The plasma had sickened her more than usual, and she'd been unable to absorb even those first few little mouthfuls.

Every day she edged closer to starvation, and these women with their strong pulses weren't helping. They were a mouthwatering temptation, her tongue swelling for a taste. *Don't drink from Macy's coworkers. Don't you dare drink from Macy's coworkers.*

"I'd offer to feed you," the second girl said, "but Mia said we couldn't. She doesn't want our blood masking the effects of yours."

Bride strode to the chair and table that had been set up for this type of thing. The woman with the basket moved in front of her, red hair fluttering around her chin; the other two moved behind Bride. They were the guard dogs, she suspected, just in case she went feral.

They were all young, no older than thirty, and pretty in their own ways. What surprised her, though, was the fact that they didn't seem disgusted by her need for blood. They had shrugged off her dislike of the plasma and would have offered themselves if possible. Where was the horror she'd always dreaded?

"I haven't seen you guys before," she remarked. Everyone who visited her was female, but never the same one twice. She'd begun to wonder if there were any male agents besides Devyn and Dallas.

"There's a waiting list to meet you," one of the girls behind her said. "We finally got our turn."

A waiting list? For her? "Why?"

"Devyn," they said in unison, and then they sighed dreamily.

Just hearing his name, the moisture in Bride's mouth increased.

"I'm Ann, by the way," the redhead said. "The brunette is Claire, and the blonde is Madison." As she spoke, she wrapped the self-tightening tourniquet around Bride's arm and cleaned the inside of her elbow.

"What's Devyn got to do with everyone wanting to meet me?"

"He decorated your cell," Madison said, her tone making it clear that should have been obvious to Bride. "Everything here, he picked out."

"He did what?" She *had* thought it odd that AIR had spent so much money on a real oak dresser and a mattress made from true feathers, but she'd never suspected Devyn's involvement.

Ann lifted a butterfly needle. "We were set to buy the cheapest stuff we could find—sorry, but it's true—when he told us not to bother, that he'd buy what you needed with his own money."

Why would he do such things? She was nothing to him. He was already dating other women. Not that he'd ever taken Bride on a date. And not that she would have said yes if he had. Really.

Ann pushed the sharp needle into her vein, blood slowly, too slowly, filling the tube attached to the other end. "Dallas told me he heard Devyn call you sweetheart."

"Yeah. So." Devyn had an endearment for everyone.

"He's only ever called me darling," Claire said.

"Me, too. Darling this and darling that. He calls Eden Black *pet,* and he's obsessed with her, but he's never called her sweetheart."

Bride's teeth and nails sharpened dangerously. "Obsessed with her? Why?"

"She's Rakan, and he's never had a Rakan."

Sounded like something Devyn would say. *I want to kill Eden Black.*

"But, anyway, he tortured that human for you." Claire stepped around the table and eyed Bride questioningly. "Even cut his head off."

"Yes. But only because I had something he wanted." She couldn't keep the bitterness from her tone.

Madison, too, veered around and faced her. "Honey, he pursued me for a week—that's the most I could resist him, and the most time he'd give me. He'd already moved on to someone else when I threw myself at him to regain his attention. Anyway, during that week he heard my partner berate me, call me names. Believe me, I had something he wanted, too, but he didn't kill Tate for me. Didn't even yell at him."

Wait. "You've been with Devyn?"

Smiling happily, Madison nodded. So did Ann and Claire.

Bride's eyes widened. "*All* of you have been with him?"

"Nearly every female agent in AIR," Ann said, and she didn't sound upset.

"Why that . . . that . . . man-whore!" Bride had known he was promiscuous, but damn. Was there no one he wouldn't screw? Probably not. Besides Bride. Her, he pleasured with his fingers and his mouth but didn't penetrate.

Why hadn't he taken her? She'd been willing. Much as she would have liked to deny that, she couldn't.

The tourniquet loosened on its own, and Ann tugged it from Bride's arm. She withdrew the needle with one hand and placed a bandage over the puncture wound with the other. "So tell me. What was he like? With you?"

All three women leaned in close, their heartbeats suddenly a roar in her ears.

Bride squirmed in her seat, sweating, now having trouble catching her breath. Her gaze locked on Ann's pulse, and even more moisture flooded her mouth. The agent's skin appeared soft, her vein full. One little nibble wouldn't—

Argh! No.

"Bride?" one of them said.

She blinked, bringing them back in focus. *No blood. Not now.* They were still staring at her, waiting. Waiting for information about Devyn. She knew they wanted to compare her experiences with their own so they could feel better about how he'd treated them. Fine. She'd give them all the gory details.

"He nearly blinded me with that glowing skin thing," she said stiffly. "I mean, really. How annoying is that?"

"He glowed?" Claire asked, brow puckering.

The three women shared a strange look, as though silently asking each other if Devyn had glowed for them. Each one shook her head no.

He hadn't glowed for them?

"Tell us more," Madison pleaded.

The words tumbled from her before she could stop them. "He tried to make me beg for it, but I refused. He gave it to me anyway, but he wouldn't let me leave after-

ward. And when *I* tried to walk away, he tightened his
hold. Talk about frustrating!" *See,* she wanted to shout.
He's not a prize. He was domineering and too determined
to have his way.

One by one, the women straightened. They shared another look. A look of wonder, this time.

"What?" she demanded, wiping at the sweat on her
brow with the back of her wrist. Her hand was trembling.

Ann was the first to shake off the awe. "He held you?
After he finished with you?"

"Yes." Why were the lights in the cell suddenly winking on and off? Light, dark, light, dark. And why didn't
the agents seem to notice?

"He couldn't get his clothes on fast enough with me,"
Madison said with a pout.

"Two seconds after he came, he thanked me and rolled
from the bed," Claire said. "He was out the door a minute after that."

Both females sounded like they stood at the end of a
tunnel, their voices thick and distant, slowed.

"He did me up against a wall and patted my head when
he was done. Then he walked away and never looked
back." Ann sounded closer, but no less slurred. "'Course,
I couldn't chase him because I was boneless, completely
sated." She paused. "Bride, are you okay? Don't take this
the wrong way, but you look terrible."

They watched her with expectation, waiting for her
reply. About Devyn? About her health? She didn't know
what to say. Clearly they thought it was a miracle that
Devyn had stayed with her after his climax, but they
couldn't know that he'd had nowhere else to go. That

he'd been waiting for Macy. That he hadn't trusted Bride to stay put.

He didn't like her, not the way they thought. Otherwise, he wouldn't have gone on a date with another female. He would have been here, claiming his kisses: Feeding her that delicious blood. Blood . . . *Need* blood.

"Bride?"

Dizziness flooded her mind, her thoughts breaking apart, unable to realign themselves. Where was she? What was happening to her? She pushed to shaky legs, but they were too weak to hold her weight, and she crashed into the cold concrete floor. A sharp pain exploded in her temple, and the world around her blackened completely.

"Open your eyes, sweetheart." Word of Bride's collapse had spread through AIR quickly, and Devyn had come running. Though he'd forced himself to remain outside headquarters these last three days, he'd never strayed far from the building.

Not even for the date he'd called a halt to half an hour into. He'd taken an agent to dinner, but before the appetizer had even arrived, he'd tossed a wad of cash on the table and left. Hadn't been right. Hadn't felt right. Bride was being drained, and he was out having fun. Well, not fun. He'd been miserable, unable to charm or flirt with his intended partner for the night.

He didn't know who he was anymore, or what he wanted.

No, not true. He wanted Bride.

It was as if, when she'd kissed him and come on his

fingers, she'd changed him. As if she'd somehow planted stronger seeds of obsession in his brain, and those seeds were now growing. He didn't know how to act anymore. Didn't know what to do with her.

He found himself thinking about her at the oddest moments. Like when he was on a date with another woman. Like when he was in the car and reached a traffic light flashing green. Like when he'd cut his fingertip and wiped the blood away.

What claimed the bulk of those thoughts was the fact that there'd been pain mixed with her pleasure. When she'd climaxed, she'd screamed, and it had not only been because of his exceptional skill. He wanted to know why she'd hurt and how to prevent it next time. For there would be a next time.

"Bride," he said more firmly. She was too pale, too still. He knew beyond a doubt she hadn't eaten in days. He'd kept tabs on her, and also knew she'd thrown up her one and only bag of plasma. "Wake up, and I'll let you slap me around. You know you want to."

A moan slipped from her, soft, barely discernible.

Of course the thought of hurting him physically had been the thing to rouse her. Her lashes fluttered open, casting flickering shadows on her cheeks. Those hazel irises were glazed, dull, but when they latched on to the pulse at his neck, they lit, swirled, once more like living emeralds, glowing.

He'd moved her to the bed, and he was stretched beside her, his head resting on his upraised palm. "You need to eat, sweetheart."

Desperately her hands pushed at him. "Get away from

me." The words were slurred, thick. Her gaze never left his neck. "You have to get away from me."

"Drink from me. Hurry, or dinner's gonna get cold."

"Go. Please, go."

"Not until you drink. It's an all-you-can-eat buffet tonight."

"I said go!"

He *tsk*ed. "I don't know why you're so stubborn about this. You're hungry. I'm willing. Maybe you'll be able to keep it all down. Which wouldn't surprise me. It's mine, after all, so there's clearly none better."

"I don't want your blood," she said, trying to scramble away herself.

She didn't, did she? His eyes narrowed. They'd see about that once he prodded her temper. "Guess what? I took a female on a date. An agent. A six-armed Delensean. I haven't had one of those in years. The prospect of having one again amused me."

"I know," she snarled, some of her color returning. "You picked her up immediately after leaving my bed and dropping me off here."

"I can't deny it."

"Did you sleep with her?" No longer was she trying to get away. Now she was leaning into him, nails clawing past his shirt and at his skin. "No, wait. Don't tell me. I don't want to know. I just want you to leave."

"You're right. I should leave. I should go on another date. Maybe with a Rakan this time. I've never had one of those, you know. I've heard they're the best, though, so I really should make an effort to—"

With a roar, she was on top of him, pinning him to

the mattress, her fangs in his neck, cutting deep, his blood flowing into her mouth. There was a sting, then only warm pleasure. He could hear her swallowing, purring as the flavor met her tongue. Finally.

"That's a good girl. Take everything you need."

Her lower body ground against his.

Already he was hard as a rock, arching up to meet her thrusts. "Just so you know, I didn't sleep with that agent."

A mewling sound escaped her, and her teeth gentled on his neck. When she tried to disengage completely, he petted her hair with firm strokes, holding her in place. "Nope. I'm enjoying this. Because I was such a good boy on my date, you have to see to my needs. That means you don't get to stop yet."

On and on she continued to drink, her purrs growing louder, her body writhing faster . . . faster, using him, taking what it needed, propelling her higher. Devyn gritted his teeth against the bliss, determined not to come like this again. A difficult task. She felt so good against him, she smelled like the sweetest flower, was finally doing something he'd commanded her to do.

Spots of color began to cloud his vision; she was taking a lot of blood, but still he didn't push her away. She needed it, and he had it to give. Even enjoyed the giving. "More," he said, the word barely audible. "Everything."

A hoarse cry slipped from her as she wrenched her mouth away. Up and down her chest moved in quick succession, her hard nipples abrading his chest. *Exquisite*, he thought. A trickle of crimson slid down her chin. Her lips were red, dewy. Her eyes no longer glowed, but her skin was so rosy it was like the petal of a rose.

"How's your stomach?" he asked. Wow. He sounded halfway to the grave.

"I—it's fine." She blinked in astonishment. "It's actually calm."

"I was . . . right then. Better than . . . most."

"Devyn?" she said with concern.

He didn't have the energy to form another word.

"Devyn," she repeated, determined this time. "I'm sorry, so sorry. I didn't mean to take so much. I didn't mean . . . I'll make it better. Okay? All right?" Slowly she leaned down and kissed him. Drops of his own blood seeped into his mouth. No, not his, he thought then. Hers. She'd swiped her tongue across her fangs, cutting the delicate tissue, and was feeding him that healing blood of hers.

Damn, damn, damn, was the next thought to hit him as some of his strength returned. He shoved her away from him and scrambled from the bed. He was panting, trembling, but he managed to maintain his balance.

"Devyn?" she said uncertainly. "I'm sorry. I didn't mean to take so much. You just tasted so good, and it had been so long . . . I'm really, really sorry, but I made it better. I did. You're already stronger. See?"

He scrubbed a hand down his face. *She knows nothing about vampires,* he reminded himself. She had no idea the magnitude of what she'd just done. Or did she? His gaze intensified on her. She sat up, smoothing her hair from her face with a wobbly hand. She wore an expression of concern and remorse.

No, she didn't know. Her ignorance didn't make it any better, though.

He'd come in here to check on her and give her blood.

And okay, yeah. He'd wanted to see and kiss her, but he hadn't come for *this*.

Maybe he should have warned her never to do it. Maybe he should have—

No. *No!* He wouldn't take the blame for this.

"What's going on?" she demanded. "Why are you looking at me like I'm a monster? You're not going to turn into a vampire. Nolan didn't. And I didn't kill you. I just took a little too much blood. Blood you commanded me to drink. You should be thanking me for pulling away in time."

Thank her? He could think of several things he'd like to do to her, but none of them ended with the words *thank* and *you,* and all of them involved his hands manacled around her neck.

"I am a monster, aren't I?" she said next, tears filling her eyes. "You're repulsed by me now."

Oh, those goddamn tears. Once again they sparked an ache in his chest.

Damn her. He would not soften. What she'd done was reprehensible. "I'm the one who should be crying. Right now the freedom I fought so hard for is gone. Everything I value is no longer available to me. And life as I know it, life as I've enjoyed it for so long, is over."

Her mouth fell open. "What are you talking about?"

"I'm talking about regrets, sweetheart. I regret that I ever met you." He scoured a hand down his face. The action wasn't violent enough, so he slammed his fists together. "God, I can't believe you did this."

"Did *what?*"

"Congratulations," he snarled. "You married a rich man."

CHAPTER 15

$\mathcal{D}$allas drained the last of his beer and chucked the bottle on the floor. Bride was gonna be pissed when she returned home and saw what he'd done to her place. Maybe Devyn would hire a few naked hookers to clean up like he'd done for Dallas. Dallas laughed at the thought.

"What's so funny?" the agent next to him asked.

Hector Dean. A hard-ass agent who knew how to have fun. He had a shaved head, arms sleeved with tattoos, and eyes like a snake's.

Currently they were lounging on the couch and watching TV—a TV that Nolan could see but couldn't watch. They had to keep an eye on him at all times, but the only way to see him, as well as the TV, was to angle the screen toward the couch and away from Nolan, who was pouting about it.

Not that Dallas cared. He'd stopped watching a while ago, but still hadn't turned the thing off. Nolan didn't deserve any luxuries.

Dallas balanced a laptop on his thighs, punching buttons, scrolling, typing, re-creating his vision to study it further. What he'd realized so far: there were eighteen McKell warriors, as Devyn had called them. The knife used to kill the Targon was made of titanium. And Devyn's body was positioned nine feet from the edge of the pier.

None of these things aided Dallas.

What good was finally accepting his abilities if he couldn't use them to his advantage?

"Well?" Hector prompted.

What had the agent asked him? Oh, yeah. "I was just thinking of Devyn and Bride."

Hector whistled. "Boy is wasted, that's for sure, and I never thought I'd see a guy like him fall."

"Me, either." Right now Bride was holed up at AIR headquarters, and Devyn was close to her, unable to stray too far—and not by force. It was surreal. Impossible to figure out, therefore not worth thinking about. *Back to the killing*. Would Bride's people hear about her confinement and come gunning for her freedom? Is that how they'd catch Devyn unaware?

"Bride's just as . . . wasted did you say? Over Devyn," Nolan grumbled. He lay on his cot, tossing a ball against the bars and catching it as it bounced back to him. "Maybe I'll steal her from him. She thinks I'm handsome, and her blood is divine."

Every morning they gave Nolan a bag of Bride's blood, hoping to keep the disease at bay. So far, it had seemed to work. "Just try romancing Bride," Dallas told him. "Devyn will cut off your head. That's his preferred method of punishment for guys who mess with his woman." His woman. Odd words when used in conjunction with Devyn. Words he'd never thought to utter.

"We're talking about Devyn, king of the Targon army and prince of a thousand bedrooms." The ball buzzed to the bars, back to Nolan. "He'll be over her in a few days, and I can be there to pick up the pieces of her heart."

"No. You'll still be locked up," Hector said.

"Maybe," was Nolan's only response.

Dallas didn't glance up from his laptop as he flipped off the alien. "You *will*."

Most likely Nolan was right, and Devyn would walk away from Bride soon enough. But Dallas had never seen the otherworlder like this. On edge, belligerent. Past few nights, Devyn had been staying at Dallas's place and had drunk himself into a stupor. Guy hadn't dated—except for that once—and hadn't had any females over.

With a sigh, Dallas brought the conversation back to the blood issue. "You craving everyone's blood, or just Bride's?"

Nolan shuddered. "Just Bride's. Not because I like the taste, but because of the way it makes me feel. Besides, yours would give me heartburn, I'm sure. You smell like stale beer."

"You're lucky you're alive—most of AIR wants you dead." Hector leaned back on the couch. "And you would be, if not for your improved health and the desire for answers."

"And Mishka," Nolan added smugly. The woman had been here every day, seeing to the otherworlder's comfort and amusement. "When's she due to arrive, anyway?"

Dallas shrugged. "Hour, tops. Thinking of winning her, too?"

"Always."

That earned a laugh from Hector. "Keep talking like that and maybe she'll kill you herself. She's batshit crazy for Jaxon."

"You don't know women, Agent Dean. I can win anyone I desire, whether they are mated or not."

Now he sounded like Devyn. Everyone who spent time with the Targon did eventually. People couldn't help but want to emulate him.

Hector stood and stalked to the mini-fridge they'd set up in the kitchen. "I may not know women, but I do know weapons, and I'm happy to introduce you to a few of mine."

Truth. Hector, too, reminded Dallas of Devyn in a lot of ways. Oh, Hector wasn't an unrepentant womanizer. Far from it. Dallas had never seen the guy with a woman or heard of someone special in his life. In fact, Hector, as fun-loving as he was, was pretty distant with the female agents. But he was emotionless when it came to killing, doing his job without hesitation or guilt.

"Let's talk about something productive," Dallas said. "Why don't you tell us where your queen's going to land?" Aka, what wormhole would she use to enter Earth. There were too many to cover all of them.

Thunk. Catch. *Thunk.* "Let me out, and I'll show you where *I* landed."

Hector reclaimed his seat on the couch, a bag of syn-chocolate cakes in his hands. "Not gonna happen again."

"The virus is no longer controlling me. I'm not going to betray you."

Mia wanted to take a sample of his blood to make sure of that, but the last time they'd taken Nolan's blood, the doctors and nurses who'd handled the specimens had had to be put down like animals.

Pretty soon, though, if Nolan maintained his current health, Mia was going to cave and do it. Dallas knew it. They needed to know if the parasite was dead. They needed to know if Bride's blood was the cure.

Dallas almost hoped it wasn't. Mia would use the vampire until her veins were bone dry, and Devyn wouldn't like it. Might even leave AIR and Earth for good. That's the kind of guy he was. If he wanted something, he considered it his. Whether he planned to keep that something or not. And he didn't like when other people messed with his stuff.

More than that, Mia might even go on a hunt for other vampires, thinking to use them as well. Anything to protect her agents. Understandable, but dangerous. Already she was asking questions. *Where are the others? How have they been able to hide for so long?* Devyn had refused to answer.

"You want to prove your new allegiance to us," Hector said, drawing Dallas from his musings, "you'll tell us where your queen is gonna be and when, so that we can kill her."

Those silver eyes narrowed on them. "The death blow isn't yours to deliver. It's mine. I'd think the two of you would understand that."

He did. And he even thought Nolan meant to aid them this time. Unlike last time, when the otherworlder had promised to help them destroy his queen and the men she'd infected but had betrayed AIR instead, leading them straight into an ambush. Now, his eyes were alert, no longer glazed as if he were hypnotized, or a puppet, and they glowed with genuine hate. Didn't matter, though. They couldn't chance it.

Suddenly Hector straightened. His ears practically twitched. "Do you hear that?"

Dallas straightened, too, concentrating on the noises around him. There, at the door, he could make out a soft scratching. Like metal gliding and twisting against metal.

Someone was trying to disable the ID lock.

"B and E in progress," he said. "Stay here and guard Nolan. Nolan, keep your mouth shut." He was on his feet before Hector could protest, silently trekking to the door. Along the way, he withdrew his pyre-gun. "Let's try to keep everyone alive today, boys and girls."

Should he let the perp destroy the lock completely and enter so that he could immobilize him—or her—here? Or should he jerk open the door and just start firing?

Here, he could keep the damage contained. But that placed Nolan in danger and would also give any stragglers time to run away.

"—possible break-in," Hector was whispering into his cell. The agent had moved to the cage, in front of Nolan, with his profile to the window and the door. He sheathed his phone, palmed his weapons. One of his guns, the semi, was aimed at the door and the other, the pyre, at the window. Just in case.

Backup was on its way.

Let 'em in, Dallas thought then. Hector could keep

Nolan safe, and this way Dallas could protect any innocents lingering in the hallway.

He pressed against the wall and angled toward the door. A minute passed, then another. Had the perp failed? Given up? And who the hell wanted Bride? Her family? Had they found her? Were the McKell warriors here? Was this the beginning of his vision? Dallas fought a wave of dread.

Finally, the metal creaked open and a man Dallas didn't recognize pushed inside as if he owned the place, his own pyre-gun extended. Dallas blasted him, a blue beam seeping past his clothes. It didn't immobilize him, proving him to be human.

As another male pounded inside, then another, Dallas and the first male launched at each other.

"Shit," Hector cursed, drawing the newcomers' attention. He was immediately blasted with stun rays himself. None affected him, either. He squeezed off a round of bullets, nailing both men in the shoulders. They grunted, jerked, but didn't fall.

Dallas kicked his opponent in the stomach, propelling him into the wall. At the same time, he elbowed one of the bleeding men in the throat. Then he spun and headbutted the other in the forehead. All three hit the ground in quick succession, their guns skidding out of reach.

"And that," he said, dusting his hands together, "is how it's done."

Except, the one he'd kicked gained his bearings, and grabbed Dallas by the ankles. With a tug, Dallas crashed to the concrete floor. Maybe his skull had cracked, maybe his brain was just rattling back and forth. Either way, a sharp pain tore through his head. He battled through it, said, "Don't shoot him," to Hector, and pulled himself to a crouch.

"Where's the vampire?" the guy snarled, kicking *him* in the stomach.

- That these humans wanted Bride enough to break into her apartment could mean only one thing. They were the slavers Devyn hoped to kill. "She's not here," he said, forcing himself to his feet. "How 'bout you dance with me instead?"

Dallas swiped out his arm, a small dagger sliding from the cuff in his shirt. His fingers curled around the hilt a split second before his hand reached the human. Contact. The tip sliced just enough to send the guy into a panic.

There was a gasp, a gurgle as blood leaked from him at the same rate as his swift heartbeat, and the man dropped to his knees, clutching at the groove. "You'll be fine," Dallas told him. "Weak but fine. Now you're going to answer some questions."

"No, he won't."

The other two must have found a reservoir of strength, because they launched themselves at Dallas, roaring, pissed as hell, and determined to end him. Their fists hammered at his head, his stomach, and his groin. Their knees slammed into his lungs, jetting the air from his lips. Hurt like a son of a bitch, but again, he pushed through.

Dallas grabbed one by the arm, twisted, and snapped the bone in two. Amid howls of agony, he ducked, ramming his head into the stomach of the only one left standing, and running. Running until the human slammed into the wall, all the while those meaty fists slugging at him. Pictures fell from the wall and crashed onto the floor.

Dallas pulled back both arms and let them fly. Teeth scraped his knuckles. Then bone gave way. Then cartilage snapped and blood gushed. The man slumped to the floor.

"Well done," Hector said, stowing his weapons and stalking over. When he reached the first guy, Cut Throat, he planted his boot directly on top of the wound and pressed. "What are you doing here, asswipe? And don't even think about playing games with me, because there are three of you, and I only need one to get my answers."

Cut Throat struggled to breathe.

"No need for violence," Dallas said. He didn't want Hector slapped with a fine for unnecessarily hurting a human. An otherworlder wouldn't have mattered.

Dallas hated the double standard. Once, he hadn't minded it. Had thought it was for the best. Earth belonged to humans, after all. Since he'd acquired his own powers and realized the full sting of prejudice, though, his views had changed completely. Just because someone was different, that didn't mean they needed to be feared. Or put down.

"What are you going to do?" Hector asked.

Letting Hector see his powers, know beyond any doubt that he was different and no longer just speculate about it, didn't sit well. Hector was one of the few people who didn't complain about working with him. Would that change?

"You'll see." Now that he'd accepted his abilities, was letting them do what they wanted, when they wanted to do it, using them shouldn't be a problem.

As he peered down at the men, he reached inside himself to the box containing his powers, no longer locked and shoved into the shadows. He clasped onto the mind control, which was twinkling like a star. The moment he touched it, its energy exploded through him and he cried out. Almost fell to his knees. It was so strong, weighing down his shoulders, shooting through his body like a boomerang, vibrating in his bones.

"Dallas?" Hector said.

Dallas held up a hand to ward him off, and they stood like that, in silence, for several minutes. Finally, things settled, and he was able to refocus. Hector was watching him with concern, though the agent didn't voice that concern. He wouldn't, either. He wouldn't want the humans to think Dallas was about to crumble.

Dallas crouched in front of the guy he'd cut, the only one still conscious. "Tell me why you're here."

The moment he spoke, the guy's eyes glazed over and he started talking, unable to stop himself. "The vampire. We want to sell her. We already have a buyer. A man. He was looking for a female vampire with a tattoo on her wrist. We were to capture her, stun her if at all possible, and take her in uninjured. But she killed Tom, my brother, and we decided to rough her up a bit before delivering her to her new master."

So. They were slavers, just as he'd suspected. What he liked least about all he'd heard was that they had a buyer ready to go. "Tell me who wants her."

"I don't know his name."

"Who does?"

"My boss."

Dallas learned what he could about the boss and then said, "Sleep." Once again the guy couldn't help but obey.

He looked over at Hector, who was eyeing him with confusion and wariness, and opened his mouth to explain what had just happened, but pressed his lips together before a single word escaped. Hector would freak if Dallas forced him to do something. Accident or not.

He closed his eyes. Focused. Tried to push the power back into its box, but it refused. It was free, now swirling through him in a frenzy and tickling his vocal cords.

Not knowing what else to do, he whipped out his cell and typed Hector a text.

Can't speak. Power. No automatic off switch.

Hector's phone beeped, and the agent pulled it out with a frown. Read the text. Paused. Nodded stiffly.

Lost another friend, Dallas thought, turning back to the couch. He would have gone to Nolan's cage and commanded Nolan to tell him everything he wanted to know, but the otherworlder had immunity to that power, as well. It seemed to Dallas that he—or anyone—only had to use their abilities against Nolan once for Nolan to learn how to combat them. First the voice, then Devyn's energy thing.

"It's okay, man," Hector said, suddenly beside him and patting his shoulder. "Your secret is safe with me." He held out his hands, spreading his fingers. A white glow started at both sets of fingertips and spread up to his tattooed wrists. Brighter and brighter the glow became, until Dallas was squinting. Then the glow seemed to break apart, de-atomizing Hector's hands.

Dallas swung wide eyes to Hector.

Hector lowered his arms, and the glow faded. "I'm human. Stun doesn't affect me, never has, but even as a kid I could do this. I can reach into someone's body and pull out their organs, one by one. For a long time, I couldn't control it, and people died. I don't know why I'm like this, but maybe more humans than we know or want to admit have strange abilities they can't explain. I mean, it's not like they'd advertise them, you know. Not after the way everyone reacted to the otherworlders." He paused, giving Dallas time to absorb his confession. "I'm telling you because I don't want you to think I'll run and tattle. I know your secret, and now you know mine."

Never had Dallas been more stunned. Psychic that he was, even he couldn't have predicted what had just happened.

"Backup has arrived," he heard Mishka say a split second before she and Eden Black pushed their way inside the apartment. He and Hector jumped apart guiltily. Both agents had their guns raised and ready for action. But they stopped and peered at the sleeping humans.

"Wow," Mishka said, looking to Dallas. "You started without us."

Behind them, the bars of Nolan's cage rattled. Dallas didn't have to turn to know Nolan had rushed to the front to get a closer view of Mishka and to listen to what was being said.

"Slavers tried to take the vampire," Hector said. "Dallas was nailed in the throat and can't talk. Ask me your questions."

He didn't have the heart to tell Hector that Mishka and Eden already knew about him. At least a little. But grateful as he was, he nodded in thanks and crossed his arms over his chest as Hector explained what happened.

"Human slavers, huh?" Eden ran a hand through the length of her golden hair. Gold from head to toe, the woman was mouthwateringly gorgeous. "We have no jurisdiction over them."

Mishka bent down and slammed her fist into the closest guy's cheek. Because her arm was comprised of solid metal, his bone instantly shattered. She dusted her hands together, job well done. "I don't care if we have jurisdiction or not. We're not giving them to the local PD."

Everyone had taken up the Devyn, king of the Targons, way of fighting dirty, Dallas supposed.

"Oh, oh. I just had an idea. The way I hear it is the vampire is aiding AIR," Eden said. "The fact that they were trying to kidnap her means they were trying to shut down an AIR investigation. That gives us all the jurisdiction we need."

"I love the way your mind works and could kiss you for it. Actually, I will kiss you for it." Mishka pressed her lips to Eden's. It was brief, without tongue, but damn, it was sexy.

Dallas moaned. It was the only way to stop himself from begging for more.

"Kyrin was right behind us," Mishka said. "We'll let him take out the trash."

"Devyn know about this?" Eden asked. "I heard about what he did to the last slaver that tried to get Bride." She shuddered, but she was grinning. "I've got to meet this woman. She'd kept the little slut from harassing me, and I owe her, well, a kiss."

Please let me be there for that, Dallas thought.

"I haven't told him," Hector replied. "Haven't had a chance."

"Hey, speaking of Devyn." Mishka stepped on the chest of each human as she walked inside the apartment. "You hear the latest news about him?"

Dallas shook his head, dread suddenly rushing through him. Had the vampires found Devyn? Hurt him already? Damn it. Dallas had tried to examine the vision he'd had with an impartial eye, searching for all the clues before acting and making things worse or causing things to happen because of his own actions.

"Brace yourself," Eden said with a delighted laugh. "Devyn told Mia he wanted Bride released from AIR custody. For good. No one was to touch her again. No more tests, even. And in return he would bring in as many vampires as he could get his hands on."

Okay, that wasn't so bad, Dallas thought, relaxing. He didn't know how his friend was going to find the vampires, but whatever. They'd do what needed to be done.

Behind them, Nolan laughed. "I guess this means Bride isn't ready for me to soothe her broken heart. Yet. Anyone wanna bet how long before she is?"

CHAPTER 16

Married?

No way in hell.

Bride had tried to question Devyn immediately after his silly announcement, but he'd glowered at her and snapped, "Not another word from you," before dragging her out of the cell. He'd left her in the hallway as he spoke to his pretty boss in hushed, urgent, *angry* tones, received a curt nod, and then had grabbed Bride up again and ushered her to his car.

Silence had reigned the entire moonlit drive to . . . his home? Had to be. It was a sprawling estate on the outskirts of town, smelled of delicious pine, and boasted gold and marble fixtures, a crystal chandelier that glistened like a thousand raindrops, and a winding staircase that probably reached heaven.

The furniture gleamed as though freshly polished. The onyx floor sparkled as though newly waxed. The walls were the perfect shade of pink, almost as if they were flushed, excited to see Devyn again.

"Kyrin en Arr, an Arcadian king, sold this place to

me so he could move into the city with his girlfriend," he said, finally breaking the silence. They were in the living room, alone, surrounded by the very wealth she'd dreamed of as a child. As he spoke, his cell phone rang; he ignored it. "Do you like it?"

He wanted to engage in small talk? Now? "Yes. But it's girly, not the kind of place I would have pictured you living."

He stopped at the bar and poured himself a Scotch. He downed it like liquid candy. "What can I say? It's the best."

And he only owned the best? Not surprising, superior as he was. She plopped on the edge of a velvet chair, the material soft against her pants. What would it feel like against her skin? *Don't go there.* "Okay, I can't stand it anymore. You were joking, right? We can't possibly be married. We didn't say vows or anything."

He didn't face her, but poured himself another drink. His phone rang again, and once again he ignored it. "Afraid we are, sweetheart," he said bitterly. "Good news is, you married a very wealthy man. Isn't that what you always wanted?"

"Yeah, but I also wanted to, I don't know, *like* my husband." Her stomach knotted. "You can't be right about this. You just can't be."

He kept his back to her.

He was lucky she didn't stalk over there and club him in the head. "How do you know about vampire mating customs, anyway? Have you married one before?"

There was a boom as he slammed his glass into the counter. "First thing the king asked me when I returned two of his cousins to their underground home was whether

I'd given them my blood. I said yes. Second thing he asked me was whether or not I had drunk from them. When I informed him that I hadn't, he slapped me on the back and told me it was a good thing, else I would have been living the rest of my life down there with my wife."

Or wives, since he'd had two. Or would he only have been mated to the first woman he drank from? God, this was confusing. "Well, I wasn't raised there, so I'm not going to live according to their customs. Same with you. You're from another planet, for God's sake. You don't have to abide by vampire customs. Right?"

"Actually, I do." Yet another call came in, its shrill ring making her jump. "*We* do. If you want to stay alive, that is."

"First, aren't you going to answer that?"

Without looking at her, he jerked out the phone and pressed it to his ear. "What?"

She could hear Macy's frantic voice on the other end.

"She's fine. She'll call you in a few hours." *Click*. He pressed a button and slid the device across the counter, away from him.

Bride's hands curled into fists. "I would have liked to talk to her."

"Too bad."

What an ass. "Second," she said, picking up their conversation where it had left off, "what were you talking about? If I want to stay alive, I'll stay married to you? We aren't even married, so I can't *stay* married to you!"

"Just . . . be quiet, damn it." He plowed his fingers through his hair and rested his forehead in his upraised palms. "I've been thinking about this since you told me about your eating problem, and I have a theory."

Silence. He raised and drained another glass of Scotch. The bottle was empty, so he couldn't pour another. Finally, he turned to her. His eyes were glowing, sparking with angry fire.

He blamed her for this and had yet to forgive her it. Well, he could suck it! It wasn't like she'd known what she'd been doing. Wasn't like she'd *wanted* to marry him. "You have a theory?"

He gave a clipped nod. "You were able to keep all of my blood down."

Yes, and because of that she was thinking clearer than she had in months, was stronger than she'd ever been, and despite the fact that her nerves were on edge, there was no sting or burn in her chest. She was keeping the thorns and the fire at bay.

None of those wonderful things were worth *this*, however.

"I knew I should have resisted you," she grumbled.

"As if you could."

That sounded more like the Devyn she knew, and she found herself relaxing in the chair. "Your theory."

"Perhaps, as slowly as vampires age, your body had finally reached sexual maturity, and in order for a sexually mature female to sustain herself, she must drink from her mate. The blood you were ingesting before me was not from your mate, therefore your body rejected it. That means you can only take from your husband. That means you'll only ever be able to take from your husband."

"First, I was able to keep your blood down *before* we mated, as you called it. Second, as you yourself said, I was unable to keep the bulk of other blood down before

I met you. And third, if you're right, that would mean we were fated to be together, and I don't believe in fate. Not like that."

"I'm not talking about fate." His eyes were grave. "I think you saw or sensed me a month ago, wanted me, and paired us in your mind. From that moment on, your body would have accepted only my blood."

"My God. Just when I think you can't get any more egotistical, you go and prove me wrong."

He didn't respond, just waited.

"This is crazy." Yes, crazy. But as she thought back to their first meeting, she remembered how she'd smelled two scents on him, both of them familiar. One had been Macy's. The other, his. Again her stomach twisted painfully.

His cell phone buzzed, disrupting the uneasy quiet. He checked the ID, muttered a curse, then placed it at his ear. "Yeah?"

A moment passed.

His expression hardened. "Don't kill them." Another pause. "Yeah, I'd love some. Tomorrow, though." There was a heavy tension-laden pause. "Later." He closed the phone and shoved it in his pocket.

As wonderfully as her ears were now working, she'd heard every word on the other end. Apparently three other slavers had entered her apartment, and Dallas had wanted to know if Devyn desired "a little alone time with them." But when Dallas had said, "Now let's talk about your promise to Mia," Devyn had replied, "Later," and hung up on him.

"What did you promise Mia?"

He blinked at her. "Excellent hearing, I see."

Had the other vampires not heard as well? Even sated with blood? "You're stalling. Tell me."

"I'm not stalling. I'm refusing to answer. Learn the difference. Right now we're in the middle of a discussion. A discussion we *will* finish."

Her eyes narrowed on him. "We're finished now. I'm not married to you. And if you're right and I need to drink from a man, a husband, to survive, I'll find someone else."

She never saw him move, but he was in her face a moment later, his nose pressing into hers, his warm breath fanning over her skin. "Maybe I'll let you. But not now. Not today. Today you're mine. You made sure of that."

"Fuck you," she growled up at him.

"Yes. You will. Many times, I'm sure." He grabbed her knees and pried her thighs apart, jerking her forward while inserting himself in the V. "You can't tell me some part of you isn't happy about this."

She gasped, but didn't pull away. "Believe me, happiness is not what I'm feeling right now."

A muscle twitched below his eye. "Well, then. I guess that makes you more like my first wife than I'd realized."

Wait. What? "You've been married before?"

"Yes. But again, not by choice."

Her confusion was only growing. "Then why—"

"No more talking. I've never been this angry in my life, and you're going to help me calm down." He arched into her, his erection brushing against her core. "Do you know how you're going to help me calm down, sweetheart?"

"I can guess." She hated how breathless she sounded. How needy.

"No objections?"

"No. I'm angry, too."

Before the last word had emerged, his lips were meshed into hers and his body was pushing her backward, against the lounge. His cock was long, hard, and thick, rubbing between her thighs, insistently this time, making her wet, hot.

Her hands were in his hair before she could stop them, her tongue thrusting against his. His decadent flavor filled her mouth, drugging her, luring her deeper into the darkness of his passion. Just then, she couldn't make their current situation or the future matter. Right now he was with her, in her arms, hers for the taking, kissing her, touching her just right, and she'd been without him for days, an eternity surely, craving him, hoping for this very thing.

He'd lose interest in her afterward. He wouldn't be able to help himself. That was just who he was. He'd forget the whole marriage thing, and then, so could Bride. Her life could return to what it had been. Only, now she had Macy.

His fingers pried at the waist of her pants. When the tie refused to loosen, he ripped it in half and shoved the material to her knees. He had to pull from the kiss to work them to her ankles, and she moaned at the loss.

"Not done with your mouth, sweetheart. Don't worry."

"Hurry." She didn't want to come to her senses and talk herself out of this. She wanted him pumping inside her, deep and hard and forever. No, no. Not forever. Today. Only this once. "I ache for you."

One boot, two, were discarded, the pants finally free of her body, and then Devyn returned, pinning her down, tongue wild against hers. "I want you. Have to have you."

She tugged at his shirt, jerking it over his head before dropping it on the floor. She traced her fingers over his skull-and-dagger tattoo. Such soft, warm skin. "I'm not going to beg you for it."

"No need. That's not on the menu until tomorrow."

She almost laughed. She did plant her heels on the edge of the lounge, widening her knees and inviting him closer. With a groan of surrender, he sank against her, the fabric of his pants wonderfully abrasive against her, the panties she wore doing little to shield her.

"Have you thought of me these past few days? Doing this? Touching you?" He kissed his way down her throat.

"I was too busy."

"Bride." It was a warning. He placed his lips just over her hardened nipple, his warm breath teasing her even through her bra, as if he wouldn't give her greater contact unless she told him what he wanted to hear.

As if she'd admit to imagining the two of them together like this. "Why do you care?"

"I don't."

"I didn't think so. So shut up and finish undressing me."

His eyes, already hot, became searing. He gripped her panties and jerked them down her legs. He bunched the hem of her shirt and tugged upward, her hair falling around her in tangles as the material left her. The bra he simply ripped in half, the front clasp no more resistant than a whisper.

Then she was bare. His gaze drank her in, his pupils dilating. His fingers inched up her naked thighs and spread her for his view. "Wet," he praised. "Pretty."

"Inside. Now."

Never one to obey, he lowered his head and licked her. She cried out, her back arching, hips shooting straight in the air. Reaching back, she grabbed the edge of the chair. It was either that or fist his hair and hold him down. Strong as she was feeling, she was afraid of breaking his neck. If she broke his neck, he wouldn't be able to finish this.

"Better than honey," he said, his voice tickling her. "Better, even, than your energy."

As he continued to lick and suck and nibble at her, he kneaded her breasts, attacking her from every angle. "Oh, God," she gasped when his wicked tongue flicked and circled in a naughty rhythm she'd never before experienced.

But then she thought, *How do I compare to all the others?* and a little of her excitement died. Did she taste as good as the others? Did she taste as good as Ann, Claire, and Madison, the three agents he'd been with and discarded? The *beautiful* agents? Did she excite him as much as the others?

For the first time in her life, Bride was self-conscious and unsure about her appeal. And she didn't like it!

Was he thinking of someone else even now? Wishing she were as violent or as sweet as someone else? Her hips ceased their frantic gyrations. Maybe this wasn't such a great idea. Maybe she should stop him. Maybe she should leave.

Then he did that thing with his tongue again, sinking it as deep inside her as it could go while his teeth scraped at her clitoris and she groaned at the heady pleasure. Maybe she could stay for a little while longer.

He inserted a finger, stretching her, his tongue now

dancing over her. Her nipples were hard, straining. Good, so good. She wanted his mouth on them, too. She wanted his mouth everywhere at once, his hands enjoying her, playing her like an instrument.

"Yes, yes, yes." She released the chair to grip his head and hold him against her; she couldn't help herself. He could live with a broken neck, which meant he could finish. "More, give me more."

He did, one hand once again kneading her breasts, the other still pumping inside her. Two fingers now, filling her up, propelling her higher. The fact that the thorns and fire were not plaguing her added to her enjoyment.

Were Devyn's hands enjoying her, though? Had they enjoyed other women more? Women who were softer? Lusher?

Her grip loosened, the hottest flames of her passion cooling. Why was she doing this to herself? Why did she care what he thought?

Things were different now, she realized. Before, when she and Devyn had made out, she hadn't truly pondered the idea of him with other women because he hadn't mattered to her. His opinion hadn't mattered. She could have left him. Now, despite everything, despite what she'd told him, she liked him.

"Bride," Devyn snarled, his breath hot against her damp folds.

"Devyn," she said. She didn't know how else to reply.

He growled low in his throat, pulled from her, and straightened. He unsnapped his pants and kicked them off, leaving his body as bare as hers. His erection was so swollen and long it reached over his navel. His stomach was so deliciously corded with muscle, her mouth watered.

His skin was glowing brightly, her desire glistening around his mouth. As she watched, he swiped his tongue over his lips, licking at the essence of her. His eyes closed, his mouth lifting in a half-smile as though he savored the taste.

"D—Devyn," she repeated.

He was on her a second later, cock at her entrance and probing. Then he was thrusting deep, all the way inside, and they were both moaning and groaning and panting at the bliss.

He pulled out, sank deeper, and she clawed at his back. He pulled out again, sank to the hilt, and she wrapped her legs around his waist, locking her ankles together. What did he prefer, though? For his women to keep their legs off him and wide? For them to drape their legs over his shoulders?

"Bride!" Despite his savage tone, he gently cupped her cheeks, forcing her attention on him. "Are you trying to piss me off?"

She shook her head, incapable of speech. What was his problem? He was getting laid, wasn't he? Or was her leg placement as bad as she'd assumed?

He growled low in his throat, once more bringing her focus to his face. "Don't look away from me. Understand?"

This time she nodded.

Slowly he thrust forward. It was heaven, it was hell, it was everything and nothing because she needed more. Had to have more. Would die without it, but would die with it. Too much, too good. Nothing compared. His eyes glowed, hypnotizing her, holding her captive. And when he moved inside her again, slowly, so agonizingly slow, she cried out, the sound echoing around them.

"So beautiful," he said. "You are so beautiful. And my God, do you taste sweet. You're so wet. Clasp me just right. And did I ever tell you how addictive your energy is? It's raw, savage, powerful, and every time I even brush against it, I find myself hard as a rock."

His words were as electrifying as a caress, and she found herself drowning in him, all that he was, her fangs elongating. "Devyn, Devyn, Devyn," she chanted. She'd already taken a lot of his blood, shouldn't take more, shouldn't want to give him more of her own.

As if sensing her thoughts, he angled his head to the side. "Drink," he commanded.

Helpless to do otherwise, she sank her fangs into his neck and gulped him back. The instant his blood hit her tongue, she climaxed, pinpricks of white lightning exploding behind her eyelids. Every muscle in her body clenched and unclenched on her bones. It was the first orgasm she'd ever had that wasn't mixed with pain, and it was paradise. Pure and perfect and shattering.

"Devyn!"

A roar split his lips, and then he was kissing her again. No, not kissing. Biting her tongue and drawing her blood, sucking that blood down his throat. Taking her inside *him.*

Just like that, Bride climaxed again, and this time Devyn joined her, shaking, jetting hot seed inside her, skin now so bright the room looked swallowed by the sun. He released her jaw to grab onto her hips, squeezing so tightly her bones might snap, but she didn't care.

He stilled and then collapsed on top of her. She lost her breath and would have complained, but he quickly rolled to the side and locked his arms around her so that she couldn't move away.

In the ensuing silence, Bride finally did regain her senses. She glared up at the ceiling, gasped when she saw a lovely mural of angels flying through the heavens, and fought to compose herself. "Devyn," she began.

"I know. It was wonderful. Now let's just enjoy the afterglow in silence."

She pinched the bridge of her nose. "You took more of my blood, you idiot."

"I'm not going to turn into a vampire, so what do you care? You nearly drained me again, and I needed to replenish."

Argh! "That's not what I meant. Last time you had my blood, you ended up married. Remember?"

"So taking more doesn't really matter, now does it?" he said, his tone devoid of emotion. "It's not like you can marry me again."

At least he wasn't yelling at her this time. "And anyway, we're not married."

"You just said we were."

"Oh, just shut up and enjoy the afterglow."

CHAPTER 17

Never had Devyn had to work so hard to give a woman an orgasm. To his consternation, Bride's mind had drifted several times while he'd had his mouth on her. And during some of his best moves, at that.

Okay, fine. They hadn't been moves. He'd been operating on instinct alone, unable to think rationally, only to feel. To give and to take. And just when he would think, *Yes, this is it, she's with me,* she would stop writhing, stop moaning. He'd wondered what he was doing wrong and how the hell he could make it better for her. He did not fail, damn it. Not at sex.

Still. Never had he doubted himself so much, and never had success been so important. He would have spent hours, days, weeks, on this lounge with her. Whatever it took. There was no way he would have let Bride leave him disappointed. His pride couldn't have withstood it. More than that, he remembered what it had been like before, when she'd come on his fingers. Even angry as he'd been, there at the beginning, he'd *needed* that again.

When she had finally fallen over the edge, he'd felt

like king of the universe rather than the king of his own world. Her eyes had closed, her lashes casting shadows over her cheeks, and her teeth had sunk into her bottom lip. She'd arched her back, sending him deeper inside her, and she'd clawed at his flesh, lost in the bliss. She'd panted his name, raspy and sweet, and it had felt like an embrace inside his ears. This time, her cries had not been laced with pain, so he'd relished them all the more.

Everything about her body pleased him. Her taste especially . . .

Once he had thought he wanted to taste a Rakan more than anything else in the world because they were supposedly like honey. But who cared about honey when nirvana was available? He'd had Bride all over his face, down his throat, in his stomach, and it still hadn't been enough. Already he hungered for more.

What was he going to do?

He hadn't wanted another wife. He still didn't. But the fury was gone, and he did like the thought of having Bride in his house, at his beck and call. He grinned at that. Bride, catering to his every whim. As if she'd really do what he told her to do when he told her to do it. Contrary female.

So what was he going to do with her? What would happen when he tired of her or turned his attentions to someone else? And he would, he just knew it. He always did. Not that he'd ever wanted a woman this intensely. Or for this long. Bride would still need his blood. Would die without it now, if the information he had was correct.

"We've been laying here for, like, ever," Bride said,

cutting into the silence. "I'm not a pansy like someone I know but out of courtesy won't name and in need of a nap. I just want to go home."

"For now, *this* is your home. And I am not a pansy. The nap was for your benefit." Of course, he ruined the boast by yawning.

She twisted in his arms, facing him. Her eyes were luminous, her lips soft and redder than usual. Strands of hair were plastered to her temple. "Sure you want to venture down that road of conversation right now?"

Meaning, she was going to argue about it. "Cut me some slack, sweetheart. I'm having trouble remembering my own name."

At that, she grinned, slowly but sweetly. "I don't know how you do it, *Brad,* but you're the only person on earth who can infuriate me one moment and have me laughing the next."

Brad indeed. "It's called animal magnetism, darling, and I have more than most."

"Oh, please."

"See. It even has you begging for more."

She slapped his shoulder, but her grin didn't slip.

Just then, it was as if they were friends as well as lovers. He . . . liked it. Liked her relaxed and teasing. Too bad he was about to ruin the mood. "Want to tell me where you were mentally while I had my face between your legs?"

That pretty grin faded, and he suddenly felt like punching something. "No," she said, cheeks pinkening. "I don't. Do you want to tell me what happened to your first marriage? Not that you're married again," she added hastily.

At least she hadn't tried to pretend ignorance about her disappearing act. "We'll exchange information, all right? I believe you remember the rules."

At first, she gave no response; her gaze simply searched his face. Looking for what, he didn't know. Finally, she nodded. "No bullshit about ladies first. This was your idea, so start talking."

"Fine. My wife." The shrew was his second least favorite subject. The first, of course, was his father. "We were betrothed at birth and married at the age of fifteen. We—she'd been raised to view sex as dirty, so we didn't get along. I left her." A glossed-over version, but the truth just the same, and easier to say than he'd expected. "Now it's your turn."

Moaning, Bride flopped to her back and threw her arm over her forehead. "You wanted to know where I was mentally while you were . . . you know." She sighed. "Well, you've been with a lot of women."

"I've never tried to deny it," he said as dread slid into his veins. He could guess where she was heading with this, and it didn't bode well for him.

"Well, I was feeling totally inadequate. How could I not, well, wonder how I compared to the others?"

Yep. His sigh mirrored hers. He'd gone through this with a few others, and he'd laughingly told them that no one compared to them. They had been words to soothe, to delight, and to move on to the loving. Here, now, he didn't want to utter such a claim. For once, he feared he might actually mean it. And if she realized that he meant it, would she then assume their marriage was forever? Probably.

He couldn't let Bride wallow in feelings of inadequacy, though. That would be cruel. *When have you ever cared about being cruel?* He just liked her confident, he told himself. She was more fun that way.

"You confuse, fascinate, irritate, and delight me," he said, "and I swear to God the only thing I was thinking about while tasting and touching you was you."

A moment passed as she absorbed his words. She raised her chin and hooked her arms behind her head, raising one leg to study her onyx-painted toenails. "Well, of course you were only thinking of me. I'm the best thing that's ever happened to you."

That's my girl. "I guess I proved that by marrying you." Now why had he said that?

She snorted. "We aren't married, moron."

"Yes, we are." *Stop, stop, stop.* "Why don't you tell me what you did for a living before scoring a sugar daddy?"

Another snort, but once again she twisted into him. This time she rested her head on his shoulder and began circling one of his nipples with her fingertips. "Are you sure you want to know?"

"Yes."

"I stole, okay. I wasn't lazy or anything," she assured him. "I was just afraid to take a job and spend time around humans. One, their smell sometimes makes me sick, and two, I was afraid they'd notice the differences in me, start to question what I was. Three, I believe I've mentioned that the sun is uncomfortable for me."

"Are you any good at stealing?"

"Hello. I'm the best."

"Guaranteed you aren't better than me, but do continue with your story."

"You steal things?"

"The hearts of women across the uni—verse. Ow!" There at the end, she had pinched his nipple. "No more of that, or you'll owe me a new one."

She kissed it better, and he had to press his lips together to stop his groan. "I started stealing full time to feed Al—Macy," she said. "She was just a kid, left on the streets like a piece of garbage. I'd never needed food, but she did, so I learned to get it for her. I'd done some stealing for myself throughout the years, clothes, shoes, that sort of thing, but time hadn't been of the essence, so I'd never really honed my skills. I just waited until an opportunity presented itself. With Macy, I couldn't wait and I wasn't always successful. Had a few run-ins with the law until I learned the best methods. After we were separated, I kept it up so I wouldn't be rusty when she returned. And well, I liked owning pretty things. What about you? What kind of childhood did you have?"

"I was pampered," he said, each word measured. He prayed she left it at that. Not even Dallas knew about Devyn's parents, about the humiliating time spent inside that darkened cell. About his shame.

She gave his nipple another kiss. "That tells me nothing. Pampered doesn't mean happy."

No, it didn't. But that kiss, so sweetly offered, without any demand for repayment, soothed the bleakness of his memories as nothing else ever had. Even sex. "I was also . . . repressed." Okay, that was enough of that. He quickly changed the subject, least he crumble and tell her everything. Would she be horrified if he did? Agree with his father that he was a bad, naughty boy in need of neutering? "How often do you need to feed?"

"To maintain top strength, I need to feed once a day, but I've gone weeks without eating before. Well, without eating a full meal."

And she'd starved. That would not happen again. Not while she was with him. "You'll feed once a day, and that's that."

"You won't be able to keep up. Who could? So I can—"

"Hell, no, you won't," he interjected. "I'll keep up." The thought of her drinking from anyone else roused the beast inside him. The thought of her enduring hunger pains because she didn't consider him able to give her more had the beast roaring. "Besides, you can't keep anyone else's blood down."

She huffed. "That's not true. I told you, the first sips are absorbed before I sicken."

"Don't even try it, Bride." His teeth were so clenched he had trouble getting the words out. He might not want forever from her, but he damn well wanted right now. "I swear to you now, I will kill anyone you drink from." Before she could comment, he sat up and tugged her with him. "We need to shower. Come on."

He stood, pulling her alongside him. Thankfully, she didn't protest. He linked their fingers and ushered her toward the stairs.

"We should put some clothes on, at least," she muttered halfway up.

"Why? We're alone. I gave the servants the day off."

Her eyes widened as she peered up at him. "You have servants?"

"*We* have servants, and yes. Eight of them." They were all Arcadians, given to him by Kyrin en Arr.

"Have you slept with any of them?"

The question had held simple curiosity rather than anger. Did she not mind the thought of him with others? He popped his jaw. He'd just threatened to kill anyone she drank from, yet she couldn't rouse a spark of jealousy?

"I'd never had an Arcadian before, so I took four to bed the very first week I moved in."

She laughed. Actually laughed. "God, you're a slut."

Serioulsy. Where was the jealousy? Why hadn't she demanded he fire the women immediately? "You're okay with that? Me, with four different women, one after the other? Women who still live in this house with me?"

"Why would I care? You're not sleeping with them now. Knowing you, you're already tired of the race. And as we already agreed, I'm the best thing that's ever happened to you."

Maddening, that's what she was. "I'll give you a tour later." She didn't deserve one now. At the top of the staircase, he veered right, passed the first four doorways, and stopped at the end of the hall. A quick thumbprint ID, and the last entrance opened. "This is our room."

Bride gasped when she stepped inside, and he bit back a smile. Just the reaction he'd been hoping for, he thought, suddenly filled with pride. The master suite was spacious, with a large bed covered in silk—real silk, not that fake shit—and mahogany furniture. There were mirrors on every wall, and portraits of naked females frolicking with each other.

Bride inhaled deeply, closed her eyes. "It smells wonderful in here."

Not as good as you. He released her hand but wasn't able to sever all contact, so he wound an arm around her lower back, spreading his fingers wide to touch all of her that he could. His pinkie sank between her cheeks. She didn't protest. She wasn't so maddening, after all.

"Bathroom is this way." He had to lead her to keep her from running into things because she kept her head turned, studying the room in wonder.

The bathroom was already open, and just as spacious. There was a claw-foot tub, a porcelain sink, and a shower stall with two waterspouts.

Again, Bride gasped in wonder. "My God. That's not . . . it isn't an enzyme stall."

"No."

She faced him, trembling hands on his chest. His cock, already thickening and desperate for another go at her, brushed the cleft between her legs. "Real water comes out?"

"Yes."

Her eyes closed, and an expression of utter ecstasy consumed her features. "I haven't had one of those in sixty years or so."

"Let's not make you wait a second longer, then," he said huskily. He walked over to the stall and worked the knobs. A gust of water burst from the nozzle, stopped, and then a continuous spray emerged. Soon steam wafted, surrounding them.

Bride didn't have to be commanded inside. She pushed Devyn out of the way and stepped into the water. A delighted laugh chimed from her as the water pummeled her, splashing into her hair and soaking its way down her body.

Never had Devyn seen a more beautiful sight. She was an angel, a siren, and a goddess, all wrapped in Temptation's skin. Her joy was palpable, and he had given this to her, he thought, his pride intensifying.

Water was expensive, but damn if he wouldn't spend his last cent buying it for her from this moment on. *Until you tire of her, right?* He stepped inside, and hot droplets beat against him, massaging his tired muscles.

Their eyes met, and she gradually lost her grin. Her gaze slid to his penis. She gulped. Shivered.

"Ready for round two already, Bradley?" Her nipples beaded, and the pulse at the base of her neck fluttered.

"Been ready. I've just been waiting for you to catch up."

She gave another of those delicious laughs.

His cock jerked in reaction. "Have you ever had sex in water?"

"No. So let's change that, shall we?"

A few blissful hours later, Bride found herself standing in front of her—old?—apartment door, Devyn at her side. He'd made love to her inside the shower, slowly, tenderly, but with an air of urgency she hadn't understood but had felt herself. She couldn't seem to get enough of him. How foolish was that? Soon her supply would be cut off, whether by Devyn or herself, and she'd *have* to do without him. Wanting more was dumb.

To be honest, she just couldn't see them lasting much longer. They liked each other now, sure, and the sex was amazing. Soon, though, someone else would come along and catch his notice. When that happened, she would leave. Bride absolutely refused to hang where she wasn't wanted. That feeling of inadequacy . . . she shuddered.

She'd experienced it only briefly, but that had been enough to assure her she never wanted to feel that way again. Ugh. Just ugh.

She would have to keep an emotional distance between them for when the inevitable break came, and yet somehow still allow herself to touch and taste him and experience the heaven that was his body. Might be difficult. The man definitely knew how to steal female hearts.

He rasped his knuckles against the metal.

"I don't understand why we have to knock," she grumbled. "It's my apartment."

"Actually, it's ours. I get fifty percent of your assets."

"Touch my books, and I'll cut off your hands."

"Ha! You need my hands more than I do."

A dark-haired, dark-skinned man opened the door, saving her from replying. She'd seen the gorgeous agent before, knew who he was, but had never spoken to him.

He flashed her a bright, white smile as he leaned against the frame. His ice-blue eyes glowed merrily. "Don't think we've met officially. I'm Dallas, the big guy's best friend."

"Bride . . ." What was Devyn's last name? Bride suddenly wondered. Did he even have one? And would he want her to use it? *Stop. You aren't really married to him.* "McKells. Bride McKells."

"Just Bride," Devyn said with a growl.

Dallas's grin widened. "Come in, come in. Macy's waiting."

Macy was here? Bride pushed past the agent without another word and sailed inside. It was her place, anyway, and she could do what she wanted. Sure enough, Macy was inside the kitchen, fixing dinner. Sandwiches. Someone must have gone shopping.

When her friend spotted her, she stopped what she was doing and rushed forward, features dark with concern. "Thank God. I've been so worried about you."

Bride hugged her tight. "I'm fine, I promise. How are you?"

"Fine." Macy pulled back and studied her. "I hear you're married. Is that true?"

"No," she said with a determined shake of her head.

"We're still hammering out the details," Devyn said from behind her.

She almost stomped her foot. "There aren't any details to hammer out."

"So anyway, it's our lucky day," she heard Dallas tell Devyn, who subsequently ignored her. "Nolan finally gave up his queen's landing point."

She and Macy shared a look of understanding, then quieted, listening to the men while pretending they were cleaning the kitchen.

"Yeah, but do we trust him?" Devyn asked.

There was a rustle of clothing. Dallas must have shrugged. "Mia's got a crew staking out the place now, ready to stun her. Nolan was stunnable that first time, too, remember? Anyway, you didn't let me finish. I went ahead and interrogated the human slavers."

Bride spun around, no longer content to pretend not to listen. The human slavers. She'd forgotten about them. "What did they say?"

Macy moved to her side and gripped her hand. One of

them was trembling, but she couldn't tell which. Perhaps they both were.

Devyn jabbed a finger into Dallas's wide chest, again ignoring her. "I told you I would handle them."

Far from intimidated, Dallas grinned. "And Mia told everyone in the building to keep you out of their cells. She didn't want their heads on the evening news. Anyway, I interrogated them in a manner you would have approved of and got the date and time of their next auction. A week from tomorrow. Bride's potential buyer is going to be there, because two other vampires have been caught."

Other vampires had been caught? They were to be sold? Enslaved? Bile rose in her throat.

Macy's arm wound around her, offering comfort.

"You know something else. Tell me," Devyn commanded.

Dallas paused, his expression hardening. "Here's the thing. Remember the vision I had?"

A clipped nod from Devyn.

"Moment I heard about the auction, something dark clicked inside me, and I knew, *knew*. If you go, you'll start a chain of unstoppable events that will not end well for you." Another pause, mouth grim. "Maybe they'll even lead to the pier."

CHAPTER 18

$\mathcal{B}$ride wondered about Dallas's comment while soaking in Devyn's tub later that evening. What chain of events? What was supposed to happen at the pier? She'd asked Devyn, but he'd distracted her with sex, the slut, and she'd gotten no answers.

When Dallas had spoken in that grim tone, his baby blues solemn, she'd experienced an overpowering flood of dread. Both men were certain something bad was going to happen to Devyn at the pier. She was sure of it. But what?

After a while, she gave up trying to figure it out on her own. Her brain seemed to be on hiatus, anyway, steam wafting around her, soft music playing in the background. A girl could get used to this.

Devyn strode into the bathroom, spotted her, and grinned slowly, wickedly. "What do we have here?"

Bubbles fluffed the surface, hiding the sudden hardening of her nipples. "Get that look off your face. We are not going for round four." Or would it be round five? "I'm relaxing." And God, it was divine. The water was warm, soothing, lapping fantastically at her skin.

Rather than leave, he perched at the edge of the porcelain. "I should join you. It's still our honeymoon, you know."

"We're not married, but I *am* going to enjoy this while I can." She sank deeper into the liquid paradise. Her hair was anchored in a knot on top of her head, so she didn't have to worry about soaking it. "Actually, I just changed my mind. We are married. I'll take this house, and therefore this tub, in the divorce settlement. What are you worth, anyway?"

He dipped in his hand and flicked several drops on her face. "A lot."

"Excellent," she said with a grin. "Half of a lot will be very nice."

"Diabolical woman," he muttered. "Thinking of leaving me already when I came bearing a gift."

"A gift?" She straightened, clapped excitedly. "For me? Really?"

"No, for my other pseudo-wife."

"Let me see, let me see."

Grinning, he reached into his pocket and withdrew a small black box. It couldn't be, she thought. Surely wasn't . . . he flipped the lid, and her eyes widened in shock. Not a ring—she was *not* disappointed—but a . . . she leaned closer. A necklace charm, she realized. An emerald, like the one she'd given Macy. Only bigger. And shinier.

"I noticed you returned hers," he said, no longer

sounding as confident as he had before. "If you don't like it, I can—"

"I love it. Give me!" She snatched the box before he could put it away and clutched it to her chest. It was the sweetest, most thoughtful present she'd ever received. Her chest was aching, and it had nothing to do with the thorns or the fire. "Thank you."

His gaze met hers, a gleam she couldn't read in his eyes. He coughed, clearing his throat as if he were uncomfortable. "You're, uh, welcome. I'll get you a chain for it. I just didn't have one handy."

"Thank you for that in advance." She bit her bottom lip. "I don't have anything for you."

"Don't worry," he said, flicking a little more water on her face. Those amber eyes were practically sparkling with sensual intent now, whatever else had been resting there gone as if it had never been. "I'm sure I'll think of some way for you to repay my amazing generosity."

Her body instantly reacted, her stomach quivering, her blood heating. She was beginning to love his inflated ego and insatiable appetite. "Ah, yes. That wouldn't happen to involve my wifely duty in your bed, would it?"

He didn't whisk her from the tub and carry her to said bed or even slip into the tub with her, as she'd halfway expected. Rather, he tilted his head, his lips dipping into a frown. The desire in those magnificent amber eyes even died.

He pushed to his feet. "I have some things to do." His voice was flat, faraway. "You'll be fine on your own."

O-kay. What had she said? "Sure you can't join me?"

she found herself asking. She might have told him there'd be no sex while she was relaxing, but she hadn't meant it. Not really.

"I'm sure." He left her without another word.

Wifely duty, she'd said. Wifely duty.

Which meant, Devyn had a husbandly duty. According to his father, that duty involved respecting her body, mind, and soul. *You don't follow your father's rules anymore.*

For the moment, she *was* his wife, and he did want to do right by her. That had become clear when she had not used his last name while introducing herself to Dallas, as was custom for humans. Her cheeks had even darkened with color. She hadn't known how to introduce herself, hadn't known her place in his life, and had most likely been embarrassed by that. That embarrassment had shamed him, even though *he* didn't know her place in his life. He'd thought, *She is my responsibility right now, and I have failed her.*

He didn't want that proud woman embarrassed in front of anyone. Even himself.

He didn't know what to do with her. Didn't know what he felt about—or for—her. All he knew was that he didn't want her thinking she meant nothing. Every moment he spent in her presence, he liked her more. When they'd returned from her apartment, he'd spent an hour thinking of ways to make her smile and laugh. That's when he recalled the emerald charm he'd purchased after meeting her. He hadn't realized at the time, but he'd bought it because it had reminded him of her eyes.

He'd given it to her and gotten the reaction he'd craved. He'd thought to spend a few hours basking in that reaction. In bed, of course, naked and straining for release. Then . . . Wifely duty. Husbandly duty.

Though she no longer showed any signs of it, her previous insecurity still haunted him. *He* had caused it. *He* had destroyed her delightful self-confidence. Before, he'd even made her cry—and he'd wanted to die! Had he not been so angry, he might have.

When he'd decided to ignore his guilt and shame all those years ago, he must have muted all his other emotions. No wonder female tears hadn't bothered him. No wonder he could kill so easily. Now that Bride was in his life, now that he had another wife, the guilt was returning, so his other emotions must be making themselves known, as well.

Damn this. He had to give Bride *something* to prove he wasn't the barbarian she assumed. It was his husbandly duty. And he knew of only one way to show her that he *did* respect her, he *did* value her, and he would care for her properly while they were together.

Devyn stripped and jumped into the pool in his backyard. He swam lap after lap, not stopping until he was panting, sweating even though the water was cold. To respect a female, a male did not press his baser urges on her. He did not press his baser urges on anyone.

"I'm telling you, Macy, after that bubble bath, everything changed between us, and by the end of the week, what I knew would happen, happened," Bride said into the phone. Devyn was gone, again, doing God knew what.

"What's that?" her friend asked.

"Devyn's grown tired of me." She tried to keep the pout from her voice. They hadn't slept in the same bed. Not once. She slept in his room, and he crashed in the bedroom next door. "He feeds me once a day, but that's it. That's the only time he touches me."

She'd tiptoed inside his chosen chamber that first night, meaning to slide in beside him and have a little fun. He'd been hard as a rock, yet he'd picked her up and carried her back. And he hadn't stayed with her! He'd immediately stomped back to the other room.

"Oh, Bride. I'm sorry. Is he seeing someone else?"

"I don't think so. I mean, he's churlish, like he's not getting any at all. Even from himself, if you know what I mean." She flung herself on the mattress, the beads on her harem costume clinking together. She, Devyn, and Dallas were due to attend the slave auction in just a few hours, something she was both nervous and excited about. Finally, she would meet another vampire. "Plus, he's not the kind to cheat. Yeah, he's a slut, but he's also brutally honest."

"What are you going to do?"

"I've offered to leave. Several times. He just hands me wads of cash and tells me to buy something pretty."

"Do you?" her friend asked with a laugh.

"I horde it, of course. But that's not all he's done. He even bought me a bowl of apples and cherries because I mentioned I liked their smell. I don't understand him!"

"Maybe he doesn't understand himself."

Maybe. "Let's just . . . I don't know, let's talk about something else. My blood pressure is rising."

Sadly, the thorns and fire were no longer content in the shadows. They'd reappeared a few days ago, probably because she'd never been so frustrated in her life, and hadn't let up since. Even now she had to rub her breastbone to ease the ache.

"Nolan is still doing well," Macy said. "Hasn't relapsed at all."

"Has he been declared healed?"

"Not yet. AIR had to kill the last doctors who tested him, so no one's willing to volunteer to take his blood this time."

"Understandable."

Downstairs, a door closed. Every muscle in her body stiffened. "I've got to go," she said. "Devyn's back."

Macy's sigh crackled over the line. "You know that I love you, right?"

"Of course. How could you not? I'm amazing."

"Now you sound like him," her friend said with a laugh. "You know that you'll always be in my life, right? No matter what happens to the two of you."

Bride fingered the emerald even now dangling at her throat. "Just as you'll be in mine. I love you, Leah Leah."

"See you tonight, Bridey Boo."

They hung up, and Bride tossed the phone on the nightstand beside a glass of water. She liked to dip her fingers in it, just to remind herself that she had access to it. She stood just as Devyn strode inside the room. He looked gorgeous in a black shirt and jeans, his hair disheveled by the wind.

He stopped short when he spotted her, his gaze hot as

it raked over her mostly bare body. Then he turned, giving her his back. "Good. You're ready." As usual lately, his voice was emotionless.

Who would have thought she'd actually miss his unabashed obsession with sex?

So badly, she wanted him to walk to her, take her in his arms, and—her eyes widened as he quickly stumbled toward her and threw himself at her. They fell into the mattress, and a gasp of delight escaped her. His muscled weight was divine.

"Finally," she purred, wrapping her limbs around him. "I don't know what changed your mind, but I'm grateful."

Frowning, he straightened, severing all contact. He looked behind himself. "What just happened?" he demanded.

Frowning herself, she eased up. "What do you mean?"

"It was like hands were on my back, shoving me forward. I couldn't stop myself."

"Wait. So you didn't want to have a quickie?"

"Can you be serious for just a minute?" he snapped.

Now *he* was accusing *her* of being lax. Priceless, she thought darkly. Just freaking priceless. "I wasn't behind you, so you can't blame me. I was standing there, all innocent, thinking how nice it'd be to touch you again"—a mistake she wouldn't make again—"and then you were racing toward me."

"No one pushed me, but I *was* shoved at you." He crossed his arms over his chest, his biceps bulging. "You were wishing me over, and over I came. That's what you want me to believe?"

"Yes. It's not like I can be two places at once. It's not like I—" Oh, oh, oh, she thought suddenly, excitedly. The thorns and the fire had been insistent lately, just as they'd been insistent each time a new power had revealed itself.

"What?" Devyn asked. "Now you look like you just won our war."

"We're still warring?" Had another power really freed itself? she wondered. Fairly humming at the possibility, she glanced at the nightstand beside the bed. "I wish I was holding that glass of water."

Next thing she knew, one of the table legs was splintering, breaking, and then the table itself was plunging toward her, the glass was sliding off it, and she was frantically leaning over and reaching out. Her fingers snaked around the base before the cup hit the floor and shattered—along with the table—water sloshing out the sides.

"All right. How did you do that?" Another demand from Devyn, but this one was gasped.

Grinning, she balanced the glass on the wooden remains of the tabletop. "Every few years, I gain a new ability. Like misting and cloaking myself. I didn't think I was due for another for a while yet, but tada! Looks like I can now make my wishes come true. How cool is that?"

Clearly Devyn did not share her happiness. He ran his tongue over his teeth as he eyed the remains of his table. "Looks like there are also consequences for your wishes."

True. Some of her excitement waned.

"Wish for something impossible," he said. "Wish for a vampire to appear in this room."

Testing her, was he? "Fine." Bride closed her eyes, wished for a tall, strong, gorgeous vampire male to appear. Naked. Expectant, she opened her eyes. No one appeared. A minute passed, then another. She wished again. Still no one appeared. Her grin faded.

"So there are limits, as well," Devyn said thoughtfully.

"Guess so," she grumbled.

"Well, there's no time to figure them out now. We need to leave. So just keep your thoughts and wishes to a minimum for the time being. That shouldn't be too hard."

Her jaw dropped. "You did *not* just call me ditzy. Because if you did, I'd be wishing all your hair fell out."

"Like that would detract from my appeal," he said, marching into the closet. "Maybe you should stay here tonight."

They were the same words he'd given her this morning during her feeding, when he mentioned going himself, then again when he'd tossed her the sequined bra and see-through pants all purchased female slaves supposedly wore to these things. "I told you. I want to go." If she didn't, she feared he would buy the vampires and give them to AIR before she'd had a chance to talk with them.

"That little wishing thing could get us into trouble." He emerged from the closet, and white-hot breath caught in her throat.

"Wow," she said. He wore a black-and-white pin-striped suit, no wrinkles, a silk tie, and leather shoes.

"Good?" he asked, spinning.

"Not bad. I guess."

For the first time all week, his lips did that twitching thing she so adored. Her heart skipped a beat. "You know I'm hot."

"Whatever."

"Anyway. Like I was saying, you should—"

"I promise. I won't wish for anything." Yet. But only because he was right. She didn't know the consequences or the limitations. Next time she was alone, however, she would find out exactly what this new ability could do and exactly what it couldn't. And she planned to have a lot of fun while she did so.

"Fine. Let's go." Devyn led her to a bright orange modified Scorpion HX in the garage. It was very old, a classic, and too gorgeous to be driven. He claimed the driver's seat, and she settled into the passenger seat, soaking up the leather smell. Rather than start the engine, he peered at her expectantly.

"Slaves don't get to sit up front with their masters." He pointed behind him. "It's back there for you."

"But I'm not really a slave. And what's more, there's no backseat."

"You are tonight. And there's an extended trunk."

If only she *was* a slave. A game of master-slave might have been fun. *Not that I'm wishing for it.* "I'll be more comfortable back there, anyway," she said, shimmying through the space between the driver and passenger side. She had to hunch over to fit.

He'd had the car updated with self-steering and programmed it to stop at Dallas's apartment. Though he didn't have to concentrate on the road, he faced forward, silent, the entire drive there.

As the vehicle slowed and idled just in front of the building, she saw that Dallas was already outside. He claimed the front seat.

"You look nice," she told him, and he did. He wore a suit identical to Devyn's, only a lighter color, because Devyn had bought it for him.

They were the epitome of wealth, while she was the tart du jour. Her hair was loose and curled wildly down her back. She'd stained her lips with the cherries Devyn had given her.

Dallas turned. His eyes widened as they scanned her. "Is my tongue hanging out? Because damn, you look good enough to eat. Seriously, I would buy you up in a heartbeat if you were for sale."

"Attention straight ahead," Devyn growled.

Dallas grinned, but he didn't obey. He winked at her. "The view's better back here."

"Everyone's going to be staring at me and my ridiculous costume when we arrive, anyway," she said. "And no, Devyn, that's not a wish."

"No one will be staring at you," he replied.

"'Cause I'll be dressed just like all the other female slaves," she said, mimicking his earlier lofty tone.

"No. Because they'll be staring at me. They won't be able to help themselves. Have you not seen the suit?"

Dallas laughed and finally focused on Devyn. "So what's my motivation for this role?"

"I told you." Devyn flicked him a glance. "You're a rich businessman, my friend, and looking for a little poptart. When I told you about the auction, you simply had to come along."

"You plan on buying anyone yourself?" Bride asked him.

"Can't. Everyone knows my penchant for variety, and it would seem odd if I purchased more of the same."

"And how long have I owned Bride?" Dallas asked.

"Like you can afford me," Bride said with a snort. "Have you not seen the bra?"

Once again, Devyn programmed the car. Autopilot kicked on, and they eased onto the road. Sensors knew when to stop and turn, so Devyn was able to spin in his seat and peer back at her. "You're a vampire, but that's not obvious, so it won't seem odd that I'm with you."

She shrugged. She hadn't been concerned with what anyone else thought about the two of them together.

He pursed his lips. "So you're good to go?"

What was wrong with him? "Yeah. For myself. Do you think Macy will be okay?" The other agents were going to be there, as well, simply hidden in the shadows, surrounding the building, watching and protecting.

"I know she will be," Devyn assured her gently, his irritation melting away. He reached back and clasped her hand, then drew it to his mouth for a kiss. His gaze never left her, was filled with fire and want.

He's touching me again! Joy burst through her, potent and sweet.

"Should I close my eyes?" Dallas asked with a laugh.

All too quickly Devyn released her and turned away.

Bye-bye joy.

"We're almost there," he said. "Bride, you are not to

leave my side. Understand? And you aren't to speak unless I ask you a question."

"I'll be a good girl, Daddy, I promise." She didn't like being told what to do, but submitting made sense. She'd never been to one of these things before and didn't know what to expect. Well, except for perverts. Better she remain near Devyn than fang someone for getting grabby.

"This is getting kinky," Dallas said, wiggling his eyebrows.

"Dallas," Devyn said, ignoring his friend's comment, "you are only to bid on vampires. Male or female."

"Great," the agent said dryly. "My luck they'll both be males, and I'll seem gay and lose my street cred with the ladies."

Looking tired all of a sudden, Devyn scrubbed a hand down his face. "If that's the worst that happens, I'll consider this a perfect night."

Devyn was on edge. He'd gone to a lot of trouble to make Bride look as if she belonged at his side, so as not to disgrace her more than would be necessary, and she didn't seem to care. More than that, he didn't like taking her to a slave auction and giving her a glimpse of his past. A past that had bruised her confidence once already.

When this was over, would she finally leave him?

Probably. With her newest ability, she could do anything she wanted. And he knew she still wasn't completely on board with the marriage.

Was he?

I don't want to examine myself right now. He wanted to examine her. He gave her money, but she didn't spend it. She hid it throughout the house. He stayed away from her bed, but she didn't seem to realize the great honor he paid her.

How long before she left him? How long did he *want* her to stay?

He'd probably hoped, on some level, that if he reverted to his old ways and cut off all sexual contact, he would grow tired of her faster. That hadn't been the case, however. He wanted her more now than ever. And he'd wanted her too damn much before.

Part of him now wanted to give her the world and watch her face light up. Like when he'd given her the necklace and then that basket of fruit. For the latter, her eyes had widened, teared, and her lips had curled into a half-smile. She'd even placed her hand over her heart. He'd felt like a conqueror, powerful and capable of anything. Over silly little pieces of fruit.

He didn't know what to make of himself. He didn't know how to handle these . . . feelings. His mouth curved into a grimace. Yes, feelings. He had them. For her. What exactly he felt, though, he didn't know. Whatever it was, it made him want to kill someone.

Tonight, he might have his chance.

If he was lucky, he'd run into the guy who had placed an order for her. Devyn planned to take his head. Then he was going to buy the vampires that were on sale and give them to Mia. Of course he would allow Bride to question them first and learn all that she wanted about her people. Then boom, done, his obligations to AIR would be over. Bride would be safe, and Mia would be pacified. Total win/win.

Only one blade hovered over his head, threatening his plans. Dallas's vision. He had to be careful. On guard. He might be confused by his current situation, but he wasn't yet ready for it to end.

"Two minutes, and we'll be there," he announced.

Dallas rubbed his hands together in glee.

"Someone told you that you don't really get to own the slaves," Bride said to the agent. "Right?"

"He's a danger junkie," Devyn explained.

Dallas shrugged sheepishly.

All too soon, the car slowed, easing to a stop. In front of them loomed a large warehouse, cars parked all around, humans and otherworlders meandering inside. The women who weren't slaves wore formal gowns. The men who weren't slaves wore suits like his. The slaves were as scantily dressed (or *un*dressed) as Bride.

He pressed a button on the car's console, and all the doors slid open. Outside, a valet stood at the ready, helping him and Dallas out. Bride was ignored. Devyn should have allowed her to emerge on her own, that was the way of things in this sinful world, but he didn't. Couldn't. He'd touched her hand earlier, and it had nearly electrified him. He needed that again, if only for a moment.

Tentatively she placed her fingers against his. So soft, so smooth, so warm. Again, electrifying. She stood, her gaze scanning left and right.

He'd once brought Eden Black to a gathering just like this. He'd wanted other men to look at her—she'd been dressed very similarly to Bride—and envy him, but he wanted to kill everyone who glanced at Bride. She was his. Right now, she was his wife.

A wife he was taking into a lion's den. *I'm seriously screwed up.*

Because of Eden, he had killed a very important man in this seedy world. Everyone here knew it, and a few had tried to keep him out tonight. But he had placed the right amount of money in the right hands, so here he was.

He released Bride and moved beside Dallas, who was no longer smiling and radiating good humor. Dallas was frowning, eyes slightly pained. A vision trying to kick its way inside his skull? Or was Dallas simply in agent mode, determined to protect Devyn from the vampires who had killed him in his latest vision?

Together they strode forward, Bride trailing behind them. He couldn't see her, but he could feel the energy she emitted. It was the only thing that relaxed him. They wound around cars, bypassing people strolling leisurely. At the front door, two armed guards greeted him. Ell-Rollises. Tall, hideously muscled, and torturously ugly. They had scaly yellow skin, and no nose that he could see. Maybe that was why they smelled so bad.

The race made the perfect guard dogs, for they were completely susceptible to their owner's commands. Whatever was demanded of them, they performed to the letter. Nothing swayed them.

"Name?" one asked in a gravelly voice.

"Devyn of the Targons. Two guests."

The guard scanned the names on his computerized list and nodded. "Armed?"

He laughed. Silly question. "Of course I am."

"All weapons must be removed," the second alien told him firmly.

"I meant I'm armed with cash, puppy. Now get out of my way."

Both sets of beady eyes roved over him.

"Can't," the second said. "Not until you're cleared." He held up a small black box and, gazing at the screen, moved it over his body. An X-ray, Devyn was sure. But he wasn't armed in any fashion that could be detected.

"Clean," the guard said, then scanned Dallas and Bride. "Clean, as well."

Both aliens moved aside.

Devyn strode into the building, certain the others followed him. He frowned. There was a strange vibration wafting through the air, a vibration that prevented him from locking on a single individual's energy, so he could manipulate their actions. It was the same vibe he'd gotten off Nolan, last time he'd tried to fight the otherworlder.

Well, fuck me, he thought next. They'd somehow done it on purpose to keep him in line. Smart of them. Wouldn't stop him from killing someone, though. His gaze shifted through the decadent world he hadn't realized until just then that he'd given up. He hadn't been in months, and hadn't wanted to come. Now he knew why. This wasn't where he belonged anymore.

The men were leering at the women, and the women—those who weren't peering dejectedly at their feet—were sizing the men up. There was more skin displayed here than usually found in his bedroom. Twelve rows with twelve seats each stretched in front of him. Only the front row was already occupied.

At the far wall was a platform with three lines of people, both male and female, all otherworlders of some sort. They were chained, their arms anchored to a beam above them, and robed. Anyone wanting a sneak peek could saunter onto the platform and part those robes, touch, even taste.

A wave of regret slammed through Devyn. Yes, regret. He'd thought living this way would keep him *from* regrets. Now, the truth hit him and hit him hard; he was looking at things as Bride must. He'd bought women who were traumatized by their treatment. Women who had been used and humiliated. Of course they'd been happy to leave with him.

Most likely they hadn't wanted him. Most likely they'd only wanted freedom from *this*.

Devyn couldn't help himself. He reached back, slid his arm around Bride's waist, and tugged her beside him. He needed to feel her, to know she was here and that she wasn't leaving him. Yet. He needed her goodness to mute his darkness.

She didn't protest as he'd expected. When would he learn that with her, he just needed to stop expecting? She always managed to surprise him. She even placed her palm on his lower back, under his jacket so no one could see, and grazed her nails over his shirt, tickling his skin to remind him of the pleasure they had shared together.

Pleasure he hadn't allowed himself to enjoy for an entire week.

Had they been alone, he might have snatched her up, ripped those pants off her, and pushed her against the wall while pounding inside the sweetness of her body. Respect be damned.

"I want to examine the merchandise," Dallas said coldly, every inch the buyer he was supposed to be.

Devyn knew he wanted to find the vampires. "This way." He released Bride and led them toward the stage, as whispers rose from the masses. Whispers about him, he was sure. What was he doing here? they wondered. Who was he with?

Before they could leave the sitting area, however, a tall, muscled warrior stood up and turned, as though he was aware of Devyn's every movement. Devyn stilled abruptly.

Though a year had passed, Devyn recognized the man instantly. McKell. *The* McKell. Power hummed from him in great waves, as though it was barely leashed.

Dread coursed through Devyn, Dallas's warning echoing through his mind. *You'll begin a chain of events . . .*

The vampire had pale skin and vivid violet eyes. Black-as-night hair. A perfect face, wide shoulders, and a thick body built for war. His fangs were so long, they protruded over his bottom lip.

Would this man, the first vampire Bride would see, appeal to her? Would she want to leave with the bastard? Good thing Devyn's wishes weren't the ones coming true. The entire place would have erupted into flame just then.

He didn't move aside and allow her to see the warrior. Not yet. If he were lucky, they'd get through this encounter without either Bride or McKell fully catching sight of the other.

"Ah, hell," Dallas muttered. "The countdown has begun."

Hell was just about right.

"Devyn of the Targons." McKell inclined his head in greeting. "I'd like to say it's a pleasure."

"As would I." He'd half admired the vamp and his cruelty until this moment. "But alas. I can't without lying. What are you doing here?"

"Many things. Since you told us of these auctions, we have come to buy back our own, as well as any meal that might strike our fancy." His purple gaze strayed to the form behind Devyn's back. Or tried to.

Devyn reached behind and ensnared Bride's arm, holding her in place so that she wouldn't inadvertently reveal herself. He'd been to several auctions since returning the girls, but he'd never noticed a vampire in the bidding crowd. "Kind of takes you out of hiding, doesn't it?"

Giving up on seeing his "slave," the bloodsucker once more met his stare. "We've already been discovered. There's no longer any risk. Instead, we are now determined to show those who wrong us the error of their ways."

Threat received. And ignored. "Well, I hope you enjoy the show. Now, if you'll excuse us . . ." He squeezed Bride's hand, pulling her beside him as he passed the vampire, still never really giving the man a good look at her.

He should have known she'd find a way to see who he'd been talking to. Suddenly she jerked backward, stilled, gasped in disbelief. Then she gasped again, in pure pleasure this time. "You're here," she said. "You're really here."

Wonderful. Devyn swung around, a wooden blade in his hand. Wood—because the X-ray only checked for metal. He pressed it into his thigh, ready to strike at any time.

McKell peered down at Bride's tattooed wrist for several heartbeats, silent. Then his gaze swung up, locking on Bride's face, seeming to drink her in. "It's you," he said. "It's really you. This is a day I have dreamed of for so long I can hardly believe it's finally here." There was awe in his voice. Awe and determination.

"What's going on?" Devyn demanded, not liking the way they were looking at each other.

McKell's attention remained fixed on Bride. "I've been searching for you, Maureen. Searching for my bride."

CHAPTER 19

Maureen.

Is that my real name? Bride wondered. "My tattoo—"

"Isn't your name," the vampire in front of her said. A real vampire. She'd known she would meet one tonight, but the fact that she had still managed to astound her. His teeth were longer and sharper than hers, and his skin was much paler. Was she the norm, or was he?

Did it matter? All her life she'd been waiting for this moment, desperate to find another like her. This man, this other vampire, was proof that she wasn't a simple anomaly, a mistake, a freak. He was proof that she belonged somewhere.

"You knew me?" she managed to work past the lump in her throat. The world around her was fading, the vampire—a real, live vampire!—becoming her sole focus. "Before?"

The warrior's gaze softened, turning the violet to a gentle blue. "Of course. You were born to be mine. The tattoo is your mark. My mark. Proclaiming what you are.

McKell's bride." He reached out, his thumb caressing the words in question.

So. The tattoo was her title. Wow. Not that she wanted to marry this man. Or belong to him, whatever that meant in the vampire world. *Her* world. A tremor began in her hands and spread to her chest, her legs.

"I have so many questions," she said. "How did I get here? Was I sent away? Did I wander off? Do I have a mother?" Bride forced herself to stop, not wanting to annoy him into silence.

Before he could answer a single question, someone passed their group from behind, and Devyn had to turn to avoid contact, which brushed his shoulder against hers and hers against McKell.

"Sorry," she muttered, tingling from where Devyn had touched her but feeling no different where McKell had. Kind of like when the warrior had traced her tattoo; there'd been no reaction. But at least the tingling from Devyn was like a jump start to her brain. Devyn. Auction. Crowd.

"No apology necessary, sweet Maureen. I welcome your touch." McKell scanned the area around them, even as Devyn growled low in his throat. "Now is not the time to talk, however."

"No, it's not, and there'll be no wishing it is," Devyn said through clenched teeth. His hand settled on her hips, his fingers spreading until they encountered bare skin. It was a possessive claim, a show of ownership. "And her name is Bride. *My* Bride."

Clearly he wasn't as happy as she was about this. He should be. McKell might be convinced to escort her to the underground, and Devyn could have his precious freedom back.

She paid no attention to the sudden ache in her heart.

McKell shook with the force of his sudden . . . fury? "You skirt the edge of death, Targon."

Oh, yes. Fury. Thankfully no one seemed to be paying them any attention, but that could change at any moment.

Devyn moved her aside, though he didn't release her, taking her place and putting himself nose to nose with the warrior. "She's my wife. We've exchanged blood. You know as well as I that she can no longer drink from anyone else. That means she is forever out of your reach."

"Actually," the warrior said, oh, so smug, "that's not entirely true. She won't die without you."

"Now your desperation is showing. I watched a female vampire die because she had lost her man."

"By choice, Targon. She died by choice. Do you really think we would have survived as long as we have if we couldn't find a way around the blood sickness?"

A hot breath hissed between Devyn's teeth.

There was a way around the sickness, Bride thought. One day she might be able to drink from someone else. Someone other than Devyn. The thought both delighted and saddened her. While she loved Devyn's blood, she didn't want to have to rely on him.

"Maureen," McKell said, "is mine."

"Boys," Dallas said when Devyn made as if to grab the newcomer by the shirt. "Enough."

Devyn straightened, smoothed his suit. "Yes, no reason for upset on my part. I've seen your moves. You need a bit more practice before you're ready for a tigress like Bride. And please, don't take offense. It's not an insult if it's true."

A muscle ticked below McKell's eyes as red bled into his irises. "Once we've weaned her off your blood, she will never again be able to see you. Never again be able to cross your path. What think you of that?"

"I think you need therapy, poor man." Devyn patted the top of McKell's head. "Such delusions are probably dangerous."

To have someone else's blood meant she wouldn't be able to see Devyn ever again? Was McKell just taunting Devyn, or was that true?

A vein looked ready to burst in McKell's forehead.

Again Devyn wrapped his arm around her, staking his claim. "You're the one who's been trying to buy her off the streets, yes?"

McKell gave a stiff nod. "You'll find that when it comes to my female, I will do anything to get her back. *Anything*."

Even kill you. The threat hung in the air, unsaid, but just as menacing. Bride tried to step between them, but Devyn was having none of that. She would have wished them apart, but was too afraid of the consequences.

"Well, you should know that I'll do anything to keep her," Devyn said.

Devyn wanted to keep her? That was news.

"Perhaps we should let the girl decide." McKell's attention settled on her, and his gaze softened. He reached out to smooth a strand of her hair behind her ear.

Devyn batted his hand away. "No touching. Ever."

McKell popped his jaw, his attention never veering from her. "My name is Victor. McKell is merely my classification."

"Warrior classification," she said, and he nodded. "So I'm a warrior, as well? Or do vampire females take the classification of who they're promised to?"

He opened his mouth to respond, but a voice from the podium stopped him. "Ladies and gentlemen, please take your seats." The overhead halogens flashed on and off. "We're about to begin, and as you can plainly see, we have a wonderful selection for you tonight."

"We'll talk," the vampire told her. "After." And with that, he gave them his back as if they were no threat at all and settled in his seat.

Devyn ushered Bride to the section of seats behind and across from the warrior. He eased into one of the plush cushion-covered folding chairs. When she attempted to do the same, he shook his head and pointed to the ground.

The twig- and dirt-laden ground? Seriously?

"Sit," he barked, clearly at the end of his patience.

Eyes wide, she plopped herself at his feet. Never had she heard so much anger in his tone. Not even when he'd first proclaimed them married. He seethed with the emotion, his muscles stiff and his face like granite. Because McKell thought he had a claim on her?

Did he? She rubbed the tattoo on her wrist. Or rather, brand. She'd been given to him at birth, he'd said. That must mean marriages between vampires were arranged.

In all her imaginings, she'd never thought her people would be so archaic. But clearly they were.

What would her life have been like if she'd married McKell? She wouldn't have met Devyn, that was for sure. Or maybe she would have. He'd once gone underground. Would they have met then? Would they have circled each other, have been challenged by the other, and ultimately have given in to the attraction? At this point, she couldn't imagine *not* wanting him. Her desire for him was now such a big part of her life.

"This sucks," Dallas said as he settled beside Devyn, drawing her from her musings. "What if the auctioner doesn't know who's vampire? I never got a chance to study the prisoners."

"Just follow McKell's lead." Though Devyn spoke quietly, she could still detect the fury in his voice. He wasn't calming down.

She wanted to soothe him, but didn't know how. Then, a few seconds later, the auction began, and she forgot all about him. One at a time, the people were paraded along the parapet, their robes parted, their bodies displayed for all to see. Disgust welled inside her. It was cruel. Some of the people cried and blushed, even looked away from the crowd. Some of the people stared straight ahead, as if they'd already endured far worse horrors, and being studied and critiqued was nothing.

To block the horror from her mind, she peered over at McKell. She didn't have a good view of him, but enough of one to make out his strong profile. A slightly longer than normal nose, unlined skin, dark hair a bit shaggy.

Not a bad piece of meat. *Ick. Now I'm thinking like the buyers.*

Devyn's palm flattened on her head, fingers digging into her scalp. "See something you like, love?"

Love. He'd never called her that before, and that he did now had her trembling. Did he mean it? Did she want him to mean it? She tore her attention away from McKell and looked up at Devyn to study him. His gaze was on the parapet. His jaw was clenched, his eyes narrowed, but oh, the fire inside them was fierce.

"Now I do," she said softly, hating herself because it was the truth.

His grip loosened, and he even stroked her hair. His expression smoothed out. Calm at last. "We have much to discuss, you and I," he said.

Much to discuss. As in their parting? As in why he hadn't touched her in a week, but the moment someone else expressed an interest in her, he talked about her as if she were his favorite possession?

Anger suddenly danced through *her*. Was that what it took to keep Devyn's notice? Have someone else desire her? Well, she wasn't playing that game. He either wanted her or he didn't.

Just then, McKell's voice reverberated through the building. Surprised, she twisted yet again. His hand was in the air, which meant he'd just made a bid. Her attention swung to the stage. A tall, leanly muscled male with pale skin and snow-white hair stood proudly. He was one of those who refused to look away from the crowd. But he didn't simply endure. He hissed and bared his teeth, yet she didn't notice fangs.

"—stronger, faster, deadlier," the auctioneer was saying. "Word of warning, though. You'll have to be careful with him. He's a biter."

A wave of laughter rose from the crowd, sickening her further.

The bidding speed increased, hands flying in the air.

"Look at these eyes," the announcer said. "Dark blue. Like sapphires. Come on, ladies. You love jewelry, you know you do. Get tired of the man, and you can wear his eyes."

"How are they holding him if he's so strong?" Bride whispered.

"Drugs, perhaps," Devyn said. "Not allowing him to drink, maybe."

McKell placed another bid.

"Now," Devyn said to Dallas.

Dallas shouted out such an astronomical sum that the crowd instantly quieted. The auctioneer gasped. McKell twisted in his seat, glaring.

"Sold," the auctioneer proclaimed with a grin.

And on and on the auction continued. McKell never bid again, but he did stiffen when a young female was brought forward. Her skin was not as pale as the vampire male's had been, but her hair was just as white, and Devyn instructed Dallas to bid. Once again, he won.

Finally, it was over, the last otherworlder purchased. Devyn and Dallas, along with the rest of the crowd, pushed to their feet. Neither of them helped Bride stand. Her eyes were dry, even though she wanted to cry for all those who had been sold and what they would soon endure.

She committed the faces around her to memory, thinking to track them down and free their "slaves" the moment she was able. Or better yet, she'd use Devyn's money and pay someone else to do it right away.

"Warrior that he is, he'll have his men try to take them," Devyn said quietly to Dallas. "Be prepared."

"And where will you be?" the agent asked behind his hand.

"Evading him and keeping Bride safe. Tell Mia I've met my end of the bargain."

The bargain. Bride's blood was no longer to be tested, in exchange for as many vampires as Devyn could get his hands on. Two, as it turned out. The sickness in her stomach churned. No way would she let that male and female be used as pincushions, their bodies drained. She'd offer herself back to AIR on a platter if necessary. She, at least, wasn't traumatized.

The two men looked at each other, nodded in silent understanding, and then Dallas was moving to the stage to collect his winnings.

"You're coming with me, and I don't want to hear a single protest," Devyn said stiffly. He didn't glance down at her, nor did he jump into motion. What was he waiting for?

"Yeah, well, you're going to hear a lot of protests." She kept her body angled away from him, as if she were talking to herself. McKell was still in his seat, facing the parapet. "The auction's over, you have your booty, so I'm done being a slave. The power is going to your head. And not the one I want! Or wanted. I don't anymore. And just so you know, we can't let these people be taken to God knows where, God knows what done to them."

"We can, and we will. If I know AIR, and I do, they'll free those they can before the new owners ever set foot into their cars."

She relaxed at that. "What about the vampires?"

"You were treated well. They will be, as well."

"How can they be treated well if they're locked up for the rest of their lives?"

A muscle ticked below his eye. He had no answer.

"AIR can have them for a week, then I want you to reclaim *our* property," she said, determined. "What's yours is mine, remember?"

"We'll talk to Mia about it."

We will. Not *I will.* Because of that, she was able to nod in agreement. "Now for the other subject I'm sure you don't want to discuss. I want to question McKell about my people."

As though McKell had heard her, he stood. Faced them.

"You're right. I don't." Finally Devyn jolted into motion. He gripped her hand and dragged her toward the exit, winding around people and chairs. "You can question our property, as you called them, at AIR. McKell will just try and take you underground."

Her heart drummed in her chest. "But what if I *want* to see the underground?" Did she have family there?

"You could be sentenced to death for living topside. Remember? Therefore, you can't go. You can't risk it." He paused for a moment, flicked her a glance over his shoulder. "If that wasn't a factor, though, you would still want to go?"

"Yes." Bride felt a pair of intense eyes boring into her back and knew who watched her. Still, she couldn't help herself. She twisted. Sure enough, McKell was watching her through narrowed lids. His hands were clenched into fists, his posture straight as a board. He wasn't following, though. He stood in place. "I've dreamed of having a family my entire life."

"Even though that family gave you to a man at birth? It's not tradition, you know. That isn't something that happens to all newborn females."

"Oh." Why had they done that to her, then, if it wasn't tradition as she'd first assumed? Payment? They just hadn't wanted her? She fought a surge of depression. "Yes," she said softly. The only way to gain the answers she sought was to ask those who had been involved. "I'd still want to go."

As they stepped outside, the musty, perfumed air inside the building gave way to the cooler, cleaner air of the night. She breathed deeply. There was a hint of car exhaust, but that was better than a gaggle of bodies that reeked of food.

"Since I can't go underground, I want to talk to McKell." He hadn't seemed to mind her questions. Had seemed eager to answer them.

"Have I told you lately how irritating you are?" Devyn increased his speed.

Her feet tripped over themselves as she struggled to keep up. "I'm a joy to be around, and you know it. Now where are you taking me?" He'd already bypassed his own vehicle.

"Whatever I end up doing, and I'm changing my mind

about every three seconds, I couldn't do it in there," he said. "They'd erected some sort of energy scrambler so that I couldn't control any of the bodies."

Note to self: buy an energy scrambler. Not that Devyn had controlled her movements since making her strip in that apartment, the bastard.

He tangled his free hand through his hair, clearly agitated. He stomped from the parking lot entirely, heading toward a fenced-off forest area. Government property. "Uh, Devyn."

"Not now."

"Then when? When we're arrested?" The more they walked, the quieter the night became and the sweeter the air. Trees. Mmm. Again she inhaled deeply, savoring their scent. Finally Devyn stopped; they had reached the fence.

He spun, gripping her shoulders, gaze frantic, a little wild now. "Are you with me, Bride?"

She blinked up at him in confusion. "I'm standing here, aren't I?"

He shook her. "Do you like McKell more than you like me?"

Did she—what? Her mind could barely process his words or what he wanted from her. "Who said I liked either of you?"

"I'll get you the answers about your family," he said, his intensity unwavering. "I'll even get you inside the underground if you want to visit, and I'll keep you safe. But you are not to engage the vampire. Do you understand? He's determined to keep you for himself."

And his point? "People don't always get what they want, now do they?"

Another shake. "Bride. Be serious. Tell me you're not attracted to McKell."

Her brain rattled in her skull, and a shocking thought seemed to pop free. "Devyn, are you . . . jealous?" This was more than simply wanting her because another man found her attractive. Devyn was too desperate. Desperate in a way she'd never seen him.

"No, of course not." His hands fell from her, but his scowl remained. "I just don't want you giving yourself to anyone else while you're married to me. For now, you're mine. I'll kill anyone who touches you," he added.

Uh, hello jealousy. She wanted to grin but didn't. He didn't deserve to know how happy he'd just made her. "Since you're so jealous, why have you ignored me this past week? Why have you slept in a different bed?"

"I'm not jealous, I said." Eyes narrowing, Devyn backed her up until a boulder stopped him. "I stayed away because I wanted you to know that I respect you."

"Give me a minute to work past your jealousy and figure out what you just said." She gasped as the coldness of the rock met her shoulders and thighs. "Nope. Still don't understand. What does denying me have to do with respecting me?"

He pushed his nose into hers. "Do you know what it's like to be locked away? To be alone, left in the dark, forgotten, the silence deafening?"

Silent, she shook her head.

"I do. As a boy I was locked away for exhibiting even the smallest hint of desire. I was told sex was dirty and shaming. For a long time, I even believed it. I got over it, but with you, I felt those old thoughts resurfacing, and I was so afraid of—"

Overcome, emotions bubbling over, Bride threw her arms around his neck and slammed her lips into his. He hadn't left her alone because he'd stopped wanting her. He'd left her alone because he'd been afraid of shaming her. She'd show him the error of that, she thought, thrusting her tongue into his mouth. At first, he didn't respond. Then he moaned. He smashed his weight into her body, and his tongue plundered deep, taking, giving, leaving her weak with pleasure.

"More," she said. It had been too long. Far too long. Despite the openness of their surroundings, despite any danger, waiting even a moment longer seemed silly. "Nothing you do to me is shameful, swear to God. Well, besides letting me suffer from withdrawals. You gave me a taste of you, then took it away."

He gave a hoarse chuckle. "Well, the first taste is always free. You have to pay for the rest."

"Name your price."

"You. Just you." His hands lowered, working at the harem pants. Didn't take much. He had them at her ankles in seconds, and ripped open his own pants. His erection sprang free. Then he was gripping her thighs, shoving them apart, anchoring them on his waist and plunging inside her. Her head fell against the cold stone, her back arching to take him even deeper.

One of his hands kneaded her breast, thrumming the nipple through the fabric of her bra. "Never deny me this again," she said. "Understand?"

He nipped at her chin and pumped into her, in and

out, fast . . . faster . . . "You're all I think about. All I want anymore."

Every forward glide took her to new heights. Every backward slide spun her mind out of control. He was touching her everywhere, even her soul. "Devyn," she moaned.

"You're . . . you. You make me hot, you make me laugh, and you make me angry. You look at me with those emerald eyes, and all I want to see is happiness inside them. You confuse me, you arouse me, you make me want to be better."

"There's no one better," she said, and hurtled over the edge, groaning, gasping, crying out his name again, holding on to him, determined never to let go.

And when she leaned up and scraped her teeth over his neck, he shuddered, and his grip tightened. She wouldn't do it, wouldn't take his blood and weaken him when they were within a hundred yards of the auction house. But she couldn't help but rasp his skin, laving it with whatever chemical she produced. Just like that, he came, sinking to the hilt, propelling her over again.

"Bride. My Bride."

She tangled her hands in his hair and forced him to look at her, to see the truth in her eyes. "Yours." But for how much longer?

The shudders left him and he stilled, continuing to pant, to hold her close. "I'm not ready to let you go."

"Then don't. We can stay here all night."

"Hear footsteps."

That got her attention. Yelping, she jerked from him, separating their bodies. "Why didn't you tell me sooner?"

As she shakily righted her clothes, she blushed at the wetness between her legs.

"'Cause I didn't want to." More leisurely, Devyn fastened his pants. He remained in front of her, blocking her from anyone's view. He was grinning, back to his usual cocky self. "McKell," he said with relish, and then he turned, clearly ready for combat.

McKell reached them. His violet gaze took in their rumpled clothes, her swollen lips and quickly rising chest. His nostrils flared. If his sense of smell was anything like hers, he scented the sex wafting from them.

"I should cut you down where you stand," the warrior told Devyn.

As he spoke, an army of vampires arrived, surrounding them. Gasping, Bride moved forward and held out her arms to shield Devyn. Without her razors, she felt naked, but that didn't mean she was helpless. "No one moves," she commanded.

Devyn was having none of that, and shoved her behind him. *She* was having none of that, and moved beside him.

"Figured you'd follow," he told the vampire. His grin became all the more evil. "Glad you did."

McKell gave Devyn an evil grin of his own and moved forward, closing the distance between them. He stopped after only three steps and frowned, then scowled. "Bastard. Using your ability against me. Well, let's see if you can use it against us all. Incapacitate him," the warrior growled to his men. "Leave him alive, though. My female needs his blood. For the moment."

The vampires, too, moved forward. They, too, froze.

"Does that answer your question?" Devyn asked smugly. Then he surprised her. Rather than strike and kill, he said, "I will let you and your men live, McKell. And in return, you will take us to your king. *If* you can guarantee that she won't be punished for living on the surface. Since you planned to take her with you, I'm assuming you've already thought of a way to bypass the death sentence."

McKell blinked, clearly startled—and just as suspicious. "I don't understand."

Neither did she. "Yeah, what's going on?" Here was a man who could and did kill without hesitation or regret. A man who clearly wanted to do so now. Yet he didn't. He was demanding to be taken underground. For her.

"She belongs to me," he continued, "and yet you feel she is your property." Devyn raised his chin, the picture of a determined male. "I don't want you chasing her for the rest of your too-long life, and she wants answers about her people. So let's take care of both matters at once. We'll petition your king and allow him to decide. You can tell her what she wants to know along the way."

And if the king decided in McKell's favor? she wondered. Hell, no. "I'm happy to go underground, but there won't be anyone deciding my fate for me."

"She will not be sentenced to death," McKell said, ignoring her. "As she was born here on the surface, the daughter of captured vampires"—his gaze shifted left and right to his men, pleading with her and Devyn not to contradict him—"her time here could not be helped."

Devyn nodded. "It's settled, then."

"Settled," the vampire said.

"It's awesome that you two are in agreement, really it is. But do I get a say in this?" she snapped. "Did no one hear me say that no one picks my man but me?"

Again, neither paid her any heed. Jeez. Was it the sequins? Put on a slave costume, and suddenly no one took you seriously.

"I'll go underground, because I *want* to go, but that's it," she said. "That's all I'm promising."

Devyn must have released the vampire from stun, because the warrior stepped backward and nodded, saying, "Do not think this will end happily for you, Targon."

CHAPTER 20

The buzzing of his phone woke Dallas. Blinking against the harsh morning light, he rolled over and blindly reached for his cell. He knocked over a glass on his nightstand. When his fingers finally scraped the cell, he latched on and dragged it to his ear.

"Agent Gutierrez," he rasped.

"Get your lazy ass up," Hector proclaimed from the other end. "Nolan escaped."

Blood freezing in his veins, Dallas jackknifed up, the urge to sleep hammered out of him with the agent's words. "How?"

"Seduced one of the female agents sent to watch him."

"That shitbag." He popped to his feet and strode into the bathroom. His still tired muscles screamed in protest. "She sick?"

"Not yet, but she's been locked up and is being watched. I've got Nolan's location, and I'm on my way to get you. Can you be ready in ten?"

"Make it eight." Though he had questions, he hung up and took care of business. He brushed his teeth, dressed, grabbed his shades, and was out the door in five. He'd planned to spend the morning thinking about his vision of Devyn, and how McKell, whose face he had indeed seen in it, had managed to stab his friend. If he had to, he'd plant himself at the pier and wait for the vampires to arrive.

The moment the idea struck, he nodded. Yes, that's exactly what he'd do. Once Nolan was taken care of, he'd find a spot and camp out. He wouldn't have seen Devyn's death if there was nothing to do about it. Dallas was as certain of that as he was that without intervention, Devyn would die. He refused to believe the visions were simply to prepare him for what lay ahead.

The way he'd botched the vision about Jaxon and Mishka was proof things could be changed—and for the better. *If* he worked them right.

The streets were lined with morning traffic; the sun was bright as people cruised the sidewalks at top speed. A few were carrying cups of syn-coffee, and the scent wafted to his nose, making his mouth water. His stomach even rumbled. How long since he'd eaten?

Hector pulled to the curb and stopped.

Ignoring his hunger, Dallas slid into the kind of sedan every AIR agent used and shut the door with a push of a button. "How do you know where Nolan is?" was the first question he voiced.

Hector programmed the car, and it eased onto the road before kicking into high gear, weaving in and out of traffic. "Remember how your friend Devyn injected himself with that isotope tracker?"

"Yeah."

"Well, get this. The vampire drank from Devyn, and Nolan drank from Bride, who was also injected, so had twice the normal amount. It's like that old game my grandparents used to play, degrees of separation or something like that. They've all got the tracker in their system now, and we've pegged all three." He motioned to the laptop resting in the back seat. "See for yourself."

"We tried the tracker on Nolan once before," Dallas said. "The virus inside him ate the isotope. We were never able to pull him into the system."

"Proof the virus is gone, I guess, 'cause we've got him now."

Finally, something in their favor. Dallas snatched it up and studied the blue screen above the keyboard. There were three black dots. Two were on the move, together, and one was stationary and in the opposite direction. Wasn't hard to figure out who was who. It was a relief to see that Devyn and Bride were still alive, though God knew what they were doing. After last night . . .

Never had Dallas seen the Targon more pissed. There'd been none of his usual charm, none of his nonchalance. He simply hadn't liked other men looking at Bride. And when the McKell had staked a claim on her . . . shit. Bastard was probably already dead.

Who would have thought Devyn the Seducer would fall for one specific female? Not Dallas, that was for sure. But no longer did he think Devyn would tire of the vampire. Not when his features softened every time he looked at her. Not when he sought her comfort above his own.

"As suspected, the little shit lied to us," Hector said. "He's not headed to the location he gave us."

"Of course not." But was he intending to help his queen or kill her? They'd soon find out, he supposed. Right now, something else weighed heavily on his mind. "So have you been to AIR this morning?"

"Yeah."

"See the new vampires?"

"Oh, yeah. Both are alive and healthy and regaining their strength."

Good. He'd thought he would have trouble with McKell, Devyn's new nemesis, after the auction, but no one had tried to stop him from taking the two vampire slaves. The moment he'd gotten them in the car and out of the parking lot, Ghost and Kitty, also AIR agents, had flanked him and escorted him into headquarters. No one had given chase, or even seemed to follow.

More shocking, the vampires hadn't complained. Hadn't fought him or tried to run. Their eyes had been glazed, though, so he supposed they'd been drugged. At the station, they'd been placed in lockup, separate cells, and given bags of plasma. Unlike Bride, they'd drained the bags and hoarsely begged for more.

Dallas had been the one to enter the male's cell. The vampire had been weak and shaky, but hadn't made use of the cot, the room's only piece of furniture. He'd stood in the corner, better able to see every angle of the cell, his white hair hanging in his face, parted only enough to give Dallas the barest glimpse of hate-filled blue eyes.

How you doing? he'd asked.

How do you think I'm doing, human? I'm in a cage.

We aren't going to harm you.

Bitter laugh. *That's what my last owner said, just before*

his guards held me down. And just so you know, I'll slaughter you and your people the way I did him and his if you think to make me your whore.

As Devyn had told him how Bride camouflaged herself before bursting into tiny bits of mist, he'd been half afraid the warrior would do something similar, but it hadn't happened. *Be at ease. That's not why you're here, you have my word. There's a virus being passed around my people, one that only vampire blood seems capable of defeating. We just want to take a little of yours and test it.*

The explanation was ignored. *Tell me about Starlis.* It was a command laced with need.

Certainly. Tell me who that is first.

That pale jaw clenched. *The female you bought.*

Starlis. Pretty name. *She's fine. Next door to you.* He shouldn't have admitted that, but wanted the warrior to relax. Not that he would have been able to do so, had the situation been reversed. *Nothing will happen to her, either.*

It better not. Because if you hurt her . . . Claws curled into a fist and cut the warrior's palm.

Were they lovers? Brother and sister? *Like I said, we only mean to test your blood.*

That desire will cost you. You should have spoken to our king rather than purchase us. The word *purchase* was sneered.

Your king is hidden from us. We don't know how to find him.

Red lips had lifted in eerie amusement. *Don't worry. He'll now find you.*

It was a threat everyone at AIR had taken seriously. Security was being beefed up, the black ops and field agents called in.

The sedan eased to a stop, and Dallas pulled himself into the present. He'd hated leaving those vampires locked up, but hadn't known what else to do. AIR needed their blood. Hell, mankind needed their blood.

Hector exited without a word, and Dallas quickly followed suit. Warm morning air enveloped him. There were several cars around them, agents outside them and staring into a government-protected forest. The same one Dallas had been next to last night, just on the other side. Coincidence?

"Weapons are in the trunk," Hector told him.

He swung around back and popped the trunk. Sure enough, there were enough guns and blades to take down an army. He sheathed the smallest and sharpest of the knives and holstered two pyre-guns. He even pocketed an extra crystal in case one of the guns misfired. He wasn't taking any chances this time.

"'Bout time you joined us," Jaxon said, striding to his side. The agent palmed a mini-grenade, measured its weight, and gently placed it in his side bag. "Thought we were going to have to win this battle without you."

"Not likely," he said with a snort. "I've got skills you can only dream about."

That earned him a laugh. "Just keep yourself alive, my man, and I'll be happy."

What was with everyone doubting his abilities? He'd screwed up once. Okay, twice. Big deal. "As you know, I can do things other people can't. I can move faster than anyone here." Besides Mia, but she wouldn't leave Kyrin's side. "I've finally given over to my dark side, so I know I can handle this." He said it with confidence, his psychic knowledge assuring him of success. He also said it without a hint of disdain.

He'd always thought he'd feel more alien, the more he accepted his powers. He'd even expected to feel regret. Instead, he felt more like himself than he had in months. "I can scout ahead and see what we're dealing with," he added. "Let everyone know what's going on before they get there."

Having heard the conversation, Hector came up beside him and held up a computerized map. "Our boy is here. It's a straight shot, dead center, and impossible to miss; he's in a circular clearing, the only clearing, where helicopters land."

Dallas nodded. "You guys circle the entire area if possible and slowly close in. I'll give a shout if he goes invisible, so you'll know to wear your infrareds and watch for him."

Jaxon slapped him on the shoulder, his scarred face still etched in concern. "Got your own infrareds?"

His gaze scanned the trunk. When he found a pair of goggles, he nodded, grabbed them up, and fitted them around his neck. "Now I do."

"Nolan's been here ten minutes and hasn't moved from his spot," Hector said. "We think he's waiting for her."

Her. The queen. The one responsible for the cannibalistic disease. Selfish bitch that she clearly was, she screwed men without a care, damning them to either death or life as a killer while saving herself. Nolan had mentioned her unparalleled beauty, but no other power. What would he be up against?

"Thought he couldn't sense her anymore," Dallas muttered. What a liar Nolan was.

Once again he scanned the trunk, looking for anything else he might need. He saw a case of bright blue syringes and lifted one into the light.

"My own special blend," Hector said proudly. "It's four different sedatives for four different races mixed together, but it's not approved by AIR, so using it could get you into trouble. Some ingredients will probably work on more than one race, so there's a possibility of overdose."

"Work on the Schön?"

"Only one way to find out."

Dallas pocketed two of the syringes, then closed the trunk and peered into the thick trees. If he got in trouble for using the sedative, he'd deal. "Electricity turned off on the fence?"

Jaxon shook his head. "But it will be for ten seconds. Soon as I see you close in, I'll throw the switch. We can't leave it off, though, just in case Nolan makes a run for it. Don't want to make it easier for him, you know."

Dallas flashed both agents a confident smile. "Don't wait till I'm close to the fence to switch it off, because you may not see me reach it. Click it now." With that, he leaped into a sprint. As he ran, he opened himself up to the power inside him, swirling and ready to be used. Instantly he propelled into hyperspeed.

A quick glance behind him showed that his friends now seemed to be moving in slow motion, barely achieving an inch per second. He reached the fence and scaled it, only cutting himself once. A minor scratch in his thigh, but it burned like hell. It was just as he was releasing the metal that the electricity kicked back on. A shock moved through him, but didn't slow him as he started running again, feet flying over grass and rocks.

He maneuvered around trees, their trunks and branches blurring into a haze of brown and green. As quickly as he was closing the distance, he was still able to see the things in front of him clearly, as if his vision tunneled ahead and his mind planned his actions accordingly, dancing him out of harm's way without incident.

Soon he reached the clearing. There was no reason to question whether or not he'd reached the right spot because Nolan was there, arms crossed over his chest as he waited. There were knives in his hands.

To aid the queen in case of trouble, or to kill her? Dallas had to wonder again.

He didn't slow but circled the area, too fast to be seen, keeping Nolan in sight as he debated what to do. Nolan had told Bride that the virus had helped Nolan dodge stun rays last time, but it had been Nolan himself who had absorbed the stun without actually freezing. Therefore, stun still wouldn't work.

He could kill him, he supposed. There was no dousing pyre-fire. But no. No longer was Nolan better off dead. Not when a cure for his disease might be floating through his system. He was a very valuable lab rat right now.

Dallas couldn't challenge him straight out, though, because the guy could go invisible, and then Dallas would have to fight him with infrareds, only able to see Nolan, oblivious to everything else around them. And if Nolan ran, the infrareds would be useless because Dallas couldn't give chase with them on. He'd slam into tree after tree. Closing in as they were, his friends could catch the bastard—maybe.

Maybe wasn't good enough.

A sheen of sweat broke out over his skin. He was going to have to knock the otherworlder out with Hector's cocktail. Or try to. While he waited for the stuff to work, if it worked, he'd have to pin Nolan down, never releasing him, never giving him the chance to escape.

A bright yellow and violet light suddenly hit the center of the clearing, as if the sun were throwing off heat missiles. The wind picked up, rustling leaves together. A soft whistle pierced the air.

Nolan straightened, stiffened.

Shit, out of time, Dallas thought. *I have to incapacitate him before she arrives.* He launched forward, fingers tightening around one of the syringes as he closed in on Nolan. The moment he reached him, he shoved the needle straight into the man's neck and pushed.

The warrior fell, shocked, the empty syringe buried deep. His body spasmed as Dallas kept him in a bear hug. Hot breath sawed in and out of his throat and lungs. His limbs shook.

"Mistake," the otherworlder gasped. "Big mistake. You won't be able to defeat her without me." But he didn't get up, and his eyelids closed. Every muscle in his body slackened.

Easier than Dallas had thought.

As Dallas released him, his own strength drained, as if he too had been injected with a sedative. He knew he hadn't. What the hell? He crawled to his knees, certain he wouldn't be able to stand and hold his own weight.

Hurry, he wanted to shout to the other AIR agents. *Something's . . . wrong . . .*

"You want to defeat me?" a soft voice said from behind him.

Dallas twisted to face the new speaker and groaned at the dizziness that assaulted him. That dizziness failed to dim the radiance of his visitor, and his jaw dropped. Standing before him was a goddess, an elfin queen. She had long pale hair tucked behind her pointed ears, chocolate eyes too big for her face, which somehow made her even lovelier, and heart-shaped lips. Her skin was several shades lighter than Dallas's, but still sun-kissed. She wore a long white robe that draped one shoulder and fell over her slender body in waves.

There seemed to be true concern on her face. True sadness at the thought that someone wanted to destroy her. This woman couldn't be Nolan's queen. His tormentor. The one responsible for the obliteration of several worlds and the death of the humans foolish enough to bed Nolan and his brethren.

"I'm sorry I had to drain you," she said, and she sounded as if she meant it. "I didn't want you to hurt me as you hurt my servant." Behind her were four warriors, all as handsome as Nolan, with the same bright eyes and symmetrical features. Each was heavily armed, watching impassively, ready to act when ordered.

Her servant. She was indeed Nolan's queen. Though everything inside Dallas screamed not to hurt so exquisite a creature—no wonder Nolan had been torn—he drew on a stubborn reserve of strength he hadn't known he possessed and whipped out his pyre-gun, thumb quickly setting it to kill, and started shooting. Better that they all died in this circle, even himself, than that they were unleashed on the world.

The men fell, new holes burned in their chests, their hearts scorched and unworkable, but Dallas's pyre-fire never touched the girl. Woman. Whatever she was. Killer. Monster. Yes. A lovely monster . . . gliding toward him, a frown on her delicate face. Irresistible, he thought. *Mine.*

Every time he'd aimed at her, the barrel moved away of its own accord, as though they were both magnets and couldn't line up together. Or perhaps he switched his aim before pulling the trigger. He didn't want to hurt her.

What would it feel like to touch her skin? To shift her hair between his fingers, those locks that reminded him of rays of sunshine?

"You didn't kill me, so I'm not going to kill you," she said in that lilting voice of hers. The word *yet* slithered between them, unsaid but there all the same. "I need to get settled, anyway. But when my need is upon me, I will find you. Very soon, I hope."

She reached out and traced a fingertip along his cheek, his jaw. Each point of contact crackled as if ice crystals bloomed. "So strong . . . so handsome . . ."

He wanted to flinch, but couldn't force himself to move. The world was going dark . . . so dark . . . her beauty fading from his view. A scream lodged in his throat. *Don't leave me. Stay.* The desire shocked him. She was evil, yet he wanted her near him, touching him some more. That cold was as addicting as a drug.

"Dallas, man. Wake up. Good job, man. You got him. You got Nolan."

"Wh-what?" He blinked open his eyes. He was lying flat on his back—when had he fallen?—and the pale blue of the sky came into view, thick clouds hanging in a line. He angled his head, peering at the clearing. It was empty. "Where is she? Where are the bodies?"

Hector frowned. "What *she*? The queen? Was she here? And what bodies?"

"The girl, yes, the queen. The guards. Four guards. I shot them. Burned them."

"There weren't any bodies when I got here, and they didn't go invisible because half of us were wearing our infrareds and there was no body heat in the area. And if you'd shot them, we would have seen the line of your fire."

Slowly he sat up, fighting the return of the dizziness. "They were here. I swear to God they were here."

Hector patted his shoulder. "You were out like a coma victim when we came through the trees. Sure you didn't dream it? Your weapon is holstered, and it hasn't been fired."

"It wasn't a dream," he insisted.

"Okay, okay." Concerned, Hector slid an arm around his waist and hefted him up. "Mishka and Jaxon are taking care of Nolan. Let's get you to medical."

CHAPTER 21

Bride expected treachery. An attack against Devyn. *Something*. But it never came. In silence, they drove to a canyon three hours away. It was a dry, barren wasteland with no resources humans needed to survive. There, they scaled down . . . down . . . into a shadowed valley of sandstone and dirt, the air almost like acid in her nose. Boulders abounded, each identical to the last.

Devyn kept an arm around her waist, holding her up. He probably thought she would have tumbled into the waiting void below if he'd released her. Wasn't like she was clumsy, but she *had* stumbled a few times. Not her fault, though. She was distracted, having to guard her thoughts to keep herself from wishing she was already underground.

Why was Devyn making this trip? He'd said he wanted her. He'd even been jealous of McKell. But that wasn't reason enough to put himself in danger like this. And he was in danger. McKell clearly hated him.

Devyn had proven he could handle the vampires, yes,

but that didn't stop her worrying for him. He was only one man. What was worse, however, was that the worry didn't stop her from being glad that he was here. She wasn't ready to say good-bye to him. They'd just started having sex again.

Sure that's the only reason you're happy to be with him?

Shut up. There were more important things to consider.

What if the vampire king tried to pawn her off on McKell? She did *not* want another forced marriage—she wouldn't stand for it. The vamp was friend material, that was all. There was no raw, animal need, as there was with Devyn.

Finally, McKell stopped at a boulder, no different from any of the others, and nodded. His men marched forward and rolled it aside, their muscles bunching and straining.

Four guards waited on the other side, each armed with pyre-guns and spears. Bride tried to step in front of Devyn, but he restrained her with his mind, the bastard. Oh, yes. She was finding one of those energy scramblers.

The guards gave their profiles when they saw McKell, deferring to his superior rank. The warrior motioned for her and Devyn to follow him.

They entered without hesitation, sharing only the briefest of looks. Hers, tension-filled. His, darkly resolved.

What are you planning? she wondered.

Bride's eyes widened as she focused on her surroundings. This could have been her home, she thought. It was murky, but no match for her eyesight; she saw everything perfectly. The walls were painted black and jagged, multiple smears of crimson throughout. Like finger marks, where nails had dragged in protest.

And the smell . . . utterly divine. Pine, water, blood, with no taint of spices or food. She smiled as she savored. That's when McKell turned back to check on them. When he saw her, his gaze softened.

Her smile faltered. She liked him, but didn't want to encourage him.

Had jealous Devyn noticed the exchange? She flicked him a glance. His eyes were closed, and he was feeling his way forward with his free hand. A frown tugged at the corners of his lips, and lines of tension marred the perfection of his face. He couldn't see in the dark, she realized.

He'd known it would be this way, yet he'd come anyway.

Sweetest. Man. Ever. How had she ever thought him detached? He hated the dark, but still he'd come. Only one reason a man would do something like that. Did he . . . was it possible he . . . no, couldn't be. Not Devyn. Devyn did not fall in love with his women. She'd known that from the beginning.

Well, if he were going to pick someone to fall in love with, he couldn't do better than Bride. *There you go, thinking like him again.* Well, it was true. She was loyal, pretty, smart, strong, and overall fantastic.

Wait, wait, wait. Do you want *him to love you?*

No. Yes. Maybe. Argh!

McKell stopped, forcing everyone else to stop as well. Devyn bumped into her and grunted. A moment later, a light flared to life. He held some sort of glowing stick that chased away the worst of the darkness. Where he'd gotten it, she didn't know. Did he carry one with him everywhere he went?

"We will journey to the palace," McKell said.

"I really want a tour," Bride said. This should have been her home, and she wanted to see every nook and cranny before she was forced to tell the king to fuck himself if he tried to force her to do something she didn't want to do.

"Bride," Devyn said on a sigh.

"What?"

"You know."

She did?

"A tour, yes," McKell said, his voice raspy, his gaze glued to her. "The king does not allow an audience until morning. We will tour the city, then wait in my home and finally talk."

Oh. Oops. Had she just made a wish come true?

"No." Devyn shook his head. "We'll see the city, then wait in the king's palace."

"Or give us the tour whenever," she said helpfully, hoping to circumvent any disaster her kind-of wish might have caused.

McKell narrowed his eyes at the Targon. He moved, so swiftly no one, not even Bride, could register, and stopped in front of them. Time ground to a halt, everything around them ceasing to exist. The guards stopped breathing, and water no longer trickled.

"I can manipulate time in shorts burst, so listen carefully. What I have to say cannot be uttered near the king or even near another vampire clan. There is a reason Maur—Bride was sent from here. If it's learned she has returned, she will be hunted. Killed." And then he was back in place, time once more ticking by.

A low growl echoed from Devyn's throat. "You told me she was safe. We *will* be discussing why she's not. Now."

Once again, time ceased, and McKell was in their faces. "I will not do this again, Targon. If I did not think I could protect her, I would not have brought her here." His offense doubled with every word. "No one will recognize her as the girl she once was."

"Your men—"

"Are loyal to me. We have fought together, bled together. We will die together. But, no, they do not know. I will not tell them. You are not to tell them, either."

Devyn nodded stiffly, satisfied with that.

"I hope you boys are having fun, talking about me as if I'm not here, 'cause I'm loving it," she said.

McKell returned to his stance before them, time kicking back into motion.

"One thing, vampire," Devyn said for all to hear, "She's *my* wife, as I've told you again and again, and you would do well to remember that. Don't forget what I'm capable of. Oh, and perhaps you should know, I texted the coordinates of your entrance to my friends at AIR. If they don't hear from me in twenty-four hours, they will descend."

It was a lie—their phones didn't work, they were too far out—but McKell clearly didn't know that. Red bled into his pupils, into the violet irises, the whites. Once more, time stopped. This time, however, even Devyn seemed to be frozen. Only Bride and McKell were aware.

The vampire launched forward, fist swinging and connecting with Devyn's eye before she could protest.

Bride snarled low in her throat. "Do that again, and I will personally slit your throat while you sleep. I'm the only one allowed to abuse him."

The vampire cracked his neck left, right, then settled back in his spot. "My apologies, sweet bride."

Time restarted. Devyn rubbed his eye, glaring suspiciously at McKell.

"The king allowed you to live the last time you were here because he trusted you to keep our secrets," McKell said as if nothing had happened. "What will he say when he learns of this treachery?"

Bride shifted, suddenly nervous again. "You risk giving away your location every time you enter the surface world. How is that any different? Besides, you said the world already knows vampires exists."

"No, the *underworld* knows of our existence. Criminals. Slavers. But they don't know how to get to us. If word spreads, human fanatics will arrive on our doorstep. War will erupt. And if that happens, we will know who to blame." A muscle ticked in his jaw, and he whipped around. "Enough of this. Come. There is a drop. You can fly, I presume?"

Fly? "No, I can't." No, not true, she thought next, but didn't rescind her claim. She could fly, but only as mist. Misting wasn't something she would do here. She would have to strip, then piece herself back together. She would be too exhausted to defend Devyn from attack.

McKell twisted to face her again, searching her features. "You do not tease? You cannot fly?"

"No." Could all other vampires? Fabulous. Already she was lacking.

Confusion flittered over the warrior's face. "Very well. I will catch you." With that, he stepped into a gaping hole and disappeared from view.

"We'll be fine," Devyn said. He kissed her temple. "I've never failed at anything and won't start now."

"But how will you—"

"I'm probably the most powerful, gifted man in the universe. Of course I can do this."

"Sorry if I'm not convinced. I need your game plan."

"Energy, love. Energy. Just as I can command other bodies to obey me, I can command the air to slow us."

She nodded, drew in a breath, and stepped to the hole. She looked down. So much darkness, so thick . . . even with her superior eyesight, she couldn't see a bottom. Couldn't hear a sound.

"I'll meet you down there, and *I'll* be the one to catch you," Devyn said, and then he disappeared.

I can do this. I can. Closing her eyes, she stepped forward. Gasped. The ground vanished, and she was falling fast, falling down. Her arms floundered for an anchor as her heart raced in her chest, beating against her ribs. Up sprang the thorns and the fire, and her stomach twisted into a thousand tiny knots. She fought past her rising panic. *Fly, damn you, fly.*

A sense of numbness suddenly blanketed her feet and spread up, into her legs, her hips, her arms. With the numbness came a sensation of heaviness, and she thought to drop faster, harder, like a stone in water, but instead she slowed. Her eyelids popped open, and she gazed around her in confusion. It wasn't her body that was heavier, she realized, it was that the air around her had thickened.

She wanted to laugh. *I'm flying. I'm truly flying.* And Devyn was responsible, the sweetie. A light appeared at her feet, and she saw that he was already on the ground, waiting for her. He could see her without the glow stick, so his hands were empty as he opened his arms; she floated herself straight into them.

"Thank you," she said with a grin. "I didn't know something like that was possible."

"Actually, you did. You've been bedded by me, so you've flown to the heavens on several occasions."

The other vampires landed behind her, in the air one moment and standing the next.

"This way." While McKell's tone was stiff, he didn't protest Devyn's hold on her. Maybe he was learning. He stalked away, forcing them to follow or be left behind.

Devyn had to push her forward to spur her into motion. This new section of the cave was spacious, with walls so high she didn't have to duck and didn't feel cramped. There were shops built into the sides, with doorways and windows and signs, everything human shops possessed. No one was about, however; the makeshift streets were empty.

"Where is everyone?" she asked.

"Sleeping," McKell answered.

How very human of them. "How do they know day versus night?"

He rounded a corner, fingers brushing the pole of a muted streetlamp. "We have a lighting system of our own, one that mirrors the surface."

They trekked down a long walkway, took several more turns, bypassed what was obviously the palace, with its intimidating size, consuming three entire walls, squished through thin slices of rock, and finally came to an iron fence decorated with interwoven circles and squares.

McKell unlocked it with a single wave of his hand and trudged forward. Again, she and Devyn followed. The guards, however, did not. They posted themselves in front of the gate. Bride soon found herself walking straight into another cave, this one separated by thin strings of beads. Or rather, bone? she wondered. The pieces were small and the same creamy white as bone, a marrowlike substance in the centers.

Inside were animal-skin rugs, a lounge and couch made from stone and draped in thick, dark fur, and a long, thin table that stretched in the center of the room. The table was the size of a twin bed and sat low to the ground. Is that where McKell slept?

"Sit, sit. Let's fortify ourselves before we begin. Are you thirsty?" he asked. Before she could answer, the warrior clapped his hands. A human girl raced through a far entryway, the beads blocking it clanging together behind her. The scent of food—fruits and nuts, no meats or spices, thank God—came with her. "Feed my guest," he instructed.

The girl was dressed in . . . peach-colored leather? No, Bride realized upon closer inspection. Flesh. She gagged, barely managed to cover the motion with a hand to her mouth. The girl wore human flesh that had been cured into leather, and the material wrapped around her breasts and hips.

Dear God. They must recycle their food when they finished with it.

This one had been tattooed around her neck, wrists, and ankles. Like shackles. The design was intricate, distinctive, with the same swirls and points that Bride had seen on the iron fence.

The human kept her head bowed, her eyes lowered, as she lay upon the table and stretched out her arm in offering to Bride.

"No, thank you," Bride said gently. Revulsion swam through her as she eased onto the floor beside the table, her legs suddenly too weak to hold her.

A tremble moved through the girl, as though she feared the rejection would earn her a punishment.

"Is she not to your liking?" McKell asked.

"I can't drink from anyone but Devyn," she reminded him.

He was silent for a moment. "Who knows? This girl might be the exception. You should try her. She's very sweet." His motions were clipped, a direct contrast to his gentle tone, as he latched onto the girl's other arm and lifted it to his lips. He bit down, hard, but the girl didn't seem to notice.

On and on he drank. First, the girl paled. Then her eyelids drifted closed. Her head lulled to the side as she sank into unconsciousness. Eyes at half-mast, McKell disengaged and leaned back, his back propping against the lounge. His lips were stained crimson. "Sure you don't want to give her a try?"

Bride swallowed back intensified revulsion. It helped that Devyn was beside her, tracing little circles along her back, reminding her of his presence, his strength. Did everyone have slaves like this?

"I'm sure," she said. "At this rate, the girl will be dead by the end of the day." There was no way to hide her disgust.

The warrior frowned. "By the time my hunger returns, she'll be completely replenished."

"How often do you eat?"

"Once a week. Every vampire here drinks once a week. Don't you?"

Once a week? Lucky. "No, I eat every day. Sometimes I was forced to go longer, but my hunger always returns with the descent of the sun."

His frown deepened, his brow puckering. "Interesting, but no cause for concern. Probably has to do with being raised on the surface." He sighed. "You have other questions, I'm sure."

"Many questions, actually." And she was more than ready to get started on the asking of them. "Where are my parents? Do I even have parents?"

The warrior nodded. He cast Devyn a smug glance, as if to say, *See, I can give her what you cannot.* "Vampires give birth just as humans do, though it is much harder for us to do so, as our aging process is so gradual. And you do have parents, yes. Or did. They're dead, I'm afraid. Your mother died of sickness. You father died soon after her in a hunting raid."

Dead. Her shoulders dipped. She didn't know them, and so didn't mourn them, but she did mourn the loss of the dream of them. "Is that why I was sent from this place? Because there was no one to take care of me?"

"No. Had they died and left you alone, there would have been a fight for you. Babies are rare and considered precious here. They were killed *after* sending you to the surface."

So she'd been sent away. Ouch. Wouldn't have stung so much if she'd accidentally wandered off.

So many nights she'd imagined a candy-flowers-and-balloons family reunion. Her parents would have laughed with joy upon seeing her, swept her into their arms, and proclaimed their undying love for her. Instead, they had willingly parted with her.

McKell noticed her upset and sighed. "Do not judge them too harshly. You exhibited signs of the"—he leaned forward, and when he next spoke, he whispered as if what he said was a curse—"*nefreti.*"

A grim shudder swept through her. "What's that?" she found herself whispering back. An Egyptian queen?

His lips thinned, as if even thinking of it were painful to him. "They are vampires who are far more powerful than anyone should be. Rather than have a single extraordinary ability, as is customary, they have *all* extraordinary abilities. They are uncontrollable, unstoppable, and because of that they are deemed a threat to the royal family, to everyone really, and killed the moment they are recognized."

Devyn palmed one of those wooden daggers he'd taken to the auction before the last word left the warrior's mouth. He tossed it in the air, as if he hadn't a care. "I don't think it needs to be said that if you touch her, I'll slice you from end to end."

"So suspicious." McKell shook his head. Thankfully he didn't erupt at the sight of that weapon. "I didn't bring her here to kill her. I'm the one who helped send her to the surface, after all, ensuring she lived. Because she had been deemed my bride, I visited her often and already loved her as my own." There at the end, he eyed her expectantly.

"I don't remember you," she admitted. "I don't remember anything about this place."

Another sigh. "No, I don't guess you would. Your mother took the memory of your time here from you, so that you would never return."

So. That's why Bride had had no idea who or what she was. "She could have just told me to stay away. I might have listened."

"We were unwilling to take that chance."

Even knowing it had been done for her own good failed to lessen the sting. She wanted to grab the dagger now resting on Devyn's thigh and stab something.

"Everyone assumes you are dead," McKell said. "As commander of the king's army, I was the one ordered to kill you. Because of my reputation, everyone assumed I would do it. And I meant to. But I couldn't. Even then, you . . . affected me. So we branded you, your mother and I, and we sent you to the surface. As I said, she died soon after."

"Of sickness. What kind of sickness? I've never been sick, so I assumed other vampires would never sicken, either."

He shrugged. "Perhaps sickness wasn't the right word. She . . . are you sure you wish to know?"

"Yes. And just so you know, I'm about two seconds away from assaulting you for the information."

Though it was clear he didn't take her threats seriously, he said, "She died of starvation."

Bride heard the underlying meaning of his words. Her mother had refused to eat. As she clutched her stomach to settle the sudden churning, Devyn pulled her tight against his body. *I was loved, after all,* she thought. The revelation soothed the hurt she'd been harboring, but also brought a wealth of despair. Her mother had loved her, but had killed herself after sending Bride away.

"I want to remember her," she said softly.

"I'm afraid I cannot help you with that. She didn't just bury your memories; she erased them. That was her ability. And I know what you're thinking. Why didn't she just erase the memory of you from the people here? There are too many people, and each day your powers would have grown. She would have had to remove their memories every day for the rest of your life. One day, she would have missed someone, and word of your presence would have leaked."

She splayed her arms. "If I have all abilities, shouldn't *I* be able to erase memories? Shouldn't I be able to stop time?"

"One would think so." He arched a brow. "You can't?"

She shook her head, wondering if she'd been sent away for nothing. Then she thought of the thorns and the fire.

The place that hurt her to even brush with mental fingers. The place that sprung up with strong emotion. The place that held many other powers.

No, she hadn't been sent away for nothing.

McKell rubbed two fingers over his stubbled jaw. "Your father was able to suppress the powers of others. Perhaps he suppressed some of your more destructive abilities to help you cope with life above."

Her father. A man she couldn't even picture, but a man who had wanted only the best for her. A pang of longing had her swallowing back a whimper.

"What other abilities are there?" Devyn asked.

"Mind reading, for one, which just happens to be the king's ability."

"Mind reading isn't destructive," she said. It was cool. Would have been cooler if she could actually do it. Maybe one day . . .

"But then again," McKell said with a shrug, "perhaps not all *nefreti* can do all things. We've never had the chance to study them because they are destroyed so early. Besides the first few, of course, who showed us their powers when they slayed the last king and disappeared. Well, and Fiona, but she lived on her own for many years before revealing herself. And now that we know of her, we cannot catch her."

Fiona. Bride wanted to meet her, talk to her. "What gives them away? The *nefreti,* I mean."

"The atomizing. Only a *nefreti* can do it. You and your mother were shopping one morning as I and my army passed. You were so excited to see me that you ran to me, and as you ran you broke apart, particles forming in your place. You swept the rest of the way to me before putting yourself back together in my arms. Too many people saw, or we would have simply hidden you down here and claimed you had died."

Oh, the horror her mother must have experienced that day. "Do you have a photograph of her?"

"Somewhere. Maybe. Because of your taint, everything she owned was burned."

A sudden blast of hate bombarded her as she imagined her mother, her poor, sweet mother, who had just given up her only child to save her, watching all of her belongings being destroyed. "Your king—"

"Thought he was protecting his family," McKell interjected before she could threaten the bastard's life. "He is not a bad man, Bride. Neither am I."

No, he wasn't. Except for his treatment of food, that is. Well, and his bitch-slap to Devyn.

"Darling," Devyn said, his tone pure sugar, "he's trying to court you. Isn't that sweet. I, of course, know you're too smart to soften."

Something clear, yet thicker than saliva, dripped from one of McKell's fangs. Bride would have laid good money on poison.

"Keep pushing me, Targon. See what happens."

"I will, thank you."

"Should I step out?" Bride said, throwing up her arms in exasperation. "Maybe let you two have some privacy for your pissing contest?"

McKell lost the worst of his anger—she knew, because his fangs dried—and looked to Devyn. "Is she always like this?"

"Yes."

The two nodded at each other in sympathy, the tension broken. What next? Bonding over beers and future conquests? Perfect. Just perfect. *You brought this on yourself.* She only hoped the king appreciated her finer qualities. Otherwise . . . No, she wouldn't think about otherwise. Everything was going to work out.

CHAPTER 22

Is this love? Devyn wondered. He must love her, or he wouldn't willingly be in the dark underground he'd vowed never to return to. A seemingly spacious world, but one he perceived as very cramped. Before and now. But Bride had wanted to come, and he'd been struck with a consuming need to give her what she desired. Even this.

He'd also hoped that if he brought her here, letting her see the vampire way of life, she would realize she could have—and would want—a life with him on the surface. A life with no regrets. Not just days, weeks, or months, as he himself had always assumed. But . . . forever?

Maybe. He knew he didn't want to let her go. He knew he wouldn't let her be with someone else. He knew no one else appealed to him. And he knew the biggest obstacle to getting what he wanted was McKell.

Obstacles must be eliminated. Always. No matter the method used.

The warrior's solicitousness was throwing him for a loop—not that Devyn trusted the man. Even a little. But damn if he didn't believe the male truly adored Bride. Still. That adoration was irritating. Bride belonged to Devyn. She filled a void inside him that he'd always denied; she made him see that there was a better way to be.

And just when he'd realized it, someone had decided to try and take her away. *Figures.*

He shouldn't be surprised that McKell hadn't yet struck at him, though. According to Dallas's vision, that would happen at the pier. Unless . . . An unsettling thought took root. Because he knew what would happen at the pier, Devyn could very well have changed the future by deciding to come here, thereby forcing McKell to try and stab him in this new location. Shit. He hadn't thought of that when he'd decided taking Bride underground was the best way to acquire the answers she sought while at the same time keeping them together—without a knife in his heart.

McKell can't kill you, he reminded himself. Yet. For the moment, Bride needed his blood. Devyn's hands curled into fists. He didn't like that there was a way to wean Bride from his vein.

Wasn't going to happen.

When they returned home, Devyn planned to take the necessary steps to ensure Bride wanted to stay with him. They'd marry in truth, by Earth standards as well as Targon. He would build an office for her books. Or rather, pay someone to build it. He would purchase a water bed, and he would sleep in it with her.

No longer would he allow his father's voice to speak inside his head, stopping him from claiming his woman. As Bride had said, there was nothing shameful in what they did. The knowledge had never been more real to him. Bride wasn't a whore, as his father would have called her. What she did to Devyn was beautiful; therefore what he did to her was the same. They could be together, be *themselves,* and still respect each other.

How had he ever convinced himself otherwise?

He didn't want her to change from the smart-mouthed bloodsucker she was. And she clearly didn't want him, flirtatious narcissus that he was, to change. After the auction, she'd almost attacked him. He smiled, remembering.

"You look smug," McKell said with a frown.

Bride faced him. His beautiful Bride. "You do," she said. "What wheels are spinning in your head, Bradley?"

He blew her a kiss before turning to McKell. "What happens to Bride if I die before she's weaned off my blood? Not that I'll allow such a thing," Devyn said, partly to remind the vampire of who Bride belonged to, and partly to learn the ways of his wife's people. As he liked being the best at everything he did, this marriage would be no exception. He would care for her properly in all ways, even if he was dead.

McKell ran his tongue over his fangs, his narrowed eyes on Devyn. "We have a potion for such matters. Once she drinks it, she will be unable to go near you, or the effects will mutate and she will die."

"Okay, next option," Bride said.

"There is also the possibility of bonding with someone else," McKell replied. "It's actually the preferred method, as it holds no danger."

"Next," Devyn said this time.

McKell shrugged. "That's it."

Then Devyn would live forever. He'd planned to anyway, but this conversation had just solidified his determination.

"I have a question," Bride said. She was still at his side, leaning into him, tensing every time she heard something unpleasant. "Can I turn other people into vampires with my blood? I mean, I haven't yet, but it's still a fear I have."

McKell regarded her strangely before comprehension dawned and he shook his head. "You've been reading surface books, I see. We have some of those ourselves because we like to be up-to-date on beliefs, in case we need to intervene or make them believe something else."

"Yes, I've been reading. It was the only way I knew to learn about myself. I had no vampire tutor, no one I could ask."

Now hold everything. "Not to call you a liar, love, but you are a liar. You're forgetting someone who did, in fact, answer many of your questions."

"Yes, and I had to pay dearly for the information," she said with a half-grin.

"Are you referring to the little striptease I forced you to perform? Well, you're welcome. I haven't forgotten how much you enjoyed yourself."

She rolled her eyes. "Like I was the only one."

With a growl, McKell tossed a stone into the wall, and plumes of dust wafted around them. "Do you not care to hear what I have to say?"

Did it make Devyn a bad person that he was enjoying the man's anger?

"Please continue," Bride said with a wave of her hand.

"It would take significant amounts of your blood for a significant amount of time to change a human or otherworlder into a vampire." McKell's ears perked, and his back straightened. "The city is awakening, and we must prepare. I have clothes for you, Bride. They are yours, no one else's. The moment I decided to look for you, I purchased them for you. They're in my personal quarters."

No way was she going into the man's bedroom alone. "First, you should know that the humans you hired to find her, the slavers, hoped to rape and torture her before handing her over to you."

The patient stillness of a predator came over McKell. He breathed in and out, slowly, measured, as if to steady himself from a deep rage. "My apologies, Bride." That rage crackled in his tone. "They will be dealt with, I assure you."

"They already have been," Devyn said, smug again. "I take care of my own."

McKell flicked his tongue over a fang. "Appropriately?"

He nodded, offended that his ability to protect his woman was in question. "While on the surface, you might have heard of a head being found. Without its body."

Now the corner of McKell's lip twitched, his anger fading. "Appropriately, then. Now go dress, child." He waved a hand toward the entrance on the far right. "I shall be waiting."

That commanding tone had to chafe at Bride's independent nature, as did the "child," and Devyn almost grinned. "There's something else. You mentioned that the king's ability is mind reading."

McKell nodded, his expression suddenly wary.

"I suspected as much, last time I was here. But if he reads minds, how are we to prevent him from learning what we know of Bride?" As he spoke, he rubbed her back to assure her that no matter what, they would do what was needed to keep her safe.

"The king can only read direct thoughts. While in his presence, in the palace really, you must be careful not to think of what you've learned here. I told you the truth only to warn and prepare you. If he even suspects, we are all doomed." A heavy sigh. "He is not the same man you knew, Targon. Remember Fiona, the *nefreti* I mentioned? She abducted his brother, tortured him in the most vile of ways, and when she tired of him and returned the prince, he committed suicide. The king has not been the same since."

Devyn wouldn't offer sympathy he didn't feel. He had not liked the prince, had considered him loathsome, always grabbing at the female servants, even hitting them. The bastard had probably deserved everything the one called Fiona had done to him.

"If the king is a mind reader, keeping me isn't an option for you, McKell," Bride piped up. "No way the two of us can keep our secrets from the king forever."

He shrugged, unconcerned. "As I explained, memories can be erased. Once we have been bonded, we will remain in my home until it's done."

Bride gasped. "As if."

Devyn stiffened. No one would be screwing with his female's mind. "You risked a lot, bringing her here."

"I have craved her return for over eighty years. Imprisonment and death would be small prices to pay for having her here." There at the end, his voice had turned husky. "Go on now. Change."

Devyn's lips pulled back in a scowl. He didn't mind the vampire paying those prices, but he did mind Bride paying them.

"But I have so many more questions," Bride said with a pout.

"And I will answer them as I show you the rest of the underground."

With those words, Devyn realized the warrior's purpose, the reason he'd allowed Devyn into the underground without a fight and with utter confidence of success. McKell hoped to lure Bride into staying with the one thing Devyn could not give her: a city of vampires. The warrior hoped she would spurn Devyn's affections, beg the king to allow her to stay, and then discard Devyn and his blood.

A sense of urgency filled him, a need to show Bride what *he* could give her. He pushed to a stand, dragging her with him. "She will change, but I will go with her."

McKell scowled at him. "You will stay here with me, and I will answer any questions you have about the care one must take with vampire mates."

Bastard. Offering something so tempting. "My bad. Perhaps I didn't make myself clear. Where she goes, I go."

Whatever the vampire saw in his expression caused him to nod stiffly.

Devyn turned, automatically locking his enemy in place. A growl sounded behind him. He didn't release his hold until he and Bride were inside the bedroom.

Then he waited, doing nothing, expecting McKell to storm inside, fangs bared. It never happened. Another shocker.

Bride spun in a circle, her gaze eating up their new surroundings, and he could only pray she liked his home better. It came with him, after all.

He took stock, as well. There was a bed of pillows and furs, two lace ribbons at the head and foot, perfect for a little game of bondage. An intricately carved vanity, a mirror, and all the things a woman could desire to pamper herself. A desk made of stone, weapons lining the wall—did the vampire not fear Devyn would take them?—and a closet filled with robes of every color.

The entire enclosure reeked of the warrior.

Devyn popped his jaw in irritation. "He wanted you in here without me so that you'll smell of him when we visit the palace."

"I don't understand why we need to visit the king. I'm not going to let him decide for me."

"Have you made a decision, then?"

"About what?" she asked, pretending to be clueless.

About me. About us. He didn't say that, however. There was another way to learn the answer he craved without sounding like a whiny, needy puss. "Visiting the king is the only way to keep McKell from coming after you." Devyn drew her into his arms. "Are you happy you came here?"

"Yes. I needed to know what it was like."

"And?" He kissed the top of her head, desperate to have his lips on her. *Anywhere* on her.

"It's not like I imagined it. The way that girl was

treated . . . the king wanting me dead . . . destroying my mother . . ." She shuddered.

"So . . . you won't stay here?"

"No. Probably not."

Thank God. "We need to figure a few things out, then. Like what to do if the king says you belong to the warrior. I honestly thought he'd side with me because we're already bonded, already married." And yeah, he'd even thought there was a possibility the king would try and force Devyn to stay here; to keep Bride safe, he'd deemed the chance worth it. Not once had he ever thought the king would try and separate them. Until now. McKell's confidence . . .

"If he does, I'll just wish him into a pile of ash," she said.

"And if that doesn't work?"

"I'll keep wishing until something does." She returned his embrace and rested her head in the hollow of his neck. Her breath was warm against his skin. "Devyn," she said, and there was a hesitance to her tone he'd never heard before. "My mother is dead, and there's no way to return my memories of her. I don't even know her, but right now I miss her terribly."

"I'm sorry, love. So sorry." He ran his hands up and down her spine, offering what comfort he could. "My own mother was more concerned with her lovers than her child, so while I'd willingly give you my memories, I don't think you'd want them."

"Oh, Devyn. I'm sorry." Her grip tightened around him. "You should have been fawned over. I bet you were adorable."

"Were?" he asked with mock offense.

She uttered a warm, rich chuckle. "Braggart. Macy says I'm becoming just like you."

"And you're the better for it."

That earned him another chuckle.

He kissed her temple. "Your mother wanted you alive and happy. More than anything else, even her own life." He cupped her chin and drew back, studying her. "You can do that for her. You can give her that."

"Yes."

Tears sprang in her eyes, turning them to liquid emeralds, and her bottom lip started trembling. Those tears . . . He was struck with the urge to fight the Grim Reaper himself, anything to give her back her mother. He couldn't exist, knowing Bride was hurting. It destroyed him, more than the darkness ever had.

What was worse, he couldn't tell her how much he thought he maybe might kinda sorta love her. Not yet. Not here. She might not believe him, thinking he said the words, those three earth-shattering words, simply to convince her to leave with him, which could in turn make the contrary female angry enough to stay.

He'd never said "I love you" before. Not to his parents, and not to one of his many lovers. When he finally admitted his feelings, he wasn't sure what he'd do in the face of doubt.

How did she feel about him? She trusted him, desired him, but did she love him?

"You're killing me," he said. "You know that, right?"

"So the big strong warrior can't stand a woman's tears?" With a shaky grin, she wiped her eyes with the back of her wrist. "I'll make a note of it for the next time I want my way and you're acting like an ass."

"I knew you were smart, but this . . . recognizing how big and strong I am. Brilliant."

Grinning, she pulled away from him and trekked to the closet, where she flipped through the robes. "This is what the females wear all day?"

"Oh, yes."

"Well, come help me pick something."

Devyn happily closed the distance between them. Rather than reach around her and grab a green robe to match her eyes as he'd intended, he cupped her breasts. "My advice? The sexier the better."

Her head fell against his shoulder, and she moaned. Her nipples hardened, deliciously abrading his palms. "Are you doing this to cover me with *your* scent?"

"That's merely a bonus. I'm doing this because I can't *not* do it." He kissed her exposed neck as his hands delved to the waist of her pants, unzipped the clasp, and sank past her panties. "It's been too long since I last had you."

"You should wait a bit longer," she said, but she didn't push his hand away. "*We* should wait."

He ground his erection into her lower cheeks. "I won't tell McKell if you won't." It was difficult, but he kept some of his attention on the doorway. Any disturbance in the energy there, and he would kill whoever walked through the door.

"If his ears are as tuned as mine, he'll hear."

"Then you'll just have to be quiet this time, won't you, love?" He sank two fingers inside her, his palm rubbing her just right.

She groaned in pleasure.

"A sound. For shame. But how wet you are. So ready for me, hmm?"

"Yes," she admitted on a wispy catch of breath. "Need you. Now." Up and down her chest rose. Back and forth she writhed.

He hadn't planned on taking her here, but he couldn't stop himself from undoing his pants and allowing his erection to pop free. He ripped the material gaping at her waist—she didn't need it anymore—stripping her luscious lower body. He kicked her legs apart, and then he was inside her, all the way home.

Trembling, she cried his name. She even reached up and back, clutching his head, placing them cheek to cheek. In and out, he pounded, driving hard and fast.

"Bite me, love."

"No." A gasp, a groan of want.

"You need the blood."

"You need the strength."

"Drink a little. Just a little . . ." Temptation, so hard to resist.

Her head turned, gaze latching onto his pulse. She licked her lips. "Well . . . maybe."

"Do it. I need it. I need your teeth in me. Shall I beg? I will. I'll beg and plead and—"

With a hoarse moan, she bit him, those fangs sinking deep, that hot tongue caressing his vein and drawing the blood into her mouth. Oh, the pleasure. He rolled her clitoris between his fingers, increased the pace of his thrusts, sweating, hungry for climax, on fire at every point of contact, euphoric, on edge, desperate.

She released him as she came, fangs emerging, fingers curling around the closet frame in front of her, nails scraping stone. Every muscle in her body tensed as her inner walls began milking him, squeezing tight. He roared, not even trying to be quiet, his hot seed jetting into her.

They stood there panting for several minutes, sated, floating on a tide of bliss. Finally reason returned, and he forced himself to pull out of her. He used one of the robes to clean them both and tossed the material to the floor.

Bride pivoted and faced him, though not really looking at him. Like butterfly kisses, she ghosted her fingertips over the puncture wounds in his neck. "Shall I try and heal them with my blood?"

She'd never offered before, and he realized it was because she'd still, on some level, feared turning him into a vampire. "No, leave them." He wanted the king to see. To know. "I'll wear them with pride, for they prove I fed my woman."

Her expression, already glazed with residual passion, softened. "Devyn, I—"

"No, don't say it." Now wasn't the time, whether she meant to discuss her feelings or ask him to slow things down. He kissed her hard and long, enjoying her sweet flavor. "Dress. I'm sure McKell is angry with us."

Her head tilted to the side, ears twitching. "He's pacing."

"And you're right. I'm angry," the warrior snarled.

He and Bride shared a smile. "Dress," Devyn told her.

Once more she spun toward the closet. She didn't bother flipping through the colors again, but snatched up the green. "Your favorite, yes?"

Knew his preferences already, did she? Adorable female.

She dressed slowly, her movements exaggerated for his benefit. When she finished, the silky material floated over her curves, leaving one delectable shoulder bare. "How do I look?"

"Breathtaking, as always," he said, surprised by the way his voice broke. "Here. Let me." He picked a gold belt from the array hanging on the wall and wrapped it around her waist, cinching the material. There was a brush on the desk, and he grabbed it. The next five minutes he dedicated to smoothing out the tangles he had caused in her hair.

She let him. He knew she needed time to mentally prepare herself for the tour they were about to take. A tour she'd waited her entire life for, but one that would not be with her family. He simply enjoyed the moment, savoring the way the dark waterfall glimmered in the light. He could have done this for hours. Days.

Finally he forced himself to set the brush aside. McKell's footfalls had grown thunderous. "Ready?"

Reluctantly she nodded.

"Don't forget, love. I'll be with you every step of the way."

Hand in hand, they rejoined McKell.

The warrior stood at the entryway, arms crossed over his middle. "I could destroy you without you ever realizing what happened."

"Hey, now," Bride said. "None of that, remember?"

McKell spun on his heel and stomped from the cave. "Come. Before I forget myself."

Just as before, he and Bride followed. Guards were still posted at the gate, and when they passed, the men fell into step behind them. Though only a few hours had ticked by, the city they next entered was nothing like the city they'd first encountered. This one pulsed with life.

Vampires meandered in the streets, their robes dancing almost magically at their ankles. Some were alone, some were paired, while others strode in groups. It was like any other city on any other planet. No one wore those glammored masks, so all that beauty was nearly blinding.

Shops were filled with clothing, food for vampires to buy for their human slaves, a bar that served the thirsty. Bride wasn't looked at twice. Devyn was regarded with hostile curiosity by the males and eye-fucked with naked desire by the females. Nothing had changed, he mused.

One woman stopped directly in front of him and invited him to her home for breakfast. He, of course, was to be the meal. She was pretty, with Bride's pale skin and bright, vivid eyes. But her lips were not as lush, her hair not as dark.

"Sorry, darling," he said, not slowing but continually stepping around her. "While I'm sure you are indeed a delicious little treat, I'm taken."

After trying a bit longer, and still meeting with rejection, the female flounced away in a huff.

Devyn glanced over at Bride, unsure of what he'd find. She was shaking her head.

"Sorry, love," he told her. "But what can I say? I'm irresistible."

"No, you're a ho. But the good news is, I'm okay with that."

And he'd once wanted jealousy from her, he thought. This was so much better. Acceptance for who and what he was. Because she knew he would always return to her?

"You would never have to wonder about *my* affections," McKell said, keeping pace at Bride's other side. "Since I began my search for you, I have given myself to no one." His voice had lowered, less substantial than even a whisper, so that only the three of them could hear.

Sneaky bastard. Devyn glared at him. *I'm going to cut out your tongue and give it to my maids to clean my toilets with.*

"Stay with me, and this could all be yours." The warrior spread his arms to encompass the city. "You would never have to hide who and what you are again."

"Wouldn't I?" she asked meaningfully. She was *nefreti,* hunted for her abilities. Deemed too dangerous to live.

That's my girl.

"You would be safe," the warrior said, "safer here than you could ever be up there. I would make sure of it. Besides, what makes you think the king would allow you to leave, placing our secrets in the hands of war-hungry humans?"

"She has lived on the surface for a long time and never revealed herself to the humans," Devyn replied. "She would not do so now."

McKell snapped his too-sharp teeth at Devyn, eyes glowing bright red.

Devyn gave him a pinkie wave and a smile.

"Not another pissing contest," Bride said on a moan. "Come on, be a good boy, McKell, and take me to my mother's home."

McKell frowned at her. "I told you. It was destroyed."

"That wouldn't stop *me* from taking her," Devyn told him.

There was a beat of silence, McKell clearly struggling to rein in his temper. "Very well," he finally said. After waving his men away, he changed directions completely, heading back toward his home. They skirted two shops and rounded three corners, and soon stood in front of a wall of loose rock. There were no people present, as though the area itself was somehow tainted. "Here you are."

Bride hesitantly, shakily stepped forward and traced her fingers over a few of the crumbles. "This was a doorway?"

"Yes." McKell nodded.

"Tell me what was inside."

"A home very much like mine. When you entered, there was a main meeting area and three doorways that branched into rooms. One was for your parents, one for you, and one for the food."

"What was my mother's name?" she asked softly.

"Ellen."

"Ellen," she repeated.

"She was beautiful, a lot like you. Same dark hair, same red lips, though you have your father's eyes. His name was Dominick, and he was a soldier like me. His strength was legend."

Her shoulders drooped a little. "I wish I remembered them."

In the distance, a clatter of bells rang.

When the last echo faded, a strained apprehension settled over their little group.

McKell was the first to break through it. He cleared

his throat. "The king is ready for visitors. Come, if we hurry, we might be able to beat the crowd."

Dread tightened Devyn's stomach as he reached for Bride. Once again, she was trembling. By coming here, he had placed their fate in the hands of a fierce king he apparently no longer knew. And all because he'd wanted to do what was right for a female. His female. Last time he'd tried to please a woman, that dark day on his mother's birthday, he'd spent weeks nursing a broken heart.

God only knew what would happen this time.

CHAPTER 23

Dallas didn't even have to knock on the metal door in front of him. Kyrin was already there, standing in the entryway, waiting. Dallas wanted to believe the otherworlder was there because he'd called ahead, which he had, but he knew better. Mia's man was as attuned to Dallas as Dallas was to him.

"I am glad you've come," Kyrin said, shutting the door behind him.

Silent, Dallas strode into the living room. Mia, lounging on the couch, flipped off the TV when she spotted him. He'd never seen her so relaxed. AIR was her life. Well, it had been until Kyrin found her.

She smiled a contented smile. "Took you long enough. *Idiot.*"

His lips curled in response. She'd always been ballsy. "What can I say? I recognize that I need help."

"You've been using your powers," Kyrin said from behind him.

He nodded. "Not as well as I'd assumed I would, but I've accepted that they're a part of me. That's something, right?"

"Sit, sit." Kyrin's arm, with pale skin that reminded him of Devyn's Bride, stretched past him, motioning toward the nearest chair.

His nerves were a little raw as he obeyed. Kyrin hadn't meant his words as a command, but that's exactly how Dallas's body took them, planting one foot in front of the other until Dallas was at the chair and easing down.

He faced his audience with narrowed eyes.

"Sorry," Kyrin muttered. The otherworlder settled beside Mia, who snuggled up next to him without shame or hesitation.

Hadn't pegged her for a cuddler. Amazing what love did to people.

"Before you guys begin," Mia said, "why don't you tell us what happened in that clearing. The full story, not the condensed version in your report."

He nodded, grateful for the reprieve. "Yesterday when I pegged Nolan with the night-night cocktail, he passed out, and a woman spoke from behind me. I turned, fell to my knees because my energy was completely drained, and there she was. An angel. There were guards behind her, and I shot them all. Didn't stun them, but killed them. I heard and smelled the sizzle of their flesh."

Dallas drew in a deep breath before continuing. "She promised to come back for me. I could feel the power radiating off her. It was like she had me in a trance. I wanted to shoot her, but I couldn't force my fingers to work. Then she was gone, the men were gone, and Hector was standing over me, telling me I must have imagined it."

The queen was part of the reason he'd finally decided to take Kyrin up on his offer of training, to prepare himself for the day she returned. And he knew, *knew,* she would return.

Kyrin frowned. He rubbed his smooth jaw with a finger, pensive. "You shot the men, but there was no sign of them when you awoke."

"Right."

"And we were only minutes behind you, so there would have been no time for her to drag them away."

"Right." But she'd been real, damn it.

"She could have walked through the wormhole again," Mia suggested, "taking the men with her."

God bless her.

Then Kyrin had to ruin it. "To my knowledge, otherworld travel is only possible through solar flares. There wasn't another solar flare after she stepped through."

Dallas's shoulders slumped. "So you're saying I dreamed her, too? Or maybe had a vision of her?"

"It's possible, I suppose. Have you ever seen yourself in a vision?"

He shook his head. "I'm always a shadowy figure. Faceless."

Once again Kyrin tapped a finger against his chin. "You don't see yourself because your decision about what to do hasn't yet been made when you see the future."

"Well, I saw myself clearly in this. I was an active participant."

"I doubt this was a vision, then." With a sigh, Kyrin leaned back on the couch. "Not a hallucination, either. We aren't prone to those. Our minds are too locked on what could happen in the future to give way to fantasies."

One small thing in his favor, at least.

"My best guess is that you spoke to this woman, and she has a power very similar to Nolan's. Not invisibility, because we would have seen her with the infrareds. Perhaps she can travel from one location to another with only a thought. My queen had that ability, as well."

Which would mean that Dallas now had a very powerful enemy. A powerful enemy he was insanely attracted to. A woman who slept with legions of men to save herself, killing them. A woman who had nearly controlled him with the same force Kyrin possessed over him.

A woman who could ruin his entire life, taking everything he loved from him.

"We'll have to place you under surveillance," Mia said, "in case she returns."

He gave a reluctant nod. Wouldn't be his favorite thing, being watched constantly, but it was better than the alternative. He didn't trust himself with Nolan's queen.

"Wow," Mia said. "I thought you'd fight me on that one."

"I'm not an idiot. Not all the time," he said, and she laughed. "I understand now how she so entranced Nolan, and why he refused to give her up."

Mia's gaze sharpened on him. "You didn't have sex with her, did you?"

"No." Had she remained, he might have let her seduce him, though, and he didn't like that. Made him feel weak.

"One thing we know. Her powers are vast, to have wiped away any hint of her presence like that," Kyrin said. "But there have been no new reports of the virus, so that is in our favor."

Mia snuggled deeper into her man's side. "When you guys are done with your training, I want a composite made of her."

"That is code for us to get started," Kyrin told him with a grin. "So tell me what brought you to this point."

At this second order, Dallas shifted uncomfortably. "First," he said, "there's Devyn. About a week ago I had a vision of him being murdered at the pier. Then, this morning, that image wiped itself from my mind as though it was no longer a concern."

At the word *murder*, Mia jolted upright. Probably arming herself mentally and figuring out the best way to watch the pier to save Devyn's ass.

"It's not. Valid, I mean." Kyrin patted her leg, and she gradually returned to his side. "You managed to change the future."

"So not all visions are set in stone?" That was news to him. Every vision he'd had before had come true.

"Not all, no. The more you allow the visions to dance through your mind, the more types of visions you'll receive, and the easier it will be for you to know what is changeable and what is not." Kyrin arched a black brow. "Were you given a new vision to take the other's place?"

"Yes." And the new one had pissed him off as much as the first, though it hadn't been nearly as bleak. "I saw Devyn chained inside a small, dark cage. He was cut up and bleeding. There was murder in his eyes." Worse, Bride had been nowhere to be seen. "There were two men beyond the bars, and they were eyeing him like he was the tastiest treat they'd ever seen."

Clearly, they were vampires. Which meant, to Dallas, that Devyn had gotten—or would get—himself captured by the warrior McKell.

Kyrin's head tilted to the side. "Tell me. Were the edges of this vision as real and colorful as the vision itself? Or were they faded, tapering into nothingness?"

Dallas frowned as he closed his eyes and replayed the scene of Devyn's captivity through his mind. He'd never paid attention to the edges of a vision before, only concentrating on the happenings. His frown deepened when he noticed that the edges were of the solid variety. "No fading. What does that mean?"

There was a regretful sigh. "That means at this point, that vision is not changeable. It will happen, and there's nothing that can be done to stop it. Devyn has already chosen the path that set him on that course and the pieces have already fallen into place."

Damn. How many layers were there to the visions? He'd never had a clue, never suspected there was more to think about than what he was seeing. He'd just thought that what he saw was what *was* going to happen.

"We've gotta get him out. He doesn't do well in confined spaces. Good news is, I can pinpoint his exact location. He injected himself with the isotope tracker a few weeks ago. Just in case Bride drank from him, he wanted to be able to track her."

Mia's grin returned. "God, I love that isotope. I'm thinking of implementing a Mandatory Injection Monday the first of every third month." She tapped her chin with a blunt-tipped fingernail. "And maybe I'll have everyone we arrest injected, as well. I mean, it's how we finally nailed Nolan. It could save us a lot of time if another escape is ever made."

Since Nolan's recapture yesterday, Dallas knew that Mia had broken down and tested the otherworlder's blood. Seemed there was no trace of the disease. Miracle of miracles, it was gone as if it had never been. So Mia had then tested the blood of the new vampires, but theirs had lacked the strong healing qualities of Bride's. Which meant that their blood wouldn't kill the disease. Only Bride's would, it seemed.

Devyn would flip when he found out. If—*when*—Dallas got him out of that cage.

"As for Devyn, we'll gather the troops and do a quick in-and-out," Mia said. "He won't be in that cage long." It was a vow. She knew how much Dallas had come to love the irreverent shithead, and she loved Dallas enough to want him happy.

If it weren't for Kyrin, Dallas would have jumped up and kissed her. "I pulled up his location this morning. It's the same as it was last night. At the canyon about three hours from here."

Her brow furrowed in confusion. "The canyon? Why did he go to the canyon? It's unlivable."

He explained how Devyn had taken Bride and run from McKell.

"No way. He wouldn't have run from the warrior." She shook her head. "Running isn't his style."

"You haven't seen how he is with Bride. It reminds me of"—he shuddered—"you guys. He wanted to protect her."

"Exactly," Mia said, nodding as if he'd just proven her

point. "To protect her, he would eliminate a threat, not evade it."

Huh. That made sense. Dallas leaned back in the chair. Shit. *I'm keeping her safe,* Devyn had said, and Dallas had just assumed the big guy had meant to hide out for a bit.

Just then Dallas felt like the idiot Mia had called him for ever assuming otherwise. But Devyn had purposefully given him that impression. Why?

The answer immediately slammed into him. Devyn had known Dallas would follow him, intending to fight the vampire army side by side, most likely losing the slaves he'd purchased in the fray.

Goddamn it! "Can I force a vision?"

Kyrin frowned. "What do you mean?"

"Can I somehow tap into Devyn's life and see what's going on right this very second?"

"You can, yes." There was no time to rejoice, because the Arcadian added, "With practice."

"Then I'll start practicing now." Determined, he closed his eyes and summoned his friend's image. There was Dev, laughing over at him. He'd probably just complimented his own beauty or the size of his cock. Dallas's lips twitched. *Come on, you can do it. Find Devyn.* Over and over he attempted to force his mind to open, to plug in and reveal. His lids squeezed tight with the force of his concentration, but the image never shifted, never became a real-life play-by-play.

Frustration was like a knife inside him.

"Stop," Kyrin said, and he did, helpless to do otherwise.

His eyelids popped open, his mind blanking. He gritted his teeth. "Do not order me around."

"You came to me for help. Therefore, I will do whatever I wish, and you will obey me in all things."

Yes, he would. He wouldn't be able to help himself. Furious, he popped to his feet. "I'm not your servant or your slave."

Pale blue eyes—eyes so like his own—narrowed. "But you are my student. Sit."

Though he was still fuming, Dallas sat, unable to do otherwise.

"If you do not want to follow my commands, learn to fight the impulse to follow them."

"How?" he gritted out.

"Practice, as I said."

Dallas pinched the bridge of his nose. Was that the otherworlder's answer to everything?

Mia threw a pillow at him. "Get over yourself. He's being generous, giving you so much of his time. Time he could be spending with me."

Kyrin clasped her hand and brought it to his lips for a kiss, though his attention never wavered from Dallas. "Have I answered all of your questions, agent?"

"Pretty much."

"Good." Kyrin stood. "Mia and I have set up a training mat. I'd like to—"

"Hell, no." That might have been the reason he'd come here, but sometime during their conversation things had changed. "I'm ready to go after Devyn and save him from that cage." Oh, yeah. And kill the people who had placed him there.

Kyrin shook his head, the picture of resolve. "You've accepted your abilities, but you have no idea how to truly use them to your advantage. You'll give me an hour or two of your time. Devyn will survive for that long. And then I will help you save him."

"Bastard!" Scowling, Dallas popped to his feet. The "you'll give me" had sealed his fate. He would stay here for "an hour or two," practicing as he'd been commanded. Unless . . . Kyrin had said he could fight the urge to obey.

Once more he concentrated. Tried to force one foot in front of the other to leave. He visualized the front door, saw himself walking out of it, but he fucking didn't move. His muscles were bunched, locked down on his bones, his brain refusing to send the signals needed for movement.

"Are you able to summon your powers easily?" the otherworlder asked him. "Can you turn them off whenever you wish?"

"Sometimes." He'd been able to race into the clearing, but he hadn't been able to bend Nolan's queen to his will. Stopping, though, once he'd started? Not really.

"That, too, will change when I am through with you. You'll summon and stop them at will."

"And just how long until you're through with me?" he couldn't help but ask with dread.

"Perhaps a year."

His jaw dropped. "A year? You're kidding me?"

Mia rolled her eyes. "You'll learn that Kyrin here doesn't have a sense of humor."

"You'll thank me for that," Kyrin said, confident.

"Thank you." The words were out before he could stop them.

Mia choked on a laugh.

Kyrin sighed patiently. "There is much to do, I see. More than I'd anticipated."

"Devyn—"

"Will be fine, like I said. The vision you had was the future. He's not yet in the cage."

Had Kyrin always been this much of an ass? "We can *keep* him from the cage, then. If we act now."

"Trying to change a vision set in stone is impossible. Doing so will only hurt *you*. I believe you've experienced that already. Devyn is going to be locked up, one way or another."

CHAPTER 24

To Devyn, the vampire palace had not changed in any way. He saw the same smooth onyx walls covered in merry murals of humans dancing in all their antique finery, same Victorian furniture stolen from the surface—walnut marble tabletops, white lace telephone chairs, and slag-glass lamps. Same ceiling comprised solely of crystal, like an endless chandelier or a rocky midnight ocean, the lights from below bouncing off the jagged shards and splashing colors in every direction. Same shields and spears decorating the walls. Same alabaster columns and statues of royalty positioned throughout.

There was a line of robe-clad women, males dressed in white shirts and black pants, much like McKell, all leading into the throne room. Guards were stationed throughout, armed with spiked whips.

None of the vamps had ever said anything to him, but he knew the whips were designed to slash through skin and vein while gripping bone, preventing the injury from healing. The subsequent blood loss weakened the captured vampires, enabling the whip to hold them in place. He could have used one of those whips on Bride when he'd lured her to his apartment, he supposed, but even from the beginning his goal had not been to hurt her.

Should have known then what she would come to mean to me. As he stood in the foyer, Bride and McKell at his sides, he tried to see the palace as Bride might: for the first time, as a home she should have grown up in, a home that had been denied her. It was beautifully dark, utterly sultry.

"The crowd beat us," McKell said on a sigh.

Bride spun in a circle, clearly awed. "Why do they wish to speak to the king?"

The warrior watched her with smug fondness, and Devyn could practically hear his thoughts: Score one for team McKell. "Many reasons. To gain permission to mate. To settle disputes with neighbors. Often a human is involved, and there has been a forbidden sampling."

She stilled, disgust replacing her awe. "Do they have to ask permission to bathe, too?"

Devyn fought a grin. Score one for team Devyn. Raised on the surface as she'd been, she was used to doing what she wanted, when she wanted to do it.

"Come," McKell said through clenched teeth. "There's no reason for us to wait in line. We will visit the king when the crowd thins."

"Why don't we just cut to the front?" Bride pointed toward the doors to the throne room. "I want to get this over with."

"That is not allowed. Not even for one of my station." McKell ushered them through an arched doorway and up a flight of stairs, comprised of the same crystal as the ceiling, only these had been ground down and polished to a glistening shine. On the second level, they turned a sharp corner, a yawning chamber coming into view.

There, the furniture was made entirely from human bones, and Bride couldn't hide her revulsion. Score two for team Devyn.

There were only three occupants. One was draped from head to toe in black, face obscured as she stood patiently in the far corner. The other two were more scantily dressed, their robes half the length of Bride's and completely transparent. He could see the outline of their nipples as they jumped from the—femur?—settee they'd been lounging on.

"Devyn," one of them called happily. She had long pale hair, chocolate eyes, and curves so dangerous they could never be fully explored.

The other clapped her hands and smiled. This one had a short cap of red curls and dimples when she smiled. She was taller, thinner, but no less desirable. "You came back to see us!"

Beside him, Bride moaned. "Great. Conquests."

McKell chuckled.

Devyn glared at him. They were tied once again, it seemed. Two to two. "You don't play fair."

His enemy shrugged, no less amused. "I play with what toys I have. I sent a few of my men to alert the princesses of their favorite Targon's arrival. They couldn't wait to see you again, and I knew you'd be just as eager to renew your acquaintance."

Devyn faced the two vampires he'd had before Bride.

The two he'd bought, bedded, and returned to their people. They were racing to him, then throwing themselves in his arms, planting little kisses over his face and neck.

To deny them would have been rude and perhaps life-threatening, as they were of royal blood, cousins to the king—a king he needed on his side. Still, Devyn untangled himself from their arms and stepped back. They frowned at him, confused. When it came to touching and sex, he'd never told them no before.

"Is this a new game?" one of the girls asked.

What were their names? "I'm married now," he explained. He racked his brain, and the answer finally popped into place. "Princess Deanna and Princess Wendy, this is Bride of the Targons."

Bride nodded in acknowledgment. "Nice to meet you."

The two females ignored Bride, speaking only to each other. "Last time he called me Demi."

"I was Elsie."

Giggling, they turned to him and shook their heads in a strange sort of unison. "Such a silly man. I'm De-Ella."

"And I'm Jalyn."

"Wow. You really are bad with names," Bride said between coughs, as if that would keep anyone from hearing her actual words.

"My apologies, ladies," he told them, trying not to laugh.

De-Ella playfully batted his shoulder. The slap would have sent any other man to his knees. She was an older vampire, and therefore stronger than most. "You're role-playing again. That's so cute."

"It's a gift."

"One I truly enjoy," Bride said.

Finally they looked at her. Really looked at her, up and down, every inch. Confusion consumed both of their features. "You married this person?" Jalyn asked.

Bride stiffened. "Hey, now. *This person* doesn't take too kindly to being insulted."

McKell drew her aside. "Come. Let's leave them to their reunion."

"No." Devyn threw out an arm, blocking her escape. "She stays."

"Yeah," Bride said. "*This person* will stay."

"She can't join us," De-Ella said with a pout. "We already have a fourth. A present for you, actually."

Grinning wickedly, Jalyn motioned the cloaked female over. Hesitantly the woman obeyed, her hips rocking more suggestively than she probably realized. Dread burned through Devyn like acid.

"This is Tadeam." De-Ella pinched the hood and slowly lifted it, first revealing a length of golden hair, thick and shiny. Then golden skin. Then a lovely golden face. The slave's eyes were downcast, but he knew they would be golden, too. "Something you've never ever *ever* tasted before but always wanted."

Yep, she was exactly what he'd suspected. A Rakan. The one race he'd been denied all these years. The race he'd tried to buy time and time again but failed. Eden's race. What he'd always thought he'd wanted.

He sucked in a breath and caught the scent of honey and spice. It was true, then. Rakans smelled like honey when they were aroused. De-Ella and Jalyn must have primed her before bringing her here, thinking it would send him into a frenzy.

Before Bride, it would have. Now, it did nothing for him. He'd tasted heaven already. He'd entered paradise. Variety was no longer what drove him. Bride was. She was the world he now revolved around. The one he sought to please, to protect, to pleasure.

She had shown him what his life was missing. Then, with her smile and her touch, she'd patched him up and made him whole.

"Remember when you painted us gold and had us pretend we were Rakans?" De-Ella traced a finger along his collarbone. "We had the McKell on the lookout, and when he found her, he bought her for us. Just in case you returned. Manus told us you would."

Manus, the king. So. He'd known all along that Devyn would return. But had he known why?

"Ladies." Bride rubbed at her chest as if pained. "I tried to be nice, but you ruined it. Now I don't like you. You are going to back away from my husband."

Her husband. It was the first time since their unexpected mating that she'd said it, and his heart swelled. *Mine. She's mine. Husband* was a title he'd once endured, detested, suffered through, and when he'd finally shed it, vowed never to take it up again. Now, for the second time in his life, he was a husband. This time he preferred the title to that of king.

Before, she'd displayed no hint of jealousy. Not even toward the princesses. Not until they'd insulted her had she even displayed anger. But knowing him as she did, she thought variety was his weakness. This entire situation had to be abhorrent to her.

The girls regarded Bride as queens would a peasant. As if she were beneath them. Had they always been so snotty? Devyn found he couldn't remember. He'd slept with them, many times, but hadn't noticed anything else about them. Hadn't cared to.

Jalyn's chin rose. "Who do you think you are?"

McKell stepped forward. "She is Bride, a vampire, found on the surface at an auction. She is mine."

"Actually," Devyn said, "she's mine."

"Well, I've never seen her before." The pronouncement came from De-Ella, as if her lack of knowledge lowered Bride's value.

Had they always been this oblivious, as well? "That's because she was raised on Earth."

"Then send her back," Jalyn snapped. "She bores me."

"Well, then. Let me entertain you with a story." Smiling evilly, teeth completely bared, Bride ambled toward her. "Stop me if you've heard this one. There once was a girl who wiped the floor with two vampire princesses. They screamed and begged for mercy, but no one helped them. The end."

"Don't come any closer." Jalyn drummed her nails against her arms. "If I must, I'll call for the guards."

McKell bent in a formal bow. "I'm right here, Princess."

"Take her away, then." Clearly assuming her orders would be obeyed, Jalyn cast a sultry gaze at Devyn. "As that's settled, it's time to see to you . . ."

De-Ella reached out and fisted his shirt. "Just give us five minutes, and we'll remind you what you liked most about us."

"I. Will. Not. Be. Ignored. Time to *show* you the story," Bride said, and it was the only warning she gave of her intentions. One moment she was beside Devyn, seemingly calm as could be, and the next she had her arms locked around De-Ella's waist, both women soaring through the air.

They crashed into the wall, De-Ella's head and back taking most of the force. When she realized what was happening, Jalyn shrieked and launched into the fray. The three rolled on the floor, punching and biting at each other, clawing and cursing.

"Bitch," he thought he heard Bride growl. She raked her nails across De-Ella's cheek, and blood welled. Pride lanced through him.

De-Ella grabbed a clump of her hair and jerked. Rage joined the pride, and he growled.

"You'll pay for that," Bride snarled before latching onto the vampire's wrist and crushing the bone. More pride.

There was a howl of pain. "I'll kill you! Do you hear me? I'll kill you!" Jalyn elbowed her in the stomach.

More rage. Scowling, he clasped onto their energy molecules, freezing all three in place. They were tangled together, Bride's eyes bright red and filled with the same intense agony he'd seen the first time she'd climaxed for him.

He was moving forward, determined to break them up and ease whatever was troubling Bride. The few punches she'd taken wouldn't cause that amount of suffering.

"No. You mustn't. She must prove her strength." McKell's clamped onto his shoulder, stopping him. "If she doesn't, if you step in, they will be considered the victors, and to the victor goes the spoils. All that is hers will then belong to them. Including you."

As if. "I'd think that would make you happy," he said, shaking off the warrior's hold.

"I won't deny it. But Bride's life here would be miserable."

"She won't be living here," Devyn said. "If you'd like me to communicate that through interpretive dance so that you better understand, I'm happy to perform."

One second Devyn's left eye felt fine, normal, and the next it felt tender and swollen again, as it had when he'd first entered the cave. As many times as he'd been hit in his long life, he knew the sensation. And he'd definitely been hit. He'd never seen McKell move, which meant the bastard had stopped time.

Damn if he didn't admire the vampire for it.

"You don't know she'll return to the surface," McKell said as if nothing had happened.

"You've seen me, right? Trust me, where I go, she'll go."

"How does she stand your ego?" McKell waved a hand through the air. "Never mind. Don't answer. Just think of it this way. If the king gives her to you, and she ever wishes to return here, which she might, she will be teased and insulted and tormented. They will never leave her alone. Nor will their friends. She will be fair game to the males, considered weak and in need of a master."

For any other lover, he would have laughed, even enjoyed the show. Catfights were fun, after all. "It's two against one." More than that, Bride was hurting.

"Yes, and next time it will be five against one. Unless she proves herself."

Devyn drew in a breath, then slowly released it—*and* the women. The fight resumed as if it had never paused.

Bride swung her leg around and kicked De-Ella in the stomach. He wanted to cheer. She spun and elbowed Jalyn in the jaw. He did cheer. The older De-Ella possessed a speed Bride hadn't yet achieved and raced behind her, grabbing her around the middle and sinking her teeth into Bride's exposed neck.

When Bride reached behind to grab the vampire by the head and perhaps snap her neck, Jalyn seized her wrist and twisted, perhaps breaking the bone.

"That will teach you to challenge your betters, little Bride."

Devyn stepped forward again, then managed to catch himself. His hands were clenched into fists. His teeth were digging into his bottom lip. *She's a fast healer,* he reminded himself. *She'll be fine.*

Bride wrenched free of Jalyn's hold, and even though her hand was damaged, she grabbed De-Ella's head as she'd first intended and jerked. The vampiress soared over her shoulder and slapped into the ground. Bride stomped on the woman's trachea exactly as he'd once wanted to do to Nolan even while dragging a shocked Jalyn to her and viciously sinking her fangs into the woman's neck.

She sucked so savagely, the vampire could not even struggle because struggling only anchored Bride deeper. Soon Jalyn went limp, and her eyes closed. Bride dropped her, spit out the blood, and lowered that gleaming red gaze to De-Ella.

Pride, much greater than before, swam through him. She'd done it. Two against one, and she'd kicked major ass. *Oh, yes. That's my girl.*

"Do we understand each other?" Bride said, rubbing her chest.

"Y-yes."

She stomped to Devyn, and halted only when she was a whisper away. The hand at her chest never ceased moving. "Thorns," she said. She sounded more animal than human—or rather, vampire—just then. Looked it, too. Blood was smeared over her lips and chin, and her fangs were longer and sharper than ever.

"Thorns?" He didn't wait for her response, but cupped her jaw, fingers spanning up and tracing over her cheeks, thumbs wiping the blood from her mouth. "Explain, and I'll kiss it better."

"Actually, you won't touch her again without *my* permission," a hard voice rang out from behind him.

A hush fell over the room. Devyn and Bride turned. Paling, McKell bowed submissively. De-Ella lumbered to her knees. Jalyn was still out cold.

The king had arrived.

CHAPTER 25

Bride struggled to regain control of herself. There was a haze of red behind her eyes, a throb in her neck and knuckles, and a burn in her lungs. The thorns surrounding the source of her buried abilities were savagely scraping against her, harder than ever before.

Despite the newcomer's demand for Devyn to keep his hands to himself, he reached out and twined their fingers, his thumb caressing her wrist in comfort. That helped enough that she was able to subdue most of her pain.

"Majesty," he said respectfully, inclining his head in greeting.

The vampire king, she realized. There was something she needed to do . . . something important . . . She drew a deep breath in through her nose, held it . . . held it . . . released it slowly. Her muscles eased their vise grip on her bones, and her gaze cleared. What did she need to—blank her mind! Yes, that was it. Blank her mind because the king, Mantus, was a thought reader.

"Majesty," she said, curtsying as she'd seen women do in movies. Her legs shook.

When she straightened, the ruler of her people came into view. He was tall, taller even than Devyn, with pale, shaggy hair and eyes of black velvet. They would have been devil eyes, if not for the thick frame of lashes around them.

His lips were stained red, as if he'd just eaten. His features were perfect, carved from marble and as pale as his hair. He possessed muscle stacked upon muscle, but that was not what gave him such an air of strength. It was the magic humming from him, so vibrant she could actually hear it singing in her ears. And her ears liked it. Wanted more.

"Your defiance is showing, Targon," the king said to Devyn. There was a slight lifting of his lips. That was it, the only hint of his amusement. His features were too hard to reveal anything else.

"And it's as lovely as the rest of me, I'm sure." Devyn, at least, sounded fully amused.

"You haven't changed, I see."

Blank mind, blank mind.

"Rise." Manus waved his fingers to punctuate his command. "All of you. Then someone must explain why I was not greeted properly."

McKell straightened. He, too, seemed carved from marble just then. "We had every intention of seeking you out, Highness. We were simply waiting until the line thinned."

Manus wore a cape of black-and-gold velvet, the material thick and plush. It billowed at his feet, though he didn't move. "There's been much thought about the Targon's arrival, but only a few have wondered at the girl with him, a stranger to our land. I didn't believe it, of course, because everyone in this room knows visitors are forbidden." There at the end, his voice had hardened menacingly. "Who and what is she?"

"She is vampire," McKell said. "Meant to remain here."

You little shit, Bride thought, wanting to slam her fist into his teeth so that he'd have trouble talking for a while.

"Is she?" Those obsidian eyes slid to the puncture wounds on the female Bride had bitten. "Raised on Earth, found by the Targon. You both want her, and you both expect me to declare who she will stay with. You both expect to be chosen."

Silence.

Thick, heavy.

Bride gulped, no longer quite so confident of her ability to tell this man where he could roast. *Mind blank.*

"Step forward, Bride of the surface."

Though she despised him for what he'd done to her mother—*mind blank, damn it*—she only hesitated for a second. Devyn released her reluctantly, giving her a final squeeze. In this underground, the king's word was law. He decided who lived and who died. Who stayed and who was allowed to leave.

When she was a few inches away, she stopped. He was just so big. His body consumed her personal space. *Mind blank.* But even as she commanded it, thoughts swam through her head. If he tried to hurt Devyn, she would tear this place apart.

He frowned down at her.

Oh, God. He heard. Beads of sweat broke out over her brow, and she stepped backward before she could stop herself. *I wish he couldn't hear my thoughts.* And she didn't care what the consequences were of that.

"Be still," he commanded. He reached out and placed his fingertips at her temples. His skin was dry and cool. His frown intensified. "Have you no opinions?"

"Excuse me?"

"Your mind is blocked to me."

It was? Her wish had worked? *Don't smile.* "Huh. Interesting," was all she said, as deadpan as possible, but she thought, *How's this for an opinion? Your people and their eating habits suck. And I don't mean that literally.*

No reaction.

She couldn't help herself. She smiled.

Sparks of white suddenly dotted the darkness of his eyes. "Your smile is lovely. However, I do not like your ability to keep me out." His head tilted to the side. "But generous as I am, I will allow it."

Wow. Finally she'd met someone more assured of his own goodness and superiority than Devyn. "Thanks."

"Guards," he called, and Bride stiffened. He didn't look away from her as a flood of armed vampires marched into the room. They lined the wall, awaiting their king's command. "Before we get to know one another, your companions must be dealt with."

"Whatever you're planning, *I* won't allow it," she said, violently shaking her head, backing away.

"Silence." The king's mouth, hard already with disapproval, hardened further. "Targon, you purchased two vampires from an auction and gave them to your friends at AIR. That is a crime against my people. A crime you knew better than to commit."

"I was going to bring them back. Eventually," Devyn said, unrepentant.

"That hardly matters." The king turned to McKell. "Thank you for projecting the information. However, your plan to ruin the Targon in my eyes has backfired, for you revealed your own involvement, as well. You allowed my people to be imprisoned without a fight."

McKell opened his mouth to protest.

"No. Not a word from you." With a nod to his guards, the king added, "Take them to my dungeon, where they will stay until I decide what to do with them."

"No! Don't you dare move," Bride cried. They ignored her, marching forward, closer . . . closer . . . "Devyn, stop them."

"Can't," he gritted out. "Their energy is scrambled."

"No!" Bride shouted. *I wish Devyn was safe. I wish Devyn was safe.* He remained in place, a target of those armed soldiers. "Please, no." Her bravado was gone. "I'm begging you." She hadn't begged for anything since losing Macy. Not even Devyn's touch. Now, helplessness bombarded her. "Please. Allow Devyn and me to return to the surface. *Please.*"

The men didn't pause, so she crouched, fangs bared, ready to fight them all if necessary. Devyn would rather die than be locked away, and *she* would rather die than let him.

"No one touches the Targon," she stated flatly. "He's mine."

"No harm is to befall the female," the king told his men, who reached their circle.

Bride grabbed hold of one and flung him away. She did the same to another, and then another, until someone grabbed *her*—Devyn, she realized, catching his wild scent.

"Do not fight this." He released her and willingly stepped back amid the guards, allowing them to tie his wrists behind his back with a whip. McKell's, too.

What are you doing! she wanted to shout. *Why are you so accepting?*

"As to why your ability doesn't work, Devyn," the king said. "I've been inside your mind before and learned how you do it. I have taken certain measures to ensure you are never so powerful in my palace again."

"Let him go, or I swear to God I will destroy you." Her mouth was so dry, her tongue felt swollen. The thorns inside her had seemingly sprouted thorns of their own, scraping at her, stinging. She had to calm down. "He didn't do anything wrong. I just wanted to see my birthplace and learn about my people. I can bring you the vampires. Just let him go. I wish you would let him go. Please."

"Too late," the king replied. "AIR now knows we exist. The damage is done."

"They would have found out anyway! Your people have been attending auctions. In fact, AIR probably already knew, since they monitor that kind of criminal activity."

"Hush, love, and go with him," Devyn told her. He even smiled at her when her gaze met his. "I'll be fine."

White-hot tears burned her eyes, blurring her vision. No, he wouldn't be fine. He would be in torment. *My fault. This is all my fault.* "I'll go with him if he lets you return to the—"

"Go with the king," he interjected, steel in the words. "Do not worry about me."

Did Devyn have a plan? Of course he did, she thought next, finally calming. It probably involved seducing a female guard, but that was okay. Freedom was the only thing that mattered.

"Fine," she said, lifting her chin. Maybe, while she was with the king, she'd remove his heart—if he had one— and set it on fire. Just in case Devyn's plan, whatever it was, fell through.

"If, at any time, she harms me in any way," the king told the guards, as if he could read her mind after all, "kill the Targon."

Bride nearly screeched in frustration and helplessness. Defeated before she'd even begun. No way would she risk Devyn's life.

What the hell was she going to do now?

Bride was escorted to a room of black velvet. The walls were draped with it, the floor covered in it, and what little furniture there was—two chairs facing each other—were dripping with it. All that soft darkness made her feel like she was floating through a night sky, no end to her torment in sight.

The king motioned her to the chairs.

"Majesty," she said, striving for a calm tone as she sat.

"Please, call me Manus." He claimed the other seat; then, with a wave, he dismissed the guard. They strutted from the room, leaving her alone with their sovereign.

I never should have come here. Being parted from Devyn was torture. Not knowing what was being done to him was agony. Thinking of him in a dark hole was anguish. Worse, it was her fault. She'd wanted to come here. She'd wanted him with her. But she would have given up both for Devyn's safety.

I love him, she thought then. *I love Devyn.*

Somehow, some way, he'd become the most important thing in her life. He was her home now. Not this place. Yes, she loved that there were other vampires here. Yes, she loved the darkness and the sweet scents and the closeness she felt to her mother. She loved that every question she'd ever had about what she was could be answered. Here, she wasn't different, she wouldn't be staked. But none of those things meant more to her than Devyn. The thought of being without him . . . she shuddered.

"I brought you here so that we may chat in private," the king said, breaking the silence.

"I want Devyn released immediately. *Then* I'll chat with you."

"He is not up for discussion," was the harsh reply. "Do not mention him again."

Or what? Bastard. "Are you used to getting your way?"

"Of course." As if that settled things, Manus leaned back, crossed one ankle over his knee, and studied her. "Tell me about your life on the surface."

"If I do, will you have Devyn released?"

She never saw him move, but the next thing she knew, her brain was rattling against her skull, her teeth were cutting into her gums, and she was propelled off her chair and onto the floor.

There was a trickle of warmth at the corner of her mouth, and she knew it was blood. Shaking with anger, burning with the force of it, she wiped the smear with the back of her wrist and glared up at the king. "You slapped me."

"I warned you not to mention the Targon, and yet you persisted." He was perched on his chair, in the same relaxed pose as before. "Persist again, and see what happens." It was a challenge.

She'd always liked sparring with Devyn. Even from the very beginning. This man? Not so much. "Devyn told me you were a great guy," she said, climbing back into her chair. "I see our definitions of *great* differ."

A muscle ticked below both of Manus's eyes. "I was not always this way."

"Your brother's death changed you." He'd get no sympathy from her. "Yeah, I heard."

"Were you also told he was returned to me missing several body parts?" The words lashed from him. "Were you told his abductor targeted me next? That I spent a week as her prisoner?"

"No," she said, and made a mental note not to look for Fiona the *nefreti*, after all. "You seem to have been returned with all your parts, though." Unfortunately. Fiona would have done Bride a favor if she'd cut off the man's hands. Her jaw ached, damn it! And she didn't need that on top of everything else.

Manus nodded, the action stiff. "I was."

"No one has a perfect past, you know? No one lives as long as we do without suffering somehow."

"And what painful things have happened to you, little Bride?"

She couldn't tell him about her mother, so she said, "Having Devyn taken from me. I love him."

"Then you are truly hurting right now, and I am sorry for that. But I will not set him free. At one time, I was forgiving. At one time, I was merciful with my people. And what did that get me? A dead brother and seven nights of torture. I do not repeat my mistakes. I do not spare my enemies, and right now Devyn and McKell are my enemies."

"They would never hurt you."

"So you say. Yet I cannot read your thoughts, so how then can I trust you?"

That's what this was about? His inability to read her? "I wish for things, and I get them, all right? When you stepped into that room, I wished you couldn't read me."

His brow furrowed. "Why?"

"Would you like it if someone knew your every thought? I don't think so."

"I couldn't read you *before* I entered the room, yet I could read everyone else. Still." His eyes narrowed, but he didn't rebuff her. "Wish for me to read you."

And let him learn that she was *nefreti*? He'd kill her and Devyn without a qualm. "I wish that you could read me." *No I don't, no I don't, no I don't. I wish that he is never able to read me.* "Okay, done," she lied. "Go for it."

He stilled, not even breathing that she could see. Invisible fingers seemed to brush at her mind, trying to get inside. He frowned. "I still cannot. Perhaps you did not wish hard enough. Try again."

She nodded as if she were obeying. "There."

His frown intensified, and he slammed a fist into his palm. "Still nothing. Are you sure your wishes come true?"

"Not always. I only discovered the power a day ago, so I'm not exactly good at it."

He sat at the edge of the chair, fairly panting with excitement. "Can you wish a person's death?"

"No," she said, because no way would she do that for him. "Why do you care, anyway?"

"In all my many years, there has only ever been one other I could not read." He settled back, excitement gone as if it had never been, disappointment in its place. "Can you guess who that was?"

Dread snaked through her. "Your mom?" she asked hopefully, though she knew that wasn't the answer.

"A female named Fiona. My tormentor. She was *nefreti.*"

Bride was proud of herself. She didn't flinch. "What's that?"

"Someone with too much power. Someone who must die."

"And you think *I'm* a *nefreti*?"

"No," he said. "She hummed with so much energy, it was like a song in my blood every time she neared. That is not the case with you. However, none of my warriors can find her because she, too, can read minds. She knows when they are coming."

"What does that have to do with me?"

"If I can't read your mind, that must mean she cannot. That means I can use you against her. I just have to figure out how."

Three days passed with agonizing slowness. Bride was allowed to see Devyn only once a day to feed. She was blindfolded until she got there, ensuring the location remained hidden, and they weren't allowed to speak to each other. A guard always accompanied her to ensure she behaved. She'd been told that for every word she uttered, Devyn would receive ten lashes.

The silence was killing her. He was suffering, she could see it in his face. His amber eyes were dull, and bruises had formed under them. Every day he was dirtier and a whole lot shakier than the last.

She realized now, he'd never had a plan. He just hadn't wanted her hurt in a struggle. Whether he knew it or not, he loved her. Rather than bask in that knowledge as she should have been able to do, guilt was now her constant companion. Luxury for her, suffering for her husband.

Whenever she would finish drinking, having tried not to take more than a few sips, Devyn would keep his head tilted, silently urging her to take more. Maintaining her strength was important for finding a way out, but she just couldn't weaken him more than he already was. He would sigh, kiss her, hug her tight, and then gently push her out of the cell.

Each time she tried to read his mind, or at the very least send her thoughts into his, but she was still capable of neither. Those powers supposedly belonged to her, damn it, but all she found were the thorns and fire. Trying to forcibly extract them was worse than when they sprang up from her emotions. It was like ripping her body in half.

She wanted to tell him she was going to get him out of here, not to worry, that she stripped and camouflaged herself when everyone was sleeping and searched the palace for the dungeon, as well as whatever was quashing Devyn's powers. She wanted to assure him that she would find it, whatever she had to do, but she *wasn't* sure she would succeed, and the words always died in her throat. They weren't worth ten lashes.

After her meeting with Manus, she'd been given a spacious chamber with a large bed and lacy canopy. The walls were bare except for a painting of Manus. There was a marble vanity, which she now sat in front of, staring into the glass, wondering when to make her next move—and exactly what move to make.

"Good." Manus leaned against the room's doorway, arms folded over the wide expanse of his chest. "You're wearing the gown I had made for you."

Her eyes met his through the mirror, and her fingers clenched around the brush's handle. "Yes." As if she would deny his wishes. It was a velvet dress that matched the cape he always wore. Black with gold trim. The material clung to her curves, soft and luscious. At his request, her hair had been curled and now hung down her back in shiny ringlets. "Word on the street is, you're single. Maybe we should find you a companion," she said. *So you'll leave me the hell alone*.

He had come to her once a day to "chat," mostly questioning her about fights she'd been in, how she'd hidden herself from humans for so long. To her surprise, he'd been a gentleman. Not because he liked her but because he thought to use her against Fiona, his enemy. Still. She didn't want him getting any ideas about the two of them.

She sighed, remembering his other visits. He'd also had

her wish for a few things—a meal to appear, her clothes to change on their own—testing the limits of her powers. For the meal, a human servant had tripped over his own feet, propelling into the room, falling and breaking his neck at their feet. For the outfit switch, her robe had brushed a lamp and caught fire. Bride wasn't too happy with this latest power and was now terrified of using it.

"Why find another when you serve well enough?" he said. "Now, come. I have a surprise for you." He held out his hand, waiting.

Slowly she pushed to her feet and turned to face him. Her heart thundered with the need to best him, but she merely crossed the distance and took his hand. Cold steel, that's what he felt like. "I want my husband released. McKell, too. They're good men. I'll take them to the surface, and you'll never have to see them again."

"How many times must I tell you? I don't want to discuss them." There was no room for argument in his tone. He ushered her into the next chamber. His. It was as ornate and lavish as hers, though it appeared uninhabited. The bedcovers were not rumpled, and clothes did not spill from the closet.

Her heart only decelerated when they exited into the hallway and headed for the alabaster columns leading into the ballroom. "You never want to discuss them," she muttered.

"Because the subject angers me. Bad things happen when I'm angry. Remember?"

Like she'd forget. "Figured out how you're going to use me yet?"

"No."

"What's the holdup? 'Cause I'm willing to bring her to you in exchange for my man."

"I've thought of that. However, while I think you can find her without her notice, I do not think you can best her in a fight. And I cannot send troops with you, because she would sense them."

Bride refused to give in to despair. There had to be a way.

A gaggle of voices greeted her ears. Then, the more she walked, the more those voices blended with the strains of music and clinking glasses. Even . . . moans? Usually all the entryways in the palace were open, easily accessible, but today—tonight?—the one into the ballroom was draped by more of that black velvet.

Manus pushed the material aside and urged her forward. Hesitant, she entered. And gasped. Vampires were everywhere. They held goblets filled with blood as they drank and laughed and danced. Naked humans lined the far wall, a buffet of choices. Males and females of every size and color. When they were chosen, they stepped forward and offered whatever body part was desired.

Hanging above them were Devyn and McKell. They were inside a cage, gripping the bars and staring over at her, as if they'd been expecting her. The princesses De-Ella and Jalyn were underneath them, laughing and throwing little pieces of human food at their feet.

A whimper escaped her as her gaze met Devyn's. *Oh, my love. I'm so sorry.* Her arm extended of its own accord, reaching for him, desperate to feel his skin against hers. Devyn reached out, too, but there was too great a distance between them.

Manus grabbed her wrist. "This way."

"No." He wanted to take her from Devyn? The rage she'd been suppressing these past three days boiled up, overflowing, burning . . . sizzling. It was like acid in her veins. And yep, there were those burning thorns, as eager to cut at her as always. "I will stay here."

"We aren't leaving the room," the king told her, exasperated. "You have my word."

Still the rage churned, free now and unwilling to hide any longer. Her gaze never left Devyn's as she stumbled her way to the dais, where two empty thrones waited. Manus motioned for her to take the one next to his, and she did, her motions jerky, clipped.

"What are you doing to them? Why are you treating them like this?" Two proud men, imprisoned, objects of ridicule. *I have to do something. Today.* But what? She was strong, but she couldn't defeat the hundreds of vampires in this room. Not at the same time. And not without getting Devyn killed. As his safety was the only nonnegotiable part of her escape strategy, that wasn't an option.

Manus tapped his fingers impatiently against the arms of his throne. "I called this gathering together to show you a softer side to this great city and its people. Look how much fun they are having."

"Yeah. At Devyn's expense."

"As well it should be. He is a traitor."

"No. He's not." There was so much rage now, it seeped from her voice, hummed from her skin. The thorns sharpened, cutting deep and hard, and warmth spilled between her breasts. She glanced down and saw that she was actually bleeding, crimson soaking the material of her robe.

"Why do you like him so much?" Manus asked, unnoticing.

She dabbed at the blood, her hand shaking. "Why do you care?"

"I don't. I'm merely curious."

"Well, for one, he would give his life for mine." Not that a man as self-absorbed as the vampire king would understand that.

"You are sure of this? The Devyn of Targonia I know is always greedy for the next female to bed."

"He was. Once," she said. "And yes, I'm sure." Look what he'd done for her already.

"I could prove that, you know? I could let him die for you." Manus clapped his hands and commanded the night's entertainment to begin. "I mean, if I were to leave him out for Fiona, a sacrifice, if you will, and she were to do to him what she did to my brother, you would do anything necessary for vengeance. You would find a way to slay her."

She ignored the new string of dancers on the floor. "I would find a way anyway, to save him from such a fate. But you know what? Now you've reached the limit. That's the second time you've threatened him, and I won't stand for another." The pain . . . oh, the pain . . . it was eating her up, consuming her. Killing her.

For the first time in her life, she embraced it, didn't try to fight it. More and more blood spilled from the wound in her chest. "The first I allowed to intimidate me. This one, I will not. This one, you will pay for."

He laughed. Actually laughed. "Already I can hear death in your tone. Perhaps I am finally on the right path."

How dare he calmly speak of Devyn's possible torture. How dare he even consider using the man she loved like that.

She sat there, panting and sweating and bleeding. "You. Will. Not!" The last was said on a scream as the rage exploded inside her. It was a bomb, destroying everything in its path, even the thorns. It destroyed who she was, what she was, dousing that inner fire with flames of its own, melting her, making her into a new creature.

"Oh, do calm down," Manus said without facing her. "I have not decided to venture down that road yet."

Her pain—gone. Her strength—unparalleled. She felt it sweep through her, a strength so potent she could taste it on her tongue, feel it singing in her blood, vibrating in her bones. She was drunk on it, dizzy.

"No. No!" Manus said, and she heard the fear in his voice. *Her body is vibrating like Fiona's,* he thought. *She is* nefreti. *How could I not have known?*

Bride could read his mind.

Still she sat, now as motionless as stone, gripping the throne, silent. A sea of other thoughts filled her head, rolling through her, some violent, some sweet, some hungry, all drifting from the dance floor. She was inside the head of every vampire present.

They were maddening, almost deafening, but she managed to ignore them. Her hands were hot, so hot, anything they wanted theirs for the taking. And they wanted vengeance.

"Guards," Manus shouted, his voice trembling. Because of the noise, no one heard him. He jumped up, meaning to run from her.

"Quiet," she told him, and his lips pressed together. "Sit."

His expression was shocked and horrified as he fell into his throne.

No longer was her ability to make wishes come true muted. No longer would there be consequences. Anything she wanted, she could have. The knowledge was there, screaming from Manus's thoughts as he recalled his time with Fiona. She could stop time, as McKell did. She could create fire with her bare hands. She could erase memories and suppress another's powers.

"Bride. Bride!"

Devyn. She recognized his voice and turned toward him. Colors winked around him, twinkling stars of crimson and azure. His energy, she thought, awed. So lovely. So pure.

Love, love, love, he thought, his voice already so much a part of her that she had no trouble distinguishing him from the others. *Thank God you're all right. I'll think of a way out of this, I swear I will. If that bastard touches you . . .*

No thoughts for his own comfort. No regrets for the torment he currently endured. All his thoughts belonged to her, for her. He truly did love her. Saw her as a cloud of bliss in the bleakness that was his life.

I'll get us out of this, she projected at him.

His eyes widened. He'd heard her, she knew he had.

And now to save him. Her gaze narrowed on Manus. As she studied him, she saw that his energy pulsed erratically, scattering all the other energy around him. Except hers. Hers was too strong. This was how he'd stopped Devyn, she realized. Through a potion that bounced particles off of each other.

Vampires, she had come to learn, loved their potions. *You will pay.* She reached inside his chest with a mental hand and squeezed. Squeezed so tightly the previously unused powers inside her recoiled. Still she held firm.

He gurgled out a pained breath, rubbed frantically at his chest, his skin growing paler by the second. He gazed at her, unsure about what was happening. He wanted to speak, but she hadn't released his tongue from her wish for quiet.

What's going on, love?

Devyn's voice hit her in a rush, laced with panic and frustration.

Everything's fine, don't you worry. I love you, she told him, never releasing her hold on the king.

I love you, too, but how are we reading each other's minds?

Surprise, your wife is one of the most powerful people in the world. I'm going to handle everything, and then we're going home.

Will you be in danger? he asked.

No. I freaking rock right now.

Well, let me have a little of the glory, at least, he projected dryly.

No way. I want to tease you about this for years to come.

Manus was gasping now, and people were starting to notice. Two vampires even approached the throne. "My king?" one asked.

So what exactly are you planning? Devyn asked.

You'll see.

—make her stop. The king's thought intruded into her mind. The closer he came to death, the louder his projections. *So important. Can't die. Can't fail Terreck.*

He'd loved his brother. Loved him more than his own life, and when his brother had been taken from him, he'd wanted to die himself. Then Fiona had come to him, taunted him. He'd wanted her head. Still wanted it, and would do anything to get it. Even lie. He didn't want to kill McKell and Devyn, wouldn't kill them. But he *would* keep them here, use them, to gain what he wanted.

With the realization, Bride released her grip on his heart.

He was panting, sweating.

So was she. Determined to finally end this, to leave and return above with Devyn, she rose. "Stand," she told him.

It was a command, and not something he could ignore. As before, there was power in her voice. Utter compulsion. It was not something he would be immune to later. No, this voice would continue to control everyone who heard it, no matter how many times they heard it.

The king stood, hate bleeding into his eyes. *Nefreti bitch.*

"Yes. I am."

Anything you speak will happen. Will become fate. Anything.

Yes, she realized, the ability to sift truth from lie making itself known. His thoughts were true.

You'll destroy the world, you know that, yes? You'll destroy your lover.

He was . . . right. She knew it, the future suddenly playing through her mind. She would return to the surface with Devyn. One day they would fight, as couples always did. She would say something she didn't mean. He would be hurt irrevocably.

Horror flooded her. She couldn't allow that to happen. Which meant, she couldn't go with him. Oh, God. She couldn't go with him.

Guards pounded toward her, their thoughts converging on her. *Must save the king. Kill her before it's too late. How could this have happened?*

She held out her hand, only that, but every single one of them went flying backward, slamming into walls and other people. There were gasps, muttered curses, then everyone stopped what they were doing and eyed her with the same horror she felt.

She could sense her ability to camouflage taking over, changing the color and texture of her skin and hair. Could feel her muscles trembling, wanting to break apart, mist and fly. To escape it all. *Not yet. Just a little longer.*

Get the whips, someone thought. Perhaps all of them were thinking it. *Have to get the whips. Only way to stop her.*

"No one move," she shouted, and even Devyn and McKell ceased moving. Soon Devyn's skin paled, turned blue. She frowned, not understanding what was happening. *Devyn?*

Can't . . . breathe . . .

"Breathe!" she rushed out. "Everyone breathe." Oh, yes, she was a menace who would inevitably hurt him.

When his color returned, she faced the king, tears

forming and streaming freely down her cheeks. "Devyn
and McKell are going to leave, and you are going to let
them. You are not to chase them. Ever. You are to leave
them alone. If you even think of hurting them, you will
suffer a pain like none you've ever known."

I'm not sure I like this.

The thought hit her, louder than any before it, and so
clear it was as if the woman was standing beside her.

Bride cast her gaze through the crowd, searching . . .
one of her new abilities allowed her to search faces with
the precision of a computer, honing in. There, in the far
corner, was a shadowy figure. She couldn't see the woman's
face, it was cloaked, but she recognized her for what she
was. A *nefreti*. Her powers matched Bride's in strength, in
beauty, the aura around her as bright as the sun.

You are Fiona, Bride said. *The one the king searches for.*

Yes.

She was also someone who could stop Bride and hurt
Devyn. *You don't like what I'm doing, fine. Tell me what to
do. I'm open to anything as long as the two men in the cage
are free and unharmed.*

Rather than tell her what to do, Fiona showed her
scenes from the past, a dark, turbulent past between two
people who wanted to hate each other but couldn't stop
the lust. Fiona's abduction of the prince, then the king.
Fiona's treatment of both. The first she had indeed tortured, but the king she had seduced.

"She's still out there," Bride told the king without
turning away, "still watching you. You can feel her, but
you can't read her and you can't stop her. But I can read
her, and she can read me. She's been an outcast her en-

tire life because of what she is. Everyone thought she was dead, killed as a child as ordered. But they couldn't do it, and sent her away. Throughout the years, she remained in contact with her sister, her twin. She loved the girl more than anything. Until your brother killed her. She retaliated. And somehow in the process, she became connected to you instead. Now she needs you to survive and has asked me not to kill you."

His eyes rounded, though the hate in them didn't fade.

"I will spare you this day. But I say again, if my husband's life is threatened in any way, I will destroy you without any hesitation."

He will not, Fiona told her. *I will make sure of it.*

Thank you.

The cloaked figure disappeared from view.

"You two." Bride pointed to the guards closest to the ropes that held the cage suspended in the air. "Gently lower the men."

Their eyes glazed as they rushed to obey, and soon the cage was settled on the ground.

"Open it."

Only I have the key, the king projected.

"Then give them the key." It was another command he couldn't resist.

He removed a necklace from around his neck and tossed it at the guards. Weak as his throw was, the key thumped to the ground several feet from them. One guard strode forward, swiped up the key, and returned to the cage. Metal scraped against metal, then the door was flung wide.

So close to victory. Just a few minutes more. "Devyn, McKell," she said.

Come on, love, Devyn said inside her mind. He still couldn't move. She hadn't freed him from her "no one move" command. *Let's get out of here and go home. I'm so proud of you. I'll even let you tease me about being a damsel in distress.*

I . . . can't. God, even thinking it was torture. *I have to . . . stay.*

What are you talking about? Of course you—

She blocked his voice—charmer that he was, he could convince her to do anything, even leave with him, and she would never be able to forgive herself when she destroyed him—and closed her eyes, sending her mind through the entire underground. Because of the thoughts of the vampires around her, still gazing at her with that horror, she knew it as intimately as she knew the surface. Knew where guards lurked. Knew where traps lay. Any and every threat, she eliminated.

And then she faced Devyn, determined, soul-sick. "You may speak. Go," she said, heart breaking inside her chest. "McKell will lead you to the surface, and neither of you will return here. Ever. You will not send anyone after me." She could have erased herself from his mind, but in this heartbreaking moment, she couldn't force herself to do so.

Both of their bodies obeyed, heading toward the entrance to the hallway that would take them to the opening to the surface. Devyn peered at her over his shoulder, clearly trying to force himself to stop.

"Come with me," he called.

She shook her head, her chin trembling too much to reply.

"Bride," he growled.

"I can't," she shouted, finding her voice. "Look at me. Look at what I can do."

And of course, he and everyone else in the room was helpless to do anything else, the compulsion in her voice forcing them to obey.

That caused a sob to gush from her.

"McKell," he shouted, panicked, desperate. "There has to be a way to contain her powers again. Tell her there's a way."

The warrior had never appeared so sad. "Her father was most likely able to do it because Bride trusted him inside her mind and allowed it. I know Bride trusts you and would allow you to do it, but you wouldn't know how. You could cause more harm than good, lock up too much."

"No." Devyn violently shook his head. "We'll find a way, Bride. I swear it. Kyrin once told me the Arcadians are like cousins to the vampires. He has powers of the mind. Strong powers. Let him try."

Hope bloomed. *Let him try* . . . it was a lifeline she desperately wanted to clutch. Then she shook her head. *You're doing it. Letting him convince you.* What if Kyrin failed? How many people would she hurt? Would she destroy Devyn's friends? Make Devyn himself do a million things he didn't want to do? He would grow to hate her. That precious love would wither and die.

"No." So badly did she want to reach for him, her hands were burning. And if she reached for him, she knew she would summon him to her, propelling him to her side with enough force to knock the air out of his lungs. "I'll stay here. I'll make sure no one comes for you."

"Bride!" There was true fear in his voice. "I don't care about that. They can chase me the rest of my life, and I'll be okay with that. It'll be fun. A game. But I can't live without you. Please!"

Her heart shattered like glass against a hammer. She didn't want to live without him, either, but to keep him safe, she would do it. "Go!" she screamed. "Just go!"

McKell obeyed.

Devyn compressed his lips into a mulish line and managed to hold his ground. She felt him push mental fingers inside her mind, knew those fingers were trying to latch on to her energy and control her, but she easily swatted them away.

That swat sent him to his knees with a pained groan. His head lifted, his eyes narrowing. A vessel had burst in his forehead, and a bruise was already spreading from temple to temple, even down his nose.

"I'm not leaving," he gritted out. "We'll battle this out if we have to, but love, you're stuck with me."

Suddenly the doorway burst open—even though McKell hadn't reached it yet. Over forty AIR agents rushed inside, pyre-guns raised. They didn't stop to see who their targets were, they just started firing. Blue beams, stun.

Bride could have stopped them with a word. She could have danced through the crowd, faster than they would have been able to see her, plucking their guns from them. But she didn't. She heard their thoughts, a jumble at first and hard to sort through, but she managed it. They didn't plan to kill the people here, or even take them all above. They planned to leave them, to let them live as quietly as they wished, form some sort of truce with them, and get Devyn the hell out.

She pivoted on her heel. She would leave them to it. She needed to find someplace to hide, someplace she would not endanger anyone but could monitor things. Perhaps Fiona would help her, after all.

"Dallas, shoot Bride," Devyn called, "and fucking keep shooting her!"

A second later, beams slammed into her, one after another, freezing her in place. She could still feel her power, but it was unusable at the moment, held captive as her body continually absorbed stun ray after stun ray.

Damn that Devyn.

The battle continued to rage behind her, blue beams constant, feet scampering, people shouting. She saw it through her mind, through the thoughts of others. Panic, so much panic. Fear, so much fear. *Who are these people?* the vampires wondered. *What do they want, what are they going to do? They smell so good, their blood rushing through their veins swiftly, sweetly. Hmm, the hunger is too much. Why can't I move? I need to feed.*

Soon the AIR agents had each of the vampires locked by stun. The battle had been easier than they'd anticipated. *Because I already did the work,* she wanted to shout. And this was how they repaid her?

Footsteps echoed behind her, then beside her, louder, and then Devyn was standing in front of her. He was grinning smugly.

"You commanded me to follow McKell, just not when I had to do it. Still, that's what I'm gonna do, but I'm taking you with me. I told you I'd find a way."

Devyn paced the confines of his bedroom. It was a mess. Wrinkled clothes littered the floor, and there were food wrappers on the dresser. Bride perched at the edge of the bed. He and Dallas had rigged a pyre-gun to the wall across from her, and it fired a continual beam directly into her chest.

It had been like this for over forty-eight hours.

He could see the rage in her expression every time he glanced at her, but he could also see the hope. Every day Kyrin came over and dug inside her mind, trying to bury the worst of her powers. So far, no luck. But if this worked . . . He sighed. *Please let this work.*

"I can't free you yet, you know that." He was babbling as he paced, but he couldn't stop himself. "Your powers are too great; even you can't control them. Plus, you'll leave me. To protect me from yourself," he added with a shake of his head. Who would have guessed his love life would come to something like this? Holding a female captive? "And that's just ridiculous, love. There's nothing you could do to me that I wouldn't like. You've met me, right?"

A knock sounded at the door.

"Enter," he called, already knowing who it was.

Sure enough, Kyrin stepped inside. Tall and leanly muscled, white hair in disarray around his shoulders as if he'd just come from Mia's bed.

I want to leave a woman's bed. My *woman's bed.* "Why isn't it working yet?" he snarled.

Ever-patient, Kyrin stopped and leaned against the dresser. He pushed his hands into his pockets. "Her powers are layered, and those layers are protected by some sort of barbed wire. Getting through it is painful."

"Teach me to do it, then." Devyn didn't care about pain. Not when it came to Bride.

"That would take years."

"Never mind." He scrubbed a hand down his face. "Just take the pain like a man, you pussy, and get this done."

"I will. But when was the last time you slept?" There was no anger in Kyrin's tone.

"I haven't. Not since returning." He'd only eaten the snack cakes Dallas had brought him. And he'd only showered each day because Macy had come to sit with Bride and talk to her, to remind her of how much everyone loved and missed her.

"You must take care of yourself," Kyrin said. "Bride will be angry when she is freed. Believe me, I've been inside her mind, and I know of what I speak. An angry Bride will not make for a happy Devyn."

Another knock sounded at the door, saving Devyn from a reply.

A second later, Macy soared inside. She spotted Kyrin and stopped. "How is she today?"

"The same," Devyn said, the words choking from him. He didn't know how much more of this he could take. He was a king, for God's sake. All of his desires should be granted immediately.

"Damn," Macy said, tossing her purse on the floor beside the door. "I was hoping for better news."

Kyrin squared his shoulders, straightened. "I'll push through today. No matter what, all right?"

"Yes, yes." Devyn nodded to punctuate his words. "Thank you."

As Kyrin pulled a chair toward the bed, careful to remain out of range of the stun, he said, "Remind me of what powers you want her to keep."

"She likes to mist. She likes to camouflage herself." And he had fantasies of chasing her around town and catching her. "She likes speaking inside my mind." At least he hoped she'd liked that. He'd liked it because he'd felt closer to her, had even *felt* her love for him.

Kyrin sat and cupped her chin, forcing her head toward him. At that point, he lapsed into silence. He always did.

The two sat like that for hours, still as statues. And with every hour that passed, Devyn became more agitated. Desperate. Macy paced right alongside him the entire time, as nervous as he was.

Bride had become the center of his world. He was nothing without her. If he had to obey her every word for the rest of his life, he would. If he had to let her control his body, he would do that too. Anything was better than being without her. That, he'd learned inside his underground cell. He could endure anything as long as she was with him.

He stopped at the far wall and banged his head against the stone.

"Hey, man." Dallas slapped his shoulder, startling him.

Damn. He needed to be a little more aware of his surroundings. He hadn't heard his friend enter. What kind of guard was he for Bride? "Hey."

"Hey, Dallas," Macy said.

"Mia's downstairs," Dallas told them. AIR was in the middle of peace talks with the vampires. They'd handed over the two vampires purchased at the auction and now wanted more of Bride's blood. Mia hoped to use it to cure the Schön queen, if ever they captured her, as well as any people the queen infected.

"Tell her to leave." No way would they take a drop of Bride's blood without her permission.

"Sure, sure. Any progress?" his friend asked.

"Not that I can see," he grumbled, motioning to the two at the bed with a tilt of his chin.

"Shit."

"Yeah. I know."

Dallas was just as agitated as he was, but for different reasons. More and more the agent was dreaming of that queen, Devyn knew. Craving her even. So far, though, she hadn't visited the agent.

At least Dallas was gaining control over *his* powers, something Kyrin was helping him do. Why couldn't the Arcadian help Bride faster, damn it?

"So, anyway," Dallas said. "I came bearing news about Bride."

Devyn grabbed him by the shoulders and shook him. "What do you mean?" Had Dallas seen Bride's departure from his life? A tortured moan escaped him, and he almost fell to his knees. If she left, he would follow her. It was as simple as that.

"Calm down. Jeez." A huge grin split his friend's face. "First vision I ever had that didn't make me want to puke my guts out, and it was of Bride biting your neck. She's going to be okay, man. Gonna wake up soon. Rushed right over to tell you, soon as I saw it."

"Turn off stun," Kyrin said, his voice raw, hoarse, right on cue.

Devyn rushed to the gun anchored in the wall and tore it loose. The bright blue beam faded. A moment later—

"Devyn."

Her voice.

He spun, his heart drumming erratically. "Bride." He strode to her, everything else forgotten. He pushed Kyrin out of the way—the otherworlder fell back weakly—and crouched in front of her. He cupped her face, not at all surprised to see that he was trembling.

"Love, can you hear me? Are you all right?"

She blinked a few times, emerald irises clearing. "Yes and yes," she said, sounding fatigued. "Hungry, though."

"Everyone out," Devyn commanded without looking away from her. There was a stream of laughter behind him, clothes rustling as Dallas helped Kyrin stand.

"I love you, Bride," Macy called.

"Love you," Bride managed.

Footsteps echoed, and then the door was shutting. Devyn gathered Bride in his arms and settled atop the mattress. "Tell me everything, and then you can eat. What's been happening? How are you?" He couldn't stop touching her. The soft skin he so loved, the silky hair his fingers always itched to sift through.

"After Kyrin made it past the thorns, we had to go through the powers one by one and decide which ones could roam free and which ones needed to be suppressed. I never thought we'd finish. Some of them didn't want to be contained again and fought us. But guess what? I can now scramble my energy so you can't control me, as well as absorb stun without any adverse effects. Well, one stream of stun, not the continuous stream you paralyzed me with, you bastard."

"You're welcome. So what you're telling me is that there'll be no forced stripping?" Could she hear the pout in his voice?

She kissed the base of his neck. "Not from me, but I bet I can make you do it. I'm still pretty much all-powerful."

He grinned, his first in days. "Is that a reminder that you saved my ass in the underground?"

"Maybe." Her warm breath tickled him. It was a sensation he'd been dreaming of for a week. "Mmm, you smell good. You always smell good."

"God, I missed you."

"I missed you, too."

He rolled, pinning her beneath him. He meant to yell at her a bit, but had to kiss those lush lips first. The moment he did, he had to taste that sweet flavor. On and on the kiss continued, hot and needy and a promise of love he freely gave.

Finally, he forced himself to pull back. "If you ever again try to leave me . . ." He let his anger and hurt shine through.

Shaking as violently as he was, she reached up and caressed his jaw. "Hate to break it to you, but you're stuck with me. I'm now stronger than you are. And just so you know, you won't even be able to force me out with a crane."

He barked out a laugh. "As if I would try. I'm a man who deserves the best, and I've finally found her."

Her gaze fell to his neck, and she licked her lips. "Now, what about this hunger of mine . . ."

He didn't hesitate. He guided her to his vein. Immediately her teeth sank inside, and she moaned. He groaned in bliss. "Oh, have I missed this."

She sucked, and he rubbed himself against her, unable to stop himself. He'd imagined having her back in his bed so many times, it was like a dream come true to actually have her there.

"For me, too," she said after she finished drinking.

"What is?"

"It's like a dream come true."

He blinked. "I didn't say that aloud."

"Oh." She shifted uncomfortably as she nibbled on her lower, bloodstained lip. "Secret's out, I guess. I kept the mind-reading thing. Kyrin tried to bury it, but I nearly scratched his mental eyes out."

"I'm glad," Devyn said, laughing.

She peered up at him, unsure. "Really?"

He nodded. "That way, you'll know what position I want you in without having to be told." As he spoke, he planted little kisses along her face.

"Pervert."

"Fine, fine. You'll also know how much I love you even when I'm flirting outrageously with someone else."

"Slut." Grinning, she tangled her hands in his hair. "I love you so much."

"And I love you. Now and always." He licked at her lips. "We are going to have some amazing children. The best this world has ever seen."

Her entire body stilled as she stared up at him. "Children? You want to have kids with me?"

"Oh, yes. You and no other. You're the only one worthy of my seed," he teased.

"Oh, my dear, sweet Bradley. I'm going to make you very happy you said that," she said, rolling him over and straddling his waist.

She was true to her word.

Take romance TO ANOTHER realm WITH *paranormal bestsellers* FROM POCKET BOOKS!

Nice Girls Don't Have Fangs
MOLLY HARPER

Jane was an unemployed children's librarian before she got turned into a vampire. Now she has a new host of problems—and a really long shelf life.

New in the SHADOWMEN series from USA TODAY bestselling author JENNIFER ST. GILES!

Kiss of Darkness

A man whose inner demons have been released must turn to a woman with magical abilities for help, despite his skepticism—and his irrepressible desire for her.

Bride of the Wolf

When a heroic werewolf is trapped in the twilight realm, only a passionate woman with a spirit as wild as his own can set him free.

Available wherever books are sold or at www.simonandschuster.com